DATE DUE

F
Man-   Manfred, Frederick Feikem   M
fred   No fun on Sunday

DATE	ISSUED TO

Other books by Frederick Manfred

The Golden Bowl (1944) (Mr. Manfred wrote under the name of Feike
    Feikema from 1944 through 1951)
Boy Almighty (1945)
This Is the Year (1947)
The Chokecherry Tree (1948)
Lord Grizzly (1954)
Morning Red (1956)
Riders of Judgment (1957)
Conquering Horse (1959)
Arrow of Love (stories) (1961)
Wanderlust (a revised version of three novels, *The Primitive* [1949], *The
    Brother* [1950], and *The Giant* [1951], published in one volume, 1962)
Scarlet Plume (1964)
The Man Who Looked Like the Prince of Wales (1965)
Winter Count (poems) (1966)
King of Spades (1966)
Apples of Paradise (stories) (1968)
Eden Prairie (1968)
Conversations (1974) (moderated by John R. Milton)
Milk of Wolves (1976)
The Manly-Hearted Woman (1976)
Green Earth (1977)
The Wind Blows Free (reminiscences) (1979)
Sons of Adam (1980)
Winter Count II (poems) (1987)
Prime Fathers (essays) (1987)
The Selected Letters of Frederick Manfred, 1932–1954 (1989)
Flowers of Desire (1989)

No Fun on Sunday

No Fun on Sunday

A Novel

By Frederick Manfred

University of Oklahoma Press
Norman and London

Library of Congress Cataloging-in-Publication Data

Manfred, Frederick Feikema, 1912–
    No fun on Sunday : a novel / by Frederick Manfred.
        p.   cm.
    ISBN 0-8061-2273-0
    I. Title.
PS3525.A52233N6   1990
813'.54—dc20   89-40738
                                                    CIP

For Herman Van Engen, peerless shortstop of Siouxland

NOTE

This story
  is not a history.
  Therefore
  it is all the more
  possible it might be a true story.

—Frederick Manfred

No Fun on Sunday

Chapter One

In May, when the grass turns green, and the lilacs fill the air with purple perfumes, and the orioles tell of orchards bursting with pink blossoms, then the boys, old and young, get out their bats and balls and run to the pastures and play the wonderful game of baseball.

The moment the twelve o'clock bell rang, the boys in the seventh and eighth grades grabbed dried-beef sandwiches out of their lunch buckets, gobbled the sandwiches as they trampled down the back wooden stairs, snatched their caps and baseball gloves off coat hooks, as well as their homemade bat and ball from behind the back door, and sallied out onto the playing field behind the grade school. Noon recess was always a great time to play work-up. In an hour's time a fellow was bound to get up to bat a couple of times.

The boys took up their positions where they'd left off the last time they played. Earlier in the week, when the first warm days began to whelm over Siouxland, they'd pulled straws to determine the order in which they'd bat. To make sure that no one could complain the pulling wasn't fair, they asked Principal Garland Ault to hold the straws. The three boys pulling the shortest straws became the first batters, the boy drawing the fourth shortest became the catcher, the fifth short straw the pitcher, and so on around the diamond, first base, second base, shortstop, third base, left field, center field, right field, and other more distant positions. If one of the three batters struck out, or was thrown out at first, or hit a fly ball that was caught, he went to the end of the line out in the field, and everybody moved up one position, the catcher became a batter, the pitcher became the catcher, and so on.

It sometimes happened that a batter was so good the boys almost never got him out. Such a batter was Sherman Engleking. Or Sherm as he was known. For this he was hated by Tuffy Janes. And what made it all the more galling for Tuffy was that when Sherm was finally put out, Sherm turned out to be a slick fielder and an exceptionally fast runner. Sherm was liked by most of the boys, because he was fair, and daring, but there were several who joined Tuffy in ragging Sherm every chance they got.

Sherm had almost white hair, slim hands, and narrow feet, with quick turning hips. When he ran he hardly seemed to touch earth, and leaping for a line drive it was as if he had been jerked up by an invisible rubber band and then magically let hang in the air for a second. His eyes were light grey, quick and piercing, and on sunny days under a clear sky had a touch of blue in them.

What Tuffy Janes didn't know was that Sherm took a lot of batting practice by himself. Sherm had fashioned himself a bat of sorts out of an old broom handle, and then of an evening, walking out to the edge of town on a new graveled road, had picked up stone after stone and swatted them out of sight.

Sometimes Sherm would pretend he was in a nine-inning game, playing for the Cubs against the hated Pirates. He'd imagine he was each player for the Cubs, singles hitter Maisal, doubles hitting Hollocher, and home run hitter Flack. When Maisal was up, Sherm formed a cunning look on his thin lips and flicked his long thin bat at a plum-sized stone just hard enough to line it over the fence along the road. The fence stood for the Pirate infield. When Hollocher was up, Sherm sighted his bat at either the second baseman or the shortstop and tried to hit the stone over them out between either the right fielder and the center fielder or the center fielder and the left fielder for a two-base hit. That meant he had to hit the stone between some cowplotches he'd spotted out in the pasture. Sometimes he allowed Hollocher a triple when the stone bounced against a wooden fence post on the far side of the narrow pasture and rolled back toward the infield. Then when Flack the cleanup hitter came to bat, Sherm would lash into the stone with everything he had, grunting like a man, and hit the stone out of sight over a fringe of chokecherry brush beyond the fartherest fence.

It wasn't easy to hit a thin stone with a thin bat. In the spring it took a while to get the timing down, closing the moment when he'd toss up the stone with his left hand to the moment when he'd take a good swing at it. In between he quick had to slap his left hand back on the bat handle just as the stone started its descent. It didn't take him long to learn that if he started out calmly, slowly, and first made easy chopping swings at the stone while carefully watching to see just how much he was missing it, just above it or just below it, he'd finally narrow the gap, until he ticked the stone, either fouling it straight up or straight down.

Sometimes farmer Okke Keatsen let his cows out into the narrow pasture before the grass was really green and then Sherm had to wait until they'd grazed across his imaginary diamond before he could go on with his crucial series with the Pirates. Twice Keatsen caught Sherm plunking one of his milk cows when, in trying for a colossal home run for Flack, Sherm would foul off the ball to the right or the left.

"Hey, kit, by Gott, we can't have that. Scaring the krep out of my cows that way. Kit, already they give only half of what they're supposed to. And with you out there they're drying up before their time."

"I'm sorry."

"Vell. Just watch it." Keatsen understood that his son Tookie was a baseball friend of Sherm's and that Sherm often helped Tookie with his arithmetic. "Watch it. And I won't klets this to your mother at church."

It was easier to hit frozen horse apples in the middle of the winter. Every street had its dribbled row of them. But the horse barn by the church had the most. Also there was room on the churchyard to hit them. Sometimes when he had Flack try for a homer, the frozen horse apple popped open like a firecracker and fibrous bits flew in all directions. At first Sherm had been a little worried that he'd carry the smell of the horse apples on his leather mittens into the house, but soon learned that the colder it was oudoors the less chance there was of stinking up the back porch where he always hung his outdoor mackinaw with the mittens doubled over in a pocket.

By the time the boys started playing work-up on the school

grounds, Sherm had finished both his winter and spring training as a batter and was raring to go.

Ma hated baseball, which she pronounced base-a-ball. It was a frivolous American game and she, just thirty years out of the Old Country, hated all U S of A pastimes. It certainly wasn't something you played, or practised, so that you could use it when you grew up to be a man. She could never understand where Sherm disappeared to in the spring evenings. She thought perhaps he was hanging out with the American bums downtown near the poolhall. And of course he couldn't tell her that he was leading the Cubs to victory over the Pirates along a country road.

When Ma got after him too much about disappearing after supper, Sherm would go out front within sight of their bay window and pick up stones and throw them at a light pole on the corner. The street had been freshly graveled the fall before and stones the size of chicken eggs lay on the surface where frost had worked them up. Pretending that he was Hollocher the great Cub shortstop, he'd dart to his left or his right, snatch up a stone and fire it on the run to his first baseman the telephone pole. Sometimes he'd pretend he was just barely able to reach the ball, and, just before he fell to earth, would fire the ball to the outstretched glove of his slick-fielding first baseman, right on the mark.

After watching him a while through the bay window, Ma would finally show up in the doorway. "What kind of crazy stunts are those, throwing stones at nothing, and then falling to the ground, getting your knickerbockers all dirty like that?"

Sherm would sigh, and sigh again. "Oh, Ma, I'm just playing a pretend game. I'm not hurting anybody, am I?"

"Well, not so far. But suppose Tante Toothache comes walking across the school yard to visit us, and you hit her?"

"Oh, Ma, I'd see her coming, for hecksake."

"She's going blind, you know."

Sherm bit back a smart remark. He had to remember Ma was jealous of Tante Toothache. When he was a year old, and Ma'd had a terrible gallbladder operation, he'd been placed in Tante Toothache's care for a time. Ma'd had her operation without benefit of ether. The surgeon had tied her arms and legs down to the operating table and had just simply cut into her and removed the gallbladder, with her bellering her head off all the while. The surgeon had offered her a drink of whiskey, but she'd refused that. She had a horror of drunks. Sherm's father, Alfred, had still been alive at that time and he'd tried to comfort her with a warm palm on her brow. When his father had offered her smelling salts, she'd cried out, "Ach, Alfred, let me faint, let me faint!" The surgeon'd had to put a drainage tube in the incision, and it'd taken several months for the cut to heal from the inside out. It was when it appeared Ma had a postoperative nervous breakdown that his father had farmed Sherm out to Tante Toothache.

"Did you hear me, Shermie?"

"Yes, I hear you. But I'm just playing."

"Anyway, supper's ready."

Sherm muttered to himself. "Yeh, same old potatoes fried in lard."

"What was that!"

"Praise the Lord."

Ma often badgered him after supper about how come he'd never had to study at home like other boys did. "You better not flunk on us now."

"Me flunk? are you crazy?"

"Well, study a little then. Other boys do. Ten minutes even."

"They're dumbbells, Ma. Sometimes I wish I was already in high school." Twice Principal Ault had arranged for Sherm to take two classes at once, the third and fourth, and the sixth and seventh, if only to keep him out of mischief. Principal Ault had once tried giving the boy books to read, but Sherm wasn't a reader. Sherm was a whizz in arithmetic and he did page through a lively book on conundrums. The only trouble was, there weren't many such books. "Ma, those kids are so dumb, they even asked Principal Ault if they couldn't skip arithmetic. Because, they said, they wouldn't need it to plow corn and raise hogs."

"So now who's got britches too big for him, heh? I'll not have an overproud boy in my house who thinks too much of himself."

Sherm got out a project he'd thought of that morning in school, and in the dim orange light shedding down from the kerosene lamp on the wall above the kitchen table, began making a base-ball. He'd found a small rubber ball, and after talking Ma out of some store cord, started winding the cord tight around the rubber ball. Several times the cord broke, and cussing under his breath, he retied the cord in a thin knot, and went on winding. He'd once snuck out after supper to see the hometown team, the Jerusalem

Saints, play the Sutherland Lords, and had seen a baseball un-ravel. When he watched the manager of the Saints examine the ball, he saw that below where the red stitching had come apart there was tightly wound cord. Later he learned that the center of the baseball had a round cork center in it.

Presently Sherm became aware that he was being watched. Looking up he saw stepfather Garland Stanhorse's warm brown eyes smiling at him across the kitchen table. Garland Stanhorse had an important nose shaped somewhat like a long slim potato and when he smiled he seemed to be smiling as much with it as with his eyes and lips.

Stepfather said, "That's going to be a baseball, not?"

Sherm winced, and flicked a look at Ma to see if she'd heard the question, then shot another look at Stepfather for him not to spill the beans. Sherm had loved his real father, but this new fa-ther was easier to live with. His real father Alfred had been very strict, and during his last years when he was dying of cancer, had looked even more fearsome with his great grey hollow eyes. Step-father had a way of starting out with a warm nose smiling and ending with a joke.

Stepfather put down the church paper he'd been reading, *The People's Friend,* and learned forward for a better look. "Where will you get the leather cover for it, boy?"

"I ain't figured that out yet."

"I have an old discarded leather shoe in the barn. You know, on the workbench next to our broom-making machine."

Sherm looked at his mother, and saw to his satisfaction that she had taken to reading some letters that had come in the mail that day and was lost in them. "Could I really have it?"

Stepfather threw a look at Ma, wiggled his big nose. "Sure. Help yourself. You know how to cut it?"

"You gotta have two patches exactly alike, with each patch looking like two moons tied together with a narrow band be-tween them."

"I think that old shoe is genuine horsehide too. You can still read the label inside it."

Sherm smiled. The old gent was up on things. Had the old boy sometims snuck out to the city diamond to watch the Saints play? "Horsehide lasts the longest."

"You're going to have to cut those two patches careful to make a nine-inch ball."

"I know. I thought I'd first try it out with a piece of paper. You know, like a dressmaker's pattern."

"Ah. Good. Before you jump across the canal, it's always good to practice jumping on the bank first."

Ma woke up from her reading. Tears were streaming down her thick cheeks and a shivering kind of shudder had started up in her fat bosom. "Shermie, it says here in your sister Ada's letter, that your sister Joan is in trouble again. They owe so much at the store in Blue Wing they can't get groceries charging them even." Ma cried to herself a moment. "What a mistake Joanie made when she married that lazy Pete Waxer, Jr. It makes one wonder if he sometimes don't forget to get up in the morning."

Sherm had little time for his sister Joan. He sort of liked her because she was family, but what a burden she was to have around. Hard luck followed her like a flock of crows. "Well, then the two of them sometimes forget to get up in the morning. Because she's no smarter."

Ma fixed a frown on Sherm. "Be careful what you say there."

"The pups that've come out of that match!"

Ma humphed. "According to Ada here, there's another one on the way."

"Oh, boy, then get ready for another dunce. With sawdust for brains."

Ma's eyes slowly opened as she just then caught on to something. "And what do you know about pups already?"

"Oh, Ma, that's all they talk about at recess time at our Christian School."

"That's scandalous!" Ma's face saddened over. "My first Shermie never talked that way. He was too smart to think dirty."

Sherm suddenly got so mad he wanted to spit. The first Sherman had died of scarlet fever a year before he himself was born. Ma often said Pa Alfred could send the first Sherman to church in his stead and the boy, still only six, would come home and repeat the long prayer and the long sermon seemingly word for word, as well as sing all the psalms. Sherm knew it was wrong to hate that dead brother but he did hate Ma's memory of him.

Stepfather got out his low-slung black pipe and with thoughtful mien began to fill it with brown strands of tobacco plucked from a pail. Stepfather made his own mix, half from a brand called Long Distance and half from wild Indian tobacco still to be found along the railroad tracks. The mix had a sweet aroma, and when Stepfather lit up the kitchen began to smell like the inside of the Roman Catholic Church after the priest had passed by down the center aisle with his censer.

Ma next began to read a letter from brother John. John and wife Mathilda had moved to Bonnie some forty miles to the northwest in Siouxland. They farmed a quarter section a few miles from Ada's place. Slowly Ma's face became wreathed in pleased wrinkles. "It says here that your nephew Alfie is housebroke at last, and now everything is running real smooth in that household."

Sherm glanced across at Ma. "Who wrote that letter?"

"Well, Mathilde did. Women always write the family letters."

"Ha. She'd never admit there was anything wrong with her family."

Stepfather puffed on his pipe like a lord, nose lifted. "When I brought our junk to the town dump, I found a pretty good fork handle there. I thought maybe you could use that instead of a broom handle, Sherman, so I brought it home. It's in the workshop."

"Hey, now you're thinking'. I can maybe even hit this baseball I'm making with it."

"What! What!" Ma exclaimed, catching on. "Garland, are you encouraging that boy with his crazy base-a-ball stunts?"

Garland smiled benignly across the corner of the table at her. "Dear woman, the boy is very active, and isn't it better he plays a little harmless game instead of learning how to shoot billiards in that bum's hangout uptown?"

Ma fell silent. But she continued to smolder to herself for awhile. She loved Garland, and had said many times over that she was far happier living with him than with Alfred.

Winding the store cord very carefully, now and then holding the growing lump up to the pale yellow light from the lamp to make sure he was winding it perfectly round, Sherm gradually built it up to about the size of a regulation National League baseball. He cut off the cord and deftly pushed the end of it down into the woven strands so it wouldn't unravel. "Now to make the two-part leather cover. But not tonight. Tomorrow's another day."

Stepfather got up and clapped out his pipe in the mouth of the kitchen range. He next looked at his gold watch. "Yes, it is time for all good Christians to go to bed. Night, boy."

10

"Night, Pa."

Ma liked it that her boy Sherman called her second husband "Pa." "Yes, boy. You didn't need to study then?"

"Ma."

In his small room, Sherm undressed in the dark. He slipped on his nightgown and kneeled beside his bed. "Father, now I lay me down to rest, may my slumber by Thee be blessed, may happiness follow my family in all the days to come, until we ascend into heaven to live in our golden home. For Jesus' sake. Amen."

He climbed into bed, drew the covers up to his chin, and nuzzled his head deep into the pillow. The full moon was glowing outdoors. Reflected light from it lit up his room just enough so he could play an old game with a big calendar picture hanging above the foot of his bed. If he looked at the picture one way, it was a train engine rushing toward him with black smoke billowing back above it. If he looked at it another way, after blinking his eyes several times, it was a handsome lady with her dark hair piled up on top of her head like those models had it in the Sears Roebuck catalogue.

He started thinking about the baseball bat he'd make out of the fork handle. He hoped it would be a handle from a manure fork because then it would have enough heft to make a pretty good stick. The bat they were using at school was an old one that Principal Ault had dug up out of his garage from his former playing days. It was cracked in the handle, which had been taped over several times, and part of the fat of the bat, due to drying, had lost part of its thickness, splintering off on both sides of the bat, especially on the trademark side. He'd have to share his bat, of course, with the other boys because, according to the principal, that's what a good Christian baseball player did. He'd even have to share it with Tuffy Janes.

Sherm thought about the new teacher they had in the eighth grade. Miss Betchworth. What a pain she was. She was as stiff and as plain as an ironing board. And the way she talked, pronouncing every letter in a word, so that sometimes when she pronounced the two letters S and T together, she actually sent out a little mist of spit from her thin lips. It was too bad Principal Ault couldn't be his teacher, strict as he was. Because one of these days Sherm was sure he'd do something naughty in Miss Betchworth's room. The notion to do so was always there.

One day out on the playing field behind the schoolhouse it happened that Sherm came up to bat when Tuffy Janes was the pitcher. It wasn't for nothing that Janes had been nicknamed Tuffy. He was as tall as Sherm, but where Sherm was slim Tuffy was heavy and muscular. No one could touch him wrestling. And despite his weight he could run. And, he could throw. His pitch came in like a streaking meteor. It also came in a little wild, erratic, and most batters were afraid to step into his pitches.

Sherm wasn't afraid. He relied on his quickness to get out of the way of a wild pitch. He took up his usual position in the batter's box, exactly in the middle, and bat cocked over his shoulder, knees slightly bent, got set. It was the first time he'd faced Tuffy that spring, and he wasn't quite ready for what happened. Tuffy threw overhanded, and the ball first headed for the outside edge of the plate, then darted inward, and then, at the last second, seemed to dip low and away. Sherm swung through the pitch. His sharp eyes saw he'd missed it a good six inches. Wow. Tuffy now had a zigzag pitch! Where in God's name had he picked that up? Had Tuffy put on so much weight during the winter months carrying heavy blocks of ice for the town iceman that he could throw it so hard? And the ball came in so fast it didn't know which way to go?

Tuffy took the return throw from the catcher. He laughed at Sherm. He flipped the ball up and down a couple of times in his scabby glove, and then with his free hand, pushed back his cap and ran his thick fingers through his golden curly hair. He'd always had the smile of a handsome rascal, and when he laughed out loud the sound of it was coarse and mocking.

Sherm stepped out of the batter's box, picked up some dust for a drier grip, and then stepped in again.

Tuffy, smiling, wound up and let fly. Once more the ball zigzagged and Sherm missed it, this time though by no more than an inch.

Sherm's lips pushed out. "Dare you to throw that one again." Sherm shortened his stance and moved his hands up on the bat.

All the other players fell silent, watching the two, knowing how much they hated each other. Principal Ault, spectacles glinting behind a window in his room, watched too. Heat from the sun pushed down on the early gray-green grass like a draft from a heat duct.

Tuffy looked around at the other players as though he expected them to cheer him on. Then Tuffy's arm came around again. The scuffed up ball wobbled the moment it left his fingers. Sherm followed it with fierce narrowed eyes. At the very last second he made a short swinging poke at it. And hit it. The ball had come in so fast, though, that even with his shortened swing he was late coming around, and he fouled it off, lofting up a high twisting pop fly between first and home.

Tuffy saw that neither the first baseman nor the catcher had taken out after it. Instantly he became a blur of motion. "I got it! I got it!" Losing his cap as he ran, Tuffy caught the ball easily some twenty feet beyond the base line. "Gotcha at last!" Tuffy crowed. "And now I catch. And you gotta go to the end of the line out in the field."

There was a mild cheer from the other players. They liked Sherm better than Tuffy, but they were also relieved that Sherm was out at last.

Wagging his head a little, Sherm said, "Not bad." A fellow had to be a good sport. Tuffy was good.

Out in the field, the thought came to Sherm that with that new pitch, the Christian School now had a pitcher good enough so they could challenge the Northwestern Academy nine. Sherm had run across town to watch the academy team practice one evening and it struck him that while the academy players were older and bigger, they really were a bunch of duffers. With their big heavy clumsy swing they'd never figure out how to hit Tuffy's new zigzag pitch. The Christian School happened to have a bunch of good players that spring, far better than usual, as Principal Ault had declared, and it was just possible the lower grade team could beat the high school team. Sherm had been curious about the academy nine because he hoped to go on to school there, despite the fact that Northwestern Academy was supported by the Siouxland Big Church Classis and not his Little Church Classis. "Wouldn't it be great if a grade school team could whip a high school team?" Man alive, that might be even important enough to get into the *Sioux City Journal*—right next to the column where it told how the Chicago Cubs had beat the Pittsburgh Pirates.

When the one o'clock bell rang before Sherm got another chance to bat against Tuffy, he sought him out as the players ganged in through the back door, laughing, joshing each other, and hanging up their gloves and caps. Sherm caught Tuffy by the elbow. "How about playing a little after school? I'd hate to go to bed tonight knowing I couldn't get a hit off you today."

"You're on. Maybe we can get a couple town kids to come out too. They don't have to do farm chores after school."

"Let's both ask around."

When school let out at three-thirty, only five other boys showed up.

"Shucks," Tuffy said. "That's hardly enough for work-up."

Sherm said, "Well, let's pretend we're having spring training like the major leaguers do. We each take three swings and then go shag flies. First you pitch awhile and then I'll pitch a while."

Once again they pulled straws to work out the batting order. Sherm suggested that since Tuffy was going to pitch first that he hold the straws. It turned out that Sherm would bat first.

As Sherm stepped into the batter's box, he fixed his whole mind on how the ball would leave Tuffy's fingers, how it would first seem to dart out, then in, and then down and away. It was agreed that the batter could call the pitch, ball or strike. Sherm let the first two go by, one was a ball and the other a strike. How did Tuffy make that ball zigzag like that? Tuffy couldn't throw it in such a way that its spin would first make it curve out, then the spin would reverse itself to curve in, then reverse itself again to curve out and down. Impossible. Like a top once set in motion, it had to keep spinning one way until it hit something, a bat or a pud.

On Tuffy's third pitch, Sherm caught on. He'd been fooled by Tuffy's motion. Tuffy had a curious elongated windup in which at first it looked like his body wasn't going to follow his arm around, and then suddenly when his body did follow it, the batter was tricked into concentrating on the body's motion and not the arm's motion. Or how the ball came out of the hand.

Making a face to himself, Sherm stepped into the batter's box for his fourth pitch. He fixed his eyes on Tuffy's fingers. And sure enough, there it was. Just a simple little hook. A dinky curve. At the last split second Sherm made a quick level swing at it, and hit a scorcher to right field.

"Lucky," Tuffy growled.

Sherm hit the next pitch straight over Tuffy's head into center field; and made his final hit a lofting fly ball well over the girls' outdoor privy.

"Lucky, lucky."

It was Sherm's turn to pitch. Sherm could throw almost as hard as Tuffy. He had no windup, and he pegged the ball more than threw it. The result was that he grooved his pitches much of the time, seeming to aim the ball for the middle of the batter's bat. By the third time around, after shortening up their grip on the bat, most of the kids hit nice little singles up the middle.

Tuffy was also a heck of a hitter. He was known to have hit the ball into the trees along the south edge of the school grounds. Just as it was Tuffy's turn at bat, they were interrupted.

"Sher-mee?"

Sherm cussed to himself. Ma. She probably needed some bread from the baker uptown.

"Sher-mee!" Ma always pronounced his name as "Share-me."

Waggling his bat, Tuffy leered at Sherm. "What a lucky excuse. So you don't have to pitch to me."

"Get in the box and I'll show you."

"Sher-mee!" Ma appeared around the side of the schoolhouse. "Sher-mee!" Eyes big and round behind spectacles, face dark from having hurried, she looked like a fat old owl. "Sher-mee! Didn't you hear me?"

Sherm lipped sideways at Ma. "Yeh, I heard you." To Tuffy he said, "Take your swing, and then I'll have to go."

Tuffy stepped into the box.

"Sher-mee! I'm calling you."

"Yeh, I know you are. Ready, Tuff?"

"Ready."

Sherm let drive as hard as he could throw. The ball went in a scuffed brown blur straight for the center of the plate; and Tuffy, timing it perfectly, caught it well above the trademark of his bat and sent it crashing into the trees along the south side of the grounds.

Sherm, angry, started walking off the diamond.

As Tuffy rounded third base, Tuffy called after Sherm, mockingly, "Sher-mee, didn't you hear me?" Tuffy made a special point of ridiculing Ma's Old Country "her" sound.

"That's sure being original," Sherm shot over his shoulder.

"Making fun of one's mother."

"You can poke fun of my ma if you wanna. She died last year, you know."

"One of these days I'm gonna kill you."

"Better let me get out a spade first."

"Why a spade?"

"So I can dig my own grave."

"Hey. That's a pretty good comeback."

During the next several weeks, as the leaves of the lilacs and the maples turned a soft pure green, the rivalry between Sherm and Tuffy continued. Sherm hit Tuffy hard, and Tuffy hit Sherm hard. Sherm had the better average, but Tuffy had the longer drives. Their play became so intense the other players also caught fire. Faces flushed, they all began to make great plays.

When Sherm proposed that the Christian grade school challenge the Academy across town to a game on the Christian school grounds, Principal Ault at first demurred. He agreed that his boys could probably make a good showing against the Academy, but he worried what his school board would say about having Little Church boys playing against those almost worldly Big Church boys. Both Sherm and Tuffy urged him to ask the board at their next meeting, and with a smile Principal Ault agreed. He loved baseball as a Christian and as a Christian fan he would ask them.

Tuffy continued to rag Sherm. "Sher-mee! Did you hear me?" he'd yell across the diamond. Soon the other boys began doing it too, though not in such a pronounced Old Country manner. Sherm knew he couldn't go after Tuffy because then Principal Ault would cancel their Academy game.

At the same time Sherm was also getting more and more sick of Miss Betchworth's mannerisms. If Ma had never married, and had become a schoolteacher, that's what she would have turned out to be, another Miss Betchworth. No sense of what a young boy liked to dream about. Both Ma and Miss Betchworth thought if a boy wasn't studying, or wasn't running errands, he was supposed to be sitting like a monk somewhere with his hands folded in his lap.

Some days Miss Betchworth was fairly decent. She actually had a little smile, much like an old brood hen might try to have with a stiff hard beak. But most days she was a tough old witch, snapping out criticisms and corrections right and left. "Mr. Keatsen, no turning around to whisper!" "Mr. Van Wyck, *i* before *e* except after *c*." "Miss Faber, comb your hair. All girls in my class must be presentable. Or else!" "Mr. Janes, sit up. Straight! I will not tolerate any slouchers in my class. Or, alas, I'll just have to send you home with a note to your parents about your behavior."

Sherm sat in the back seat of the middle row, and Tuffy sat right next to him. Both had once sat up front, where Miss Betchworth could keep an eye on them. But they'd managed to be so well behaved, as well as managed to get the highest marks in class, that she'd seated them in the back of the room. This left her free to move the dumbbells up front where she could give them special attention.

The school day was almost over when Tuffy raised a hand.

"Yes, Mister Janes?"

"Can I please leave the room."

Miss Betchworth looked at the pendant watch pinned to her gray blouse on the left side of her bosom. "Mr. Janes, there's only a few more minutes left. Can't you wait?"

"But I gotta go bad."

"Mr. Janes!" Her green eyes turned white-edge grey. "We are never to be that explicit about our bodily needs in front of others. No!"

"But, Teacher—"

"No! I said. And if you ask one more time, alas, I shall have to write that note to your parents."

Everybody sat a little more erect. For goshsakes.

Ten minutes later the last bell rang.

"All right, class. You can now put your books away. Quietly. Quietly. No slamming of the desk tops please." She glanced up and down the six rows. When she saw all was in order, everybody sitting bolt upright with their hands on their desks, desk tops clean, she allowed herself an end-of-the-day pinched smile, and began the dismissal ritual. "Turn."

Everybody swiveled to the right, feet in the aisle.

"Rise."

Everyone got to their feet and stood erect beside their desk.

Sherm did like the rest. And standing up, thinking how ridiculous the strict formality of the dismissal was, he said, in a low voice, mostly to himself, but just loud enough for Tuffy and others nearby to hear, "Turn, rise, pass, the old man died with a cob—"

"Whoops!" Tuffy let fly; and then quickly clutching at the front of his trousers, added, "Alas!"

Instantly everybody nearby clapped a hand to their mouth.

"What was that! in the back of the room there?" Miss Betchworth snapped. "What? What?"

Smothered laughter. There were brave attempts to put on an innocent expression, boys and girls both.

"Tuffy? Was that you?"

Hand over his mouth, legs crossed tight, he shook his head.

"Sherman? You?"

Sherm shook his head.

She glared at Tuffy. "I distinctly heard your voice, Mr. Janes. What was so funny that you had to blurt out something and then laugh?"

"Nothing, Teacher."

"Nothing?"

"Nothing."

"Well, Mr. Janes, we're all going to stand at attention here until you tell us. Even if it takes us well past suppertime."

Tuffy turned stubborn and red.

"Mr. Janes?"

Tuffy was in double agony. He pushed something down inside the front of his brown knickerbockers and then recrossed his legs, tight.

Miss Betchworth swept forward in her long gray dress, heavy high-heeled kid shoes klokking sharply on the oiled hardwood floor, until she was within a step of Tuffy. "I'm waiting."

Tuffy stared at her with a wonderfully torn expression.

"Mr. Janes." It looked like she was about to slap him.

"I ain't tellin'."

"Then we're all standing here until dark."

"I gotta go real bad, and if you don't let me go, I'll pee right here on the floor."

"You will, will you?" Then she did slap him. The sound of it was like someone hitting a baseball for a single.

Tuffy lived up to his name. Purple-faced, he said bravely, "It's the Lord's will that I have to pee, Miss Betchworth, and that's just what I'm gonna do." He reached for the buttons of his fly.

Just then Principal Ault showed up in the doorway. "Miss Betchworth? I notice that your class still hasn't been dismissed. What's going on here?"

Miss Betchworth said over her shoulder. "Mr. Janes started to laugh when I began calling out, 'Turn, rise, pass.'"

"He was, was he?" Principal Ault turned on his pointed toes and stepped around to the back of the room until he stood behind Tuffy. He was wearing a dark blue suit with a gleaming white shirt and a flowing hand-folded red bow tie. One hand in his pocket, he smiled hypnotic at Tuffy, gold teeth showing. "My boy, what was so funny that you had to laugh?"

"It wasn't funny so much as it was that I had to go somewheres."

Principal Ault noted how Tuffy's legs were crossed and where his hand was placed in a pressing manner.

"My boy, needs are needs. Why don't you just tell Miss Betchworth what you were laughing about and then we can all go home?"

"I can't. I ain't no squealer."

"I am not a squealer, you mean."

"Yeh."

Miss Betchworth offered, "I think, if I mistake not, that Mr. Janes used a dirty word to rime with 'pass.'"

"Is that true, Tuffy?" Principal Ault demanded.

"I ain't sayin'. And please let me go to the privy. My ma will be real mad if I come home with a—"

"That's enough in that direction, Tuffy." Principal Ault took his hand out of his pocket and then began rubbing both hands together.

Sherm watched Tuffy's misery with a superior smile. It was good to see Tuffy suffer a little. It made up for the way Tuffy ragged him about the way Ma called him Sher-mee. But at last Sherm began to feel sorry for Tuffy too. Poor sucker. Sherm turned from where he was standing stiff at attention. "Mr. Ault, I'm the guilty party. I'm the one who tried to say something funny. And Tuffy was only letting us know what a relief it would—"

"Enough!" Principal Ault barked. "Mr. Engleking, you come with me my office. Tuffy, you go take care of your needs. Miss Betchworth, you can now dismiss your class."

Miss Betchworth nodded. "Thank you, Mr. Ault. All right, class, pass."

Principal Ault took Sherm by the elbow and in front of everybody ushered him out into the hall and then around the corner into his office. The office was pin-neat and sparkled with furniture polish. There was a sharp smell of after-shave cologne. Principal Ault pointed out a chair for Sherm to sit in and then sat down himself behind a blond oak desk.

"All right, Sherman. Just what was it that you said that made poor Tuffy laugh?"

"Well, I finally got so sick of the way Miss Betchworth always says"—quite deliberately, in an excessive way, Sherm mocked her old-maidish manner—" 'turn, rise, pass' that before I knew it my tongue said it."

"What did your tongue say?"

" 'Turn, rise, pass, the old man died with a cob'—"

"Enough. I get the picture."

"You wanted to know."

"Yesss." Principal Ault squinted in thought, so sharply it pulled up his red nose. "Well, we can't let this go by without some kind of punishment, now can we?"

"I suppose not."

"You knew of course that I like your family very much."

Sherm shrugged. Principal Ault had given Sherm's sister Ada an expensive wedding present because he'd been partly in love with her.

"What do you recommend that I do, Sherman?"

"I can say I am sorry."

"But there has to be more than that."

Sherm waited. What he'd suggest might be worse than what Principal Ault had in mind.

"By the way, are you sure you didn't say that dirty word? The one that rimes with 'pass'?"

Sherm shrugged again. "Well, I might have to myself. But Tuffy said 'whoops' so loud, and then 'alas,' that I don't remember hearing it."

"Nevertheless, it was in your mind, wasn't it?"

"I guess so."

"That's just as bad as the actual saying of it."

"If you say so."

Principal Ault drummed his pink manicured fingers on the glass top of his desk. "Just writing some lines for me is not going to be enough. It's got to be something short and sweet, and something you won't forget right away." Principal Ault fixed

Sherm with his mesmeric shiny brown eyes. "Aha! I have it."
From a drawer he got out a piece of school stationery and, taking
up a desk pen, rapidly scribbled something on it. He signed it
with a flourish. "Here. I want you to take this to either your
mother or your new father, and have them sign it so that I know
that they've read it, and then you return it to me. Tomorrow
morning."

"Oh." Sherm took the paper.

"You better read it so that you know what you're in for."

Sherm read it:

"Dear Mr. and Mrs. Stanhorse:

Your son Sherman was guilty today of causing a disruption in
school. It involved a dirty word that rimes with the word 'pass.' I
shall leave it up to you to give him the proper punishment. All I
ask it that Sherman return this paper with either of your signatures.
                                                    Principal Garland Ault"

"You may go, Sherman."

Sherm's nose came up a little. "Thanks." He folded up the
paper and slipped it into his shirt pocket.

Sherm trudged out into the hallway, then down the inside
stairs, then outside down the cement steps facing east. He headed
across the street for home.

Sherm muttered to himself. "Well, at least I showed him I
wasn't afraid of him." He picked up a stone from the graveled
street. "I wonder if he ain't sticking it into me because he couldn't
have my sister Ada. That horny old bastard." Sherm threw the
stone viciously at a telephone pole. "Well, I'll show him."

But Ma had better not see that note from the principal. That
would really set the dolls to dancing. Nor could he show it to his
stepfather. As a respected janitor of their church, Stepfather
Stanhorse would take the side of authority. Also Stepfather might
think the words "the old man" referred to him. Sherm shud-
dered. Of course he'd never think of stoppering up the old man
with a cob.

"I gotta think of something to get out of this pickle."

He entered the house. "Ma?"

"Yes, son."

"Need anything from town?"

21

"Ya. I think we better have some more of that dark roggenbrea. Pa's been complainin' a little about being stopped up."

Sherm nodded. He liked rye bread himself. Especially if it was well buttered with sugar sprinkled on.

Ma went to the cupboard and took down a fruit jar from which she extracted a green dollar bill. "Two darks. And one raisin bread." Ma smiled warmly. The warm smile had to work its way through her natural scowl. "And because you offered to go, you can spend the rest for a treat."

"Thanks."

Sherm walked slowly toward downtown. That folded paper in his shirt pocket felt hot. Somehow he had to get a signature from either his ma or his pa without them reading the letter. It was wrong not to let them read it, a sin even, but it was far worse to have them mad at him. If Ma found out, she would for sure tell him he couldn't go to Northwestern Academy next year.

He cut across the courthouse lawn. Every sidewalk there had been laid by his real father Alfred. Because of that Sherm always admired the great pillared courthouse. He liked its pink and gold stones, the gilded tower, the high sparkling windows, the flight of broad stone steps on the east side. It was also the building where his real father had gotten his citizenship papers.

Sherm snapped his fingers. "Aha. I got it." He turned it all through his mind once more. "Yep. That's the clear thing. You bet."

He stepped into the aromatic bakery and bought two loaves of dark bread and a loaf of raisin bread. Then he stepped across the street to buy himself a treat at Pool's Drugstore.

Mr. Pool had the look about him that he knew an awful lot of bad things about people in town. "What can I do for you, son?"

"Got any sweetwood?"

"Yes. Just got in a fresh packet of it today."

Sherm placed a dime on the glass counter. "How many sticks for that?"

"Ten." Mr. Pool slipped ten sticks into a paper bag.

"Thanks." Sherm removed one of the greenish yellow sticks from the bag, doubled it over and popped it into his mouth. Ah. That wonderful puckerish sweet taste as his teeth slowly shredded the fragile twigs. It was far better than gum. Gum lost its flavor after a while but sweetwood kept giving off an earthy taste for a long time. Sweetwood also filled one's nostrils with a heady scent. So a fellow got double value out of it.

The single stick of sweetwood was still giving off its flavor as he stepped past the great cottonwood in the alley behind Ma's lot. As he entered their backyard, he noticed that the door to their privy was open. That was something Stepfather didn't like. That door had to be closed or the wind would slowly bang it off its hinges. Sherm went over and closed it and very carefully set the turnknuckle crossways to secure it. When he noticed the turnknuckle was quite loose, he got a hammer from Stepfather's toolshop and pounded the nail on which the turnknuckle rotated until all was snug. Then he closed the door again.

He placed the bread on the kitchen table. "Here you are, Ma."

"Good. What are you chewing there?"

"Sweetwood."

"Ach. Something you've learned from the Americans."

"Wanna try a stick?"

"Good Gertie, no. It tastes like a horse manger."

"Where's Pa. I want to ask him for a favor."

"Pa? Garland?" Ma smiled widely. She sure was in love with stepfather. It hurt to think about what they might be doing in their bedroom at night. "Garland is still at work, son."

They had a supper of fresh herring. When Ma broiled herring it was pretty hard for her to ruin it. Sherm had two fish along with some boiled cabbage and two slices of raisin bread.

While Ma washed dishes and Stepfather got out his underslung pipe, Sherm got out a tablet of linen paper and a pencil and began writing.

Ma said over a heavy shoulder, "Ah, at last some homework from school."

Sherm wriggled his nose.

Stepfather took a deep puff and then tongued out a perfect smoke ring. The smoke ring headed for the weather clock above the kerosene lamp. For a moment it completely enveloped the old-man-with-the-good-weather-clothes and then slowly dispersed against the ceiling. "What's that you're writing, Sherman?"

"We're supposed to find out from our parents what it was like living in the Old Country."

"Aha. Well, we're ready to hand if you need information, ha, Ma?"

"Yes, Garland," Ma said as she placed the shining dishes back in the cupboard.

Sherm wrote several paragraphs of made-up stuff. Then, when neither Stepfather nor Ma were looking, he slipped Principal Ault's letter into the tablet under the sheet he was writing on. He slipped the letter up high enough so that only the very bottom edge showed. Right away, though, he could see it wasn't going to work having it stick out an inch. He tore the sheet he'd been writing on from the tablet and then pushed it up along with Principal Ault's letter. That was better. Principal Ault's letter now looked like it might be part of the tablet. Almost the same kind of linen paper.

"How you coming there, Sherman?" Stepfather asked.

"I got a couple of questions. First, in the Old Country, did you really always wear wooden shoes there when you went outdoors?"

"We did."

"What did you wear in the house then?"

"Heavy woolen socks. With sloffies over them. Slippers, you call them here."

"Did wooden shoes cost much?"

"A dollar or so."

Ma picked up *The People's Friend* from the top of the old sewing machine and sat down at the table with her men. "Anything else you want to know, son?"

"Yeh. Did women wear bloomers there?"

"Och! Son. What a question. I suppose next you'll be wanting to look under my dress here in America."

"I meant in the Old Country."

"Of course. They're further ahead there than we are here."

Sherm wrote that down.

Stepfather asked, "Anything else?"

"Ya, Pa. I think it would be nice if I could show my teacher a sample of Old Country penmanship. Could you sign your name at the bottom of the page here?" Sherm got up and went around the table behind Ma and then placed the tablet in front of Stepfather. He did it in such a way that only the bottom of the page showed. It was actually the bottom of Principal Ault's letter. Sherm placed his hand over what he'd written so that the two edges wouldn't show.

"Can't I see what you've written so far?"

"No, Pa. Not until after I get my mark."

"But don't you want to see if I think what you've written is accurate?"

"No. Just sign your name."

Stepfather took the pencil from Sherm and signed his name with Old Country flourishes.

"Ah. Good. Now I've got a good paper. Thanks so much. Boy, will Principal Ault be glad to see this."

Sherm didn't sleep very well that night. He had the signature, but he also had the bad conscience. It really was awful to hoodwink one's parents. But it would be an even worse thing if Ma said he couldn't go to the Academy that fall. Life surely was riddled with sins. Something was off with God's world when a fellow had to choose between two wrongs instead of two rights. The picture on the calendar at the foot of his bed remained an onrushing locomotive all night no matter how hard he tried to make of it a handsome woman. In one of his dreams his foot got caught under a railroad tie and no matter how he struggled he couldn't free it as a huge steam engine loomed up over him. He woke up to his own scream.

He left early for school the next morning and reported to Principal Ault in his office.

"Ah, Sherman. You have my letter signed by your mother?"

"My stepfather signed it."

"May I see it?"

Sherm handed it over. It surprised him to see how cool he was about it all. Maybe that awful nightmare had helped to steady his nerves.

Principal Ault examined the signature. "Hmm." He held it up to the light of the window behind his shoulder. "Looks authentic. With all those fancy Old Country spirals it would be pretty hard to forge that. Eh?"

Forge? It was beginning to sound more and more that he'd done something criminal.

"What did your father and mother say?"

"Well, they thought what I done was pretty awful."

"Did they punish you?"

"You mean, like hit me?"

"Something like that."

"I ran some errands for Ma."

"Did they ask you to do any extra chores?"

"Well, I fixed the turnknuckle on the privy. To keep the door from slowly banging off."

"Anything else?"

"No. I don't have mean parents."

"Well and good. But."

Sherm waited.

Principal Ault tapped the edge of the letter on the glass top of his desk. "I've had some further insights about what your punishment should include. And I've decided, for various reasons, among them the disruption you caused, that our Christian School baseball team shall not play the Academy team this spring."

"What!"

Principal Ault slapped the flat of his hand on his desk top. "Now. Now. There'll be no argument about this! It is an absolute order."

"Well, let our team play them without me then."

"Nope!"

Sherm let his shoulders sag. There was no way a person could change the principal's mind once he'd made it up. The principal was known to be so bullheaded that even the school board was afraid of him. The only reason the board tolerated him was that they knew with him in charge there'd be good discipline in the Christian School. Sherm let himself smile a curved smile. "Well, if we don't play them we won't be breaking any records then. And there won't be any story in the *Sioux City Journal*."

"That's right. There won't be. You may go."

"What shall I tell Miss Betchworth?"

"I'll tell her that a punishment has been exacted that fits the crime."

"Thanks."

When Sherm ran out back to the playing field to play some catch before the school bell rang, he saw Tuffy Janes coming through the trees. Before he could figure out what to tell Tuffy now that there'd be no Academy game, Tuffy waved at him, and with his jeering jackass smile called out, loud, "Sher-mee, did you hear me?"

"He didn't even remember that I saved his neck the other day," Sherm thought.

Chapter Two

That summer Sherm spent part of it visiting first his sister Ada on their farm near Bonnie and then visiting his sister Joan near Blue Wing.

It was always fun to go to Ada's. Ada was a sweetheart. She never seemed to get into an uproar. Always calm and smiling. She had a way of making her lanky husband, Alfred, look like quite a man even though he couldn't read or write. And their oldest boy, Free, three years younger than Sherm, was always a lot of fun to be around. Free was already a pretty good ballplayer. He was a little overgrown, but he sure could hit and throw. And was he full of schemes about games they could play! Best was when they went swimming naked in the Little Rock River below the cliff east of Bonnie. They were so full of it—joy—they would yell all afternoon long. In the evening their ears still ached with it.

Going to Sister Joan was different. Joan's kitchen seemed to be crawling with kids and cats and puppies, and all kinds of sick little pigs and chicks, and one week even a sick calf. The smell was like an uncovered city dump. The worst smell came from sour milk and from dirty diapers in a pail under the sink.

In late August, when Sherm returned home, Ma had to know all the news. She was glad to hear that all was hunky-dory at Ada's house. When Sherm told Ma that her grandson Free had shot up so fast he was now taller than he was, Ma shook her head. Ma said that Ada had better put a big stone on Free's head or he'd grow up to be as tall as King Saul.

But Ma shook her head sadly when she heard about Joan and her family. "Ya, that's what she gets for marrying that lazy dumb-head. Your Pa warned her."

Sherm sneered a little. "Joan didn't have any choice. She had to get married."

"Och, boy, that you should know about such things already."

"Oh, Ma, I know where I come from."

With both hands Ma covered her belly. "Such snotnoses these days."

Sherm buttered a slice of raisin bread, then reached for the sugar bowl and sprinkled some sugar on top of the butter. "Mmm, good, good."

"Boy, boy, how often must I tell you that if there are raisins in bread you don't need more sweet stuff."

Sherm crooked his head. "What Joan and Pete need is a foreman to run their farm. A farm boss of some kind. Who'd figure out what crops was best to put in. How many cows to milk. How many hogs to feed. Run it like a business. Instead of by guess and by golly. Ma, they live worse than the hoboes do out by our railroad tracks."

Ma began to cry. "Joan is a sorrow, all right. I knew from the moment I was strengthened by your father Alfred that when I bore that child it would be a mistake. I already knew it then in my womb."

Sherm finished his slice of sugared raisin bread. "Someday somebody better step in there and straighten out that mess."

School at Northwestern Classical Academy started on the first Monday in September. Sherm found himself a member of a class of twenty-nine, twenty-three boys and six girls. He was quite surprised to see how old some of the boys were in his freshman or "D" class. Two of them were past twenty-one. They'd been hired men for farmers for seven years, and had finally got sick of pitching manure and milking cows. They wanted something better out of life. They claimed they'd been "called by the Lord to minister unto a Little Church congregation somewhere." Ministers lived like lords, had much influence and power in little Siouxland towns. Their girl friends of course were happy with their ambition. They'd be the queen bee at Ladies Aids and other women societies in church.

Sherm was quite startled to see Tuffy Janes also enrolled in the freshman class. Was that pickle puss going to be a torment all through high school?

Three days after school started, Professor Beckering, who doubled as the athletic coach for football, basketball, and baseball, put out a call for football practice.

Sherm didn't tell Ma right away about the football. It turned out that when Cocah Beckering saw how fast Sherm could run and what good hands he had he made a halfback out of him. Sherm was also designated as the passer in the backfield. Interestingly enough Tuffy Janes was made center. To Sherm's surprise, Tuffy's manner around Sherm changed magically. No longer did he razz Sherm with that jeering call of, "Sher-mee, did you hear me." Instead what Sherm heard was, "Okay, buddy boy, let's push 'em back into the end zone," or, "Sherm, intercept that pass!" It was enough to make Sherm cough up a choked laugh.

The second week, practice became so vicious that Sherm came home with torn britches. Ma had specially bought him brown worsted knee pants at Wolfwinkel's Mercantile.

"What happened to you, boy?"

"Nothing. Just tore 'em a little, is all."

"Look at those terrible rips. Were you in a train wreck?"

"Of course not."

"How did it happen then?"

"Oh, I was just fooling around after school."

"So I notice. You come home so late I can't send you to town for bread because by then the stores are closed."

"Why don't you bake our bread then?"

"Smartnose! Telling me what I should do in my own kitchen."

"Can't you easy sew this up?"

"No. And now I want you to tell me what happened. Or else."

Sherm's upper lip almost touched the point of his nose. "Well, if you must know, I was playing football at the Academy." It was a shame that the Academy was so broke it couldn't furnish football clothes.

"Foot-a-ball? In heaven's name, is that another one of those crazy American games they play in this wild country?"

That evening, after dark, Sherm snuck an old pair of overalls and a shirt out to the privy. He hid them behind the door. In the morning he'd start for school by taking the alley, as he sometimes did, and once he was past the barn he'd quick whip around the back of the privy and retrieve the overalls and shirt, and then on to school where he'd place them in a locker.

To his great astonishment, the next morning after he'd hurried around behind the barn, and then the privy, and as he stepped into the privy, there stood Ma, holding that bundle of his old overalls and old shirt, a triumphant smile on her wide red face.

"So!" she cried. "You thought you was gonna play foot-a-ball after all, ah?"

"Why, Ma! The idea of seeing one's mother busy in the privy."

"Pretty clever you are, huh?"

He feared what was coming next.

"After you went to bed last night, I called on Principal Timmer. You know, where he lives around the corner from us? And told him that I have not given permission for you to play foot-a-ball. And I told him that if you do not obey me on this, I'm taking you out of school."

Sherm was suddenly so mad he thought of hitting his mother. Or screaming. Or throwing a fit. Or pretending he was dying of a heart attack.

"Now you get on to school. I put a treat in your lunch bucket to make up for not playing foot-a-ball." She pointed at the shiny lunch pail he was carrying.

Sherm stared at her.

"Why you should want to play with a ball that looks more like a bloated pig with no legs or head . . . what fun can there be in that? Why, it won't even roll."

"Does Stepfather know about this?"

"No, he doesn't. And it isn't any of his business either."

"What will you do if I tell him?"

"Then you can go to bed tonight without supper."

"Oh, Ma, I thought you were long past that for punishment. I'm going to high school now. I'm halfway to being a minister. Like you want me to be." Sherm actually had no intention of ever becoming a man of the cloth. His notion of being a great man was in quite a different direction.

"Look in your lunch bucket to see what that surprise is."

"No. You're not bribing me." His first impulse was to brush past her and throw the lunch bucket and its contents down a hole in the privy, but her bulk was too formidable. Instead he set the lunch bucket down on the wooden plank path. "I'm telling you one thing though, Ma. Next spring I'm gonna play baseball. Or else."

"We'll see about that when the time comes."

"Ma, I can be just as stubborn as you. I can run faster than you. And maybe I'm even stronger than you. You better be careful when you tell me what I can't do."

"What! A child strike his parent?"

"Maybe a child finally has to when his parent has no sense about what a young boy wants."

"Show me in the Bible where a child ever struck his parent! Even the bad ones in the Bible never did."

"Ma, I'm willing to give up basketball this winter because I don't care much for that game. But baseball? Never." Sherm shook his head. "Boy, is Mr. Beckering going to be mad when he finds out I can't be his passing halfback. He was depending on me. Specially on me."

Sherm turned, and without his lunch started hiking towards school.

Before Sherm showed up for football practice, Mr. Timmer already had a talk with Mr. Beckering. Mr. Beckering only shook his head, sadly, and remarked that some Christian parents just didn't understand the innocent American way of life.

At the end of the semester in the first week of January, Sherm brought home his report card. Ma was at Ladies Aid, so Sherm showed it to Stepfather. Garland Stanhorse solemnly ran his finger down the typed list: Algebra, Bible Study, English, History, and Physics. Blinking, he finally looked up, took a deep puff on his pipe and exhaled a huge smoke ring, and then, licking his lower lip, said, "My boy, this is most remarkable."

"Yeh, school is easy for me. Or else those others are so dumb I look good by comparison. When the profs put the curve on us."

"You have a perfect score. A 100 in every one."

"Yeh, well, maybe I've become a teacher's pet, now that I can't take up sports at school. But by golly, I'm gonna play baseball come spring."

31

"Yes, my boy, you and I will have a talk with your mother about that."

"Then you're really not against sports?"

"Sherman, I am a man, not a woman. Women just don't have it in them to like sports."

"Yes. And what really burns me is that Tuffy Janes was allowed to play football. And he was allowed to play basketball this winter too. Ochh!"

One day in February, Professor Lena Lyzen asked to see him after class.

"Yes, Professor."

"Sit down, Sherman." She was a lanky woman, always well groomed in well-designed gray dresses, always wore a necklace of milky pearls, always had her blond hair done up in a Grecian knot. She had a smile for him, an unusual event since she was known to be a crab who was very strict about class attendance and class behavior.

Sherman took the chair beside her desk. Behind her, the handwriting on the blackboard was so perfect it looked like it had come out of their algebra textbook.

"Sherman, I have a favor to ask of you."

Sherm waited.

"I notice you're always prepared for class."

"Yes, Professor."

"You must be diligent about doing your homework then."

"Not really."

"Oh?"

"I get it all done in study hour."

"What?"

"Yes."

"Then that means you were born with a talent for mathematics. God-given."

"Yes, Professor."

"I also notice you're the first to respond to questions addressed to the class."

"I get so tired of waiting for those other oatmeal brains to wake up."

She smiled some more. When she finally unbent, it was like having the sun break through on a cloudy day. "Sherman, Sherman. It's wonderful that you're such a good student. But you see, if you jump in first like that, you don't give the other students a

chance to work it out for themselves. They'll never learn anything this way. As it is now, they depend on you for the answers."

Sherm waited.

"Thus I am asking you to no longer respond unless I pointedly
ask you. I want you to remain silent. You and I will know that you
know the answers."

"You mean I got to sit there like a dumbbell?"

"That's right."

"Oh, Teacher, that's going to be awfully hard to do."

"Nevertheless, in as nice a way as I know how, I'm ordering
you not to respond. Please?"

"Professor Lyzen, you know what I wish?"

"Yes?"

"That I could have a class alone with you. Could I? In your
home, if it would look funny here at school?"

A further smile opened her face and her light-blue eyes, a morning glory blooming for the first time. "I would love that very
much. But it would be against regulations. Also, you couldn't afford to pay me for private tutoring."

"Too bad." Sherm shook his head. "So I guess I'll just have to
sit here and suffer." Sherm shook his head some more. "What
with Ma crabbing all the time about me wanting to play baseball,
and now this, maybe I should just quit school. I'm sick of it all.
Why, Ma don't even want me to act in plays. Or sing in the school
chorus."

Lena Lyzen placed a hand on his hand where it lay over his
knee. "Oh! don't ever think of quitting school. You have a bril-
liant future. As a professor somewhere. Or a scientist."

"I dunno, Teach. Sometimes I don't think much of myself."

She patted his hand. "You're different, Sherman. Look at you.
You always have your hair combed neatly. Your nails are well
manicured. No dirty milking rings." She gave him the warm
smile of a lover. "You surely have wonderful hands, my boy.
Slim and pliant. A pianist's fingers. Have you ever thought of
taking up music?"

Sherm studied her face.

"Miss Folkers says she heard you singing in chapel the other
morning and thinks you have a good voice."

'Ha. I'm still a silly boy soprano. What she don't know is that
sometimes my voice croaks like a frog."

Another gleaming look of understanding suffused her face.

"That happens to all boys, doesn't it?"

"My brother John said his voice changed when he was fourteen. No, all I can do pretty good now is whistle. That is, without my whistling suddenly dropping down an octave."

She realized she'd let her hand rest on his long enough. She picked up a pencil. "You're thirteen, then now?"

"Yes. Last October."

"Well, you'll soon be a man. I can see that. And now I have papers to mark. You will remember not to respond to questions addressed to the class as a whole?"

"Yes, Professor."

In late April, Professor Beckering put up a notice on the bulletin board that candidates for the baseball team should report to the diamond west of the school building the next day, Wednesday, at 3:30.

As Sherm read it he instantly made up his mind. Either Ma was going to let him play or he was going to quit school. Absolutely.

When Wednesday morning came, Sherm dug out his baseball glove from the commode in his room. He saw that it was stiff from all the gobs of spit he'd rubbed into its pocket the previous summer. Luckily his stepfather had a bottle of neat's-foot in the cabinet under the kitchen sink. Sherm had poured a little puddle of the pearly stuff into the pocket when Ma, finished with filling his lunch bucket, saw the glove.

"Och, boy, not that again!"

Sherm set his neck against her.

"Are you taking that to school with you?"

Sherm worked the neat's-foot deep into the pocket as well as up the sides of it.

"Did you hear me?"

Stepfather reappeared in the kitchen doorway. He'd paid a visit to the privy. Or, as he always put it, he'd been out to see if the morning star was still shining. A quick flick of his warm brown eyes and he caught on. "Wife? I shouldn't interfere in this matter, he is your son, not mine, but—"

"Then keep your nose out of this."

"But I'd like to put in a word for your son." Stepfather rubbed his hands together as if getting ready to bless the people. "Your boy has been a model student all year long. Exceptional, in fact. Beyond even what you have a right to expect. I think the boy deserves a reward for that. Let him play a little baseball. It isn't going to hurt him. If anything, like I've said before, it'll keep him out of trouble. It is an innocent sport. When he gets older, he's bound to take up some kind of grown man's work."

"But if I let him play base-a-ball now, he won't grow up to be like the first Sherman. Och! That first Sherman, how he could remember whole sermons, and the long prayer, and all the psalms, and repeat them for his dying father Alfred. And och! how he dreamed of becoming a missionary someday, a preacher of God's word, so that we might all receive salvation in the afterlife, where there shall be peace and love everlasting."

Sherm had enough. He jumped to his feet. "So that's what your scheme is, Ma, to make me over into that first Sherman. Oh, how I wish he hadn't died of scarlet fever, was alive yet today, because then you could have your preacher son and I could be your baseball son. He could've even played catch with me sometimes."

Ma hid her face in her hands. "That I should live so long as to hear such heresy from the lips of a child born of my own flesh—"

"Ma! That's enough. All right, I won't play ball this spring then at the Academy. But I'll tell you something. Just as soon as school is over in June, I'm running away. You and I will be fighting every day like this until I'm twenty-one. And that I cannot and will not take." Sherm folded up his wonderful glove and stomped off to his room. He was about to drop the glove in a drawer, when, Ma's sneaky way of nosing through his things, he tossed it up on top of his mahogany wardrobe. She was too fat to get up on a chair and find it there. Then he went back to the kitchen and picked up his lunch bucket.

Ma stood with head bowed over the dishpan. She was crying, face flushed, eyes closed.

Stepfather filled his pipe and lighted it. He raised his head. He looked a little like those times when, in an imperious manner, he carried a glass of water down a side aisle of the church to the pulpit, just before the minister, followed by six elders and six deacons, marched into the church through the door of the consistory room. "Boy, are you going to leave you mother this way this morning? If you do, it will only fester the more."

Sherm lashed out. "I hope it festers real bad." A mental picture of a carbuncle on the back of brother John's neck popped into his mind. "And turns from a boil of trouble into a carbuncle of endless sorrow." That running carbuncle had dirtied John's pillow for almost a half a year.

Stepfather's mouth fell open, showing gold-capped teeth. And Ma continued to cry, hands adrift in dishwater.

The moment Sherm finished his last exam, in History, he made plans to disappear. After some thought, he decided he'd go live with Joan and Pete near Blue Wing. He'd show Ma he wasn't just a snotnose, but was old enough, and wise enough, to run his sister's farm and help her husband make some money. A couple of years of helping them, and saving up money, he could then disappear once more and try out with the Cubs when they held their spring training on Catalina Island off the coast near Los Angeles.

Somehow Principal Timmer got wind of what Sherm had in mind. He came over, with Professor Lena Lyzen, around nine o'clock one evening, right after Sherm had secretly finished packing a suitcase.

Both Ma and Stepfather were pleased to see them. After a few polite remarks about the lovely June evening, Ma led them into the parlor, Sherm following them with dragging feet. Ma pointed to the dark blue plush davenport for the two guests, took a rocker herself, while Stepfather sat in his smoker's chair beside the bay window. Sherm took the only other chair left, a hardbacker by the open door.

A sweet breeze came in from the west, carrying on it the aroma of freshly cut alfalfa from the Keatsen farm near town.

Sherm turned in his chair as if to jump up and fly out of the open front door.

Stepfather cleared his throat in warm warning.

Sherm settled back in his chair.

Both Principal Timmer and Lena Lyzen gave each other a look.

"Nah," Stepfather said, taking on the role of the head of the house, "what is it that we can do for you?"

Principal Timmer tok a sheet of paper from his inside jacket pocket, opened it, perused it a moment, then said, "Well, Mrs. Stanhorse, you know of course that your son Sherman turned in a wonderful record of scholarship the past year. Never in the history of our school has anyone, anyone, had a perfect hundred for every one of his classes in one year. Both semesters. Ten in all. Now, I am hoping that you are planning to send your son to school this fall."

Ma lifted her head proudly. "God has given my boy a great talent, and I will not permit him to bury it in the ground. Like that man did in the Bible."

"Then you do intend to enroll him this coming fall?"

"Naturally."

"Good." Principal Tammer looked at Sherm. "Well, and what do you say to that?"

Sherm ran his tongue inside his upper lip. "Hey, what makes you think I ain't going to school this fall?"

Principal Timmer turned to Lena Lyzen. A loose fold of skin edged over the top of his starch-white collar. "Lena?"

Lena Lyzen reached out and touched Sherm's knee, in gracious love, and then remembering where she was, with a delicate motion withdrew her hand. "Sherm, if you don't go on to school, it will be a serious loss to us all. You have so much to give. And as time goes on, that gift will become all the more precious to us. You must not lightly ignore God's intention. With that wonderful mind of yours he put you on this earth for a special reason."

"Why am I getting a lecture like this?"

Lena Lyzen crooked her head ever so slightly, as if to suggest that she and he knew something. "I gathered from your attitude in class you were unhappy about something."

Principal Timmer nodded. "And I heard the rumor in school you weren't coming back this fall."

"I never told anybody."

Lena Lyzen smiled the smile of the cat that had just spotted a mouse where the cat knew there was going to be one. "Ah."

Sherm squirmed. Lena Lyzen wasn't only just a nice lady, she was also a clever one. Sherm looked out of the bay window, at the telephone pole he'd once played was the Cubs' first baseman. He turned and glared at Ma. "That mother of mine thinks that taking part in sports is a sin. She won't let me play baseball, my favorite sport. When I dream about baseball night and day."

Ma pounced. "See? 'Night and day.' That base-a-ball has got

so deep in you you'll never get rid of it even after you grow up. Maybe it'll be in you like lust long after you're an old man." Ma nodded emphatically, chin doubling over obscenely. "You're going to school this fall. That's God's will. And you're not playing that boys' game. That too is God's will."

Sherm thought: "Well, we'll see about that. No old lady, even if it is my mother, is going to keep me from doing what I like to do best."

Stepfather tried to smooth things over with an old man's wise smile. "My boy, sufficient unto the day is the evil thereof. Why don't we all wait until early next spring and then we'll see again."

Sherm shook his head, looking black down at his hands. "I know my ma. She's even more stubborn than Simon Peter the Apostle."

Ma gasped. "I've never told lies like Simon Peter, denying he ever knew Christ three times before the cock crowed!" Ma's face slowly thickened and turned pink, then red, and in a moment her tight-closed eyes squirted tears in the corners, so that little rivulets of them began to run down her cheeks to the drawn corners of her white-edged lips. It was a sight that always upset Sherm. He couldn't stand it. For one thing it always meant that she was really hurt, at the same time that she was using it to get her way.

Stepfather Stanhorse took over. "Nah. Perhaps at this point we should pray together. Before one of us says something that the other one will never forgive."

Sherm didn't kneel in prayer at his bed that night. Instead, he checked the pockets of his brown knee pants to make sure Ma hadn't looked in them and found the fifteen dollars he'd quietly saved up the past year. He also made sure that his baseball glove and the baseball he'd made were tucked in the bottom of his suitcase. Next he checked the advertisement he'd clipped out of *The People's Friend* giving the times when the Chicago & Northwestern passenger train, going north, stopped in Alton three miles away. Reassured that there would be plenty of time to catch the 6:10 if he got up at four o'clock, he set the alarm on his little bedside clock and slipped off into a fitful sleep.

Again that night he dreamt a train was aboout to run over him because his toe had got hooked under a railroad tie. The more he struggled to free himself the farther his foot worked under the tie. A demon in him took over then, and whispered in his ear with a wise old leer, "Never give up! Never give up! You're going to be somebody important some day. Very important."

In dream he glared up at the great owling eye of the locomotive as it slowly chuffed up.

A tinny rattling awoke him. he rubbed his eyes. The engine had a little tin bell? Impossible. He blinked his eyes. Ah, it was his alarm clock. Four o'clock. Time to get up. Quickly he reached for the clock to shut it off before the sound of the alarm had worked its way through the wall that separated his room from Ma and Pa's bedrooom. Thank God the alarm bell on top of the clock was hardly bigger than a thimble. He picked up the little brass clock and stuffed it in his suitcase under the bed.

He rolled his blue nightgown up over his shoulders and head, folded it neatly, and stuffed that too in his suitcase. He pawed around on the floor until he found his underwear and socks, put them on, then reached for his shirt and brown knickerbockers draped over a chair. In the deep dark he slipped on his tie.

Picking up his brown shoes and his suitcase, he tiptoed out into the living room, then through the kitchen onto the porch. Carefully he pushed the door closed, holding the knob over until he was sure the latch had caught without a sound. He sat down on the bench outside the porch and slipped on his shoes. Then, looking at the eastern sky, seeing that a pearl-grey had begun to push up into a purple-black, he set out for Alton. He took the back alleys most of the way across town to make sure no one, and for sure not the town constable, would spot him.

Ma would go wild when she'd learn he wasn't in his room. Or nowhere around the house or barn. And she'd first call Principal Timmer; and in turn Principal Timmer would pretty soon call the constable; and then everybody would be in an uproar—but by that time he'd be safely set up at Joan and Pete's place as their new hired hand. By then not even Ada would be able to talk him out of it.

A mile out of town, as he walked past the lane of a farmstead, carrying the heavy suitcase, he heard roosters waking up; first a couple of hoarse crakings, then what sounded like someone blowing through a wet whistle, and then, at last, throat cleared, a beautiful cock-a-doodle-doo, ending with the boastful cock-a-hoop cock-a-whoop.

Dawn spread swiftly all across the eastern horizon, blue becoming pink becoming an exploding yellow. Windmills and tall single cottonwoods stood sharply etched against the blooming light, almost as if someone had taken a scissors and had cut out their silhouettes from black paper and had set them up against the streaming atmosphere.

"Serves her right."

When Sherm came to the city limits of Alton, he skirted along the west edge, then along the south edge, until he hit the Chicago and Northwestern railroad tracks coming up from Le Mars.

The sun bounced up over the horizon just as he stepped into the waiting room of the yellow depot. He snigged up his nose at the dead smell of cigar smoke. There was also another odd smell that he couldn't name. The big clock on the wall to the right showed 5:56.

When the ticket window opened, Sherm bought a one-way ticket to Blue Wing. He asked, "Train on time?"

The stationmaster listened a moment to the clattering of the telegraph transmitter behind him, then said, "Last I heard." His voice had a curious metallic catch in it.

Sherm sat down on a gray bench by the dooor.

The big hand on the wall clock tocked slowly but inevitably around its rust-streaked white dial.

Sherm crossed and recrossed his knees. Would Ma be up by now? Stepfather would be up, making coffee and setting out the plates for Ma. Ma wouldn't look to see why he wasn't getting up until she had the oatmeal and fried eggs ready. He could see his folks very clearly in his head. Just so he was safely aboard the train by the time they checked his room.

There was a long blast of a steam whistle, followed shortly by two quick short toots.

Sherm got to his feet, picked up his suitcase, and walked out onto the cobblestone platform. Looking southwest down the pair of rails shining silver in the slanted morning light, he soon saw, bubbling up over a grove of trees, black smoke, then gray smoke. In a moment the big round dark front of the locomotive nosed into view, followed by the coal car, then the dun-green baggage car, then the dun-green passenger cars. As the train approached, and enlarged, he found himself excited that he was actually going on a trip. The big black engine coming down the tracks right in front of him was an awful lot like the big black engine of his nightmares.

Th brakes of the train clamped on, and slowly the big wheels dragged on the rails, and the driving rods of the steamer made an iron-banging clamor, followed by a squeal of steel sliding on steel; and then all locomotion stopped. Steam hissed out of the engine's petcocks and out of the connecting hoses between the cars.

A conductor with a silver medallion of some kind on his black cap stepped down between the second and third car and placed a portable set of flat broad steps on the cobblestone platform. The conductor bawled, "Board!"

Sherm was the only passenger boarding that morning. Quickly he mounted the steps, turned right into the third car. The car was about two-thirds full. Sherm found an empty seat halfway down on the right. He slid across it to sit near the window. There was a toot from the engine's whistle, and with a light lurch the passenger car began to glide forward, winching sounds cracking below. Looking out of the rain-and-soot-streaked window he saw the depot moving backwards. He was on the way. Actually on a real trip all by himself.

Within minutes the big wheels began to click below him, faster and faster. The passenger car rolled slightly from side to side, not enough to make him sick to his stomach, but enough to let him know he was beginning a whole new way of life. And, only thirteen years old. He could feel his heart pound in his chest, almost hear it. He wondered if the other passengers had noticed anything funny about him. Cautiously looking around he found that most of the passengers were trying to sleep.

"What they don't know is that someday I'm going to be a famous man. Not even the great Walter Johnson will be able to get me out. While Grover Cleveland Alexander, Old Pete himself, will be happy to have me making great plays behind him at shortstop."

Wisps of speckled gray smoke, whipping back from the smokestack of the engine ahead, brushed against the rattling stained panes. Soon he could smell the acrid burned carbon. The smell of train smoke reminded him of those times when he'd had the miserable skitters, sitting on a privy hole, bent over, head between his knees, groaning out of what seemed the bottom of his soul.

The train stopped to pick up two passengers in Hospers; in Pas-

41

sage, to pick up a family of five; in Ashton, an old bewildered woman who resembled Ma; in Yellow Smoke, two dapper salesmen. The country between the towns was almost flat, except where the deep creeks ran. The Floyd River meandered back and forth under the railroad right-of-way, like an errant thread of silver woven into the tight weave of a green-checkered sweater. At every railroad crossing the swaying thundering engine let go with two longs, a short, and one long.

From Yellow Smoke north the train seemed to pick up speed.

The conductor came by and took Sherm's ticket.

Sherm said, "I see we're really going now."

"Behind a couple of minutes, bub."

They rounded a lake, and there in front of them opened the south edge of Blue Wing: elevators, a tall courthouse, a considerable hotel. Before Sherm was ready for it, the steamer let go with a long toot, followed by two short toots, and then the brakes slowly clamped down and they came to an iron-anguished stop.

"Blue Wing!"

Sherm stood up, picked up his suitcase, and shuffled down the aisle, and then into the vestibule between two cars, and then down the steps onto the platform in front of another yellow depot. A drayman stood waiting with a red-wheeled wagon and a perfectly matched set of mottled gray horses.

Sherm started out walking towards Joan's farm three miles to the west.

The day was a good one, as perfect as a dream in June: clear skies, smell of mown greens, children already oscillating in swings under tall elms, some women hanging out the wash on wire clotheslines.

The suitcase soon became heavy no matter how often he shifted it from his right hand to his left hand and back again.

He stopped on a cement bridge over a braiding creek, sitting down for a moment on the round steel railing. He combed back his blond hair with trailing fingers. In so doing he caught sight of a smudge under his elbow. Darn. Must've got that when he leaned on the windowsill in the train. That passenger car sure wasn't soot-proof.

Out of the corner of his eye he caught movement in the running water. Minnows. Hundreds of them with slowly wiggling tails, all managing to keep to the exact same position despite the moving water. Looking down more sharply he made out several blue-black crabs lurking in the shadows of water grass.

He kept hoping some car or wagon would come along so he could hitch a ride the rest of the way. None came. Finally, arms rested, breath caught, he trudged on.

By now Ma and Stepfather would have discovered he'd flown the coop. He could imagine Ma fainting, and crying out to the Lord, Did she deserve this? With Stepfather soothing her with his imperial janitorial air and steady voice. No doubt by now Ma had called sister Ada in Bonnie long distance as well as brother John. Good thing Joan couldn't afford a phone. Or was it that they'd owed so much to the country telephone cooperative that their phone had been disconnected?

Presently, behind a rise, he made out Joan's farm on the right, first the grove of box-elder trees, then the high barn, and then the house. And just like last summer, it was still a run-down place. The paint on the barn had almost been weathered off, so that it resembled a horse that had been skinned, with here and there a vein of old red showing. The house no longer had any color at all. The sidings had about the same color as the old faded shingles on the roof.

As he approached, other things caught his eye: chickens every-where, in the ditch, in the garden, up on the manure piles behind the barn and the pig house; hogs sleeping in wallows of mud; horses standing in the night yard their bay hides matted and un-curried; and cows with dirty flanks just then swaying their way out to the pasture.

Then he saw the children on the back porch, two little boys, a little girl, and a baby in diapers. Joan was some six years younger than Ada but already she had as many kids. He tried to remember their names: Paul, wasn't it? and Alfred? and Janna? and finally Barry the baby. The children spotted him coming down the dusty road and stared at him with the stilled intensity of squirrels sitting upright at the opening of their burrow.

Sherm turned into the rutted dirt lane. No sign of either Pete or Joan. Just the kids and the animals. Well, this was going to be his home the next while.

"Hi there, you young whippersnappers, I'm your Uncle Sherm."

There was no sign the children understood.

43

"Don't you recognize me, Paul? Remember when you and your pa and ma came to visit Gramma in Jerusalem? On the train? The toot-toot?"

A wiggling finally stirred in Paul and a smile opened his sunburned blond face.

Sherm set his suitcase down at the foot of the porch. "My my. How you've grown, Paul. And you too, Alfred. You were only so high when I last saw you. But now you're almost grown up enough to be a first-class hired hand. And Janna, my! You're on the way to becoming a lady."

Alfred was almost an exact duplicate of Paul. But Janna was a shy fat little thing with a thick-lipped smile. The boys were wearing faded overalls with penny nails fixed into their suspenders instead of buttons, while Janna was wearing what had to have once been a Sunday dress, white, but now it was an unwashed yellow with several tears and evidence in back she still wasn't housebroke.

Sherm stepped onto the porch. "And little Barry the baby. What a cute little twerp you are." The baby's gray diaper was still dry, but it had been pinned on in a careless manner with one end sticking out obscenely. "But we can't have this. You looking like a pony stud." Sherm bent over, loosened the safety pins and reformed the triangle of the folded diaper neatly over the child's bottom, and then repinned it. He was careful to slip a finger on the inside of the diaper so the safety pin wouldn't prick skin below. "There. That's better. Now you can pass for the Prince of Wales himself. Who by the way, in case you care to know, is a second cousin of yours ten times removed." All through Sherm's ministrations little Barry smiled softly shy blue eyes at him.

There was a cry in the doorway to the kitchen, and out burst a bubbly fat woman. Her face was contorted by surprise and joy both. "Shermie!" It was sister Joan. My God. She'd picked up even more weight since he'd last seen her. By comparison Ma was only a well-set-up woman. Joan swarmed over him with her thick arms and hugged him so hard she lifted him up off the porch. She kissed him all over his face with thick-lipped wet smooches. Sherm couldn't help but smile to herself, and he let his body go limp. For pete's sake, did she think he was some sort of prodigal son finally returned from the fleshpots of Gramma's town? He tried to shrug his way out of her voluminous embrace, but instead found his nose thrust into the top opening of her faded blue dress and in between her hanging loaves of titty. Her flesh smelled like trapper sourdough. Spook, Ada called it. With an effort, Sherm placed his hands on her belly and pushed herself out of her embrace. "Hey, you almost smothered me to death."

"That's because we love you so much, Shermie." Joan's light-blue eyes were almost light-grey from all the tears. Mottles of flushed red moved up her thick cheeks. She turned to her children. "Did you kiss your Uncle Shermie hello? Huh? Huh?"

Paul and Alfred, abashed, slowly shook their heads.

"Well, we can't have that. Too, give your uncle a nice warm kiss."

Both boys, embarrassed, looked down at their bare feet.

Sherm said, "That's all right, my little uncle-sayers. We can kiss each other tomorrow, huh?"

"Well well," a man said in a soft-mannered way. "So, it's you, Sherman." It was Peter Waxer. Pete was still the same easy-does-it fellow. He was dressed in a pair of new blue overalls and a light-gray cotton cambric shirt and shiny black dress shoes.

Sherm smiled. "My gosh, Pete, you going preaching somewhere?"

"Na." Pete smiled, lazily. "Just going to town a minute."

Joan said, "We're out of bread and salt, so Pete has to go a minute." Then a wondering thought struck her. "Hey, how come you came here?"

Sherm slowly looked around at the children; then quickly, almost furtively, up at the wire strung between the house and a telephone pole out along the road. "Oh, I see your phone is hooked up again."

Joan jerked back, offended.

Pete only smiled a little. "Naw, not yet. It don't hardly pay for us to."

Good. At least they couldn't have got a frantic call from Ma that he'd run away.

Joan asked, "Did you and Ma have a fight again?"

"Hey, what's wrong with your brother coming to visit you once in a while?"

"Nothing."

Sherm shifted from one foot to the other. "No, I tell you, I thought maybe I ought to go visiting my sister and her husband and help them make a million dollars."

Joan's face took on a look that for her was a shrewd one. "Well, we could use a hired man all right. But we can't pay him much."

Sherm crooked his head to one side. "How much?"

"How much would you expect?"

Sherm pawed the porch with the toe of his shoe. "Oh, I should have a dollar a day plus board and room."

Pete ran both hands up and down his new suspenders. "Sounds okay to me."

Joan continued to look at Sherm with quirked eyes. "Too much. Ten dollars a month plus board and room."

Sherm had expected much less. Had in fact expected just board and room for a while. Ten a month wasn't bad. Provided they could actually pay him. Sherm held up a hand and saluted the sky. "Say, since you don't have a phone, I better go along with Pete and write a letter at the post office to let Ma know I got here safe."

Pete buttoned up the side buttons of his overalls. "Why don't you set your suitcase in the kitchen a minute then. I'm going right now. I'm a little behind in the cultivating so we mustn't waste too much time."

"Correcto. Be with you in a jiff."

Soon Sherm and Pete were strolling out to the corncrib, where the car, an old Model T Ford, stood in the alley. All four children trailed after them. Alfred, the boldest, tugged at his father's hand. "Bring us an ice cream cone, Papa."

Pete smiled softly down at his son. "Why, boy, it'll be all melted by the time we get home."

"Then bring us some all-day suckers."

"We'll see."

The old Ford leaned a little to the left. Looking, Sherm saw that the tire on that side was partially flat. Sherm said, "We better pump that up a little."

Pete looked. "Naw. Them's rubber tires and they can take a lot of beating. I have to get some gas and we can have the gas station blow it up for us. They got a new air pressure hose there."

Sherm stepped around to the front of the car. "Shall I spin her tail for you?"

Pete shook his head. "No, better let me. She kicks back sometimes and you gotta know how to hold the crank handle. Like so." Pete took hold of the handle and was careful to keep his

46

thumb back and off to one side. "She can break your arm if you don't hold it like so." Pete nodded his head toward the steering wheel. "You get behind the wheel and pull the gas lever all the way down and the spark partway. And the minute she catches, pull the spark all the way down."

Sherm climbed into the old Ford sedan. "It's already done, captain."

They were in luck. The old engine started on the first spin of the crank. When Sherm pulled down the spark, the four-cylinder engine roared up like it wanted to break free of the chassis. The window in the door rattled.

Pete climbed in past Sherm, and set the gas lever until the engine idled down smoothly. With a smile, Pete backed the car out onto the yard, and, working the foot pedals, started off without a lurch.

Sherm watched Pete carefully. Sherm made up his mind that soon he'd be driving Pete's car to run errands for the family.

Pete drove just fast enough in high so the motor wouldn't kill. Sherm kept pressing his feet down on the wooden floorboards to hurry them along. He wanted some speed. There had to be some difference between the speed of a fast horse and a car.

In Blue Wing, Pete pulled into Ole's station and left instructions to have the tank filled with gas and the tire pumped up. Then he and Sherm went off in different directions to do their errands.

In the post office, Sherm bought a penny postcard, and going over to a slanted desk wrote a note to Ma. The post office pen had a scratchy point and the black ink was so thin it was hardly darker than coffee. Several times Sherm had to write the words over:

"Dear Ma:
Arrived safe and sound at Sister Joan's place. Found all well. No runny noses for once. If you called Ada, call her again to say I'm all right. Maybe they can drive over sometime and visit Joan's. Call our John too.
                                                                              Best, Sherm
P.S. Don't write me any letters telling me you want me back. My mind's made up to help Joan and Pete. Their place is a mess and they talk like they're almost broke. S."

When Sherm got back to the gas station, Pete was still out shopping. Sherm spotted a sign across the street on a one-story building: Henry Engen, County Agent.

"Hey," Sherm murmured to himself. "Now there's a guy who can help us. He's bound to have some pamphlets on how to raise crops in this part of the world."

The county agent was out making the rounds, but Sherm helped himself to various booklets: how to prevent erosion, how many kernels of corn to plant to the hill, what brands of oats grew best around Blue Wing, what fertilizers to apply, how often corn should be cultivated, what kind of grain shocks worked best in wet weather. The agent's secretary gave Sherm a heavy manila envelope in which to carry booklets.

Back at the gas station, Sherm found Pete waiting for him.

On the way home, Pete leaned his nose toward the envelope in Sherm's lap. "What's that, presents for the kids?"

"No. But maybe a present for all of us."

"Like what?"

Sherm explained they were pamphlets to help a farmer make more money.

"Ha. From the county agent, I bet."

"Yes."

"He was out visiting us last month. The nosey nut. He didn't win any friends with us, letting us feel we didn't know how to farm. When, ha, I've been farming all my life."

Sherm decided right then and there he was going to hide the manila envelope for a while. He could read the booklets later on.

"Ha," Pete went on. "He told us we'd probably do better working as moppers in our local creamery."

"Pete, don't worry about the agent. We'll show him."

"That's what I want to hear."

Soon they reached the east end of Pete's farm. Sherm looked out over Pete's fields. "You started cultivating the second time yet?"

"No. That's why I was in a hurry today."

"I'll climb into my old duds the minute we hit the yard." Looking off to the south, Sherm could see from the darker bands of freshly turned black loam that most farmers were well into their second time through the corn. "With the two of us we'll soon catch up with your neighbors."

"I never worry about my neighbors. I go by what I can do."

"Well, we got a whole month to get it done. And a game ain't over until the last out in the ninth."

"You like baseball."

"You bet."

48

"Lazy man's game. Good way to get out of work."

Sherm smiled. Look who's talking.

As Pete turned into their yard, the four children tumbled down off the porch and ambled after them, following the car into the alley of the corncrib. Sherm expected them to be jumping up and down. Instead they stood quietly in the door opening. If Sherm didn't know better they could have been children who'd been beaten regularly. Sherm decided that it must be they weren't eating right.

Albert asked, "Did you bring us some all-day suckers, Papa?"

Pete climbed out of the car after Sherm, then reached in back for a box of groceries. "I sure did. Here you are." Pete doled out hard round candy about the size of red marbles. "You want one too, Sherm?"

"Nope. Hard on your teeth."

"Oh, one won't hurt you."

"Shall I carry the other box?"

"If you please."

Looking in the package, Sherm saw four loaves of white store bread. No wonder those plump kids had no pep. They'd been feeding on what Ada's husband, Alfred, called paff. Sherm shook his head. Here was another thing he was going to get after Joan about—the human body needed good grub just like a steam engine needed good coal to run right.

They had an early noontime dinner of boiled potatoes, fried strips of fatty bacon, store bread with rancid homemade butter, and flour gravy. No vegetables. Lots of thin coffee with skim milk for cream. A long prayer asking for a blessing before the meal and a long prayer of thanks after. No reading from Scripture.

They were in the field by two o'clock. It took a while to get the second cultivator for Sherm ready. The cultivator, once painted red, had stood so long in the grove it was almost totally covered with rust. The four shovels had to be cleaned off on an emery wheel. The wooden shear bolts were so old they had to be replaced with new ones whittled from a branch of ash. The wheels and all working parts had to be greased and oiled.

Sherm worked grimly. He wasn't going to admit he's made a mistake going to work for Joan and Pete. In a couple of weeks his peppy way would, by example, help get them on the right track. All they really needed besides get-up-and-go was some extra brains.

They'd made two rounds before Sherm caught on how to operate the cultivator. If one pushed down on the shovels too hard, the curved shovels wanted to go visit China to let the Chinese know what the Americans were doing on this side of the earth. If one didn't push down hard enough, the shovels hardly scratched the gray loess. As brother-in-law Alf would say, a person could pull a chicken backwards through the field and expect to do as good a job.

By nightfall the two of them had made quite a dent in the back forty acres, a broad strip of freshly turned dark soil, in contrast to the light gray-brown of the rained-on first cultivation.

As they unhitched their horses in the yard near the horse door of the barn, Sherm knew he was at last a farmer. His muscles ached over his shoulderblades all the way down to the tops of his feet. He also had a row of white blisters in the palms of both hands.

Sherm said, "We're gaining on 'em."

"Ya, mabbe so. But I don't mind being last and happy."

Chapter Three

A couple of glances through the booklets from the county agent told Sherm it was already too late in the year to make changes in the way Pete operated his farm. Too bad Pete had set his shoulder against the county agent. But come spring, perhaps Pete might be educated into doing the smart thing.

They managed to get the cultivating done four days after the last farmer in the area had finished his final time through the corn. Sherm wanted to get busy with the harvesting right away. But Pete dawdled around several days, giving as his excuse that the conveyor canvases on the binder needed repairing, that two teeth in the cutting blade had to be replaced, that they really ought to put up the alfalfa first.

"But, Pete, look out there. The oats is dead ripe."

A square field of sixty acres of oats undulated off to the north in soft gold waves.

Pete nodded. "I know. But the alfalfa is about to flower and if cut in flower it don't taste so good to the cattle."

"But a storm with a powerful wind will flatten the oats. And then you won't be able get at it with your binder."

"We'll just have to trust in the Lord."

"But golly, Pete, I hate it when all the neighbors are ahead of you. It don't look good."

Joan meanwhile was as happy as a robin fat with night crawlers. The way Sherm was helping to make the place look snappy was one of the luckiest things that had ever happened to her. She hoped that pretty soon they could invite sister Ada and her family over, and brother John and his family, and not feel ashamed of their home. But until everything was trim and orderly Joan kept delaying writing the letter inviting them to come. Someday Joan wanted to be the one to start the custom of having family reunions.

Joan got after the two older boys to help her with the washing of the hands and faces of the littler kids before each meal. She cleaned up the junk on the back porch and hauled it out to the junk pile in the box-elder grove. And miracle of miracles, she began to wear a fresh apron each day, and combed her gold hair into a tight knot on top of her head, and actually cut down on the amount of fat and butter and store bread at mealtime.

Sherm noticed that the table milk seemed to curdle soon after milking. Sour milk he could never stand. It was worse even now that he sometimes burped the baby. So he talked her into scalding the milk pails, as well got her to set them up on a rack, the mouth of the pail open to the sun.

Every chance Joan got she gave Sherm hugs and kisses. Sherm thought her a pest, worse even than their shepherd puppy with its pink tongue always ready to lick a person.

Ma wrote a series of letters full of lamentations. He was throwing his talent away. He'd been a very bad boy to run off like that. Someday he'd pay for it because the Lord didn't like disobedient children. "And oh my son, someday long after your mother has been laid away in her grave you'll remember her tears. And you'll feel so sorry, be so full of grief, you'll waste away before your time."

Sherm made it a practice to delay reading her letters for a day or two, until he was ready to handle her complaints. He usually folded up Ma's letters, unopened, and stuck them in the watch pocket of his overalls. When he finally did read them, it was usually while paying a visit to the privy, using the weak light coming through the half-moon cut in the door. In the privy he was sure no one could see him read his mail. Finished, he always tore up the letters into tiny pieces and, with a shrug and half a laugh, dropped them into the next hole. As time went on Sherm gradually began to associate the texture of Ma's letters with the urine-stained edges of the heart-shaped privy holes.

But Joan had to know. One noon, dog-tired from pitching alfalfa hay all morning long, Sherm took a nap on the west porch. Presently he sensed a monkeying around with the front of his overalls. At first he thought it was their shepherd puppy trying to snoozle up on his chest. Or maybe baby Barry. Little Barry had the curious notion that uncles liked to have babies sit on a person's nose with their little butties.

The monkeying around stopped; and then it was as if the puppy or the baby were playing around with a piece of paper.

Paper? Sherm's eyes wicked open. God in heaven! It was sister Joan sitting on her fat haunches beside him slowly opening Ma's last letter with a thick finger.

Sherm's right hand struck like a cat pouncing on a mouse. "Here you! What's the idea?" He snatched the letter from her. "You got a lot of nerve."

"Well, I was only wondering how Ma—"

"Don't you know it's against the law to read other people's mail?"

"Who says?"

"The President himself."

"Well, you're not of age yet, and as your older sister, and as your guardian, I have a right to know what kind of mail you're getting."

Outraged, Sherm jumped to his feet. "You? My guardian? When it's really me who's really your guardian getting your life straightened out . . . you got a lot of guts."

Joan stood up, her hips making a popping sound. She turned so deep a red her eyes seemed to color over with it. "Well, you're too tight with our family news."

"That's my news. And I'll decide when it's your news."

"You snotnose, saying you're straightening out—"

Sherm whirled away from her. "Shut up. I ain't gonna hear no more. Time to finish with the haying. We're already a week late cutting the oats. Tempting the Lord like this hoping it won't rain on that super-ripe grain." Sherm stomped off toward the barn to get out the horses.

"Little snotnose," Joan said, low, not quite daring to challenge Sherm too loudly, since he'd really been of great help to them. And cheap help too.

As he stepped past the water tank, he saw an astounding thing. A mottled bull snake was arched up off the ground lipping at drops of water that were squirting out of a leak in the upper part of the tank. Actually. For a second the mouth of the snake looked like the opened red beak of a rooster. For godsakes. So snakes drank water too. And what a lot of guts that snake had to venture into the barnyard where animals could trample it to death.

Sherm hated snakes. The sight of even a little garter snake made him shiver. He was about to get a club, when he saw something that was even more of an eye-opener. About two feet back from the mouth of the snake, in the middle of its torso, was a bulge, a huge one. Had the snake swallowed a gopher?

Just then Pete stepped out of the barn. "Hey, what you lookin' at?"

"Look. A bull snake having himself a drink after he's had dinner."

Pete stepped over for a closer look. "Yeh, I've seen that snake do that before. He's et one of our pullets."

"You mean this snake right here?"

"Yeh. See that scar on his tail? That's where I once chopped him with a hoe."

"Too bad you didn't kill him."

"Not really. The Lord has a purpose in giving us snakes."

"What purpose?"

"Well, a bull snake can be a real friend in your garden. He'll snap up all the bugs and worms. And catch gophers. Nose out moles. Let alone remind us what a mistake Adam made in the Garden of Eden when he listened to that snake and ate of the tree of the knowledge of good and evil."

"Ha, you can say that again."

Finished drinking, the swollen bull snake swung away from the tank and rapidly began to sinuate across the pock holes made by horses and cows, and despite its lump of a belly disappeared through a hole in the wooden fence dividing the cattle yard from the hog yard.

"I still say we should have killed it."

"No, no."

"Anyway, let's hurry and get in the rest of the hay. And maybe we can make a couple of rounds yet today with the binder." Sherm looked around up at the sky. Some wispy mare's tails had come drifting in from the west. "That stuff up there means we're gonna have rain by tomorrow night."

"I ain't gonna worry. I'm leaving everything up to the Lord. He'll provide."

"Ha. Provided we do the work."

"You know, Sherm, sometimes you come close to blaspheming a little."

They got the last load into the haymow at three. They had a

quick sandwich and a cup of dark tea, and then pushed the binder out of the machine shed. Pete got out four of his strongest horses and hitched them to the binder. Sherm didn't think much of Pete's horses. They could pull all right, but they weren't matched well, neither as to color or temperament. The big gray mare was clumsy, the bay mare was jumpy, the black mare was a dumbbell, and the sorrel gelding could still remember when he was a stallion and sometimes tried to mount the mares even when they had their harnesses on.

The first time around the field Pete had to cut a swath against the fence. Sherm followed him, hopping and hurrying after, picking up the bundles out of still-standing oats and throwing them out of the way against the fence. Sherm was out of breath when they arrived back at the gate to the farmyard.

Pete looked down from his seat high on the binder. "You don't have to work that hard, boy."

"We want to win this ball game, don't we?" Sherm threw a look up at the slowly thickening trails of the cirrus clouds. "If we hurry we can still pull her out in the ninth."

"For godsakes, boy, you're not proposing we work through the night?"

"Why not? There'll be a full moon out tonight. See it above the windmill there? Moonshine will follow right after sunshine."

Pete bindered and Sherm set up shocks until five o'clock.

Sherm rushed Pete through slopping the hogs and milking the cows. He rushed Pete through supper. It was Sherm's turn to read a portion from Scripture, so he chose the short Psalm Twenty-Three. When Pete walked out on the back porch to rest a little, Sherm gave him a dirty look, then to shame him stalked out to the barn and curried Pete's other four horses, harnessed them, and hitched them to the binder behind the granary.

"Pete," Sherm called across the yard, "if you shake a leg, we still got a chance to win. Remember, tomorrow we're getting that big storm."

After a while Pete came trudging slowly across the yard, still working a toothpick in his teeth, nose drawn up to show he didn't like being hurried along on his own yard. But Pete was also aware that Joan was watching him through the kitchen window over the sink and that Joan was on Sherm's side of the argument.

It cooled off around eight, and by nine o'clock, in very clear glorious moonlight, the four horses began to show pep, and went around and around the field hardly showing sweat. And Sherm shocked steadily.

At two in the morning, Pete pulled up behind the grove near the gate to the field, and slowly, groaning, stepped down off the binder. Sherm was shocking nearby. Pete said, "I don't care if it rains buckets by morning, but I'm tired. And the horses are dead tired. So we quit for now."

Sherm glanced at the grain still standing. It was a golden square of about six acres. The moon was about to set in the west, a huge round silken pincushion. Its silver shine tinted the gold grain just enough to make a person wonder if he wasn't looking at a field of platinum pencils. "Aw, gee, Pete. Just a couple more hours and the game is ours."

"Nope. Not me." Pete began to unhitch the horses.

Slowly Sherm helped him, now and then glancing at the perfect standing grain still left to cut.

When they had the four horses in the barn, and had unharnessed them and fed them corn and hay, Sherm wondered out loud, "I'll bet I can get the first four horses we used into the barn if I call them."

"What for?"

"Well, I was thinking, I'm still not sleepy. Maybe I can finish the cutting with those rested horses. While you catch up on your sleep."

"Nope, I say no. Too bad, boy. I'm boss here."

"Okay. Let's hope the rain holds off."

"God's will. Let's go to bed, for godsakes."

As they entered the kitchen, Sherm said, "Could I take your alarm clock to bed with me?"

"What for?"

"I still want to win this one. I'll get up first for you."

"Take it. I'm sleepin'."

Sherm set the alarm for five o'clock. Then, kicking off his work shoes, and with overalls and shirt still on, he lay down on his cot in the hot attic. Joan had wanted him to sleep in the same room with the two oldest boys, but Sherm said he was used to privacy and he wasn't going to change that. He fell asleep immediately.

Several dreams misted up in him. In one of them he found himself inside a bull snake, with the snake trying to enter a mousehole and getting stuck in it, and it became so tight Sherm couldn't get his breath. In another dream Pete was bindering away in a

56

field that instead of getting smaller kept getting larger and larger. And finally he dreamt he was up to bat in a game behind school where of all things Ma was pitching. He couldn't believe what he was seeing. Ma was throwing curves that looked like twirling corkscrews, and no matter how much he choked up on the bat and watched her motion, he couldn't hit her. She was a better pitcher even than Tuffy Janes. Just as he was about to come up to bat for the third time, Tuffy Janes showed up around the corner of the schoolhouse and called out, "Sher-mee? Can you hear me?" And then the alarm went off.

Sherm had fed and harnessed the first set of four horses, and had them hitched onto the binder, before Pete came out of the house.

Pete's blond hair was still tousled from sleep. "Don't tell me you've already milked the cows?"

"No. I thought maybe you could do the milkin' while I finished the cutting." Sherm turned on the cool steel seat of the binder and nodded toward the west. "There sits that bank of clouds."

With the sun shining on the front side of the oncoming anvil-shaped clouds, instead of behind it, the clouds were remarkably dark. That was going to be a real soaker.

"You mean to tell me you think you can run that binder?"

"Sure. I've been watching you."

"You'll have a runaway, kid."

"Nah. These plugs are too tired to think of that. After the way we pushed them yesterday."

Pete shook his head. "All right." Pete was already sweating. "Boy, if it don't rain today, it's gonna be hotter than deepest hell."

Sherm was careful not to let the horses know he was nervous the first round. He kept steady lines on them, didn't say giddap too often; and once when he aimed the edge of the revolving platform too deep into the standing grain he kept himself from swearing out loud. A couple of inches of missed oats wasn't going to hurt all that much.

It was old stuff by the third round, as if he'd been cutting grain all his life. He let up on the lines a little, clucked up the horses when they lagged on the corners. He found himself steering the whole assembly of horse hooves, bumbling bull wheel under the center of the binder and the scissoring platform as straight as a plumb line.

By the fifth round he could occasionally take a long look at the oncoming threatening sky. The several anvil clouds slowly swelled towards each other, until they formed one huge towering system. The storm's bottom dragged black along the horizon some twenty miles off. It wasn't going to be a line storm, thank God. Line storms always came on with a great rush of wind, with raindrops flying level. It was going to be more of a long heavy downpour, good for the pastures and the haylands.

Around and around he urged the horses. Soon he could see he had only two more rounds left. Hurray. They were now in the bottom of the ninth and had to score only two more runs to win the old ball game.

About then Pete showed up. He lifted his straw lid and scratched his ropey hair. There was a slow scowl on his face meant to be a smile of sorts. "Pretty good, kid."

"Don't mention it."

"You can step down now and I'll finish her."

Sherm stiffened, made a face at Pete. "Aw, let me finish her. After all, it was my idea to beat that sucker up there."

"Get down. This is my farm and my binder."

"Pete, when a guy is pitching a great game, you never take him out in the ninth. A good manager let's him finish."

"Get down." Pete stepped up on the first rung of the little ladder to the high seat.

"Shoot," Sherm said, thinking of a dirty word. "I guess at that you're the head stud around here." Sherm tied up the lines on the lever to the platform and then leaped lightly down to the stubbles below.

Pete unwound the lines and took up command. As he did so Pete spotted the strip of grain Sherm had missed on an earlier round. "Hey, what happened there?"

"Nothing. I was just being too careful to take a full swath. Didn't want to waste any time."

"Yeh, that sometimes happens when you're new at it." Pete wiggled his broad butt around in the steel seat trying to find a cozy set for himself. "There's some breakfast left over for you."

"Thanks."

When Sherm stepped out of the house, wiping the taste of eggs from his lips, he saw through the grove that Pete had just finished the cutting. Sherm hadn't taken a dozen steps toward the gate of the field when the gravid black cloud let go. Huge drops hit the dusty yard so hard they sprettled up miniature volcanoes. Sherm ran out to help Pete unhitch the horses. Before they could get the horses and themselves into the barn they were sopping wet. Even their feet in their shoes made sucking sounds.

"Well, we won in the ninth."

"Yeh," Pete said, pulling his wet shirt here and there away from his skin, "if we don't get pneumonia."

Three weeks later, when it was Pete's turn to be threshed out by the thrashing ring, it turned out that the Farmer's Elevator in Red Wing declared Pete's oats the best of the year. It had the fattest and heaviest kernels.

"See," Pete said as he sipped his evening tea on the back porch, "it don't always pay to be first in the neighborhood."

Sherm said nothing.

When it got dark, Pete said, "Yah, well, I think you and me deserve a good time, kid. Have you ever gone fishing?"

"No."

"Time you learnt that too. Tomorrow we'll wind up the tail of my old tin can, pull back both her ears, and let her rip all the way to Lake Okoboji."

"Just you and me?"

"Just you and me. Joan and the kids can do the chores for once. When we come home with a bucket full of bullheads, they won't crab much."

Sherm began to feel better. "On the way through town maybe we can cash that check of mine."

Pete clammed up.

"You know, my wages. I've been here now two full months and I got twenty bucks coming."

Pete lifted his teacup to suck up the last drop.

Sherm turned in his folding chair and faced Pete. "You are going to pay me, aint' you?"

Pete finally drawled, "Seems kinda funny to be paying wages to a relative."

"Hey, you and Joan ain't thinking you got me for nothing this summer, are you? Specially when I've helped you two get organized."

"We'll have a lot of fun fishin', kid."

Here was something else to worry about. From what Joan had let slip, he knew that Ma had twice written Joan to say that she was thinking of asking her own sheriff to ask Joan's sheriff to have him sent home. By law.

59

"Pete, I want that check. Today. Or by golly, I'm pulling up stakes and going to my brother John's. I know he's been thinking of renting an extra eighty acres and I can help him with that."

"Don't get your water hot, kid. We'll work it out."

"You ain't overdrawn at the bank now, are you?"

Pete got to his feet. "Time to go to bed, kid."

Sherm hated being called a kid.

Pete stepped into the kitchen a minute to tell Joan that he and Sherm were going fishing the next day. There was a brief spat between Pete and Joan, but Joan abruptly gave in when she heard the harsh gravel in Pete's voice. She'd learned that when Pete finally got mad, he sometimes pounded people.

Pete stepped out on the porch again. "Before we hit the hay, kid, we better get us some night crawlers. I'll go get us the flashlight and I'll show you how to catch them."

"I thought you looked for them under wet boards."

"Those are just angleworms. What we want are the big ones. And they're awfully tricky." Pete got himself the flashlight and brought Sherm a fruit jar for the night crawlers.

It had become rusty dark out. The earth smelled sweet after the rains. Pete led the way onto the lawn behind the house, between the privy and the kitchen door, where Sherm had every now and then that summer pushed an old clattering lawn mower. It improved the looks of the old farmstead to have a neat lawn around the house.

Pete whispered, "Now, we mustn't walk too loud. You see, a night crawler is a pretty careful critter. He don't take chances. He's got to look around for sweetheart crawlers, but, at the same time, he keeps his tail hooked in the ground so he can quick jerk hisself back into his hole in case of danger."

"Hooked?"

"Yeh. He thickens his tail until it's sort of gets wedged tight into the opening of his hole. I've seen 'em already where they were seven, eight inches long, fat, and then when they felt a footstep near, they folded back into theirselves like an accordeen. And then they're gone." Pete scratched his side. "We'll stand here a little while until they get used to us. Then I'll quick snap on the light and then you reach down and grab 'em before they retreat."

Sherm was sometimes surprised by Pete's language. Most of the time Pete talked like a dunce. But every now and then he'd let fly with a big word like "wedged" and "retreat." There was more to Pete than just animal grunts.

"About now they should just about be kissing," Pete whispered. "Worms has got it over us. They can kiss with both ends of theirselves. They're 'maphrodites and can even make babies with both ends."

Sherm thought: "Good thing we human beings can't. Or the world would be even more full of dumbbells."

Pete whispered, "Okay, now let's both squat down easylike. And when I snap on the light, make sure you grab 'em by the tail close to their holes. If you don't, they'll slip away like a greasy rubber band."

Sherm slowly knelt down.

Then Pete snapped on the flashlight. And there they were, dozens of them, pale pink wonderfully agitated bands of life. Sherm quickly grabbed up two and dropped them into the fruit jar. Pete, more practised, managed to lift up a half-dozen, gently, and let them unfold into the fruit jar. The worms made Sherm feel squeamish.

Pete snapped off the light. "We'll wait a while again. Should really have fifty or so for a fishing trip." Pete whispered some more. "I see you let a couple get away on you. You wanna plop your hand down quick and hold 'em in place, even push down on 'em a little, steady, until they let go of their hole. Don't bruise 'em though. We want them crawlers full of pep, so that when we hang 'em in the water, they'll wiggle around like the dickens and catch the eye of a bullhead."

In a half hour they managed to catch some sixty. Pete got a handful of damp crumbles of dirt and dropped it amongst the worms.

The next morning, slipping into their town overalls, and clapping on their straw hats, Sherm and Pete climbed into the old Ford and headed for town. Sherm wasn't too surprised when Pete first pulled up to the First National Bank and went in and cashed his last cream check. Sherm had also heard Pete and Joan arguing in their bedroom downstairs during the night as to whether or not Sherm should be paid his wages right away. It sounded like Joan was even more convinced than Pete that it was funny to be paying wages to a relative.

Back from the bank, Pete handed Sherm his wages for two months, four five-dollar bills. Sherm carefully folded them into the watch pocket in the bib of his overalls. He quietly resolved he was going to hide that money somewhere in the house. After catching Joan snitching Ma's letter from his pocket that noon when he was taking a nap, he no longer trusted her.

"Trouble is," Sherm murmured to himself, "a fellow ain't no match for sneaky dunces, no matter how smart he is. They'll spend night and day for weeks slyly working up a scheme to rupe you, while you're busy thinking about the great game you're gonna play, and then when you least suspect it, they spring the trap." Sherm held his head to one side. "Well, with all us smart bozos around maybe that's the only way they can get their fair share."

As they drove through Blue Wing, Sherm spotted a sandwich board standing in the middle of downtown. On it someone had scrawled in chalk:

> "Baseball tonight!
> Blue Wing vs. Whitebone.
> Come one come all."

"Hey," Sherm cried, "I didn't know Blue Wing had a team. If I'd 've known that, I'd 've gone to see some of their games. Walked into town even."

"Going to ball games is a waste of time."

"I'd rather go to a ball game than go fishing."

"When you grow up you'll know better."

"And you'll know better when I start playing for the Chicago Cubs someday making fifty thousand dollars a year. Besides enjoying life."

Pete leaned over the wooden steering wheel and looked up at the sky. "Gonna be a great day for fishin'. Hardly any wind. And that in the southeast. A nice soft day."

"You never played ball, did you, Pete?"

"Oh, I triedt it once. But I t'row like a woman."

That accounted for it. Sherm felt a little sad that the glove he had in his suitcase hadn't been used all summer long. Next year he was going to change that. Come next March he was going to tell Joan and Pete that he wanted twenty dollars a month in wages, payable always at the end of each month, plus the right to try out for the Blue Wing baseball team and, if he made the team, the right to play shortstop for them on those nights when they had a game. Meantime, he was going to find himself a discarded broom handle somewhere and go out to the gravel road and hit stones again. Somehow he had to keep his batting eye real sharp.

They were the only boat out on blue Lake Okoboji. There were no waves, not even a single slow undulating ripple. The whole lake was a huge limpid blue eye on the body of the land.

Pete showed Sherm how to hook on the fat night crawlers, catching them twice through their limp bodies and in such a way they could still wriggle pretty lively. Next he showed Sherm how to swing out the hook slowly with the weight and the dobber in such a way that it landed gently on the surface of the water and well away from the boat. He also warned Sherm to be careful not to get the hook caught in his neck or ear. Out on the lake Pete's blue eyes took on a lively glinting deep blue.

Pete knew too where the fish were. Pete pulled up one bullhead after another, and hooked the stringer through their gills, while Sherm had no luck on his side of the boat. When Sherm complained that he was on the wrong side of the boat, Pete smiled, and changed sides with him, and continued having great luck. And Sherm still didn't get a single nibble.

Sherm muttered to himself. "Them dang fish must know I'm a greenhorn."

"No," Pete said, letting the soft parts of his speech purr a little, "no . . . trouble is, you're still dreaming about baseball and not about fishing." Pete hauled in another bullhead with a steady sure pull. He unhooked it and put it on a second stringer. "You see, kid, what you gotta do is think like a fish. You gotta go down and become a fish. In this case, a bullhead. Be hungry for a worm like a bullhead. You mustn't think about church, about planting corn, about making a baby with your wife. You gotta think like a bullhead."

"Hmm. Well, I'm hardly ready to make babies yet."

"You see, a bullhead actually thinks he's God. And in a way he is, so far as he can think. Now that's the way you gotta think. Then you'll catch fish."

Sherm decided not to say more.

Around noon Sherm got his first nibble.

Pete swung around to have a look. "Wait," he whispered,

"wait now. The first two nibbles he's just testing to see if he likes the taste of the worm. But on the third nibble, he'll want to gobble it down. That's when you give your line a jerk to set the hook."

Another nibble.

"Wait."

Third nibble.

"Nab him now!" Pete whispered sharply.

Sherm gave his pole a lifting jerk. Then, easily, he pulled a fat bullhead out of the water. "I'll be jiggered. My first fish." He unhooked the bullhead, careful not to get pricked by the bony spike on either side of its wide head, and slipped the metal end of his stringer through its gill. He thought the skink smell of the bullhead wonderful. "Someday, when I hit my first homer with grown-ups this is the way I'm gonna feel."

Sherm snagged three more, and then Pete decided they had enough. Together they'd caught sixty bullheads and had thrown back fifteen as being too small.

Back on the yard, with the kids and Joan hovering near, Pete showed Sherm how to skin them. Bullheads didn't have scales. Pete cut a circle around the fish just behind its head; then, taking a pliers and catching hold of the end of the skin, jerked the skin off towards the tail, where he chopped off the rest with a hand axe.

Pete handled the whole operation like a master. "Great eating fish," Pete said. "No bones to catch in your throat. It's a little like eating a small pig."

Joan said, "I suppose I better fry 'em all up so they won't spoil." With a sly accusing look at her husband, she added. "So long's we ain't got an icebox. Yet."

Sherm hated bickering. He had been sick of it with Ma and he was sick of it with Joan and Pete. Oh, to live with some family someday where everybody tried to get along without trying to stick it into somebody. Sherm turned to the boy Paul. "How would you like to play catch with your Uncle Sherm?"

"Uk, uk," Pete warned. "There'll be no ball playing for my kids."

"Not even play catch?"

"Nope. Joan?"

Joan nodded. "We don't believe in sports."

Sherm sneered. "Against your religion, I suppose. Seeing as you get up too late on Sunday morning to go to church."

64

Joan said, "Shermie, sometimes you're kind of a smartass."

"Well, around you poeple I have to be. A little."

Joan went on. "We do go to church Sunday afternoons. Getting us all dressed for church is a lot of fuss and commotion."

"Trouble is, you start dressing the kids a half hour too late. Hehh. I sure get sick of having to march up the aisle all the way through church and wind up sitting in front. Right under the minister's beak. Where he sometimes spits on us when he starts ranting and raving."

Pete said, "People who sit in back like to sleep a lot. We at least have got to stay awake and listen to the preaching of the gospel."

Sherm said, "I still don't see why your kids can't play around a little with their uncle."

Pete jerked the skin off another bullhead with a hard wrenching motion. "We don't even want them to get started playing base-a-ball."

That night the whole family gorged on bullhead meat. Sherm had to agree that Joan sure knew how to fry them. She dipped them in a mix of four and cornmeal, and then dropped them in a kettle of boiling lard. She knew too just when to take them out, so that the bullhead flesh melted in one's mouth like soft cake.

The next couple of months Sherm and Pete got along reasonably well. There was no need to rush to keep up with the neighbors. After the grain harvest farmers generally took their time hauling manure and getting the fall plowing done before corn picking time. Pete told Sherm he wouldn't have to do any yard chores if he would do the plowing that year.

Sherm quickly learned how to operate a two-share Emerson plow with five draft horses. After a little juggling, Sherm decided which two horses made the best lead team and which three made good pullers in back.

Sherm found himself an old broom handle, and taking along a salt sack full of pebbles, often took batting practice when he stopped to blow the horses on the far end of the field. He was careful to do it out of sight of the yard. There was no need to rile up Pete. Sherm was also careful to sometimes rest the horses on the yard side of the field so Pete would know he was good around horses.

When Sherm rested the horses near the gate to the yard, the children came tumbling out to greet him. Though all four were a little on the slow side, around Sherm they were active enough to want to sit on his lap or play they were plowing by sitting on the steel spring seat or pet the horses' noses.

All through September there was but little rain. Mornings were almost always yellow clear with fall light. Swallows swept the house lawn for bugs and flies, flying a foot above the mown grass in long circling ovals. Their blue feathers glinted black in the forenoon light. Faintly their beaks went click-click click-click. Evenings were cool the moment the sun set in the west. Thrushes in the wild gooseberries behind the grove sang their evening-mood lullabyes, a soft flutelike song with falling notes, ee-o-lay, ee-o-lah.

Carrots and onions harvested from the garden tasted at their very best. Sherm helped Pete butcher two pig fatteners and one steer, and helped with pressing out the lard, and making sausages, and hanging beef and ham in the smokehouse behind the house. Life on the farm with relatives seemed to have turned out pretty good after all. Pete was shaping up into a good farmer.

Sherm was also pleased that Pete paid him his ten dollars a month on time and that Pete did it with no grudging remarks or any show of reluctance. By the end of September Sherm had saved up four five-dollars bills out of the forty dollars he'd earned that summer. He'd spent twenty dollars for socks, a new straw hat, new shirt and overalls, underwear, and ice cream cones for the kids when they went to town Saturday nights.

Sherm asked Joan if he could use an old trunk of theirs for a chest of drawers in the bare attic. She said it was okay. They'd inherited it from Pete's father, who'd taken it with him from the Old Country. The trunk was made of black-painted oak. It had knobby ornamental brass guards on all eight corners. Sherm noticed that the guard on the bottom right side, in back, didn't fit tight. There was a little gap between it and the wood.

Sherm studied the gap a moment, and then, with a knowing shake of his head, decided it would make a perfect place to hide his four five-dollar bills. He folded the four bills into a tight wad and shoved the wad into the gap. The wad just fit, with the ends barely showing. A person would've had to know exactly where to look to notice them.

Every so often Sherm extracted the four bills to count them, and then stuck them back into the gap. He did notice after a while that the sharp edge of the brass guard had rubbed off part of Lincoln's nose on the outside bill.

The day of his birthday in October, the tenth, just as Pete and Sherm were about to start picking corn, Joan and Sherm had an awful blowup.

Pete had mentioned at breakfast that he and Sherm had probably better go to town to buy themselves some double-thumbed mittens. Since it was up to the hired hand to buy his own mittens, Sherm decided to go along. He went upstairs and extracted two fivers from his wad, from the inside of it, and then put the other two back in the gap. In town, Sherm discovered that a pack of twelve pair of mittens cost him only four-eighty. While he waited for Pete to finish shopping, he got himself a malted milk for ten cents and two candy bars for a dime.

Coming back to the yard, Sherm said he'd be right down and help Pete catch the four horses, a team of two for each wagon, and then they'd be ready to tear into the cornfield. Sherm hurried upstairs, tipped up the heavy black trunk, and kneeling, withdrew the wad to fold into it the fiver he hadn't spent.

The wad felt thinner than he expected. What? Unfolding it, he saw there was only one bill left. For pete sake. He examined the remaining bill carefully. By golly. The outside fiver with the worn Lincoln nose was gone. In godsname. Had Joan somehow found his secret hiding place? It would be just like her. Again he remembered the time when he'd caught her rustling a letter out of his bib pocket while he slept on the porch. At the same time he had to be careful not to make a false accusation. Suppose he himself had somehow mislaid the fiver with the bruised nose, and she hadn't stolen it. It would ruin what warmth had grown up between himself and Joan. And Pete would get pounding mad. So he had to be careful. He made up his mind to wait and have a good think about it.

Dutifully he went downstairs, said nothing to Joan, who was noisily getting dinner ready, and went out to the barn. He helped Pete round up the four horses, and curried and harnessed them, and fed them.

Pete noticed Sherm wasn't smiling. "Something the matter, kid?"

"No."

"Worried you won't be able to keep up your end of it picking corn?"

"No."

"What's eatin' you then?"

"I'm busy thinking."

Pete houghed up a laugh. "Be careful, kid. I know when I hit a knot in life, too much thinking makes me thin."

"We'll see."

Pete finished buckling up the last harness strap. "Let's tie on the feed bag while these old plugs finish their dinner."

Right after Pete had asked God to bless the food set before them, Joan smiled with an especially fat smile at Sherm, "Well, brother, how does it feel to be fourteen?"

"Fine."

Joan looked at Pete, then at her two youngest children, then back to Sherm. The two older children were off to the country school on the corner of their farm. "Tisn't every day a person gets to be fourteen. I remember when I got to be fourteen years old."

Sherm couldn't resist stinging her with one. It was about something brother John had told him. "Wasn't that when our pa told you not to come home from a date with a pants on over your head?"

Joan flushed. "Why you snotnose you, talking that way to your older sister." She threw another look at Pete. Pete had also reddened. "I got half a notion not to give you your birthday present."

"It's okay by me," Sherm said. "No sweat off my nose."

Pete helped himself to some mashed potatoes, two slices of bloody beef, and poured on the flour gravy until the whole mess resembled a huge mound of ice cream covered by pale chocolate. He passed the platter of food on to Sherm. "Help yourself to the spuds, kid. Lots of 'em. Picking corn is going to be hard on you. In a month you'll be so thin you'll look like a pair of pencils."

"Thanks."

Joan's red face gradually returned to normal. "Ain't you curious at all about your present?"

"No." Sherm did wonder a little when she'd had the time to buy him something.

"Well, I'm gonna give it to you anyway." She reached inside her pale gray-green dress and drew from between her loaves of breast a folded bill. "Pete and me didn't know what you'd really like, so we decided to give you money instead. That way you could buy what you wanted." She held it out to him across the table.

Sherm stared at the bill. It was a fiver.

"Take it," she said. "And congratulations."

Sherm was afraid to look closely at the bill. But he finally did take it.

Joan said, "We had to do a lot of pinching and scraping to come up with those five dollars, what with all the kids we got to raise, and bills to pay, and the minister's salary too yet."

"You wouldn't kid me now, would you, Sis?"

"What do you mean, kid you? We did pinch a lot to get up your gift."

Sherm opened the folded bill and turned it over. There it was. The bill was the one where part of Lincoln's nose had been worn off. Sherm slowly lifted his eyes and glared at Joan. "Yes, you did pinch a lot. Five bucks' worth."

Once more Joan flushed, red rising from her neck up over her cheeks, all the way to the roots of her blond hair. "You better not look a gift horse in the mouth, little brother."

"No, but I am looking at the nose of this horse." Sherm looked down at the picture of Abraham Lincoln. "Begging your pardon, sir." Sherm lifted the bill so Joan could see what he meant. "See this spot here where the bill looks almost worn through? Right over this president's nose? I recognize that as belonging to the bill I had on the outside of a wad of bills I hid in the gap in the brass guard on the bottom right side of that old trunk. The wad was a little too thick for that gap and taking the bills in and out it wore off on that nose." Sherm pointed. "See?"

Joan was dumbfounded. So was Pete. Their look meant that both knew she had rustled through his things, in and around the trunk, and had done so while Sherm was in town.

"You stole this, Sister."

"Are you accusing me of being a thief?"

"What else? I've got the goods on you."

"Why you little puckersucker you! And that after all we've done for you. Giving you a home when you ran away from Ma's. Teaching you how to farm. Helping you—"

Sherm popped to his feet, sending his chair flying against the wall behind him, scaring the two little children so that they began to cry. "The gall of you two! First you steal my money, then you give it to me as a gift, pretending it was a hardship for you. And then you say you did me a favor putting me up all summer . . . when the truth is, I've made a respectable farm family out of you. Got you straightened out from your lazy ways. Today, because of me, your milk doesn't curdle any more. Because I got after you about that." Sherm could feel his face burning he was so angry. It was awful to have to say such mean things about one's own flesh and blood. But there it was. The truth. "In fact, I've had enough. I'm leaving. And the little you owe me for this month, the first couple of weeks, you can stick it up you know where."

Chapter Four

As Sherm walked past the stockyards on his way to the Blue Wing depot, Sherm spotted a red cattle truck. On the front of the rack was a small sign:

Troy Barb

Bonnie

Trucking done cheap.

"Hey," Sherm said aloud. "Maybe this Barb fellow just hauled in a load of stock and will start to head back to Bonnie yet this afternoon."

Just as Sherm rounded the red truck, a man in gray coveralls and wearing an engineer's gray cap stepped out of the Buckeroo Cafe. The man was carefully picking his brown-stained teeth.

"Something for you, kid?"

"You going back to Bonnie soon?"

"Right now."

"Do you know John Engleking there?"

"Fat or Slim."

"Well, my brother sure ain't fat."

"You a brother of Slim John then?"

"Guilty. Could I ride with you to Bonnie?"

"Sure thing. Hop in." The trucker looked down at Sherm's suitcase. "Better not throw that inside the rack. Still some fresh steer plops in there. Hmm. I think there's room for it behind the seat in the cab."

They headed west out of Blue Wing down Highway 16. The land spread before them in long rising and falling waves. Plowed land lay in purple rectangles. The faded gold tassels of the corn-fields drooped in tattered shreds and the fat hairy ears hung down like pony tails. The only thing left green were the pastures and the alfalfa fields.

Troy Barb said, "You play baseball?"

"You bet."

"Figured you probably did. All you Englekings are good at it. Your brother John. Your cousins Garrett and Alfred. Even Fat John. What a catcher he is."

"You sometimes see them play then."

"Your church team plays the town team."

"You play?"

"Nope. I'm all thumbs. But I sure like to watch them two teams play. They fight like bulls. But then, when the game is over, they visit around like friendly old cows."

What a picture. Sherm laughed.

Presently they began to coast down from a height of land. Below in a valley lay Whitebone, a pretty little city so thick with trees it was hard to make out any buildings, except for downtown. A river curled twinkling past the powerhouse and flowed serenely south. Two miles north of town the land surged up toward a huge outcropping of lichen-covered scarlet rock. The upthrust crest resembled a range of little mountains.

"Hey," Sherm said, "what's that?"

"Them's the Blue Mounds. Lot of wild prairie left up there. A fellow can raise fine fatteners on that buffalo grass. I know. Because I trucked some heifers down to Bonnie one day. You should've seen how the hair on them Shorthorn heifers shone. They was as pretty as one of your speckled Frisian-Holstein champions at a county fair."

"Bet you can see a long ways from up there."

"Our Bonnie banker once took the Bonnie Omaha train up to Whitebone here, and rented a horse and carriage and drove up there on a picnic. He says a feller can see thirty miles in all directions. Even all the way to the tip of the water tower in Sioux Center."

Sherm whistled. "It would be like looking down at the land from a U.S. Army balloon."

From Whitebone they drove south on the old King's Trail, following the river valley, through Rock Falls, past Lakewood, and finally into Bonnie.

Troy Barb said, "Tell you what. I'll drop you off at Garrett

Engleking's hardware store. From there you can ring up your brother."

"Many 'bliges."

"Don't mention it."

Sherm stepped into the hardware store. Shining galvanized pails and several new red wheelbarrows were arranged neatly in the big glass-front display windows. There was the smell of a freshly oiled floor. The aisle down the middle was packed on either side with washing machines, iceboxes, kitchen cabinets. Open drawers full of various sized nails lined the west wall, and shotguns and shells the east wall.

A handsome man with pompadour gold hair stepped out from behind a wall of rolls of linoleum. "Well, look what blew in with the tumbleweeds. Sherm."

"Garrett." How good it was to see his cousin. Sherm had always liked Garrett, had felt sorry for him when he heard that Garrett's wife had died. There had been something of a mystery about her death, a mystery Ma wouldn't talk about. Garrett attracted women like a prince might; and that wasn't funny because Garrett did resemble the Prince of Wales. The Englekings and the family of the Prince of Wales came from the same part of northwest Germany.

"It's been a while." As Sherm shook hands with Garrett he remembered something else. The Englekings shook hands in a funny way, lax, as if they didn't believe in a handshake, as if it was beneath them.

"Yeh. At the family reunion at Bosch's grove near Hello. The same time all the churches in our classis happened to hold a Fourth of July picnic there." Garrett looked at Sherm's hands. "You still play ball?"

"Ask me if I still eat."

"Good. We need a shortstop for our church team."

"Just my dish."

"Too late to play any more this year. But next year we'll get 'em. The town team is getting too proud of itself."

A powerful-looking man wearing a ridiculously small panama hat stepped in through the front door. He too right away recognized Sherm. "For catsake. Every time you look around there's another one of us whiteheads."

Sherm had always liked Fat John too. Fat John was known to

have lifted a barrel of salt onto a bobsled without help. Instead of shaking hands with him, Sherm reached out and patted Fat John's belly. "Better get rid of this."

"Oh no! I just got it."

Garrett said, "Fat, if you went and lost fifty pounds, you could catch for our team again. And I could go play center field."

"No can do." Fat John fondled his barrel of a belly. "This is my insurance policy."

"Fat lot of good that's going to do your family when you die. Who'll cash it in?"

Fat John stood with the sides of his new blue overalls unbuttoned. "Well, my wife can always sell me as a tub of suet to a soap factory."

Garrett started to laugh as a way of apologizing for what he was going to say next. "You know what the guys along Main Street are saying these days, don't you, as they watch you and wife Etta get into your old Dort?"

"I wouldn't care to know. I've just about heard it all."

"They'd give twenty-five dollars just to see you and Etta fornicate."

"Ha. They wouldn't see much. My business is all fizzed out. And her business, you can't find it."

Sherm was a little shocked. He knew about Uncle Great John's children had been raised different, full of rough laughter, as compared to his father Alfred's family.

Fat John heaved his bulk around. "Sherman, what brings you to this old burg?"

"I'm on my way to my brother John's."

Fat John reset his little white panama hat on his huge globe of a head. "I'll be going home in a minute and drive right past his place. If you're not too proud to be seen with me you can ride with me."

"Well, seeing as that your father and my father were brothers, maybe I can stand it."

"I got my Dort parked east of the bank. I'll go pick up the groceries at Rexroth's and meet you there." Fat John left.

Garrett asked, "Did you take your glove with you?"

"It's right here in my suitcase."

"Wanna practice short hops by yourself?"

"Sure."

Garrett reached under a counter and came up with a tennis ball.

"Here, take this. It's been pretty well roughed up, but you can still bounce it against a garage door and play you're shorthopping a grass cutter."

"You play tennis?"

"You tell 'em. We got a court east of the Millinery Shop."

"I didn't think Bonnie was that up on things."

"Bonnie is on the move. Someday we're going to be the great astonishment of Leonhard County. If not the world."

"Ha. An Engleking is never licked. Somehow we always manage to pull it out in the ninth."

"Now you're talkin'."

Soon Sherm was rolling east out of Bonnie with Fat John. The Dort was a small car and seemed hardly strong enough to support the vast bulk of his cousin. The Dort leaned to the left as it ground up and down several slow hills.

Two miles out of town, Fat John let the engine gear the car down and turned right down a narrow road toward a small grove of box elders and several old apple trees.

Just before Fat John turned into Slim John's lane, he said, laconically, "I hear you went to the academy a year in your ma's town."

"Yeh."

"Like it?"

"Ma crabbed too much for me to like it."

"She agin education?"

"No. She didn't want me to play ball after school."

"Maybe it's just as well. Education after the eighth grade don't do you much good. Once you know how to count pigs and read your bank statements, you don't need more."

Fat John pulled up at the end of a cement walk. The walk led to the kitchen door of a two-story L-shaped country home painted cream and green. A slim man, brother John, was sitting on the front stoop slipping on his workshoes.

Sherm grabbed his suitcase and stepped out of the car. "Thanks, Fat. Someday when I get my first car I'll give you a ride."

"Don't buy a Dort then. Buy a Pierce Arrow." Tipping his white panama hat, Fat John let out the clutch and the Dort with a crushing grind of gears groaned off.

Brother John finished tying his shoes and stood up. He pretended shock. He called back into the kitchen. "Wife, bring me a heart pill."

75

"I figured this might be a shock to you."

Slim John came up and put his arm around Sherm. "It's always good to see you, bud. Especially a bud off the same branch." Slim John wasn't much for shaking hands either. "Here, hand me your suitcase."

Sister-in-law Matilda stepped out onto the stoop. She had straight light-brown hair done up in a knot in back of her head. Her eyes were big and wide and very blue. "Why, if it ain't your brother Sherm."

Slim John reared back on one leg. "Well, if he's somebody else, I'm gonna have to get spectacles."

Matilda dried her hands in her green apron. "And you've grown up so," she went on in her flat-out Frisian way. "Though of course you ain't gonna be as big as John."

Sherm wagged his head. "Thanks a lot. And here I was thinking I was gonna pass him by a good foot."

Matilda asked, "What's up that you should favor us with a visit at exactly this time?"

Sherm made a face. He didn't want to talk about Joan in front of Matilda. Matilda was just dying to get the goods on members of John's family. Matilda was especially jealous of sister Ada and her family. "Nothin' really. I'll tell you about it in due time."

Matilda said, "Who was that brought you here?"

"Fat John."

"Oh, him. He owes such big bills all over town."

Both Sherm and Slim John winked at each other.

The screen door behind Matilda opened and out rambled little Alfie. "Uncle Sherm!"

Sherm settled on his heels and placed both his hands on little Alfie's shoulders. "Hi."

"You come here to help my dad haul 'nure?"

"If that's what he wants me to do, sure."

"Pheasant 'nure too?"

"Even cat manure if that's what he wants."

Matilda's nose for news wasn't to be deflected. "I bet you had a fight with Joan."

Slim John raised a hand. "All in good time, wife. Right now, let's just be glad that the very thing I was talking about this morning, that I needed a man to help me pick corn, just walks on my yard, nonchalant, ready to go."

Sherm stood up. Little Alfie placed his hand in Sherm's hand as if they were already old pals.

Slim John looked at Sherm's hands. "I better go to town and buy you some double-thumb mittens."

"If you'll look in that suitcase you're holding, you'll find I'm already all set."

"Then you did have a fight with Joan."

Sherm let down a shoulder. "Their milk was always turning sour. Even before we could use it at the table."

Matilda's head snapped down. "See, I knew it, knew it."

Sherm said, "Then I got a job here with you?"

Slim John said, "Six cents a bushel and board and room?"

"Sounds perfect to me."

"Wait a minute," Matilda said. "Don't I have something to say about this?"

Slim John smiled at Matilda. "You want to pick corn for me instead?"

"Good Gertie, no. That's man's work."

Slim John went on. "If your brother Lew should happen to traipse onto the yard here, looking for a nest to land in, do you think I'd question it?"

Matilda grimaced.

Sherm pursed up his lips. It was beginning to look as if he'd jumped out of one hot frying pan into another hot frying pan. Though there was a difference. There were no liars in brother John's house. Or thieves.

Slim John looked Sherm up and down. "Matilda is right. You sure have shot up since I last saw you. If you didn't drink their milk, what did you eat then at Joan's? Because you're about ready to be put out to stud."

"Every time I went to town I snuck in a malted milk."

Matilda said, "You won't find any sour milk in my kitchen."

Sherm said, "Then I really am welcome?"

Matilda found a smile. "Well, why not. I'd rather have a relative as a boarder than a stranger."

Sherm said down to Alfie, "Son, would you know what room your mom's gonna give me?"

"Sure do."

"Good. You show me, and I'll go change my pants and then help your dad with the milking."

"Hey," Slim John said, "now you're talking. With you pitching in with the chores it's going to help a lot."

Matilda said, "But it ain't gonna help me much."

Slim John said, "Why not? You'll have a happier husband in the house."

"It means I'll have another mouth to feed."

Sherm fashioned a rueful Engleking smile. "Why, Tilda, didn't you know? I'm one of those heavenly beings that doesn't need to eat. Why, I don't even need a thunder mug under the bed. I'm blank there. More even than a steer."

Matilda decided to go along with the joke. "Aw, you."

Alfie tugged at Sherm's hand. "Are you coming?"

"Sure." Sherm took his suitcase from Slim John. "Let's go."

"You're gonna sleep with me," Alfie said. "We always keep the guest room for when Gramma comes."

Sherm changed into his yard clothes. He helped John carry the milk pails and the big shining nickel milk can into the dull-red barn. Together they called in the cows, six of them, red-and-white Shorthorns, all with heavy bags. One of the older cows, hipbones holding up her fur hide like two tent poles, had an udder so full she squirted four tiny jets of white milk every time she took a step. The two men locked the cows in by slamming the wooden stanchions shut.

Slim John found a one-legged stool for Sherm. "Tell you what. You milk those three on the end there and I'll milk these three here. That way we'll each have a fresh cow, a cow just bred, and a cow I should dry up."

"Sounds good to me." Sherm studied his three. "The one way over there you're drying up, not?"

"Right."

"I'll try her first. that way I can ease into it, and she can tell the next two ladies that I am a gentleman with gentle fingers."

"Sounds like you already know about women."

"Brother, after my experience with Miss Betchworth, and my wrangle with Ma, and my row with Joan, I am an absolute jackass when it comes to women."

"Well, the same thing happened to me when I was your age. But when I got to be eighteen, I couldn't keep 'em off me." John settled under his first cow. "But I was so green about it I let myself be snared by the first one."

Sherm in turn settled under his first cow, sitting down on his one-legged stool and putting his feet out to either side to make a three-point seating, while catching the pail between his knees. He started on the large two front tits, stripping them lightly at first, calling out gently, almost in a whisper, "Whoa, baas, old girl, no stunts now."

The cow turned her spreckled white head around and fixed him with a wondering onion eye. "Mooo."

John said, "Everything okay there?"

For answer Sherm began to ping-pang streams of milk down into his empty pail.

When the foam had risen a couple of inches in his pail, Sherm began to whistle a tune, "Coming Through the Rye." When John didn't object, Sherm next swung into "In The Sweet Bye and Bye."

John finished his first cow, stood up and emptied his pail into the tall five-gallon can. He looked down at Sherm with a pleased smile. "Mister, you sure can whistle. I wish I could."

"Sing instead then."

"If I could I would. But I sing like a squeaking hinge. And as for whistling, Tilda says I sound like a pullet that's lost its tongue."

"Then you really don't mind if I whistle a little?"

"Heck, no. Cows give more milk when you give them some music. So tootle away, bud. It's money in the bank for me."

Sherm finished his first cow, emptied his bucket into the big milk can, settled under the cow just bred. He let his head nuzzle into the cow's red flank. He could smell the sun in her fur. It was good to be with his wonderful older brother again. They'd always been pals; had shared jokes against the world. Sherm whistled more tunes, slipping in several double notes by setting his tongue just past the edge of his teeth against the edge of his upper lip.

When they were almost finished with their second cow, John said, "What really happened there with Ma?"

Sherm told him.

"Well, she sure was mad. She called here, you know, and wanted to know if it was all right if she got hold of the sheriff to find you."

"Ha," Sherm said, "Then she didn't right away guess where I'd gone."

"No. But then you wrote that card and she cooled down."

"I figured she would. She knew Joan and Pete were dumb knuckleheads when it came to farming. That they could use a little wise sense on their place."

"And what happened then with Joan just now?"

Sherm hesitated. "Better not tell your wife what I'm gonna say."

"No chance of that. I've come round to where I never give the wife extra ammunition."

"Well then, it's that Joan is a sneaky thief." Sherm told about how Joan had found where he'd hidden his money, had taken a five-dollar bill, and then later had given it back to him as his birthday present.

"Not really!"

"She did."

John let go with a strangled laugh. "It don't surprise me one bit. She always was a sneak, you know." John milked in silence a minute. All six milk cows chewed on their own little pile of ground corn-and-oats. "But maybe it was her way to keep up with us. Our sister Ada, you know, was Pa's favorite. And I was Ma's favorite. So Joan was left with a hind tit."

"Ha. But where did that leave me?"

"Well, I tell you, bud, both Ada and me began sharing a little of our portion with you."

"Wonderfully kind of you."

"Oh, we weren't that kind. It was mostly that you were such a cute kid. And also, when you came along Ma didn't cry as much anymore about how she'd lost that first Sherman. That is, after she'd healed up after that awful gallstone operation."

Sherm mewed up his lips. Always being compared to that first Sherman. "John, tell me honestly now, was the other Sherman quite a kid?"

"He was. And I miss him. And what fun you and me would've had with him."

"My name would've been different then, wouldn't it?"

"Guess so. Probably either Garrett, after our great grandfather, or Kort, after Ma's cousin."

"Hmm. Kort Engleking. Hmm."

"The other Sherman was smart like you too."

"Maybe smarter?"

"No. But different smarter. He might have become a preacher

the way he could remember a whole sermon and repeat it after we came home from church."

"I wonder, would he have been against playing baseball?"

"I used to play catch with him."

"Was he good at that?"

"Not as good as you."

Sherm finished his second cow and emptied his pail. "Well, I tell you, dear brother, and maybe this'll come as a surprise to you, but I've made up my mind to try out for the Chicago Cubs someday. As their premier shortstop."

"You'll have to play on Sunday." John in turn emptied his pail into the tall milk can. "Have you thought about that?"

"I've thought about it." Sherm settled under his third cow. He liked her big tits right away. His long fingers fit exactly around them. Milk streamed down into his pail in thick white spurts. "I'll hatch that egg when I come to it."

"Our church will be agin it. Let alone Ma."

"I know. But the church ain't always right. In the Academy, I studied a little church history, and there I found out that our church fathers changed their minds a couple of times. So that tells you something. It's mostly ordinary human beings like ourselves making up our church rules and not necessarily God. Though our preachers like to tell us that God only talks through them. And not us. Until there's a revolution."

"Hey, it sounds like I got me a Bolshevik here in with my cows instead of a bull."

"One thing the Academy taught me, and that is, if you get an idea, and you've worked it out pretty well, and you're sure you're right, you should speak up."

"But what if you're overruled by people you respect?"

"Either fight to win or become a silent martyr. But I intend to be such a good shortstop, and a moral one to boot, that no one will question whether or not I have the right to play ball on Sunday."

John fell silent.

Sherm sensed that what he'd just said hit home. What a relief it was to be living with a brother who didn't fly off the handle the minute he heard a wild idea. Away from the house and out on the yard or out in the field, he could speak his mind and no one would send the law after him.

John finished his last cow and got out from under her and threw his one-legged stool to one side. "One thing I'll tell you though. The worst is going to be with your sister Ada. She hates baseball, you know. Almost more than Ma. And when she shakes her head a little, with that little smile of hers, man, do you start to feel guilty."

Sherm said, "Because she's such a great gal, that's why." Sherm finished too. "Really though, the worst is going to be with Ma, not Ada. I'm closer to Ma because I've been living more with her. I'm not scared of Ada. But I am of Ma."

"That goes back to when you was having titty from Ma. You probably bit her a couple of times and she glared down at you and told you not to be naughty. Those kind of mean looks that early can queer you for life."

"Yeh."

"Anyway, let's bring in the milk and separate it. Tilda will have supper ready about now. And she don't like having you set down to that table one minute late."

They did the separating. Then while Sherm fed the calves, John hung the separated cream deep in the cistern behind the house to keep the cream fresh until the cream hauler came around to pick it up. They washed themselves thoroughly on the porch with a bar of tar soap and combed their blond hair with a part to one side, and, removing their shoes, stepped into the kitchen.

Matilda looked up at the clock over the stove. "Well," she said, "I see it does help to have a hired man. You're on time tonight."

When John didn't say anything, Sherm decided to keep his silence too.

All through a supper of fried potatoes, fried homemade sausage, boiled cabbage, bread and butter and wild plum preserve, and dark tea, little Alfie rattled away from where he sat on a high stool next to John.

"Next year I'm going to school, Uncle Sherm."

"You are, eh."

"And Pa's gonna give me my own calf to raise."

"Good."

"'Course I'm gonna have to haul my own calf 'nure."

"That'll give you strong muscles."

Matilda said, "And stinky shoes." She was feeding little Nell, the baby, where it sat next to her in its high chair. Matilda first mouthed the food, making it soft and mushy, and then gently ladled it between baby Nell's little pink lips.

Alfie said, "Say, Ma, when you polish the parlor table don't your hands stink then too?"

"Why you little snot you. John, you ought to give him a biff over the ears for that remark."

John held his head sideways as if to make a baffle of his right cheek against the solar glare from her blue Frisian eyes. "Now, wife, out of the mouth of babes. . . ."

"Don't you go throwing the Bible at me."

"If the text fits, then like Mary, you should take these things unto your heart and ponder them."

Matilda lay down the baby spoon. "I'll pounder you if you keep talking any more that way."

John winked at Sherm. "Brother, put this in your cup of tea. Take your time about getting hitched. You'll be much better off just shaking hands with Madam Palmer. For one thing, Madam Palmer can't talk back."

Matilda stared from John to Sherm and back again. Then she caught on and turned red. "Such disgusting talk by Christian men. For shame."

Little Nell reached for the baby spoon, and when she couldn't quite take it, began to cry.

"Shh now, shh now, little darling. Mama was only trying to make gentlemen out of her menfolks."

Sherm finished his dish of sliced pears. He began to wonder if he shouldn't have gone to Ada's instead of John's. At Ada's he would've had his nephew Free to play catch with, as well as brother-in-law Alfred. Only trouble with that was, Alfred didn't need any hired help with all those sons of his around.

John helped Matilda clean off the table; helped her with the dishes, drying them neatly and carefully until they squeaked, and putting them away in the kitchen cabinet.

Sherm meanwhile got down on the floor under the kitchen table with Alfie and played city with him, making an elaborate structure with blocks, until one of the buildings reached almost to the cross supports of the table.

Alfie surprised Sherm. "Is that the tower of Babel?"

"Ha. It sure looks like it."

"Then the top of the table there is heaven."

"Sometimes it is. When the lady of the house serves her prize-winning plum preserve."

Matilda managed a pinched smile. "Now you're trying to butter me up, Sherman."

"Plum preserve on fresh bread tastes supreme."

Presently Matilda got out the broom. "Nah, you two under the table there, you better put them blocks away so I can sweep up."

John said, "Can't you wait until just before we all go to bed? Tain't often Alfie has his uncle around to play with."

"No. I want to sweep up right now. Then I'm done for the day. I like to be done too, you know."

Sherm put his arm around Alfie. "We can build us a Tower of Babel some other time, not?"

"Sure."

When Matilda had everything pick-thread neat, she threw the dust into the stove and set the broom behind the cabinet. "Where did you put our local astonisher?"

John pointed. "Where I always put it. Up on the rack there."

Matilda went into the living room with *The Bonnie Review* and sat down next to the flower stand near the bay window. She rocked as she read. The rocker made the squeaky noises of a happy cricket.

Slowly the talk in the kitchen began to sparkle again. John leaned back in his swivel chair and told about the big fish they'd caught with a seine in the Little Rock River on the east end of his land. Sherm, sitting across from him, told how Pete Waxer showed him how to catch bullheads.

John fixed his blue eyes on Sherm. "Why didn't you keep on going to the Academy? I always wanted to go on to school. And you had your chance. What a fool you was to give up that chance. Or is there a reason I'm not supposed to know?"

"Ma wouldn't let me do anything at the Academy except just study hard. No fun at all."

"Sherm, a man's gotta learn he mustn't always listen to women. Sometimes they're right. For women. But they sometimes sure miss it when it comes to what's good for men."

Alfie sitting in his high stool by the table had been looking through a biblical picture book. When he finished he began to fidget around. "Pa, can we make some popcorn for the company?"

John glanced at Sherm. "You like popcorn?"

"Heck, yeh." Sherm ruffled Alfie's wispy gold hair. "My middle name is Popcorn."

Alfie turned to his father. "Is Uncle Sherm pulling my leg?"

John looked under the table. "Not so far as I can see."

"I dunno, Pa. He likes to tease too."

John got up from his swivel chair and dug out a paper sack of popcorn and a wire popper. He put some more red cobs in the kitchen range. Soon the top of the black range turned pink and the popcorn began to jump inside the popper like a bunch of crickets gone wild.

Sherm said, "Man, does that smell good."

Alfie said, "Wait'll Pa pours some butter over it."

Matilda's rocker quit squeaking. "Do I smell popcorn?"

John winked at Sherm. "If you do, wife, you got a pretty good smeller."

"What! And that right after I swept up the kitchen nice and neat?" The old rocker groaned as Matilda popped up out of it. "Well, we'll see about that." She showed up in the doorway to the kitchen. "What are you making popcorn for?"

"You know how Alfie likes popcorn. I didn't see any harm in it. And he wanted to do his visiting uncle a favor."

"I don't like it. Because now I'll have to get out the broom again. You men, you never think about how hard we women got it in the house. Especially on a farm. All we do, night and day, is clean up, sweep up, wipe up. Hehh."

Wrath slowly turned John's blue eyes hail-white. A dark flushed filled out his cheeks.

Matilda demanded. "Well, what are you going to do about it?"

John said, "Wife, this is what I'm going to do about it." He opened the top of the popper and, waving it around, sprayed popcorn all around in the kitchen. Both Sherm and Alfie ducked, raising up an arm against the white fusillade. "There," John said, "now you got something to sweep up, if that's what you're worried about."

Matilda stared at all the popcorn scattered around. Then she began to cry, and sagged down into a chair.

Sherm began to whistle. Because of the excitement of the moment, he managed to execute several double notes and a couple of overquavers. In the tight kitchen the whistling sounded clear and charming.

A twisting smile relaxed John's face. "If I could whistle like that, I'd give a program in church. I've tried and tried, but somehow it just won't come."

Sherm said, "That's because thin-lipped fellows whistle best. Fellows like you can't quite shape their thick lips into the right kind of flute. I didn't want to say it before."

Matilda said, "My husband doesn't either have thick lips."

John knew what she was thinking. He sat down in his swivel chair and laughed a little to himself. He picked up a couple of popcorn kernels from the top of the table and nibbled at them, and gave his shoulder a lift as if he might be admitting he was guilty of some happy bedroom fun.

Sherm couldn't stand to see Matilda crying in her chair. He got to his feet, and searching out the broom and dustpan, began sweeping up the feather-light white kernels.

Alfie watched it all. Finally he said, "Whatcha gonna do, Uncle Sherm? You gonna make some white 'nure out of that for Mama's flowers? 'Cause you can't eat it now."

Chapter Five

John warned Sherm not to go too fast the first week picking corn. "You can easy sprain a wrist and then you won't be any good for the rest of the season. So ease into it."

Sherm nodded. "A little like with the Cubs. They always have spring training for a couple of weeks in sunny California before the regular season begins."

"Yeh. The only thing is, we can't have a couple of weeks lalling around in the sun. On the prairie that first blizzard can come awful quick."

The first morning John picked a three-box wagonful, thirty-six bushels on the nose. Sherm picked a two-box wagonful with a small extra pile, for twenty-seven bushels.

When they went in for the noon-hour dinner, John picked up Sherm's right hand. "Sore?"

"Nope."

"It's your right wrist that goes first."

"Coach, I could've easy picked as fast as you. But I didn't want to embarrass you."

"And you stay back. If you try to keep up with me, by Thanksgiving you won't have enough body left to cast a shadow. You'll be down to just plain bones."

Matilda did them justice by serving up a sumptuous meal: baked potatoes, boiled sausage, boiled cabbage, onions boiled in milk, homemade bread with butter and plum preserve, and a huge slice of apple pie.

John said from his end of the table, "Eat until you can't anymore. Cornpicking is the hardest job on the farm, and we've got a good six weeks of it ahead."

Matilda liked it that her men ate like heroes. "I have more fresh bread, Sherm. Bread'll stick to your ribs where meat won't."

Sherm had already eaten so much he felt flushed over his cheeks. "Thanks."

In the afternoon, when John saw that Sherm was trying to keep up with him anyway, he deliberately slowed down. The result was they both came in with thirty bushels each.

When they went to milk the six cows, John pursed up his lips. "We'll find out now if you was trying to show off this afternoon."

"Don't worry. I'm not a fool. While it's true I sometimes go after a ball I shouldn't be able to get, and still get it, I never go so far as to break my neck."

John smiled. "I can't wait for you to play shortstop for our church team. Boy, will that town team be surprised when we finally lick 'em."

As he milked, head tucked into the hollow of the cow between her hip and her rib cage, Sherm idly watched his hands work. After a dozen strokes of milk he knew he was all right.

They finished their first cow at the same time.

John picked up Sherm's right wrist once more, gave it a hard squeeze in his big calloused hand. "Hurt?"

"Nope. Say, our cousin Garrett gave me a tennis ball when I came out. Do you mind if I bounce it against the door of the corncrib alley and do a little shorthopping with it?"

"You mean to say you got enough pep left to play ball after picking corn all day?"

"You tell 'em."

"I'll be a beat-down dog. Well, do it your way then. I don't want to be guilty of too much olderbrothering."

"John, a fellow's got to play the game and not worry about fame."

"Looks like I better outfit you with a full thirty-six-box wagon."

The next day Sherm decided he wouldn't go all out to stick close to John's heels. After all, his brother wouldn't have got to where he was if he hadn't known what he was doing. At noon John finished his two rows a good twenty yards ahead of Sherm. John backed up his team and picked out one of Sherm's rows.

When they finished at the end of the field, John had thirty-eight bushels and Sherm had thirty-four bushels.

Sherm did the same thing in the afternoon, again finishing some twenty yards behind his brother.

By the end of the first week, though, both were going at it full blast. John came in with two loads of fifty bushels each day, and Sherm came in with two loads of forty bushels each.

For four weeks, the weather was wonderful: a little hoarfrost in the morning, clear and sunny all day, and the evenings cool. The only thing troublesome were the trailing single spider threads wafting off the standing corn. They tickled one across the eyes and nose all afternoon long, so that a person had to stop now and then and wipe them off with the back of a mitten, and so lose time.

Sunday noons, between the morning church service and the afternoon service, Sherm sometimes visited sister Ada and her family for dinner. It was usually warm enough for Sherm and his whitehead nephew Free to play catch awhile. Ada didn't like it they threw the ball around on Sunday, but since they were only boys she decided to overlook it. Sherm's visits were good for Free. Free was a smart kid, and restless, but when Sherm came over Free seemed more himself and didn't get into trouble as often with his father.

After they'd played burnout for a while, until the palms of their left hands stung, Free and Sherm took turns pitching to each other, using the outside wall of the calf pen as a backstop, and an old scuffed-up baseball and a bat made out of a fork handle. Free could already throw curves, out, in, drop, and his various pitches helped Sherm sharpen batting eye. Since both were Cubs fans, they had to pretend they were playing for other teams, Sherm for Gramma's town and Free for Bonnie. Both were always trying to win in the bottom of the ninth. Not to discourage Free too much— Free was after all three years younger—Sherm let him win once in a while. They had different spots marked out on the yard where, if the ball landed on them, it went for a single or a double or a triple or a homer. Because Sherm couldn't get anything on his fast ball, still couldn't make it spin enough, Free turned out to be a pretty good fastball hitter. Free was growing too fast to be smooth but he had the good hands and the good eye. They played furiously against each other, all the while praising each other on good plays made and laughing until their bellies hurt when one or the other pulled off some great nutsy game-saving stunt.

Sherm had trouble hitting Free's inshoots. Free's ins made Sherm fist the ball. One day Sherm read when Free was going to throw an inshoot, and quickly adjusting his stance, and swinging his bat close to his body while coming around a bit late, hit a low line drive that shot past the corner of the white garage and with a crinkling sound of green glass breaking landed in Ada's kitchen.

Silence and two living statues on the yard.

"Boy," Free whispered, "are we going to get it."

"Not if I admit I did it," Sherm said. "Your dad won't dare lick me and your mother is my sister."

Sure enough, tall powerful Alfred was the first to show up in the porch door. "Hyar! Who did that?"

Sherm waggled his head, and smiled his winning Engleking smile. "Like George Washington, I cannot tell a lie. I did it."

That slowed Alfred down. "Oh." But Alfred still glared at Free.

Ada next showed in the porch door beside Alfred. "What happened, Free?"

Sherm gave Ada his best smile. "Like Abraham Lincoln, I cannot tell a lie. I did it, Ade."

Ada brushed back her blond hair from her forehead, allowing herself a smile. "Well, be a little more careful after this. Dinner is ready."

"Hey," Alfred said, "I thought it was George Washington who couldn't tell a lie."

Sherm said, "I'm sure Abraham Lincoln must have said it too sometime or other. After all, no president is allowed to lie."

Alfred said, "That's what you think. Didn't that darn Woodrow Wilson lie about us not getting into that war in Europe?"

Ada said, "Glass all over the kitchen floor. That's what you get for playing ball on Sunday."

Sherm said, "I'll pay for the window. I'll get a pane at Garrett's hardware and put it in myself."

Alfred said, "Naw. You don't have to do that." Alfred had to smile at last. "I'll bet I can throw an inshoot you can't hit either."

"Now now," Ada said quickly. "No more ballplaying today. I said dinner is ready."

Noon hours, while brother John discussed family matters with Matilda, Sherm got out his glove and tennis ball and played short-hopping the ball against the corncrib door. John had several old tires lying in the junk pile back in the grove and one day Sherm took one of them and hung it under a box elder tree. He practised throwing the tennis ball through the old tire from every possible position, flipping it underhanded, snapping it sidearmed, pegging it overhanded, running to his right, running to his left, falling down, slipping in loose dust, still pretending all the while he was Hollocher the great Cub shortstop.

Watching him from where he sat putting on his shoes on the front stoop, John shook his head. "Sometimes, brother, I wonder what's gonna become of you, all those crazy tricks throwing the ball."

"You won't say that the day I send you a train ticket to Chicago to come see me play in the World Series."

"Anyway, it's time to pick corn. So far the good Lord has been most kind to us with this good weather. One more week of hard picking and we got her out."

"Think you can afford to pay me that big check when we jerk out that last ear?"

"You worried that our brother-in-law Alfred is going to charge you for that window after all?"

"Hey, how did you find out about that?"

"Our sparrows gossip a lot with their sparrows. They just live across the river from us, you know."

"So that's what those sparrows are talking about with all their chitter-chatter. Can you teach me their language?"

"The sparrows tell me they don't think much of Academy students, especially when they talk Latin."

Sherm made a face. "I suppose for the rest of my life I'm gonna be razzed about that year I went to high school."

John smiled. "Actually, I'm jealous."

They got the corn out five days before Thanksgiving Day under a threatening sky.

Looking across the river, Sherm could see that on the eastern slope Alfred was picking his last rows too.

Sherm's horses followed John's wagon home. Both wagons were heaped with mounds of knobby gold. Both men had had to put on an extra ten-inch sideboard. It was late afternoon and the men and the horses were aching tired and the reaches under the wagons made cracking sounds every time a wagon wheel nobbled over lumpy ground. It was always a sweet time when one rode home sitting on a huge load of corn. Muscles and bones and tendons felt wonderfully used.

Sherm called ahead. "Say, is this the earliest you ever had the corn out?"

"Sure is."

"Aha. So we're still breaking records all over the place then."

A smile broke through John's smut-darkened face. "Wait until you weigh yourself tonight after you take your bath. You won't believe the pounds you lost this fall. That'll be another record you broke."

They elevated the corn into the crib. They did the chores and milked the cows. They went in to eat supper. And for once they found Matilda in a happy mood.

After the supper table had been cleared, John got out his green record book and on a piece of brown butcher paper began to do some figuring. Sherm across the table from him got out his own little record book from his bib pocket.

Presently, after wetting the point of his pencil stub several times, John was ready to talk. "If I ain't forgot my grade school 'rithmetic, I got you down for 2,892 bushels you picked. At six cents a bushel that comes to $173.32. How does that square with what you got?"

Sherm pretended to restudy his figures. He held his head first one way then the other. John was actually right down to the last penny.

Matilda paused in her sweeping. "That much, John?"

John shrugged. "Our bud here picked hard and fast."

"But that's more than Garrett picked when he helped you get out the corn last fall. And Garrett's older than Sherm."

"I know."

"And Garrett's the fastest picker around, you said."

"But Garrett couldn't pick on Saturdays. That's when he had to be at his store. Remember?"

"But that much money for this young fellow?"

"If he earned it, he's got it coming."

"But can we afford it?"

"What? You're not thinking that because he's family he don't get paid? Like Joan was thinking?"

"Well, no, I guess not. But I had my heart set so on a new commode. And a full-length mirror."

"Don't worry. You'll get it if you need it that bad. After all, we totaled nearly six thousand bushels this year. And when we shell part of that out, we'll be rolling with the Apostles in heavenly clover."

"Then we had a good year at last, John."

"The Lord has been kind to us."

Sherm put the money in the Bonnie First National Bank. He immediately bought a new baseball bat in Garrett's hardware store, a black stick with the color shading off into gray toward the handle. The bat had a soft cork grip. The moment Sherm hefted it he liked it. When he smelled it the odor of it reminded him of the wooden shoes his father Alfred used to make in their little shop behind the house.

Garrett had to laugh. "You're worse than a woman out shopping the way you inspect that bat."

"I was just trying to smell out how many four-baggers there was in this black beauty."

"Homers, eh? Well, come next Decoration Day, the Singles team can use a couple of those when we play those old Married stiffs." Because Garrett had lost his wife June he could play with the Singles team again.

A couple days later, after supper, with a blizzard moaning outside, John got out his green record book again. After some more figuring, he lay his pencil stub to one side. "Say, bud, I got a proposition for you."

"Fire. But please use blanks."

"You know I'm farming three eighties here. One hundred sixty of my own and an eighty from the Siouxland Insurance Company."

"Yeh?"

"How about it, instead of wages, you rent that eighty with the profit yours? You get three-fifths, the insurance company gets two-fifths. And you keep up the fences."

Sherm slowly sat up straight. Already at his age a regular farmer?

"Course, you'll need machinery and horses. If you'll help me with the chores, milking and such, I'm willing to throw that in with your board and room."

Matilda turned from where she was mixing bread dough on the cabinet counter. "John, don't I have something to say about board and room?"

"Like what?"

"Like maybe your brother can help me with the dishes now and then. And make his own bed."

John let a smile turn up his lips. "What, give him my job of drying dishes when I like it so much? Because it gives me a chance to jolly you up and get you ready for what follows afters?"

Matilda blushed. After all their years of married life she still had not got used to the way her husband could melt her cold bluntness down with warm humor. "Your brother doesn't have to know everything about us."

Sherm said, "Matilda, I thought Alfie and me have done pretty well in that department. When haven't we made our bed?"

A smile opened her lips. "Well, that's true. Only your brother here sometimes forgets the woman's side of marriage. A wife has rights too, you know. Should have a little say in how we run things."

John said, "Well, Sherm, what do you say?"

"I'm willin' if you're willin'."

"Done. Tomorrow we go to the bank and make arrangements there with the insurance company."

Matilda wasn't done. "Does that mean he's going to stay here all winter and earn wages?"

John turned to Sherm again. "Usually the way it's done around here is, during the winter until March 1 you get board and room for helping with the chores. But no wages."

"Okay by me. Except that a couple of springs from now I have the right to hike out to Catalina Island and try out with the Cubs."

"You sure got that in your head, ain't you. What are you going to do about Sunday ball?"

"I won't be the first one in the major leagues who couldn't play on Sunday. A fellow by the name of Parson Lewis had it written in his contract he didn't have to pitch on Sunday."

"He probably wasn't much good."

"Parson Lewis won twenty-five games for Boston around 1900."

"Well, but, since he was just a pitcher, his manager probably arranged his pitching turn around Sundays. But a shortstop plays every day."

Matilda butted in. "You mean to say a preacher once pitched for a major league team? In what is really only a boys' game?"

Sherm said, "I think Parson was just his nickname. Because he was so religious."

Matilda sneered. "That I'm going to be related to a baseball bum."

"Leave my brother alone," John said.

"John, if you had the chance, would you play on Sunday?" Matilda demanded.

John said, "If I was good enough."

"Not married to me you wouldn't. On that Ada and I agree."

During the winter months, when it wasn't too cold, Sherm practiced shorthopping in the alley of the corncrib. It was a little tough throwing the ball while wearing a fuzzy cotton mitten, but Sherm thought maybe it might be a good thing. Just like it was always good before going up to bat in a game if a person took a couple of practice swings with several heavy bats.

When it was around zero outside, Sherm got out his father Alfred's Old Country skates with the turned-up ends both front and back and sallied down to the frozen river and went skating for miles, usually south towards Bonnie. A couple of times on a Saturday he talked Free into meeting him at the frozen swimming hole, each walking a half mile, and from there swinging along together as they explored the new turns in the river north towards Yellow Smoke. Free had skates that had to be clamped onto leather soles and often the clamps let go just when he and Sherm were sailing along in great high joy. At the end of the day, as Sherm trudged home, he was sometimes so tired he found himself walking bent over like an old man. But boy! how he could eat after he'd helped John with the chores. One evening he broke his own record when he ate seven thick slices of buttered fresh bread topped off with blood-red plum preserve.

The two brothers became thick friends. With a quick look, or a wink, they'd share the humor of a situation without having to say a word. They found it easy to slyly poke fun at Matilda. She so often left herself wide open. But both men knew it really wasn't all that fair. Also, it was no fun eating burnt potatoes. The two men developed secret male talk. Matilda sometimes sensed they were hinting wicked thoughts. When she guessed what they were thinking she would try to stick it into them. But both men became past masters at letting her blunt attempts at sarcasm slide off like water off a duck's back.

One thing didn't happen. Sherm didn't ape his older brother's way of walking. All those days of shorthopping the ball helped Sherm to develop an athlete's way of striding along, springy off his toes, not heavy off his heels. When John bought Alfie a pony, Sherm played with his nephew, pretending he too was riding a pony, and on foot would race the boy on his pony in short sprints. The result was Sherm became an extremely fast runner.

Chapter Six

When the Young People's Society met one Thursday evening, Garrett studied Sherm as he practised with the single men on the nearby Christian School grounds. It didn't take Garrett long to see that in Sherm they at last had a real slick-fielding shortstop.

The Decoration Day church picnic was held in Fat John's pasture along the Big Rock River. Families arrived around ten in their carriages and buggies and flivvers. The men promptly tumbled out and began throwing baseballs around, while the women set up folding tables for potato salads and golden-topped vanilla cream pies. Fat John's two older boys went around with a wheelbarrow, and each with a shovel scooped up the cowplotches and the horse apple piles from a diamond-shaped playing area.

The Marrieds were favored to win. The Singles just didn't have many good players. The Marrieds also had the best pitcher in Ed Van Driel. Van Driel, a submarine chucker, could so buggywhip the ball that it looked like a rising white streak on its way to the plate. By the time Van Driel tired in the seventh inning, the Marrieds usually were so far ahead they could safely bring in Free's father, Alfred Alfredson, with his quick hook and wide smile.

When Garrett made out the Singles lineup, he found he was short a man. Tapping the point of his pencil on his white teeth, he mused out loud. "By golly, we only got eight men."

Sherm overheard him. "Why not play Free?"

"But he's only eleven. Still all calf legs."

"So what? He's got sticky fingers."

"Well, all right. We'll stick him in right field. The Marrieds won't hit too many over there off Pete Haber." Garrett slowly shook his head. "Pete throws like a woman."

When they got ready to play, Sherm discovered brother John

97

was playing first base for the Marrieds. Sherm gave Garrett a nudge. "Watch this." Sherm formed a trumpet with his long fingers. "Look who we got over there on first. The great Frank Chance himself."

"A pantsful to you too, buster." John spat a big gob into his first baseman's mitt and greased it in good and deep. "Garrett, where'd you find that baby-haired bat boy? You really gonna let him play with grown-ups?"

Garrett laughed. "You tell 'em. And we've even got 'em younger than that. Wait until you see our right fielder."

The game started. And immediately, Pete Haber walked three men in a row. That brought up cleanup hitter John. John took some huge warmup swings with his bat. "Let me at 'em, let me at 'em."

Garrett took off his mask and trotted out to the pitcher's mound to have a talk with Pete Haber. Sherm ran in from his shortstop position. Garrett said, "See how John holds his bat? Cross-handed? If you'll keep the ball close on his fists he'll never hit it."

Sherm said, "He drives his car that way too. If you don't watch him, he'll drive on the wrong side of the road."

Garrett said, "Can you remember that, Pete?"

Pete worked his loose red lips. "I'll try."

Pete did get his first pitch in on John's fists. But the second pitch headed for the outside corner of the plate, and John, hunching himself up, swung with a great grunt and walloped the ball, elevating it out of sight over a row of cottonwoods. The married women, lined along the first base line, let go with a trilling alto cheer. Four runs.

By the time Van Driel's arm began to hurt him, the Marrieds were leading 17 to 4.

But several good things did happen. The first time up Sherm struck out. The ball was by him before he even started his swing. The next inning, while the Singles took their turn at bat, Sherm studied Van Driel's motion. Van Driel threw the ball much harder than Tuffy Janes. And where Tuffy Janes seemed to throw a zigzag ball, Van Driel threw a ball that suddenly appeared to jump almost into the batter's face.

The next time up, Sherm stood deep in the box, shortened up on his grip, and determined he'd swing the width of the ball above where it looked like he should swing. Also he'd swing earlier. "C'mon, Black Beauty, let's show these clodhoppers how we hit a ball."

Van Driel wound up, kicking his left foot high, then dropped his arm and snapped it with a quick wrist action. Out of his fist came the ball, rising like a gray-white pea becoming a white egg, then becoming like a fat dragonfly as it darted in.

Sherm chopped down at the pitch, met it squarely, his black bat making a melodious crack of a sound. The ball just missed Van Driel's surprised face and sailed over second base into center field. The single women, lined up along the third base line and sitting on the fenders of their boy friends' flivvers, let fly with a shrilling cry of glee.

Garrett too was surprised. He jumped up, once.

Safe on first, puffing a little, mostly out of excitement, Sherm waited for John to make some kind of teasing belittling remark. But all John had for him was a sly look. And in a moment Sherm found out what that look was about. John had apparently given Van Driel a stealthy signal. The next thing Sherm knew, as he led off first a few steps, Van Driel whirled and made a snap throw to John, hoping to catch Sherm napping. But Van Driel's throw was high and Sherm easily made it back to the bag. John had to make a leaping lunge up for the ball, and managed to snare it in the webbing of his mitt.

Garrett, always fair, called out, "Now that's the way to play first base."

Free didn't do too badly either. He batted last, and just as he was about to step into the batter's box with Sherm's new black bat, Garrett called him to one side. "Listen. You're still pretty much of a runt compared to the rest of us, so you don't have much of a strike zone. And to make it even smaller, I want you to scrunch over, at the same time pretending you're going to hit the ball all the way over into Hack Tippett's pasture on the other side of the river there. But! And listen carefully now. Because if you don't, I'll get after you later on. Tell your dad about some of the crazy stunts you pull at school. This is what you do. Don't swing at the ball. At all! Get it? You won't be able to hit Van Driel, so we got to hope he'll walk you. Got it?"

Free nodded.

"I mean that now. Don't swing at all."

"All right."

Out of four times at bat, Free walked three times and scored two runs.

Also out in right field, Free pleased Garrett with the way he handled the only fly ball hit his way. It was one of those flies that seemed to want to pair up with the faint full moon hanging in the western sky. The gray ball hung up there and hung up there. Free took one look, and trotted over to his right a dozen steps, and waited. The bases were loaded at the time, two were out.

Sherm was tempted to run over and call out advice. But decided against it. It might only take Free's attention off the ball. The kid was on his own once that ball was up in the air. That was the great thing about baseball. Every now and then a whole game would hang on one play that only one man could handle.

At last the ball dropped straight down, a gray pigeon hit on the wing. Easily, with a little give in his wrists, Free caught the ball in the pocket of his glove.

As Sherm ran in to their bench, he gave Free a clap on the butt. "Atty old kid. Keep playing that way until you get married. After that you can muff the ball."

Free walked around thinking he was quite a big potato.

Garrett said, "You were right about him, Sherm."

Sherm said, "You ought to see the curve that kid throws."

Garrett considered the idea. "No, he's too young. Give him a couple more years and we'll try him out as a pitcher."

"Garrett, the only trouble with that is, by that time you'll be a Married again."

Garrett next tried to arrange a game with the town team. But they declined. Their pitcher, Hooks Hansen, had suffered a broken arm while cranking his Ford and wouldn't be able to pitch anymore that summer.

Making several telephone calls, Garrett finally did set up a game with the Little Church team in Rock Falls, on the fourteenth of July, a Saturday.

While blowing their horses at the end of the field, Sherm and

John talked about the coming game. It was a grand day out. A cool breeze slipped down off the northwest height of land. It ruffled the foot-tall dark green corn and cooled a man's hair inside his straw hat.

John said, "I suppose Garrett expects me to play first."

Sherm said, "After that leaping catch you made at first, who else?"

"And we're playing them in Rock Falls?"

"Last I heard."

"Wild Bill is bound to be there."

John and Wild Bill Alfredson had married sisters. Where friendly John had married a bristly Frisian golden blond, hot-tempered Wild Bill had married a smiling Frisian silver blond. John had often said that Wild Bill should have married Matilda while he himself should have married Bill's wife, Eve. Wild Bill and super-critic Matilda deserved each other. While he and Eve could have cooed each other right straight into heaven without having to work at it.

Sherm asked, "You two ever come to blows?"

"Not quite. We've both made it a point not to go to the wife's family reunions."

"Too bad Eve can't control him."

John picked up a clod. With a powerful pinch he pulverized the clod into a burst of brown dust. "Not even a sweet-face angel straight from heaven could cool Wild Bill down when he flies off the handle. He can be smiling at you but the truth is his fuse is already fizzing."

"Man, if he and Matilda'd 've got married, they'd probably both be dead by now."

"You better hold that thought. Because I don't dare hold it. As a Christian, I can't."

The next few days the Bonnie church team practised in Aunt Josephine's pasture across the road from John's grove. They warmed up playing catch a while; then Free's father, Alfred, hit towering fly balls, short steep ones for the infielders and long far ones for the outfielders. There were shouts of encouragement when a fellow dropped a ball: "Better luck next time." Later, when Sherm made a fine stop deep in the hole, Garrett cried out, "That's digging them out of the cowpies there, kid!" Finally there was some batting practice. They used the east side of the hog house for a backstop. First Van Driel threw the ball a while; then lanky Alfred. The word was that Dink Scholler would pitch for Rock Falls. Dink sometimes pitched underhanded, sometimes overhanded.

The practice always ended on a note that Sherm and John didn't like. All of Uncle Big John's boys were homebrew beer drinkers. Sitting on the pasture ground in the deep dusk, they had to have a drink, at least a quart each of the powerful stuff, before heading home. Some of the other men on the team were in the Little Church consistory. But even though it was against the law to drink any kind of liquor that tested more than three percent alcohol, they didn't think it wrong. Their preacher sometimes railed against homebrew beer. But everyone seemed to feel that for once the law was wrong.

As they walked home one night, John said, "Someday them drinking homebrew is gonna backfire. I've noticed how in the past even before a game they like to have a bottle."

Sherm agreed. "They say they need that drink to relax from having worked hard all day."

"Trouble is, it relaxes them too much and they drop the ball, and then they give you that sheep-eating grin of theirs."

Finally Saturday the fourteenth of July came around.

All the farmers had finished cultivating their corn and their oatfields still weren't quite ripe. Sweeps of gold had begun to show over the grain on the hills but down in the draws dark stippled green still prevailed.

John and family, and Sherm, left at twelve sharp. The game was to start at one o'clock at the fairgrounds, where a diamond had been laid out inside the race track oval. When the Bonnie team arrived, the Rock Falls team was already out taking infield practice and a fat tub of a man was hitting fungoes to the outfielders. Some fans had settled in the stands at the race track finish line.

As the Bonnie team sat on their plank bench, putting on their spiked shoes, they studied the other team. Sherm and Garrett in particular watched pitcher Dink Scholler warm up. Dink was one of those smiling fellows with a lazy sweeping motion.

Just before the game started, both John and Sherm were shocked to learn that Wild Bill Alfredson, who'd shown up late, was going to umpire the bases.

Garrett spotted it too. He walked over to talk to the manager of the Rock Falls team, Jim Albers. "I thought you told me you'd get two out-of-town umpires. That Wild Bill is a member of your Little Church, not?"

"Well, ya, he is." Jim Albers had a heavy red wattle. "But we couldn't get anybody else. So we had to take him. He was willing to do it for free."

John overheard what was said. "Ha," he snorted. "Wild Bill would, the minute he learned I was going to play. And the worst is, he'll be standing near the first base bag most of the game, right behind me, breathing fire and brimstone down my neck."

Lanky Alfred, Wild Bill's cousin, didn't like it either. "None of us Alfredsons have ever been able to get along with Wild Bill. When he gets his head fixed on something, it sets in as hard as cement."

Sherm had a question. "What about that umpire at home plate? He ain't an out-of-towner, is he?"

Garrett said, "That's Doc Maloney the dentist. He's okay. He gets more trade from Bonnie than he does from Rock Falls. He has a way of saying things that rub people the wrong way, but I like it."

Four of the Rock Falls church team were wearing baseball uniforms; the rest new blue overalls. All the Bonnie boys were wearing overalls, some of them not so new.

"Play ball!" Doc Maloney bawled from homeplate. "Battery for Rock Falls, Scholler and Albers; battery for Bonnie, Van Driel and Engleking! May the best team win!"

The couple dozen fans in the stands let go with a weak cheer. Two women fluttered lace-edged handkerchiefs.

For three innings there were no runners. Both pitchers were sharp.

Sherm struck out his first time up. He'd never run into a pitcher who threw slip pitches. The arm came around fast, but the ball seemed to dally on its way to the plate. The first time Sherm saw it he swung too early. When Sherm set himself to time the slower pitch, Dink Scholler fired a fast ball by him for the third strike.

The next three innings both sides got runners on base but couldn't drive them in. On his second time at bat Sherm punched out a single over first base on a fast ball.

Neither John nor Sherm could complain about a single one of Wild Bill Alfredson's calls. Wild Bill wore a light gray summer cap tipped back, revealing a high sloping forehead. His tight smile slit back into his cheeks, giving his chin the same slope as his forehead.

In the top of the ninth, with the score tied one to one, Sherm was first up. He decided to look for the slip pitch instead of the fast ball. Dink was bound to show it somewhere along the line. Sure enough, with the count one ball and one strike, there it was. Sherm held himself back as long as he could, then lashed into it. He lined a screamer just inside the third base line. The ball bounded all the way to the race track fence on the east end of the oval. Sherm ran with long elastic strides, and slid into third just head of the throw. Nobody out and a runner in scoring position.

Catcher Albers called time. He strolled out to the mound for a conference with Dink. The first baseman and the shortstop joined the two. There appeared to be some fumbling around with the baseball. The catcher gave the ball to the pitcher, and the pitcher shook his head and gave it back to the catcher, but after some vigorous talk the catcher gave it back to the pitcher. They'd only had one good ball to play with during the game so far, and by that time, the ninth inning, it was pretty well scuffed up and stained a tannish brown.

The catcher and the pitcher and the other two men finished their conference. All four returned to their position. Dink, who'd been smiling through the whole game, was now frowning, and had an uneasy air about him. He stared in for a sign. And stared in. Garrett, up to bat, waggled his bat menacingly. Sherm took a short lead off third. Dink slowly wound up, came to a complete stop, then suddenly fired at third. Wild throw. The ball sailed high over the third baseman's head.

Lanky Alfredson was coaching at third. He yelled, "Run, Sherm, run!"

Sherm ran.

As Sherm approached home plate, Albers the catcher threw off his mask. Albers smiled at Sherm, and extracted a baseball from his back pocket. He tagged Sherm.

"Out!" everybody on the Rock Falls team cried. "Hurray!"

Albers pretended to be sorry. "You're out, Sherm. Because this is the real ball."

Garrett erupted in the batter's box. He whipped off his cap and slammed it to the ground. His bold pompadour hair seemed to lift. "What! Then what your pitcher Dink threw at your third baseman was not the ball in play. You can't win on a trick like that."

Within seconds, both teams were milling around home plate. Shouts. Curses. Roars. Waving fists.

"He's out!"

"He's safe!"

"He can't be!"

"He is!"

Finally Umpire Maloney stepped on home plate and waved his arms up and down. "All right, everybody, shut up!"

It quieted down.

At that point Wild Bill strolled over from where he'd been standing near first base.

Umpire Maloney pursed up his mobile lips, rolled his brown eyes heavenward as if he were giving it all one more review, and then rendered his decision. "I'm calling a balk on the pitcher. The runner is safe."

The faces of the Bonnie boys opened, and then they cheered loudly. And Sherm quickly tagged home plate to make sure he'd scored.

The Rock Falls boys groaned.

Wild Bill turned to confront Umpire Maloney. "What did you say?"

"Runner is safe. The pitcher committed a balk."

Wild Bill's slit smile cut back even deeper, sharpening the point of his chin and his nose. "How do you figger that?"

"The object thrown wild over the third baseman's head was not the ball in play. It was a potato. And a potato can never be a legitimate part of a baseball game. So the pitcher made a false move towards third."

Wild Bill turned white with rage. "You really are calling it a balk then?"

"Yes, I am. I'm the head umpire here and what I say is final."

"That's what you think." And before Umpire Maloney could defend himself, Wild Bill lifted a haymaker from his hips and caught Umpire Maloney with four farm knuckles on the chin. Umpire Maloney tumbled to the ground.

Wild Bill stared down at Umpire Maloney. "Now, that sure should've shook up your piles."

Umpire Maloney lay perfectly still.

"But what's more important," Wild Bill continued, "is that I say, the runner is safe on the grounds of . . . let the buyer beware."

John moved in a step. " 'Let the buyer beware?' What's that got to do with baseball?"

Words seethed out from between the teeth of Wild Bill. "Maloney may be the head umpire, but I'm the strongest umpire. So what I say goes."

Umpire Maloney came to. Slowly he got to his feet. Umpire Maloney looked around at the wild flushed faces circling him. "I want all of you to go back to your positions. Or to your bench, if that's where you belong. I want a private word with my fellow umpire. Okay?"

Gradually the players from both sides retreated a dozen steps.

Then speaking in a low voice which neither side could make out, Umpire Maloney whispered fiercely in Wild Bill's ear. The satanic smile cutting back into Wild Bill's cheeks didn't leave, but Wild Bill's feet turned him around, and slowly he headed back to his spot just off first base.

Sherm said low to John. "Wow! I wonder what he told him?"

Garrett snorted. "Probably reminded him of the big dentist bill he owed. That if he didn't shut up, he'd sic the sheriff after him to collect the bill." Garrett also had a private grudge against Wild Bill. It went back to the time when Wild Bill used to brag uptown how he'd seduced Garrett's sister up in the haymow while the rest of the family was in church.

"Whatever it was," Sherm said,"it sure worked."

"For now," Garrett said.

Loose-lipped Pete Haber with his thick sly eyes quietly slipped away from the Bonnie bunch and going around behind the backstop all the way beyond third base, retrieved the potato where it had rolled into deep grass. When Pete came back he gave it to John. John, with a smile, dropped it into his back pocket.

In the bottom of the ninth, two out, with a man on first, the Rock Falls cleanup man, Buster Broene, came to bat. Buster was a left-handed hitter and had the nickname of Wagontongue because of the huge homemade bat he swung. It looked like it might be forty inches long and in the meat part was as thick as a car piston.

Wild Bill couldn't resist making a comment. "If Wagontongue ever connects, pulls it low, look out. He'll take your head off, John."

John backed up a couple of steps. "I'm ready."

Garrett called time and strolled out to the mound for a conference. John, lanky Alfred, and Sherm gathered around Garrett and Van Driel.

Garrett said, "Van, old boy, think you can hold 'em?"

Van Driel flashed his rectangular smile and rolled his right arm around. "I think I got a couple more good pitches left in the old soupbone."

"I'd put Big Alfred here in. But I think Buster will have more trouble with your underhand rising ball on his fists than Alfred's soft curve."

"Hey," Alfred said, "I like that. If you need a hard curve from me, I can give you one." Alfred rolled his right arm around too. "That old I ain't."

Garrett said, "Slim, what do you say?"

John said, "Nope. You're the manager. One Alfredson mad at me is enough."

Garrett rolled the old scuffed-up brown ball around in his hand. Finally he placed the ball in Van Driel's hand. "All right, here goes nothing'. We'll take a chance on you. Now remember. The strike zone is the width of the plate from the kneecap to the shoulders. So get that pitch in close to his Adam's apple."

Van Driel gritted his big white teeth. "He'll feel the wind of it under his chin."

"All right, let's get 'em."

Van Driel looked in for the signal; then, with a glance at the runner on first, wound up quickly, and snapped the ball towards home. To the horror of catcher Garrett, Van Driel's toe had slipped a little off the pitching rubber, and the ball headed straight for the center of the strike zone.

Buster Broene blinked, surprised to see the fat pitch coming where it was; recovered; swung mightily. There was a sickening sound. Out of the swing came a screaming line drive. And it almost did decapitate John. Then it climbed towards right field, rising, rising, where Pete Haber started to yell, "I got it, I got it." Of course Pete Haber wasn't within a mile of it.

The runner on first started to streak around the bases, second, third, and headed for home. Buster Broene followed close behind. The two men would be the tying and winning runs.

John woke up to the coming disaster. He stiffened. He absolutely couldn't have his brother-in-law Wild Bill crow over him. A mischievous smile broke across John's lips. He reached back into his handkerchief pocket and extracted the hot potato and yelled, "Garrett! Garrett! Here's the ball." And threw it.

Garrett, mask off, was already standing on home plate. His blue eyes widened; then he caught on. A grimace of sorts set on his lips. He hunched down, set himself for the catch. Then, potato caught and clutching it, he whirled and dove for the incoming sliding runner and tagged him on his shoes. In so doing he managed to block the plate.

Everyone expected Umpire Maloney to make a call. But Umpire Maloney didn't. He stood smiling, looking down at Garrett holding the potato, and at the runner.

Meanwhile the real baseball fell to earth. By chance it hit one of the fence posts in the railing around the race track and bounced back toward Pete Haber. Pete Haber slid to a stop, picked up the ball, whirled, and hurled it with all his might toward John. John leaped up and caught it; then he in turn hurled it towards home plate. Again Garrett set himself, all the while blocking the plate. The ball landed in Garrett's pud with a flat whacking sound. Then Garrett tagged the runner a second time.

Umpire Maloney rose on his toes, jerked his right thumb upward, roared, "The runner is out!"

"Hurray! We win! Two to one. Hurray hurrah!" The Bonnie boys jumped up and down in glee.

Men from the Rock Falls bench converged on Umpire Maloney, roaring, swearing, pushing, "What!! What!!"

Again Wild Bill advanced on Umpire Maloney.

Silence.

The Bonnie players ran up to see what was going to happen next.

Wild Bill's thin lips foamed over. His lips were drawn back so tight they'd turned white. Eyes slitted in rage, chin and brows more pointed, he looked more satanic than ever. "Did you call him out?"

"I did."

"But their catcher tagged him with a potato."

"I know. But he also tagged him with the ball."

"How come you didn't call this a balk too?"

"I couldn't. The pitcher threw the ball the way he was supposed to. And the batter hit it the way he was supposed to."

"But you can't tag a man out with a potato."

"I know."

"Well then?"

"He also tagged him out with the ball."

"But it was a trick again."

"I know. But the runner just lay there after he was tagged with the potato. He should have kept on trying to touch the plate. With his foot. Or with a hand. But since he didn't, and since the catcher has a right to protect the plate, and since the real ball finally showed up, he was tagged out."

"Tain't fair!"

"Besides, I've called him out. And an umpire never changes his mind. A call is a call."

"Well, we'll see about that. Because I'm gonna help you change your mind." Wild Bill cocked his hand near his hip.

Before Wild Bill could swing, John couldn't resist taunting him. "Well, Bill, how do you like them potatoes?"

"Why you! . . . Wild Bill turned and went after John instead. Again he cocked his hand near his belt.

Sherm couldn't let Wild Bill hit his brother. He dove for Wild Bill's ankles.

Wild Bill tried to step forward; couldn't; cursed, trying to step out of Sherm's hobbling embrace.

The Bonnie boys woke up, and first Garrett, then Van Driel, then hunching Pete Haber jumped on Wild Bill, bringing him down with a loud thump. Garrett settled on Wild Bill's right fist, Van Driel on his left fist, and Pete Haber squatted on his broad back. Wild Bill kicked up with his heels several times, but Sherm hung on. Wild Bill kept squirming and cursing and wriggling under the four bodies.

Umpire Maloney stood over them. Finally he said to Manager Albers of Rock Falls, "Maybe we better call the sheriff after all." He said it more down at Wild Bill than at Albers.

"Maybe we better."

After a moment, Wild Bill quit squirming.

Garrett said, "You had enough, Bill? Because if we have to, we can sit here on you all night."

Wild Bill muttered something into the chalky dust.

"Did you say yes?"

Silence.

Umpire Maloney said, "Let him up. And we can all go home."

Wild Bill got up slowly, brushed off his clothes, cast those nearest him a glittering silverish look of hate, then stalked off to his car.

On the way home, John asked Sherm, "Where'd you ever get the idea of grabbing him around the ankles?"

"I learnt that at the Academy. I went out for football there, for one day, before Ma told me she wouldn't let me go out for sports."

"Well, at least that wasn't wasted on you. Besides your *amo, amas, amat.*"

Sherm laughed. "It's a case of where if love doesn't conquer all, a good tackle can do the job."

Chapter Seven

Sherm didn't get much chance to play the next several years. Hard times hit Siouxland. In 1924 there was too much rain, and the grain and corn suffered. In both 1925 and 1926 the skies rarely clouded over and hot dry winds burnt the crops. Naturally that meant hard times also hit Main Street. Merchants had to lay off help. Three of the best town players had to leave Siouxland to find work.

The usual Decoration Day church games between the Marrieds and the Singles though were held. The Marrieds always won by lopsided scores. What hurt the singles was that Garrett finally got hitched again, one flesh and one bone. It was too bad, Sherm felt, that Free with his twisting sidearm curve was still really too young to pitch against grown-ups.

Sherm went to visit Free across the river to practise with him. It was June and the sun was about to set. There was a sweet musky smell of freshly cultivated cornfields riding the evening air coming in from the northwest. Opened earth smelled like a blooming coneflower.

Sherm sometimes had to pitch to Free too to give him his fair share of batting. But Sherm continued to have little or nothing on the ball except great speed. His pitches still went in hard and true straight for the center of the plate.

"Doggone it," Sherm said. "If only I could throw a little bitty curve, you wouldn't hit me so easy."

"It's not too hard to learn, Uncle." Free dropped his bat and picked up the ball. "Here. I'll show you. Like so." Free gripped the ball deep in his long young fingers and then pretended a throw, arm coming around with the wrist lifted up level, fingers pointing up. "You want to make sure the spin is level, and that by snapping your wrist like so, the ball spins like the dickens. Faster even than a top. The faster you make the ball spin the more it will curve away from a right-handed batter."

Sherm tried it, throwing the ball against the side of the barn.

Free said, "Don't look at where it's going to go so much, Uncle, but instead look at how it comes off your fingers."

Sherm just couldn't get that sidearm snap motion down. "Oh! The heck with it. I'm a shortstop and that's it."

Free had to laugh. "Well, in a way I'm glad. Because now I can be the Cubs great pitcher while you're being the Cubs great shortstop."

Sherm said, "But there is one thing I can teach you. You've got to have more of a k-nick in your swing. You know, just as you hit the ball. With those long arms of yours, you're a little slow starting your swing. Which is all right. But you got to learn to make your swing pick up speed, and then just as you hit the ball put the k-nick into it."

"How do you mean?"

Sherm picked up the bat and took several practice swings. "See? Like so." Sherm went out of his way to grunt loudly just as he was about to hit an imaginary ball. "You sort of bunch yourself all up into one big muscle. Like a cat hunching itself up as it gets ready to jump on a mouse." Sherm handed Free the bat. "Here. Try it."

Free took several slow wide swings.

"Go for that mouse! He's getting away."

Free swung faster.

"Still no k-nick in it. Darn. How can I explain it better." Sherm frowned, pushing out his lips until the set of them looked like the snout of a pig. "Here, give me that bat again." Sherm studied his lovely black beauty of a bat, how the slim cork-covered handle slowly swelled out into the fatness of a homebrew bottle. "Hey. I know. Is there anybody in school you hate?"

"Nnn . . . not really."

Sherm pursed his lips out again. It was true. Free was a softie. The only time Sherm saw Free angry was when someone had been unfair to his younger brothers. "You remember that time when Cornie Tollhouse was ragging your brother Everett pretty mean? And you punched Cornie on his big chin and knocked him down? Even though he was older than you?"

"How did you find out?"

"Cornie's brother Hank told me about it. Cornie is always acting tough with his brothers too, you know, and all they do is laugh at him. Hank said it was time somebody clocked him one."

Free smiled.

"Now. Remembering how you got mad at Cornie, see if you can't get that into your big swing just as you connect. You get that k-nick in there and the ball will jump a mile off your bat."

Free took several more swings, each time getting more of his butt and forearms into it.

"That's it. Keep practising that way and pretty soon that k-nick will come naturally. Because then, if you don't make it as a pitcher for the Cubs, you can play first base for them. You already got the good monkey hands. And you'll make a good target at first base for me."

In late August, finished with shock threshing, John and Matilda with their children decided to go visit her brother Lew Westraw for a week. Lew lived on a farm in the south part of Siouxland.

Sherm asked Free if he couldn't come live with him that week. That would give them a chance to practise every evening after supper. Lanky Alfred demurred. Alfred said it was time Free learned to run a sulky plow. Sherm suggested that Free could learn to plow with the sulky on John's stubble fields. When John learned of Sherm's idea, he offered to pay Free a dollar a day. When Alfred heard about the dollar a day, he agreed. Free could use the money to buy textbooks for his senior year at Western Academy.

The first couple of days plowing, Sherm and Free tended to the business of making straight furrows and taking advantage of every inch of the width of the plowshares. The first furrow was always the one that would tell how the rest of the field would plow. Sherm started on the west end of the eighty-acre field north of the grove and standing on the frame of the Emerson plow aimed his lead team straight for a single chokecherry tree on the east end of the field near the Little Rock River. After a dozen rods Colonel, the horse on the right of the lead team, seemed to catch on and, head down a little, black mane flowing, headed straight for the mark. At that Sherm let up a little, though he kept a firm line on both sets, the lead team and the back four.

Birds flew by overhead, but Sherm watched them only peripherally. A big flop-eared jackrabbit, roused out of its nap in the stubbles, began bounding away in a zigzag course toward the cornfield to the south, but Sherm ignored it. Free called once behind him about something, but Sherm pretended he didn't hear him. Sherm resisted the impulse to look back to see how straight he was plowing. To look back was a sure way of getting a wriggle in that first furrow.

When he hit the end, before he could kick out the two shares and pull on the lines, wise old Colonel had already begun his veer to the right and, the two shares up, kept veering tight, drawing the other five horses with him. The plow turned too, tight, hobbling on its three little wheels, with Sherm balancing on it as he stood watching the whole operation narrowly. When Colonel straightened out against the just-plowed two furrows and started heading west, still drawing the other five horses with him, Sherm kicked in the two shares, and once again they were turning over golden stubbles and covering them with shining black earth. Angleworms, upended, began wriggling desperately. Orange-nosed white grubs lay stunned. Mouse nests, riven in half, tumbled open, exposing white-gray baby mice to sudden light.

Colonel followed the furrow to perfection. Sherm, relaxed, sat down on his steel seat again, and, twisting around, watched to see how Free was managing the turn. But he needn't have worried. The big-boned kid handled his three-horse team with the ease of an old hired hand. When Free kicked in his single share, it immediately began to cut its full width. Good. That way the ends of the field would always be plowed straight, not bent in because the driver had been laggard.

All went smoothly the first couple days. They managed to milk the cows six o'clock on six o'clock. They had a breakfast of eggs and cornflakes. They had a noon hour meal of home-canned beans, home-canned sausage, fresh cabbage from the garden, homemade

114

bread with butter and plum preserve, fresh milk cooled in the cistern, and home-canned pears. They had a supper of fried potatoes, a sandwich of smoked drief beef, more milk, more pears. And then it was out on the yard, using the machine-shed door as a backstop, to play their imaginary game of Cubs against the Yankees in a World Series game. Babe Ruth up to bat was always a terrifying sight, and Sherm and Free were constantly scheming on how to pitch around him. But Lou Gehrig, up next, was almost as bad, and sometimes they had to walk both Ruth and Gehrig, and pitch to Meusel and Lazzeri.

To make it even more real, they took turns batting left-handed for Ruth and Gehrig. Both Sherm and Free were natural right-handed batters, but Sherm felt it made them better right-handed hitters if they now and then swung from the portside. It helped them fix in their minds what the true strike zone should be, the width of the plate from the knees to the shoulders. Sherm also thought it was good for Free the pitcher to learn to pitch to left-handed swingers. He was going to have to pitch to them someday.

Sometimes Free pretended he was scared of Ruth and Gehrig. So Sherm had to walk in from his shortstop position to buck him up. That helped. And they usually beat the dreaded Yankees. After a time Sherm developed the air that the Cubs had already won the game before it had started. Well, Lou Gehrig couldn't stand Sherm's attitude and tried to hit one past Sherm at short, but failed. Babe Ruth, of course, was mad, and his cheeks were all swole up like he had a big red beet in each cheek.

Sherm and Free studied the pictures of the two men that showed up in the sports pages of the *Sioux City Journal,* especially those pictures that showed their batting stances. So far as they could see, neither man had a batting weakness. Lou Gehrig had the steadiest set of nerves and you couldn't shake him up much with taunting chatter from the field. Babe Ruth was a kind of a show-off and in many ways he was also a kind of baby. But oh boy how that Ruth could swing that heavy bat. Free would sometimes get two strikes on Ruth and then, instead of being struck out, Ruth would catch hold of one of Free's inshoots, which really were outshoots for left-hand hitting Ruth, and bam! Home run. No wonder Ruth was called the Great Bambino.

The fourth day, with all the horses working smoothly and knowing what was expected of them, Sherm and Free began to have fun out in the field. When Sherm spotted Free staring at the earth flowing off his share, Sherm would reach down and catch up a firm clod of dirt and throw it over Free's horses and hope to hit him. And then he'd quick pretend he too was looking down at how his plowshare was working. It didn't take long for Free to catch on to that game, and soon Free in turn was lobbing chunks of dirt at Sherm, and then quick pretending that he'd actually been looking back up the black furrow.

Once when Free hit Sherm on the back of his straw hat, dirt crumbling down Sherm's neck inside his shirt collar, Sherm pretended great rage, and tying up the lines on the big lever to the shares, letting the horses go by themselves, ran back and pulled Free off his seat and wrestled him to the ground. Both their straw hats flew off. In a moment though Free with his longer arms and his powerful thighs got the leverage on Sherm and rolled him over on his back. Free at fifteen was already six two, an inch taller than Sherm at eighteen. In sheer raw strength Free was much stronger than Sherm. But Sherm was quicker.

With Free sitting heavy on him, Sherm, his head pressed down into the stubbles and prickly wild roses, finally let up on his pretended rage, and began to laugh. And then Free laughed too, and rolled off him, stretching out on the ground beside him.

Finally Sherm bethought himself. "Hey! Our horses!"

Both popped up and looked downfield.

The two sets of horses were going along quietly and minding their own business of pulling, switching their black tails, now and then bobbing their heads to get rid of the nose flies. The two Emerson shares up front and the sulky share in back were still cutting their full width and turning over the black earth.

Sherm and Free dug into it and ran to catch up, and hopped aboard their plows like they might be cowboys catching hold of the pommel of a saddle and then throwing a leg over.

What Free didn't know at first was that Sherm had a reason for lobbing clods at him on the east end of the field, and only on the east end. Pretty Allie Pipp lived north across the road. She was the sister of Laura Pipp, Garrett's second wife. She was the youngest of the Pipps, tall, with long flowing dark auburn hair and sometimes mischievous brown eyes. Sherm had been thinking of dating Allie on Sunday nights after Young People's catechism. He knew she was dating Cornie Taylor, who'd just gotten a new Chevie from his father. The Taylors were rich. Sherm still drove a horse and buggy Sunday nights when he couldn't get his brother John's car.

Sherm knew Allie'd been watching them plow. Several times she'd made it a point to hang out the wash on the south side of the new Pipp cream-colored bungalow just as he and Free arrived on the east end of the field. He should have taken it as a hint that, yes, he should ask her out. But he didn't know quite what to do, since it was his dream to become the best shortstop that had ever played the game. Would Allie fit into those plans? Her parents, Mr. and Mrs. Drew Pipp, were quite religious, like his own mother, and like her they would be sure to be against having their daughter marry a baseball bum, and one who, worse yet, played ball on Sunday.

Sometimes, after he and Free had wrestled in the stickle stubble field and he'd discovered that they'd wrestled for nothing because Allie hadn't come out to hang up the wash, he'd instead stop at the very end of the field to blow the horses and get off the plow and go lean on a fence post. He'd look at the glinting river below the clay cliff and try imitating the whistles of the meadowlarks in the pasture and the cardinals in the willows bordering the ford where the river turned.

One day Free joined Sherm, leaning on the post next down the line. "Uncle, I've often wondered where all those green spots in the pasture come from. You know, where the grass is tallest."

"That's where I spilled it on the ground."

"You mean like Onan in the Bible?"

"Something like that."

"When?"

"Actually it's where the bull spilled it."

Free thought this over. "What about the cows?"

"Well, yeh, them too. The first year it burns out the grass a little, but the second year, boy, does it come back."

Some cows were lying in the grass across the fence, and at that moment with groans they got up, rising rear end first.

Free said, "Horses get up front end first, don't they?"

Sherm was busy with another thought. "You know, I think that this fall, after I shell my corn, I'm gonna buy me a car. It's time I got going with a woman."

"Allie Pipp?"

"Hey! You caught on."

"I'm getting ready to like the girls too, Uncle."

All too soon the week was over and Free had to go back home. It also ended baseball practice for the year.

Right after they'd finished picking corn, Sherm shelled out the ear corn from his eighty. With the check from the Farmers Elevator in hand, Sherm deposited it to his account at the Bonnie First National Bank, and then went down the street to Wickett's Garage and bought a secondhand Ford Roadster. It was the kind where one could fold back the top behind the seat. It made for fun in the wind in the summer, but in the winter was always cold, no matter how tight the side curtains might be buttoned up.

The next Sunday night, right after catechism let out, Sherm caught Cornie Taylor by the elbow just as they were about to enter the old church barn together to relieve themselves. "Cornie, got a minute!"

"For the next ten minutes or so, yeh." Cornie was a shorty, already bent over from too much farm work too early in life. He had a narrow face with very close-set dark eyes, low forehead, and a considerable mop of very wavy brown hair. "What can I do for you that won't cost me too much."

"Can I beat your time with Allie Pipp?"

Cornie coughed in shock. He got out a pack of cigarettes from a shirt pocket, offered Sherm one, and when refused, took one himself and lit up with a long match in an elaborate gesture. The sudden flare of light coming out of his cupped hands emphasized in glowing gold the ferret look of his face. Finally, swallowing, he said, "Sure. Go ahead."

"Thanks. I thought it only right that I should give you fair warning." Sherm started to walk away.

"Hey. Wait a sec." Cornie took a mighty puff of his cigarette; blew out a little fog of smoke in the near dark. "Whatever gave you the idea of asking her?"

"You two ain't engaged yet, are you?"

"She been flirting with you?"

"Not that I noticed." Sherm thought of those times when Allie hung out the clothes across the road from where he and Free were plowing in John's field, and wondered if the good Lord would hold it against him that he'd just told a lie.

Cornie took another deep puff. "You gonna ask her then right now tonight?"

"You bet."

Sherm wound up the front tail of his tin lizzie, and along with a dozen other swains began purring up and down the street between the Little Church and downtown Bonnie. There was only one sidewalk the length of the street, on the east side where most of the houses were, and for a little while it was always choked with trios and duos of whispering and laughing girls.

It didn't take Sherm long to spot where Allie was walking. She was paired with his cousin Josie Engleking. Good. That might help. He tooled along in low gear behind them a ways, and then when he saw where they'd have to cross an intersection, he pulled up in front of them. He goosed up the motor a few times and pretended he was having trouble holding back a wild horse. Finally, with a smile, he pushed up the gas lever to let the motor idle down to a smooth tumbling purr. "How do, gals."

"How do," Josie said shortly.

Allie only smiled.

Josie said, "What do you want? You know Allie is going serious with Cornie Taylor."

"Hey, what a cousin you turned out to be. Because I thought you'd be on my side in this case."

"Case?" Allie said.

Sherm said, "Let's hope it still ain't an affair."

Allie said, "I'll say not."

Sherm tried out a laugh on them. "You gals are kind of snippish tonight."

"Well," Josie said, "we thought you was Harm Jolley." Harm Jolley had a roadster exactly like Sherm's. "And him I don't wanna see." Everybody in the catechism class had been buzzing over the fact that Harm Jolley had asked Josie for a date every Sunday night for the past two months and every Sunday night Josie kept turning him down. Josie had been known to say that she wouldn't date him if he was the last man on earth, not even if he and she were the last two mortals on earth and the human race was about to die out if they didn't have kids. She was not going to be an Eve to his Adam.

Sherm said, "In a minute when I pick up Allie here, what are you going to do? Walk home alone then?"

Allie crooked her head at him, long brown curls swinging away from her shoulders. "I suppose you think I'm an easy pickup."

"I didn't mean what you think."

"So you think I think that way."

Sherm deliberately assumed the air of a confident shortstop about to pick up a hot grounder. "Hey, I better keep my eye on the ball and catch it while I'm still ahead."

"I'll say you better." Allie laughed at him to let him know that while she liked him she also liked to stick it into him.

"In other words, my fair lady, you're turning me down."

"I guess I am."

"You're not sure?"

Josie broke in. "You're almost as bad as Harm Jolley. Won't take no for an answer."

Sherm showed his teeth at Josie. "You're rubbing me the wrong way, young lady."

Josie's nose came up. "Oh, for catsakes, Mr. Hoity-Toity."

"Yeh." Sherm turned to Allie and shaped up his best smile. "My lady queen, will you favor me with your presence in my chariot?"

Allie shook her head.

Sherm cocked his head to one side. "Looks like you ain't my gal after all. Okay. Watch my dust." He goosed up the motor several times, loud; then, starting out with the low pedal pressed down, let the motor catch in high gear. The motor almost choked; recovered; then, its power leveling out, it catapulted the car down the street. With a wave of his hand, as though he were dismissing peasants, Sherm was gone.

Sherm smoldered over the turndown for several days. And one night, while milking cows with John, when the two men were often at their most confidential, Sherm said, "What would you say of your favorite brother if he started dating Hettie Nabor?"

John finished milking his cow and stood up. He stared down at

Sherm. "You mean, Hettie of that wild Nabor family living across the section from us?"

"Yeh. I hear she's easy. One of those fast girls. And it's about time I learned."

John turned to pour the milk out of his pail into the big five-gallon can. He set down his one-legged stool and sat on it a minute. He held his head sideways, started to smile. "Tell you. And I wouldn't want this to get back to Matilda. But I've looked at Hettie Nabor myself, and the truth is, I wouldn't mind sleeping with her. 'Course, I'd want to be awake."

Laughter burst from Sherm. "Well, I sure intend to be awake my first time."

John stared down at the clean gutter behind the cows. "You know, you and I, we're blessed with the Engleking curse."

"What's that?"

"With our long fat ones."

"I presume you mean when our children grow up."

"Don't 'presume' me now, with that Academy talk. You know what I mean."

"Speak for yourself, John."

"Ha. I've seen you when we went swimming naked in our swimming hole. What you don't know is that whenever we go dipping there, all the women on our line start to rubberneck, wondering if they shouldn't go sneak down through my tall corn and have a peek at us."

"Dreamer."

"Just the same, you should hear Matilda complain. She's said several times our name should be Stingleking, instead of just Engleking. Oh, we're a scourge to womankind, boy."

"A thorn in the flesh. So to speak."

"Yeh."

"John, I think our dear departed dad would say that now we're about to brag."

"Good point. And sitting here ain't gonna get the cows milked."

Sherm nodded his head against his cow. "Well, if I do go look up Hettie Nabor, I'm gonna do what the town boys say:

> 'Find 'em,
> Feel 'em,
> Frig 'em,
> Forget 'em.'"

Free came over for a visit during Thanksgiving vacation.

Sherm welcomed him with a good clap on the shoulder. "Maybe you can help me with a conundrum I've run into."

"You? Puzzled? Impossible."

"This is one, though, where if I don't come up with something quick, my name is mud. It's Thursday and I still haven't got a program ready for Young People's tomorrow night. It's going to be a Basket Social in our Christian School building. In that empty room upstairs. And Reverend Tiller asked me to provide some entertainment afterwards."

The two of them were sitting in John's living room. They could hear John joshing with Matilda in the kitchen where the two of them were washing the Thanksgiving Day dishes. Matilda was in a gay mood. It was curious but she'd often turned merry when Free was over.

Free scratched the end of his nose. "Maybe you can pull off what I saw last week at Western Academy. It was a shadowgraph."

"What's that?"

Free explained.

Sherm popped up out of his rocker. "Hey. Wow. That'll rattle the rafters. It's time we shook up this bunch in Bonnie. Harm Jolly is supposed to help me. I'll call him and tell him to meet us at the Christian School yet tonight where we can practise it."

Sherm next went into the kitchen and asked Matilda if she had an old sheet, one that she was thinking of tearing up into rags. She did.

Soon the three of them, Sherm, Free, and Harm, met at the Christian School. Besides the sheet Sherm also brought along a gas lantern, a hay rope, a hatchet, a cleaver, a butcher knife, a balloon, a fieldstone in the shape of a heart, and a teakettle. They went upstairs to the classroom of the sixth, seventh, and eighth grades, next to the empty room.

Harm was a blond six-footer, with a high red forehead which almost gave him a bald look, light gold hair, light blue eyes, and a strange heavy mouth. As Sherm explained what a shadowgraph was, Harm looked dumb, but when it finally popped into his head how it was to go, after Sherm had gone through it a second time, a huge raw smile broke across his face.

Harm said, "Kind of like a movie then."

Sherm said, "I wouldn't know. Movies ain't come to this part of the country yet."

Free said, "Mostly because of our church."

Harm said, "We better not let slip to anybody what we're up to, or we'll have both the minister and the church consistory after us. Excommunicate us."

Free said, "Nobody got excited at the Academy. And that's a Little Church school."

Harm said, "But we're out in the sticks here."

Free said, "Well, not so far out that we don't know about baseball and the breaking of the Seventh."

After Sherm set up the sheet over a frame and lighted the gas lamp, they practised, with Sherm acting as director, and Free and Harm as actors. They also indulged in a few practice runs they couldn't show because of the ladies, over which they laughed and laughed.

When they were about to go home, Harm had a favor to ask. "Think you guys could find out for me which'll be Josie Engleking's basket? Because I want to buy it, and for at least during the time when we eat the contents she'll have to sit with me."

Sherm said, "Harm, let me give you a piece of advice. I know you won't like it, but here it is anyway. Josie ain't worth your time. She's gonna be an overpersnickety crab wife no matter how nice her husband is to her; even no matter how much in love with him she may be. She was born with her wires crossed."

Harm said, "I still want to give it one more try. And if that don't work, I'm going after Hettie Nabor."

Sherm said, "I'll find out which is Hettie's basket."

"No, I want to give Josie one more try. If it don't work, then I'll make Hettie my corncob girl."

The next night turned out to be a fair November evening. Temperature in the twenties. Night sky thick with glittering stars. No wind. Flivvers and Chevies and Dorts, and horses and buggies pulled into the churchyard a half hour early. From there the young people walked across the frozen lawn over to the Christian School on the corner. There was heavy laughter from the boys, as they swaggered along in twos and threes, hands in their pants pockets, wearing their best new overalls and dress shirt with tie and the jacket of their second-best suit. All the girls wore calf-length skirts with the colored belt fastened low over their hips. The girls had by that time managed to talk their parents into letting them bob their hair. Some of the girls wore puff bangs low over their foreheads.

A single large bulb burned in the entrance to the school, as well as in the hallway and at the head of the stairs. The empty west room upstairs glowed with extra light. Harm Jolley had brought over from his house across the road two gas lanterns. The girls sat on folding chairs and the boys stood by the windows smoking cigarettes. The girls kept looking at where their baskets stood waiting and the boys kept watching to see which baskets the girls were looking at. There was laughter, teasing talk, storytelling.

Sherm sat down next to Josie. "Well, Josie, I see you're all set for a big date tonight."

Josie's hair had been specially primped up with curlers. Head arched back, she sat with her nose lifted as though she had absolutely no time for small talk with bores. Josie prided herself on the clothes she wore. With her friend Nelda Brewer she sometimes took the train to Sioux City and bought herself a new dress and new slippers and the latest stylish chapeau. She claimed that the local stores in Bonnie were always a couple years behind New York and Paris. The mail-order houses Monkey Ward and Sears & Sobbock were even more behind the times. She sometimes also thought of going to a movie in Sioux City to see what Hollywood was up to in the latest styles. The trouble was, going to movies was against her religion.

Sherm said, "Didn't you hear me, Josie?"

"I heard you."

"That barber from Amen you been going with, he here tonight?"

"He had to work."

"Maybe I should bid on your basket then."

"But you're my cousin."

"So what? If I buy yours we don't have to get married, do we?"

"I just don't think it's a good idea to play with fire."

"Hey, I never knew you felt that way about me."

"Sherm, if you only knew. All the girls are nuts about you. From the way they cheer you when the Singles play the Marrieds you know that."

"Which basket is yours? Please?"

"Hmp. I'm not telling you. You'll run right over and tell your buddy Harm Jolley."

Sherm noticed as she talked that her eyes flicked around at the gaily decorated baskets set on several card tables on the far side of the room. Her glance seemed to linger on the basket on the far end of the last table. "What makes you think I might tell him? When I want to buy it myself?"

"I heard about you and Harm and Free. That you're giving the program tonight. I'm almost afraid to watch the kind of naughty high jinks you three will pull off." She glanced at the end basket again. "I'm surprised you're not trying to worm out of me which one is Allie Pipp's."

"Hers? Ha. She had her chance with me."

"Pretty snooty."

After a while Josie got up and went over to talk with Nelda Brewster. What she really was up to was to show off her new calf-length shimmering blue dress with its red velvet belt and her new silver slippers and the latest in hose from New Jersey.

Josie's fancy white stockings caught Cornie Taylor's eye. He whistled, and jeered, "Detroit! Detroit!" The past summer his father had given him the money to take the train to Detroit, where he bought a new blue Chevie at factory price, not what the local car dealer would charge him. While in Detroit he learned it was the thing for young swains to whistle at women wearing white hose into which a red arrow had been woven, an arrow which pointed upward from the instep.

Josie whirled around. "You trying to poke fun of me, Cornie?"

"Detroit! Detroit!"

Josie stepped up to Cornie and pushed her pointy nose into his dark squirrel face. "You better tell me what you mean by that or I'll hate you forever."

Cornie laughed. "Boy, I'm sure gonna worry about that."

"Just what do you mean by 'Detroit'?"

"In Detroit it means 'detour.' Where the highway department has put up an arrow pointing ahead to where they're putting in a bridge." Cornie looked down at her ankles. "See where your arrow is pointing?"

Josie burned red. She slapped Cornie.

The boys nearby let go with a series of hoots and whistles. Even Sherm and Free looked at the red arrows in her white stockings, and cheered. Only Harm Jolley kept a straight face. He didn't think it very funny. Presently Sherm felt sorry for Harm and told him which basket was Josie's.

Reverend Tiller showed up, pink face beaming, high forehead shiny under wavy gold hair. He had a big smile for everyone. He shook hands with some of the boys, particularly the trouble-makers, and bowed to the ladies, especially the prettier ones.

Reverend Tiller acted as auctioneer. Laughing, sometimes praising the prettied-up baskets, sometimes apologizing for the way he waved the basket around, thus possibly mixing up the contents, finally in some cases putting in a bid hmself when none were forthcoming, he chanted in a singsong manner, "Remember, the money raised here is for a good cause. It's all going to missions. We must somehow bring the message of Christ to the heathen Oglala Sioux in South Dakota."

Finally there were only three baskets left. And of course everyone knew by that time whose they were. They watched carefully to see what would happen next. When Reverend Tiller picked up the third from the end, and asked for a bid, Sherm offered a dollar. Cornie Taylor promptly bid two dollars. Yep. That had to be Allie Pipp's. The two young men bid furiously, until the price went up to twenty dollars, Cornie's bid. Reverend Tiller waggled the basket at Sherm. "Going? Going? . . ."

Sherm said, "Let Cornie have it. He's richer than I am."

". . . Gone to Cornelius Taylor for twenty dollars."

Allie Pipp looked disappointed.

When Reverend Tiller held up the basket at the end, Josie turned red, and she glanced apprehensively at Harm Jolley to see what he would do. No one bid on it at first. All the boys knew she didn't think much of the Bonnie boys. Finally Harm offered five dollars. Reverend Tiller, understanding what was going on, quickly snapped, "Sold to Harm Jolley."

The last basket had to be Hettie Nabor's. Hettie waited to see if Sherm would bid on it. She sat like a desperate rabbit, thick lips parted, eyes a glistening amethyst. She understood all too well that she had the reputation of being wild. None of the local fellows would date her. Boys from other towns around heard she was easy and often drove over to see if they could pick her up. She finally learned to say no the first night. But the second night she'd melt and say yes. Sherm, besides lusting after her, also felt sorry for her.

Sherm raised his hand. "Five dollars."

"Sold!" Reverend Tiller cried, glad to be done with the auction. "To Sherman Engleking, premier shortstop of the Bonnie Little Church." He handed the basket to Sherm. "And now I see that I don't have one."

Allie Pipp smiled her mysterious dark-eyed smile. "Oh yes there's one for you, Reverend. We didn't forget you." She went over to where the girls had piled their coats on a discarded recitation bench, and from under it dug out an especially gaudy basket. It had been decorated with various colored ribbons. "This is for you, Reverend."

The Reverend's pink face opened in genuine surprise. "How very kind of you young ladies."

Allie said, "When we found out from juffrouw that she wasn't coming, we decided it wouldn't be very nice for you to be sitting here watching us all eat."

Every one slyly watched Josie sitting with Harm. Face an almost apoplectic red, she opened the basket for Harm, set it on his lap, and disdained to eat from it. Eyebrows went up. It was the custom for the girl, after she'd opened the basket, to dole out the contents, cookies, cake, pie, fruit, to the swain who'd bought the basket. Josie didn't quite turn her body away from Harm, but did avert her face. Harm meanwhile did try to eat, but had trouble swallowing, with the result that his mouth filled up until it looked like his cheeks would explode.

Free saw Harm's dilemma. He happened to buy the basket of Thila Oxart, the fattest girl in church. "Need some help, Harm?"

"Mmmllp?"

Free whispered, "Go out in the hallway and open a window and spit it all out. Then start over."

"Gdllp." Harm excused himself with a gesture and left for a minute. When he returned, his cheeks were back to normal, in color and size both, and he did start over. He managed to down the next bites.

Josie all the while held herself so erect she sat more on the points of her buttocks than on the roundth of them.

When all were finished eating from the various baskets, Sherm and Free and Harm excused themselves and went into the east classroom to set up their act. Harm turned on the overhead light as well as lit a gas lantern.

Sherm surveyed the room. "The audience can sit in those desk seats in back of the room. We'll put up the sheet here in front of the first row. And then do our act on the principal's desk." Sherm cleared the desk of a row of textbooks as well as the blue blotter. "And we'll set the lantern here on this stool next to the blackboard. That way, by putting you two between the lantern and the white sheet, your shadows will fall perfect on the sheet. And the people on the other side, all they'll see is your shadows in action."

Harm and Free sat down on the desk, their backs to the sheet. Sherm pulled up several chairs and placed on them the various props they'd use.

"All set, you think?" Sherm asked.

"Good as we'll ever be," Free said.

"Is this the way they had it at Western Academy?"

"Prexactly. But I wonder about something."

"How so?"

"It might be a little strong for some of our Bonnie kids. They might take it for real."

Sherm said, "Naw. I think everybody here can guess pretty straight."

"I don't want to be blamed for any heart attacks."

"Hey, I thought you said nobody got excited at the Academy?"

"I meant the profs there. And the Hello consistory."

Harm said, "Maybe at last we'll get Josie to feel sad about me."

Sherm laughed. "Let's hope so." Sherm picked up his coat, which he'd hung up earlier in the room, and threw it over the props. "We're all set then. I'll go call them in."

Soon all were assembled in the back rows of the east classroom. All were silent, full of wondering as to what was coming, even Reverend Tiller.

Sherm stood to one side. "All right, everybody. In a moment I'm going to douse the overhead light. And the only light on will be that lantern standing on the stool there behind the white sheet. I'm the director of this show. There will be two actors. This is a story about two very good friends who've never had a fight. But you know how things work out in life . . . they at last had a falling out. And then . . . And then . . . Well, that's what we're going to find out as we watch the shadows on the sheet. It's all pantomime. No talk by the actors. Of course the audience can do as it wishes. Cheer. Hoot and holler. Boo the actors to the rafters. Give 'em the old razzberry. Whatever your merry hearts desire."

Sherm reached up and pulled the cord to the overhead light, and suddenly, except for the lantern light behind the white sheet, the room was dark. Sherm sat down on a front desk seat to keep an eye on how well his boys pulled off the shadowgraph show.

It started tame enough. Harm and Press sat haunch to haunch, laughing with their shoulders, now and then putting an arm around each other, nodding, leaning back and laughing.

But then Harm seemed to mention something Free didn't like. Free held up a big fist and shook it at Harm. Harm in turn got mad and shook his fist at Free. Free then picked up the hatchet and threatened Harm with it. When Harm didn't back down, Free swung the hatchet and seemingly hit Harm a great thunk over the head. Sherm of course knew that Free had kicked the side of the desk at the same time the blow seemed to land. It sounded hollow and awful. Harm slowly fell over. Sherm knew that Harm would lay himself down on the desk while Free would slide forward a foot. Their new positions would allow Free to perform all kinds of seemingly brutal acts in shadow without touching Harm. Harm, stretched out, let out a long moan. Free next picked up the cleaver and pretended to dismember Harm, as a butcher might do in a slaughterhouse. Harm let go with the most agonizing groans in the world. Sherm smiled. Harm really was putting on a show. Harm sounded exactly like a dog that had been run over by a truck. He yowled. His shadow form jerked and wriggled.

The audience behind Sherm let go with several "oh dears" and "for godsakes," their seats creaking; then fell into a stiffened silence.

Free next picked up the curved butcher knife and slowly pulled out of Harm what looked like intestines, really of course only a hay rope; then a stomach that looked exactly like a balloon; and then, of all things, a teakettle. There was a moment when it appeared the teakettle was even steaming. Finally, Free pulled out a heart. The only trouble was the heart wasn't beating; it was as dead as a stone.

It was all so wonderfully real Sherm wanted to laugh. But since everybody behind him was sitting in total shocked silence, he felt it might not be in keeping.

129

The next thing Sherm saw on the sheet was the shadow of Reverend Tiller. What? Quickly Sherm popped to his feet and stepped around to the lighted side of the sheet. "Reverend?"

Reverend Tiller looked gravely at Sherm, then at Free and Harm. "This show has got to stop."

"But why?"

"Snap on the light and you'll see."

Before Sherm could pull on the light cord, the strangled silence in the back of the classroom erupted into females crying and weeping, and males cussing and swearing.

Especially piercing was the way Josie carried on. "That darn Free. He killed Harm. Oh, poor Harm, now he's dead. And here I've been turning him down. Even tonight. Oh. Oh."

Sherm couldn't believe it. What a bunch of dumb jacks and jennies. All of them. And that Josie, he was ashamed he was related to her. The way she yanked around, it probably meant she was a little interested in Harm after all. But of course, because she was an Engleking, poor Harm Jolley was beneath her. It really was something to laugh at. Because where did that put Harm? When he was worth two of her?

Free said, "Sherm, what do we do now?"

Sherm's lips curled. "Why, turn on the light of course." He reached up and pulled on the light cord. Instantly the classroom was awash with glaring illumination. "Let there be light in the firmament, to banish ignorance from the minds of the Bonnie bunch forever."

"Now, Sherman," Reverend Tiller warned, "no blasphemy. Please."

"You!" Sherm snapped at the good reverend. And then Sherm turned to face the upset bunch of young people. "And the rest of you! You make me disgusted. Couldn't you see it was only a pretend show? Did you dumb jackasses really think that our Free, our good-hearted softie Free, would really hit Harm over the head with a hatchet? And butcher him? God! It's unbelievable that you'd think that. You guys are not only living back in the sticks here, you're even more backward than the redskins out on the reservation."

Dennis Nabor mumbled, "Wull, how was we to know it wasn't for real." Dennis was Hettie's brother and was known to be a regular rip of a fellow around women.

"Ochh!"

Mortified, angry, the young people quickly coupled up and grabbed up their baskets and clothes, and clattered down the stairs in the main hall and vanished into the night.

All except Hettie Nabor. No one had taken her arm to see her home. She stood smiling a little. Like Mary Magdalene of the Bible, she was both experienced and saved, and she understood the show.

Sherm turned to Harm. "If you've got any brains at all, you'll take this beautiful girl here, Hettie Nabor, home. And keep taking her home after this. Because if you don't, I will. Josie ain't worth even one of your toenails."

Harm nodded. "That's what I found out tonight."

As Sherm watched Harm and Hettie leave, he said to Free, "Well, well. Maybe it was worth doing after all."

Reverend Tiller finally smiled. "Yes, Sherman, perhaps you taught us all a lesson tonight. Because frankly, I didn't know what I was going to do about Hettie. I had all I could do to keep the consistory from calling her in and reading her out of the church."

The next day, Saturday, Sherm went shopping in Tillman's Mercantile for winter yard gloves. The moment he stepped in through the door, Tillman began to laugh and laugh, and slap his knee. He stroked his blond hair back from a broad sloping forehead.

"Sherm, Sherm, what you boys did last night."

Sherm pretended surprise.

"You fellows. I hear the girls' laundry bills doubled overnight. Ha."

"What I wonder is, what Reverend Tillman is going to tell the consistory."

"Don't worry. What you guys did was good for this old turtleback burg. Especially our backward church."

Too bad Tillman wasn't a member of the consistory.

That same Saturday night, Sherm ran into Free on Main Street. they started to laugh the moment they spotted each other.

Sherm asked, "You didn't happen to get Hail Columbia at home, did you?"

Free said, "Oh, Pa heard about it but he didn't say anything. Only Ma got a little excited. She didn't mind us having good fun; she just didn't like it that we scared the girls so. She said we should have remembered that the local gals ain't all that up on things. And, she was a little worried that we were aping one of the Devil's clever inventions, the movie."

"She'll get over it. She's a wise old gal and there's plenty of stretch to her."

"I think what I better do is bring home some of my books for her to read. That'll help."

Sherm watched all the young girls parading up and down the street, tripping along arm in arm, stopping now and then to window-shop, full of secrets and giggles, throwing arch glances at where the boys lolled in the doorways of the two cafes.

Sherm felt restless. Too bad he'd sicced Harm onto Hettie Nabor.

Just as the thought of Hettie came to him, he spotted Cornie Taylor tooling in low gear through town, going so slow with the motor barely purring that the new blue Chevie now and then chugged a little. And sitting in the front seat with Cornie was Allie Pipp. Darn.

Free said, "What I can't get over is that it's still so warm out this time of the year. We could almost play catch."

"Yeh. The farmers all got their corn in ahead of the first snow. Now all they have to do is wait out the winter." Sherm wriggled his shoulders. "What do you say we do a little trolling up and down our lovers' lane to see what we can see."

"Okay by me. But I better tell Pa I got a ride home."

They found no parked cars in the lovers' lane on the north edge of town. Sherm had hoped they might spot Cornie's car there. If they had, Sherm was going to pull up at right angles to the new blue Chevie and let the headlights of his flivver blind the two of them, especially Allie Pipp.

Free said, "Let's check the Catholic Church. I hear there's sometimes some wild doings going on in those weeds in the empty lot north of there."

Sherm said, "Father Cobden planted some popcorn there this year."

"I suppose that'd be picked by now."

"Nnn. Let's go look." Sherm wheeled the Ford roadster around and headed for the Catholic Church. To his surprise, they found the little patch of popcorn hadn't been picked. Also there was a touring car parked in the shallow ditch beside the still-standing corn. "By golly!" Sherm exclaimed. "That's Dennis Nabor's jalopy. And there's nobody in it."

Free said, "Would they really go into that cornfield and neck? With the ground a little chilly?"

Sherm said, "Well, when you're in love and all het up, you don't pay attention to such little details."

"Hey. How would you know about that?"

"I got ears and I listen good." Sherm whirled the steering wheel over. "Let's go to the east side of the patch of corn and then drive down through the middle of it and see what we can see. That patch slopes downhill and it'll be easier driving through it from that side."

Sherm took the corner easy, and then halfway along the side of the patch, turned left. Instantly, ears of popcorn began to fly off in all directions as the radiator of the car breasted through the five-foot deep growth. It was also rough going over the hard cultivated rows. Sherm and Free bounced up and down as the flivver jounced along. Gradually the still-standing popcorn slowed the car . . . when of a sudden they came upon a clearing where the popcorn had failed to grow, and up off the ground rose two bodies, a boy and a girl, the boy with his trousers down around his ankles, which hobbled him as he desperately tried to get out of the way to the right; the girl with her panties down around one ankle, from where they flipped back and forth as she tried to skip out of the way to the left. Almost everything worth looking at was naked to see. Dennis Nabor and Nelda Brewster! Sherm was so startled he failed to step on the brakes. The two surprised lovers just made it. The front fenders on both sides of the Ford just missed their buttocks. Then again, as the Ford entered the farther wall of standing corn, ears began to fly in all directions, several even hitting the windshield. And bumping and bouncing, Sherm and Free came to the end of the patch of popcorn and sailed slowly through a shallow ditch and climbed up onto the graveled street. They rolled on a dozen yards before they collected their wits, and then, eyes wide, mouth open, they began to laugh, and laugh so hard Sherm had trouble keeping the jitney in the middle of the street and Free slopped over against the curtain on the door.

Sherm finally pulled up for fear he'd run into something. He braked the roadster and stopped in front of the First National Bank.

They laughed off and on for some time. Just when it looked as if they'd got control of themselves, one would look at the other and they'd start all over again.

Sherm said, "Of the tree which is in the midst of the garden of popcorn, God hath said, 'Ye shall not eat of it.'"

Free said, "Neither shall ye touch it lest ye die."

Sherm said, "The Devil said, 'In the day ye eat thereof, then your eyes shall be opened; and ye shall be as gods, knowing good and evil.'"

Free said, "'And the eyes of them were both opened, and they knew that they were naked.'"

Sherm said, "Yeh, but they never got a chance to sew 'fig-leaves together and make themselves aprons.'"

Free said, "We better be careful or we too will hear the voice of God on Main Street here."

Of a sudden they did hear a voice speak to them. "What the hell are you two rapscallions laughing about this late at night up-town here?"

Sherm instantly recognized the voice. At least it wasn't God, thank God. "Hi, Constable. What can we do for you?" Constable Koltoff liked to pretend he was a tough lawman, but actually he was a pretty good old skate.

"Well, what was you two laughing about?"

"Oh, just a private joke."

Constable Koltoff leaned in suddenly, sniffing Free's breath.

Sherm made up a friendly laugh. "No, Constable, we haven't been drinking."

Constable Koltoff touched his nose. "Some of you Little Churchers like to drink homebrew beer, though."

"Not us. We're ballplayers and you can't drink and play good."

"Well, all right. It's late. You guys better head on home now."

"You got a point there." Sherm turned to Free. "Well, Buster, I better take you home before you get into trouble with your pa and ma."

As they rolled towards Free's home, Free asked, "Do you think those two popcorn lovers recognized who we were?"

Sherm said, "Do you mean, did they see us? No. But I'm sure Dennis Nabor knows the sound of my motor and he'll know. And of course his gal there, Nelda Brewster, she'll ask him if he knows. Ha. The next time I see either one of them they won't dare to look me in the eye."

The second Sunday after Thanksgiving Day, Sherm decided it was time he got a final yes or no from Allie Pipp. If it was going to be no, he wanted to know right away, so he could think of going after other girls. He was nineteen and most boys his age were already going steady. All his frank talk with brother John had ripened him for the role of a lover. And watching John's bull sneering up the smells of ripe heifers in the pasture also helped Sherm make up his mind.

And there was one other thing. It was the memory of what Sherm had seen the past summer. He was shocking oats near the high riverbank above John's swimming hole when, about to pick up a pair of bundles, he heard voices below him. He straightened up and listened. Light voices. Young women. And one of those voices was Allie Pipp's. Swimming? That he had to see. Slouching, he slinked across the stubbles and, kneeling, pushed his way very slowly through a wall of ragweeds bordering the riverbank. It was where John couldn't get his horses to go closer with the mower. Gently Sherm opened the last fringe of the weeds and looked down. Allie. With her sister Laura. The one who'd married cousin Garrett Engleking. Holykaboly. Where Laura was stocky and jolly, Allie was slender and wistful. Sherm instantly noted some other things. Allie had breasts like two lazy little kittens asleep, and her pudendum looked exactly like two fingers of a child curled over a knee. Allie was beautiful.

Laura was teasing Allie. "You sound like you might be in love with Sherm."

Allie said, "I'm dating Cornie now."

"Suppose Sherm'd ask you out, then what?"

"I think he thinks he's too good for me."

"What kind of silly talk is that?"

The two women were standing in the sandy edge of the flowing water, up to their ankles, and now and then they reached down to cup up a handful of the amber river and let it spill over their breasts.

Presently Allie stepped out of the water and reached for a

135

towel. She stood with her toes curled up. What was bothering her that she should be so toe-uptight?

When Allie and Laura began dressing, Sherm cautiously retreated butt first through the rag weeds until he hit the stubbles again. He stood up, removed his battered straw hat, wiped his brow. Whew. What a sight. Wonderful.

He also knew that in a minute or so they'd climb up the animal pass a dozen rods to the north, and then they were bound to see him shocking grain. That he couldn't let happen. He didn't want Allie to know that he might possibly have seen her in her birthday suit. Later on, after he got to know her better, he might tease her about her lazy kittens. He looked around, spotted some chokeberries growing at the edge of the field. Quickly he skipped across the stubbles, past rows of shocks he'd already set up, and hid himself behind the chokecherries. Soon Allie and Laura climbed the riverbank and headed across the end of John's oatfield for home.

Right after Young People's Catechism, before Cornie could approach Allie, Sherm stepped into the bunch of girls crowding around the front door of the church, gently pushed Josie and her friend Nelda aside, and confronted Allie. He smiled winningly, then said with a little toss of his head, "I'm taking you home tonight."

"Says who?" Allie demanded.

"Says me. Now I tell you something. I'm asking you one more time. Only one more time. And if you don't say yes, I'll never bother you again. Won't ever look at you again. So, can I see you home tonight?"

All the boys and gals within earshot stared.

Cornie Taylor smiled to himself as he lighted a hand-rolled cigarette.

Allie tried to be perky about it. "And you won't do any more of those silly stunts while plowing with Free?"

Sherm stiffened. "I'm waiting."

Allie tried to hold up to his fierce eyes. But it could be seen that he meant exactly what he said. Slowly she softened, and finally she said in a subdued voice, "I guess you can."

"Guess?"

"Yes. I mean, yes, you may."

With a little swagger, Sherm stepped up, took her arm, and said, "Come then. My chariot waits and the horses under the hood are chomping at the bit."

The lighted cigarette fell from Cornie Taylor's lips. Nervously he hoisted up his trousers with his elbows. The young men of the day fancied it stylish to wear their belt below the hips. "Well, I'll be a sonofabitch!"

Sherm took his time with Allie. He took her home three times after Young People's before he kissed the back of her hand. He asked her a lot of questions about her family. He gathered that her brothers and sisters didn't like Bart the firstborn Pipp. Bart had a high-nose way of smiling as though he knew something about you that you should be ashamed of.

Twice Sherm dropped in on Allie in the evening by strolling over from John's house. It was below zero and it was just too much fuss to get his roadster started. Dressed in a warm sheepskin coat he didn't mind the walk. He wanted to see what she was like when she least expected him. The moment he showed up at the door, her father and mother vanished into their bedroom. But what he saw of them he liked. Banty Drewes Pipp had done quite well with his boys, except for Bart. But Ma Pipp was the tower of strength in the family. She was almost twice the size of Drewes, and though very firm had twice his warmth for their children.

The first time Sherm dropped in on Allie she was ironing in the kitchen. He right away knew he'd never forget the sweet smell of almost scorched cotton shirts as he watched how careful she was to get the collar absolutely flat and smooth. They didn't say much that night. After she made a cup of hot chocolate for him, he walked home.

The next time he walked over she was just emerging from the kitchen door carrying a lantern and a basket. The yellow light from the lantern whelming up over her face gave her the look of a nun out on an errand of mercy.

"Hi, Allie."

She jumped. "Och! You scared me."

"Sorry."

A shudder raised her shoulders. "I guess I'm just scared of the dark."

"I didn't mean to scare you."

137

"I know." Her eyes remained square with fear.

Sherm wondered about it. Someone had probably scared the pants off her when she was a little girl. "What's the matter? Lose something outside?"

"I forgot to get the eggs today. And Dad was afraid they might freeze in the chicken house. I told him not with the hens sitting on them."

"Where's your brothers?"

"They all went to town."

"Come. I'll help you. Let me carry the lantern. You carry the basket."

Most of the white chickens were already asleep on their roost. A red-combed cock in front began to crake in challenge at Allie and Sherm and that woke up the hens.

Sherm said, "If those hens were women, they'd be shooing us out of here, instead of us shushing them down."

Allie began checking the nests. There were no eggs in the empty nests, but every hen sitting in a nest had an egg under them. She'd collected a dozen when a hen at the end pecked her hand. "Hoo!" she cried, and dropped the egg. The egg cracked, and opened a little. "Oh dear."

Sherm said, "It's all right." Taking off his mitten he reached down and carefully picked up the cracked egg, making sure the egg white didn't run between his fingers. With a smile, he said, "We'll just wing this one into the kitchen for the cook to use when she bakes me a cake."

Allie relaxed. And laughed. "You sure know how to make a person feel good, don't you, with your wisecracks."

"Was that a wisecrack? I thought I was just talking sense. A couple of weeks from now that yolk really would've had wings."

Sherm had supper at the Pipps on Old Year's Eve. Around eight Allie's brothers and sisters took off for a New Year's Day party at the neighbors'. Around nine her father and mother went to bed; they declined to see the New Year in with a glass of port Sherm brought over.

Sherm and Allie sat on the davenport in the parlor. A fat candle burned in its holder on a side table. Allie got out the family album and showed Sherm pictures of herself when she was a little girl. There was one where she was sitting on the knee of her oldest brother, Bart, and that one she quickly skipped over.

The hard coal burner in the next room made soft sounds as the coal settled into the blue-hot embers in the firepot.

Allie finally had a question. "How come you haven't been fresh with me?" She ended her query with a nervous laugh.

"Hey, I thought we were friends."

"What do you mean by that?"

"Friends can touch each other, can't they, without it being called fresh? When friends love each other it's just natural that after a while they'd want to touch each other."

"How come you haven't touched me then yet?"

"Because I got the feeling you're not exactly sure you want that yet with me."

"You sure are different from Cornie Taylor."

"I should hope so."

"The first date he tried to be all over me."

"Like a ferret, sort of, huh?"

"Yes. I had to fight him off all night."

"I knew that. And that's exactly why I decided I'd be different with you."

"But pretty soon you're gonna be just like him, ain't you?"

"Hey. Suppose we intend to get married? Wouldn't you want me to touch you somewhere along the line?"

"Well, I guess so."

"And wouldn't you want to know before we got married if I had it in me to be that way?"

"I suppose so."

"Wouldn't you want to make sure I wasn't a deadbeat?"

"You sure know how to argue, don't you?"

"Living with John and Matilda you learn that."

Allie sighed. And sighed. "I guess you're a nice fellow after all."

Sherm noticed the way two of her fingers curled over the edge of the red cover of the album. It reminded him of the time he saw Allie swimming with Laura in John's swimming hole. "Tell you. I decided I wasn't going to kiss you until you'd first kissed me three times."

She stared in disbelief at him.

"So I'm waiting for at least your first time. Right now. And then around eleven o'clock your second time. And finally at the stroke of midnight, New Year, your third time." He smiled at her.

"Right now means right now, you know"

She let down. "Such a funny man. At least we're gonna have a lot of laughs together." A smile slowly lifted the corners of her curved lips. "I remember how you and Free used to throw clods at each other. I'd laugh and laugh about that." Impulsively she leaned toward him, long wavy hair flowing around his face, and kissed him. "There. There's the first one." The aroma in her hair was that of a flowering milkweed. Her full lips opened around his lower lip. Then she leaned back and laughed merrily. "You never expected that, I betcha."

"I sure did."

"What?"

He waggled his head like a lord. "We Englekings usually win out in the ninth."

"Some of the kids in church don't like that in you."

"So what? They don't say anything when I hit a home run to beat the Marrieds."

"But I like it in you. Because you're not mean with it. Who wants a man at the head of the table who has already given up before he begins?"

At eleven o'clock, as he was telling her about Ma and how Ma with her strict rules caused him to quit Northwestern Academy, he once more found himself whelmed over by her flowing wavy hair as she kissed him a second time. "Holykaboly! When you finally make up your mind you come on like a sweet summer shower."

"Now I suppose you think me sex mad."

"In this part of the country you can never have too much rain."

They talked awhile. He was careful not to let his hands fall in the wrong places. Not that he didn't want to. Lord, it was an agony to wait.

When the clock on the mantelpiece struck twelve, they both got to their feet and smiled at each other. The fat candle behind them had burnt down to its last inch.

"Happy New Year, Allie."

"Happy New Year, Sherman."

He waited, smiling.

"You rascal. Well, here's your third time." She kissed him softly, with a little smile.

"Thank you, my lady. Now here comes my promised kiss after

those three." He took her gently in his arms and held her close, until he could feel her kitten-soft breasts against him; and kissed her, until her lips opened under his. He drew back his head. He didn't smile. It was serious. "And now," he said, "how about a glass of port to celebrate the New Year in."

Chapter Eight

Sherm was sure that he and Allie could make ends meet living on the eighty. The problem was, the eighty had no house. Also, he'd have to get permission from Ma if he was to get married before he was twenty-one. Ma might just be ornery enough to say no. He really hadn't made up with her yet. And that was probably a mistake.

If he did marry Allie soon, that year or next year, and if he decided to be a baseball player instead of a farmer, would Allie be willing to live in rambunctious Chicago with him while he played for the Cubs, she who became uneasy even going to town in Bonnie on Saturday nights with its 574 souls?

And if he didn't marry her and played for the Cubs, would Cornie Taylor try to sneak in there again?

Also, if he played in the majors, would he play ball on Sunday? He'd have to make up his mind about that too one way or the other.

One night, milking, Sherm once more brought up the subject.

John didn't say a word until he'd finished his last cow. Then he placed his one-legged stool in a rack behind the cows and leaned against a crusted partition. It was ten below outside, but inside the barn it was warm. The sweet smell of ground corn and musty cow fur hung in the air. Light from the lantern hanging above John shed around him like a golden parasol. "Would you really like to hear what I really think?"

"What else?"

"I'd go for it."

"You mean, marry Allie?"

"No, not that. 'Course she's wonderful."

"You mean, head for the Cubs at Catalina Island yet this spring?"

"You bet."

"And leave you to farm my eighty? That I've already rented and signed for?"

John pushed up the bill of his dark-blue Scotch cap. The gold lantern light caught the thrust of his blond brows and his nose. "If I could play like you, yes sirree. Which of course I can't. I'm cross-handed and maybe even got some wires crossed in my head. And, I can't run like you."

"What about breaking the Sabbath and eternal damnation?"

"Listen, bud. The good Lord wouldn't have given you the talent to play baseball the way you do if he hadn't intended that someday you could play in heaven. That God-given talent wasn't given for nothing. He must've had a reason for it."

"The only trouble is, I haven't played much the last year or so. And I'm bound to be rusty."

"Well, then ask Alvord if you can play for them, if you need practice."

"You mean, play in a half-dozen games around here and then head for the Cubs? When they've already started playing in Chicago?"

"Something like that, yeh."

Sherm finished his last cow, got up, dropped his stool in the rack besides John's. "I better sleep on this."

Early in February, he made up his mind. He would play as many games as possible the coming season for Alvord, or Amen, or Whitebone, and then come February of the next year, when he was twenty, he'd head for Catalina Island and the Cubs' spring training.

But first he had to make sure that Bonnie would not have a team. It would be ever so much more handy if he could play for Bonnie just a few miles away.

Sherm went in to see Garrett in his hardware store.

After they'd said their hellos and mentioned the weather, Sherm came right to the point. "You say our church team don't have enough good players anymore."

"That's right."

"Same with the Bonnie town team?"

"Right."

"Why don't you and Jimmy Wales at the First National put together a bunch of the best players from both teams? I betcha Bonnie could just about lick anybody if we did that."

"You're antsy to play, huh?"

Sherm hadn't told Garrett about his dream to play for the Cubs. "What else? Playing baseball is just about the most fun you can have in life."

"Tennis is a lot of fun too."

"Yeh, I know. You and your white shoes and white balls and white lines and white net. If you'd turn that pep into baseball you'd have a lot more fun." Sherm liked Garrett. Soon he and Garrett, besides being cousins, would also be brothers-in-law. "The point is, if you and Jimmy can't get together on a joint team, I'm going to play for Alvord."

Garrett frowned, and fell silent.

"I really mean that, Garrett."

"Well, we can't have that. I'll talk to Jimmy come Monday. Though who's gonna pitch for us? Hooks Hansen never did get his arm back after he broke it. And Van Driel is too old. And to win ball games you've got to have a good pitcher."

"What about Free? I tell you, I practised against him last summer and I had a heckuva time hitting him. And you know how he beat you Marrieds last spring."

"He shouldna pitched those eleven innings though. That wasn't good for his arm."

"He's never complained about it."

"And that big curve of his, after the first go-round, you know what to look for."

Sherm shook his head. "You should see that inshoot he's got now. He throws it exactly like he does his outdrop."

"All right. You talked me into it. We should be able to arrange games in which we only play during the week and not on Sunday."

By the middle of March, Garrett and Jimmy Wales agreed that Bonnie could field a combined team. They also agreed who should play on it. There was some protest from a few of the Little Church boys who thought they were good enough to play, as well as from some of the worldly town boys. But Garrett and Jimmy got tough and ignored the complaints. "Just jealous," Garrett said. "And just not good enough," Jimmy Wales said. Both agreed that either they'd get up a good team or drop the idea.

The next good news Sherm heard was that Garrett and Jimmy talked the Velvet Paint Company in Sioux Falls into providing them with eleven baseball uniforms, free of charge. All the Bonnie team had to do was agree to wear the lettering *Velvet Paint* on the back of their baseball shirts. In addition, the Velvet Paint Company agreed to put the lettering *Bonnie Boys* on the front of the shirts.

They began practice early in May whenever the weather was warm and dry enough. Garrett and Jimmy took on the role of co-managers to keep the peace between the churchgoers and the worldly ones. Within a week it became apparent that Bonnie would be able to field nine good players: Frankie Wales, 2b, Wimp Tollman, 3b, Sherm Engleking, ss, Garrett Engleking, lf, Jimmy Wales, c, Spider Bont, 1b, Stiffy Lawson, rf, Sleepy De-Boer, of, and Free Alfredson, p. Peter Haber and Fritz Engleking were named subs. Pete, erratic, had the pep and cheer, and that was good to have on the bench. Fritz, also erratic, had keen eyes and often drew walks. And once on base, Fritz was a terror. He had short stumpy legs and as he ran they beat on the base paths like a snare drummer gone wild.

They played their first game at home on the high school grounds. It was against the hated Hello Homebrews. Early Monday morning Garrett set up a sandwich sign in the center of Main Street with black handwritten letters on a white background:

BASEBALL
Bonnie vs Hello
Wednesday
June 6
5:30 P.M.

The first thing Sherm did that week was to make sure his brother-in-law Alfred would let Free off early from cultivating. Alfred was all for it; in fact, said he himself would be there with bells on. Alfred remembered the great old glory days when Bonnie had a super team who could beat everybody for a hundred miles around. That was when Bonnie had its baseball diamond in

Harry Foxhome's pasture west of the Cannonball depot. Alf
too had once dreamed of becoming a great baseball player
pitcher with a rising fastball. Now that Alfred and Ada
moved their family to a farm just east of Bonnie, near the to
water tower, with Main Street tailing off into their lane, it
been easier for Free to walk to baseball practice and to You
People's at church.

Everybody selected for the team tried out their new uniforn
home, and when it didn't quite fit, got the lady of the house
make alterations. Sherm's fit him to a tee, but Free, who by t
summer had shot up to six seven, had trouble getting his to
His long arms stuck out unnaturally and the pant legs just bar
reached his knees, revealing skinny calves. Ada frowned at all
fuss over wearing special clothes for what was a boy's game,
a man's game; but with a forgiving sigh, she did let out
sleeves and the pant legs so Free wouldn't look like Ichab
Crane.

The gods of country baseball decided to smile on Bonnie's f
attempt to field a uniformed team, and Wednesday opened
and cool.

When the Bonnie Boys ran out on the field for their prega
warmup, a big crowd was already on hand, up on the woo
seats behind the backdrop, and on the grass from the visito
bench out beyond first base, as well as from the home bench v
beyond third base. A large contingent of Hello fans had dri
over in a snaking caravan of jitneys, and it wasn't long befc
from the first base side, they began taunting the Bonnie fans.
Hello fans in particular razzed the Bonnie team for daring to w
uniforms when everybody knew Bonnie had been settled
Christian roughnecks and worldly outlaws. Bonnie fans beh
the third base line, true to their reputation, shouted coarse ch
lenges across the diamond at the Hello fans.

Garrett and Jimmy Wales, anticipating there might be qui
wild time in the old burg during the game, asked Consta
Koltoff to umpire behind home plate and Deputy Sheriff S
vester Hasselmore to umpire the bases. A couple of badges in
form of silver stars would have a cooling effect on the m
raucous, rabid fan.

Garrett was a little upset when Wimp Tollman didn't show
for the pregame practice. He asked Pete Haber to go over t
neighboring house and telephone the Tollmans to see what

146

up. Pete soon came back to say that Wimp had to milk his share of the cows before his father would let him off the yard.

Garrett consulted with Jimmy. "What are we gonna do? Haber can't play third. He's even lousier in the outfield. And Fritz is left-handed and I never yet heard of a left-handed third baseman."

Jimmy's black eyes rolled in thought. "Tell you what. I'll get Free to pitch in such a way that no balls get hit down to Haber at third. Until Wimp shows up."

Sherm was sometimes involved in Garrett's and Jimmy's strategy sessions. "If you want me to, I can shade over behind Haber a couple of steps."

The Homebrews took the field for their pregame warmup. Noise from the Bonnie fans quieted down when the Homebrews pulled off several slick practice double plays. It didn't look good for Bonnie.

With five minutes to go before game time, Free warmed up with Jimmy Wales along the sidelines. Free had grown so fast, six inches in the past year, that he was still somewhat awkward. But his pitching motion was smooth. His arm came around long and sweeping, and his wrist and fingers were quick and flexible.

Sherm took a good hard look at the Homebrew pitcher warming up on the first base sideline. He was a fellow by the name of Lefty Groten. Upon graduation from the Hello high school, Lefty had tried out with the Des Moines Bruins. One look and the Bruins signed him up and put him in the regular pitching rotation. He won six games in a row, throwing two three-hitters as shutouts and averaging less than two runs permitted per game. Then something happened which was never explained, either by Lefty himself or the Des Moines sportswriters. He won only one more game, and before the season was over he was cut from the team. There were rumors about some odd behavior in the locker room. Also that his teammates didn't like him. There was even one story that one winter he'd been caught by his farmer boss leaning against a cow. Lefty was a handsome young man, slim, blond, as smooth in his motion as a ballroom dancer, carrying himself with boyish hauteur.

Precisely at 5:30, Constable Koltoff stood on the white home plate and, looking at a card, bawled in a cracking trumpet voice: "Batteries for the day! For Bonnie, Free Alfredson and Jimmy Wales. For Hello, Lefty Groten and Jabber Jurgens. Play ball!"

Sherm rolled the practice ball on the ground toward the Bonnie bench and then strolled over to confer with Free. Jimmy came out with the new game ball and placed it with a little flourish in Free's black glove. Free, standing on the mound, towered a good foot over Jimmy. Free wore his gray baseball cap pushed back, revealing a throw of almost white blond hair. Jimmy wore his cap backwards with the bill resting on his neck. His black pompadour was caught neatly under the cap.

Sherm gave Free's right shoulder a friendly shake. "There's eight of us behind you, so just get the ball over the plate and we'll do the rest."

Jimmy said, "One finger for a straight ball. Two for your inshoot. Three for your hook. And four for your knuckle ball, in case we have to use it. It's up to you to decide how you want to throw your hook, sidearm or three-quarters overarm."

Sherm touched the gleaming white ball in Free's glove. "Remember all those pretend games we used to play? How we always felt we'd already won the game even before it started? But that we were willing to play the game to let the enemy get in some batting practice?"

Free nodded.

"Let's go get 'em then."

Jimmy reached up and gave Free a pat on the butt. The gesture drew a laugh from both benches. Then Jimmy ran back and slipped on his mask and squatted down behind home plate to give his first signal. The first batter up was Cecil Sweep. Jimmy called for a fast ball and began his chatter behind his mask. "Pitch to me, baby. It's just you and me now, baby."

The Homebrew bench began to chatter too. "Make him pitch to you, Cecil."

Free wound up and fired. Ball one. Too high.

The Homebrew manager, Ted Herman, let out a yell. "He's got 'em higher than that, Cecil. Keep your eye peeled."

Free wound up again. Ball two.

Ted Herman cried, "Hey! The pitchin' poet is already blowing up. All poets are a little crazy, you know."

Sherm called from his position, "So what if you write a poem now and then, Free. Tain't everybody that can do that. Just pitch us a good poem of a game."

Jimmy chattered, "C'mon, baby, let's play the batter ain't even there."

Free fired again. Ball three. Again. Ball four. Runner on first. The Homebrew bench and fans cheered.

Jimmy called, "Free, baby boy, pitch it to me. Let's give him one he can't hit."

Calls came from all around the Bonnie infield and outfield. Some calls came as chirps. Some as whistles.

When Free next walked Meylink, the second man up, Sherm called time and ran in to have a talk with Free. Jimmy took off his mask and came up too.

Sherm said, "What's the matter, boy?"

Jimmy said, "Get the goddam ball down, Free."

Free said, "It's this mound. I've been used to pitching from a hole in the ground."

Jimmy said, "Adjust. Adjust."

Free said, "I'll try."

The Homebrew fans set up a roar while the Bonnie crowd fell into a choked silence. Manager Ted Herman of the Homebrews cupped his hands around his mouth and bellowed, "He's blowing up all right. We're gonna knock him out of the box in the first inning. Hey hey! C'mon, Gorselman, swing that big bat of yours!"

Free did try to adjust with every pitch. It took a while to get used to having his left foot come down late. And in adjusting, he threw his first pitch to Gorselman so wide it skimmed off Jimmy's reaching pud and it hit the backstop. Both runners advanced, to second and third.

Free did manage to get the next three pitches within Jimmy's reach, but they were all balls. Bases full.

The Homebrew fans began to pound their board seats. Some of the Homebrew fans sitting in their parked cars blew their horns.

Sherm picked up a little stick out of the grass and threw it behind him. "Come on, Free, settle down now."

Loose-lipped Pete Haber at third, leaning forward, swinging long arms back and forth, called out, "Don't try to fan everybody, Free. Let 'em hit. Remember, we're all behind you."

Jimmy called for a different pitch, the big hook. Free nodded, wound up, carefully eyeing the runner at third, and let fly. The ball started high and then dropped over the outside corner of the plate.

"Strike!" Umpire Koltoff cried.

The Bonnie fans finally had something to cheer about and they awoke with a roar.

Free wound up again. Then, just as he threw, in the momentary hush, his father, Alfred, let go with a clarion cry, "Here comes his big outdrop again." Alfred was standing behind third base in the front row of fans.

Jabber Jurgens, the batter, quickly adusting, went about Free's outdrop. He caught it square, and hit a sharp bouncer toward Pete Haber. Pete charged the ball as though after a rabbit. He lowered his glove, loose lip hanging; and missed the ball. The ball swerved into left field.

Sherm cursed. And took out after the scooting white ball. He beat left fielder Garrett to it and picked it up and whirled and threw it to home plate. Too late. Two runs scored; men on second and third. Still nobody out.

The Homebrew bench and the Homebrew fans were ecstatic. "The big boy is blowing up. Blowing up. Ya-hoo, ya-hey!"

Garrett called time and came running in. He and Sherm and Jimmy conferred with Free. Garrett said, "We can't have Free's dad call the pitches from the sideline. Somebody's got to go over and tell him to shut up."

Sherm said, "Don't look at me. His wife is my sister and I don't want to get into a fracas with him."

Jimmy said, "How come he can read your pitches, Free? Can't you hide them better behind your glove?"

Free said, "He plays with us kids every day. So he knows me forwards and backwards."

"Dammit," Garrett said. "I'll go over and talk to him a minute. After all, I worked for him one summer and he used to listen to me."

"Good," Sherm said. "Do it."

Umpire Koltoff came waddling up, his constable star shining in the setting sun. "How much more time you guys gonna waste here?"

"Constable, I'm gonna trot over and tell Free's dad to shut up and then we can play."

"Okay. But hurry it up."

Garrett walked over and took Alfred by the elbow and led him to one side and spoke to him emphatically. After a moment, a wide smile breaking across his face, Alfred nodded and made a wiping motion with his hand over his lips.

"Play ball!" Umpire Koltoff cried.

Both Sherm and Jimmy gave Free a pat on the butt and ran to their positions.

Heavy-hitting Art Cruellen was up, waggling a big bat.

Jimmy called for another outdrop. "C'mon, Stretch my boy, he can't hit 'em if he can't see 'em."

Free wound up and fired. Everyone waited for Free's father to announce the pitch. When Free's father only smiled, Sherm relaxed. The pitch slid down over the outside corner of the plate, knee high. Cruellen watched it all the way. Cruellen stepped out of the batter's box a moment, considered to himself a moment as to what he'd just seen, then stepped back in again. His gray eyes glittered and his lantern jaw pushed out.

Jimmy's black eyes behind the mask glanced up at Cruellen. He called for an inshoot.

Hands hanging free, Sherm was ready to dart in either direction. "Throw him the pitch he'll misunderstand. The old dark one."

Free threw. The ball speared straight for the middle of the plate, belt high, then, just as Cruellen swung, it jerked inward, riding over Cruellen's fists. Two strikes.

"Now you're pitchin', kid."

Jimmy next called for the outdrop. Cruellen, swinging mightily, nubbed the ball with the end of his bat, sending a squirting ball towards Pete Haber. Again Pete Haber charged. The white ball with its crazy spin zigzagged like a baby jackrabbit. Pete once more completely missed the ball, and after it passed third base, it spun off across the foul line into the Bonnie crowd. Sherm ran over and somehow fielded it. By the time he threw it towards home plate, two more runs had scored and Cruellen wound up on second base. Hello Homebrews 4, Bonnie Boys 0.

Roars from the Homebrew side of the field. Silence from the Bonnie side.

Digusted, Free walked the next two batters, rightfielder Cager and centerfielder Manning. Bases loaded. Still no outs.

Another conference on the mound, with Sherm, Jimmy, Garrett, and Spider Bont over from first, surrounding Free.

Presently Spider Bont offered to pitch. He had speed. Also, he was a mite jealous that Free had been named the Bonnie pitcher.

"What do you think?" Sherm said.

Garrett slowly shook his head. "Actually, Free hasn't pitched all that bad. All the runs so far are unearned because of Pete

Haber's blunders. God, how I wish Wimp would show up."

Jimmy said, "Sorry, Spider, but not you. You're wilder than a woman and right now with the bases loaded that won't work. Besides, you're better at first than Free."

Sherm looked over his shoulder at the sun. It was still high in the sky above the row of ash trees bordering the school grounds. Pretty soon the sun would slide northwest and set over the corner of the schoolhouse roof. Sherm placed a hand on Free's shoulder. "Listen, buddy ol' boy, suppose we do lose this ball game. So what? It'll be the only one we'll lose all year. So settle down. And pitch to these bozos like you used to pitch to me on your dad's yard."

Noisy Ted Herman was up next. He was a dentist and well liked in Hello. Some of the Bonnie fans had gone to him for dental work, and they had a smile for him remembering his witty remarks while they lay at this mercy in his dental chair. Herman waggled his bat as though he meant to hit the ball over the white Congregational church across the street from the high school.

To keep everybody on his team awake, Jimmy began firing the ball around to the various bases after each of Free's pitches, sometimes to first, sometimes to third, even to second, where either Sherm or Frankie Wales had to cover the bag.

Sherm noticed that Herman kept glancing in Pete Haber's direction. Something was up. Sherm once more took several steps towards third to help Pete Haber out. Sherm had been careful not to move to his right or his left until just after Free began his windup for fear of revealing what catcher Jimmy had called for, a fast ball or a curve.

Jimmy called for the curve. Free threw. The ball started for Herman's head; then swung down and over the plate. As the ball approached him, Herman suddenly shifted his stance in the box, shortened up his grip on the bat, and bunted the ball towards third. He bunted the ball softly and perfectly, and it rolled a dozen feet down the line. Pete Haber once again let go with his loud loose-lipped yell. "I got it, I got it!" This time the ball found the pocket of his glove, by great luck. Pete Haber was as startled as anyone else that he had the ball, and ran on a few steps before he realized he should do something with it. It was too late to throw home, so he heaved it towards Spider at first. Pete Haber for all his crudeness did have a powerful arm, and he threw a hard rising ball that climbed well above Spider's leap for it. The ball rose into the leaves of some ash trees far behind first base. All three runners scored and Herman slid into third base before Stiffy Dawson could retrieve the ball and throw it back to the infield. Homebrews 7, Bonnie 0. Man on third.

Slick-mannered Lefty Groten was up next. He was the first left-handed batter Free had to face, and Free walked him on four pitches. Free's inshoots tailed away from Groten, and his big hook came in too low near Groten's ankles. Lefty Groten's elegant sneer also got Free's goat and made him try too hard.

Sweep, the Homebrew leadoff man, came up for the second time in the inning. On the very first pitch, following the big hook down over the plate, he too bunted it softly towards third. Pete Haber, sensing that Herman was running almost beside him, step for step, miraculously picked up the ball and let fly with a huge windup straight for Jimmy Wales waiting on home plate. The ball drilled in so hard and so quick it not only snapped the pud off Jimmy's catching hand it also knocked him over backwards. Herman scored, and Sweep wound up on second base and Groten on third. Still nobody out. Homebrews 8, Bonnie 0.

Garrett yelled in from left field to call time. He came walking in slowly and met Jimmy and Sherm near third base.

"Yeh?" Jimmy said.

Garrett said, "I think maybe we better try Pete in left field and I'll take over third. I know I don't have the arm anymore to throw across the diamond, but maybe I'll have better luck with all those bunts."

Jimmy agreed. "Good idea."

Garrett and Pete Haber switched places after Garrett announced the changes to Umpire Koltoff.

Second baseman Meylink came up for his second time. He wasn't much of a hitter but he could bunt with the best of them. Garrett moved up several steps.

Sherm held his glove to one side of his face and called, low, urgent, "Throw him high and tight, Free. It's harder to bunt a high pitch. He'll pop it up."

But Meylink fooled everybody. Instead of bunting, he chopped at the ball. And even though it almost fisted him, he still got a good piece of the ball and hit a little liner just over Garrett's outstretched glove. It landed fair and then squirted over the foul line

153

and rolled into the street ditch. Pete Haber in left field took out after it, caught up with it, tried to pick it up, failed; tried to pick it up again, failed. When he finally did grab it, he hurled it blindly towards home, when he should have thrown it to Sherm, the cut-off man. It took off over Sherm's outstretched glove, and farther along also took off over Jimmy. It just barely caught the top of the backstop, and dropped to earth. By the time Jimmy scrambled for the ball and picked it up, Lefty Groten and Sweep had scored easily, and Meylink racing around the bases slid in and also scored. Homebrews 11, Bonnie 0. The Hello fans went wild, cheering, shrieking in glee, and blowing car horns raucously.

Sherm picked up a pebble from the skinned part of the diamond and threw it behind him in the grass. Holykaboly. He threw a look at the subdued Bonnie crowd. They ranged six deep from the backstop out behind third base, some sitting on the ground, some kneeling, some standing. Bonnie fans sitting on the fenders of their cars sat with their head slumped.

Then Sherm spotted Wimp Tollman standing near brother-in-law Alfred. Hey! Sherm ran in. "Ump? Ump? Time."

About then Garrett at third also spotted Wimp. "Hey, Wimp. Got your glove? Good. Take over third here. And I'll go back to left field. Pete, you go over and help Fritz on the bench keep score."

Pete Haber's lips hung even looser. "Shucks. Shite. And here I was hoping I could at least bat once. Because I'm a good hitter."

"Listen, Pete. I want you to keep track of the Homebrew batting order. Make sure they bat in the order they gave us. So they don't sneak up one of their better hitters a notch."

Pete's thick brows came up. "Say, that's a super idea." Pete generally was a good old sock.

The next batter, Gorselman, decided to try Wimp with a bunt. It was another good one, placed down softly. But Wimp, with his naturally slumped shoulders, leaned in on the run, wiggling both his gloved hand and bare hand as if they could be easily detached, and then with both hands abruptly steady, pounced on the ball and aimed the ball for first on a line with a shotputlike motion. He got the runner by three steps.

"Atta boy, Wimp! That'll teach 'em to try bunting."

Pete Haber, a good team man, cheered too. "That's showing 'em how to play the hot corner."

Jabber Jurgens came up next. Free fed him two lazy round-house curves that just missed the outside corner. Two balls.

Jimmy, disgusted, began firing the ball back at Free harder and faster than Free was pitching it. Jimmy showed Free a fierce face, and shook his fist at him. "Let's not have any more of those Christian pitches, big boy! Burn it to me or we will put Spider in."

Sherm stuck it into Free too. "Don't you care? This is our first real game in real uniforms, boy."

Free stepped back off the mound and picked up the rosin bag and powdered his fingers with it. His lower lip stuck out, mad.

Jimmy called for a fast ball. "C'mon, Free, let's bust that bat out of his hands."

Free laid it in there, over the center of the plate, knee high.

Jabber guessed fast ball and around came his bat and it caught the ball solidly with the sound of a four-inch firecracker going off. The ball just missed Free's hand, kept drilling like a musket ball another hundred feet, and then, catching air, began to rise. First there was a silence from both sets of fans, and then the Homebrew section exploded.

Sleepy DeBoer, who'd been pretty quiet all along, took one look, then turned and began running with his back to the infield, running with a strange scoochy slouched stride. He ran past the southwest corner of the high school building, crossed the sidewalk, and then, just as he was about to crash into the base of a towering ash tree, turned and easily caught the ball. Two out.

Sherm had been running out towards Sleepy to get the cutoff throw. He had trouble believing what he saw. "Holy sockdolager, Sleepy! Now we're playing ball."

Sleepy's eyes closed in smile as he threw the ball in.

Sherm called over to Garrett. "Did you know Sleepy could field like that?"

Garrett said, "You tell 'em. Before the game I tried to hit a couple of fungoes over him and he got every one."

Sherm brought the ball all the way in to the mound. He noted that the new game ball had already picked up some grass stains as well as dirt marks. He placed the ball in Free's black glove. "After that catch, my boy, you can't say we're not behind you."

"A little late."

"Listen, we still have nine at bats coming."

"But against Lefty Groten? Western Leaguer?"

Sherm slapped Free on the shoulder. "You get 'em out from here on in, and we'll catch up with 'em. If you got any Engleking blood in you at all, you're never licked."

Free tried to smile out of a deep tired frown. "Yeh, and when we walk on the diamond we've already won."

Jimmy finally had a smile inside his mask. He looked up at the next batter, Art Cruellen. Cruellen was known for his big swing, sometimes lunging after the ball. "C'mon, Free old boy, let's do a little tatting around the edge of the plate." Jimmy called for three inshoots in a row. "He can't hit 'em if he can't see 'em."

Free licked in three perfect pitches, which started for the center of the plate, then jumped up and in over Cruellen's hands. Side retired. At last the Bonnie fans had something to cheer about.

From then on Free pitched with confidence.

In the bottom of the fourth, the Bonnie bats woke up. Frankie Wales, leadoff man, while not as big as his brother Jimmy, always had a good swing, and he caught one of Lefty Groten's slants and dumped a dying quail over shortstop Sweep's head into left field. Wimp, next up, lashed viciously at one of Lefty's fast balls and drilled it past Lefty's nose into center field. Two on. That brought Sherm to the plate.

Just as Sherm stepped into the batter's box, he caught a whiff of some lady frying hamburgers with onions in one of the houses across the street. The smell mingled wonderfully with the smell of just-mown grass and parched dust off the street. Sherm said down to catcher Jabber Jurgens, "What a great evening for baseball. Can't be beat for real fun."

Jabber gave him an arched look. "Yeh." Then Jabber gave Lefty a series of signals from between his crouched knees.

Sherm had been studying Lefty's pitches. The first time up Lefty had got him out with a big curve tight on his fists for a pop-up. Sherm decided that the next time he saw that big sweeper coming toward the plate, he'd step in the bucket and pull it to left field. Lefty wound up, and, yep, there it was. Sherm moved his left foot back and swung hard and quick. Sherm had bought himself a new light blond bat, a Louisville Slugger, to speed up his swing. He caught the ball with the fat part of the bat and there it went, on a line over the third baseman's head, rising, rising, heading for the row of ash trees beyond the sidewalk. Sherm watched it go as he ran to first base. The only question was, would it stay fair? Sherm had rounded first base when he saw it catch the topmost branch of an ash and then start trickling down through the leaves of the tree.

Umpire Hasselmore called it. "Fair ball!"

Garrett, standing in the on-deck circle, let go with a whoop. "Wow! A second-story shot into the trees."

As Sherm rounded second and headed for third, he could see that it would take the left fielder another dozen steps to catch up with the ball—enough time for him to make home. Leaning inward, Sherm touched third and flew home. He saw Jabber the catcher looking out to left field as if he were silently urging his left fielder to hurry up. Garrett took up a position near home plate and signalled for Sherm to slide. Sherm threw his feet forward and made up his mind to kick up as much dirt as he could to confuse Jabber.

"Safe!" Umpire Koltoff roared.

Bonnie 3, Hello 11. Bonnie fans stomped on their plank seats, waved their hats, punched car horns.

Free settled down even more. The next two innings he struck out the side twice. His inshoot kept pushing the batters away from the plate, and when Jimmy figured they'd been pushed back far enough he'd call for the fast-falling outdrop.

Bottom of the sixth, Wimp Tollman was up first and he kept fouling off Lefty's slants until he drew a walk. That brought up Sherm again.

Jabber called time and walked out to have a talk with Lefty. They conferred with their backs to Sherm. But Wimp on first base, who'd learned to survive the elbows of two tough brothers by reading their expressions beforehand, read Jabber's and Lefty's lips, and when Jabber ran back to his position behind the plate, Wimp signalled with a single finger that Sherm was going to get nothing but fast balls.

Good, Sherm thought. Those I can hit even farther. And sure enough, the first pitch came right down the pike. Sherm caught it three inches beyond the trademark and drilled it. It cleared the center fielder's head and smacked into the south wall of the schoolhouse and then caromed toward the left fielder. The left fielder almost stumbled over a gopher sitting at the edge of its hole watching the game. The gopher popped down into its hole and the left fielder righted his balance and picked up the ball. Sherm pulled into second base standing up. Wimp scored easily.

Garrett too went after the first pitch and bent a liner over third base that landed fair and rolled far enough for him to make second. Sherm scored easily.

Enraged, petulant, Lefty Groten with his elegant pitching motion struck out Jimmy Wales and Spider Bont. He next got two strikes on Stiffy Lawson. But then Lefty made the mistake of throwing a knuckler, which came in just slow enough for Stiffy with his old bones to hit a squirter past Sweep and out between the Homebrew left fielder and center fielder. Then suddenly, to the astonishment of everybody, as the ball slowed down, it disappeared in the grass. Both the left fielder and the center fielder stopped to stare down at the ground. Garret scored from second. When Stiffy saw that for some reason the two fielders couldn't pick up the ball, he kept going. He trotted in his stiltlike stumping stride around second, and around third, where Coach Fritz Engleking waved him on home. Stiffy did make home because the ball never arrived. Bonnie 7, Hello 11.

Everyone, both on the field and along the sidelines, wondered and exclaimed about what might have happened out in left field. Finally base umpire Deputy Hasselmore strolled out to see what the matter was, and after a minute came back and told Umpire Koltoff that the ball had rolled into a gopher hole, and did anybody have a spade handy so they could dig out the game ball? Laughter erupted all over the place.

Sherm said, "I often wondered what they meant when they talked about a gopher ball. But now I know."

At that point, with things looking better for Bonnie and the crowd in an amiable frame of mind, Garrett sent his brother Fritz and Pete Haber through the crowd each with a hat asking for contributions. He told them should any one ask, What for? to say it was to pay for the game ball, any broken bats, catcher's equipment, and a new ball for the next game. Before the inning was over, the two men reported they'd collected $18.50, along with a couple of hairpins, two soggy quids of tobacco, and one sack of Bull Durham tobacco.

Free seemed to get even stronger. He continued to shut out the

Homebrews, allowing no hits, walking no one, striking out two, with his teammates playing errorless ball behind him.

Several times Manager Herman of the Homebrews questioned Umpire Koltoff's calls at home plate. Herman argued that Jimmy was slickering the umpire by the way he caught some of Free's pitches that, in his opinion, were just off the plate. "Ump, he sticks his pud out a little extra far, and then as the ball comes in, he jerks his pud real smooth back in as if the ball was over the plate after all."

Umpire Koltoff took off his mask. "You get back to your bench or I'm kicking you out of the game."

"Okay, Ump. But I just want you to watch him carefully. Because I know that slick-fingered sonofabitch. Cashiers are all that way."

Sherm smiled. He'd seen Jimmy Wales counting bills at the bank with those swift-flipping fingers of his and often wondered what he could do in a card game. Jimmy could easily have been a card shark.

Jimmy sat listening to the colloquy between Herman and the umpire. When Herman called Jimmy a sonofabitch again, Jimmy threw off his mask, stood up, and snarled, "Who are you to call me names, you lecherous wretch, remembering what you've done to women patients you put under in your dentist chair? Hey?"

At that moment Sherm was shocked to see their minister, Reverend Tiller, standing nearby in the crowd. But Reverend Tiller's amused expression hardly changed. Sherm's respect for his pastor went up. Reverend Tiller seemed to be more of a man of the world than he'd let on in Young People's meetings.

Herman gave Jimmy a sick smile that looked like a capital *W*. Then, satisfied that he'd stuck a question into Umpire Koltoff's stolid constable mind, Herman retreated to his bench.

In the top of the ninth, Sherm wandered over to the mound to check Free's arm. "Think you can hold 'em for three more outs? Give 'em the old horse collar?

Free smiled. "I still have a little more lace left to tat around that plate."

"You're sure now?

"I haven't begun to cut loose."

"Okay. Let's go get 'em. Because we're gonna score five runs in the bottom of this inning."

Free said, "Well, even if we don't, I'd still like to shut 'em out for eight straight innings. Just to know I can do it the next game we play."

"Atty old attitude, kid. Make me proud of my long-legged uncle-sayer."

True to his word, Free fell into his smoothest motion. Jimmy called for nothing but fast inshoots, figuring that the Homebrew batters would be worrying about Free's big outdrop; and Free bored them in, the ball starting for the outside corner of the plate and then flitting over the inside corner.

After Free struck out the first two batters, Manager Herman got to his feet and strolled over the umpire.

Umpire Koltoff took off his mask. "This better be good. Or out you go."

Herman said, "Well, I think this will be a legitimate complaint. Just to be fair, you ought to make that long-geared apple knocker out there pitch from a spot four feet behind the pitching rubber."

"Why?"

"Look at that bean pole carcass of his with those long orang-ou-tang arms." Herman made it a point to talk up slowly and very loud at the same time that he faced Free. "When he lets go of the ball, his hand is four feet closer to home plate than the hand of our Lefty Groten when he lets go of the ball. That gives us that much less time to see the ball."

Sherm ran in. Even from where he stood out on the field he could hear Herman clearly. He gave Free a big head-cocked-to-one-side smile. "You know what Ted Herman is up to, don't you?"

"Don't worry," Free said. "Meylink is up next and I want to get him on strikes. In the first inning he cleaned the bases with that dinky hit of his."

Umpire Koltoff stood thinking to himself as he tried to picture what the Homebrew manager was trying to tell him. When it finally became clear what Herman was up to, Umpire Koltoff abruptly let out a roar, and pointed to the cars behind the stands. "You're out of the ball game! Get off this field. Back to your car. Or I'm forfeiting the game eleven to nothing in favor of Bonnie!"

Manager Herman shrugged, winked at his bench, and slowly stepped behind the backstop towards his car.

"All right, play ball!"

Free cocked up his long left leg as high as his head, and then

160

let drive, his arm coming around last like the snapper at the end of a bullwhip. He whistled in three incredibly swift rising in-shoots. Meylink missed them all by at least a foot.

"Great!" Sherm shouted. "Now to go get 'em."

In the bottom of the ninth, Sherm, first up, choked up on his bat. A home run wouldn't win the game. He noted that the sun had begun to set into the trees behind the schoolhouse and that it was getting hard to see the dirty ball. He picked on the first pitch and lay down a perfect bunt towards third. With Ted Herman out of the game, catcher Jurgens had to put substitute Ted Coleslaw in to play third, who wasn't much better than Pete Haber. Cole-slaw did pick up the ball but he threw it over first baseman Cruel-len's glove and Sherm ran all the way to third. Garrett, next up, also dumped one down the third base line and Coleslaw once more overthrew his first baseman. Sherm scored and Garrett wound up on second base. Bonnie 8, Hello Homebrews 11.

Jabber called time and walked out to the mound. Lefty Groten was having a fit. He kicked the rosin bag towards second base. He spat on the ground. He swore out loud. After some talk, Jab-ber, like Garrett had once done, called in his left fielder to play third and sent this third baseman to play left field. The next sev-eral Bonnie batters weren't known to hit the long ball.

When the game resumed, Lefty was still up in the air about Coleslaw's two wild throws. He proceeded to walk Jimmy Wales and Spider Bont. Bases full.

It was the Bonnie players turn to roar. "The slicker's blowing up! The slicker's blowing up!"

Lefty Groten stuck out his tongue and thumbed his nose at the Bonnie side of the diamond.

Jabber took off his mask and again started walking toward Lefty Groten.

Lefty stopped Jabber with a pointing finger. "You get back be-hind the plate! I'm now gonna strike out the side. They're nothing but a bunch of hayseeds anyway."

Sherm remembered some baseball history he'd read in the *Sioux City Journal*. Sherm had taken over as the Bonnie coach at third. "Hey, Lefty, why don't you pull a Rube Waddell and call in your outfield and then strike out the side?"

The crowd picked up Sherm's challenge. "Hey! Yeh. Call in the outfield, Rube."

Being called a "rube" made Lefty all the hotter. His handsome

161

pettish face turned red. Ignoring the three runners on base, he began to throw like a topnotch Western League pitcher. He didn't even both to take a signal from his catcher. The moment he got the ball back from Jabber, he stepped on the rubber and whipped in the ball. And proceeded to strike out Stiffy Lawson and Sleepy DeBoer on six straight pitches, all strikes down the middle, belt high. Some six feet in front of the plate the pitch took off and rose a foot. He made Jabber's pud pop like a shotgun. Two out.

The Bonnie crowd quieted. The Hello crowd began to crow again, getting ready to celebrate the victory.

Next up was Free.

Sherm called time and took Free by the arm to one side. He turned Free around so both their backs were to the players on the diamond. Sherm said, "You've pitched great guns so far. Now I'm wondering if you can hit great guns."

"I'm gonna try."

"Are you big enough to take some advice from your uncle?"

"Sure."

A month earlier Sherm and Garrett had driven to Sioux City and looked up a sporting goods store. They bought a new catcher's mask and chest protector, each a new bat for themselves, several baseballs; and in particular bought a new bat for Free. Both had noticed that Free had taken a fancy to an old cracked Babe Ruth model, a 40-ounce 36-inch long Louisville slugger. Free was strong, but his long arms were too slender to wield such a heavy bludgeon. They found a slim 32-ounce 36-inch bat for him, a Travis Jackson model. Garrett pointed out that the lighter long bat would give more balance to Free's big swing.

Sherm said, "Your new bat suit you?"

"You bet. The more I use it the better I like it. It fits me like your black bat used to fit me when I was a kid."

"So I noticed. You got wood on the ball three times."

"Yeh. Two grounders and a single. Not counting the walk I got."

"How's Lefty been pitchin' you?"

"He always starts me off with his big outdrop on my fists."

"Well, he's mad now and he'll start you off with one of his swifts."

Free nodded. "I'd decided to look for his fast one on the outside corner. First pitch."

"Good. And now one more thing. About your stance. You stand in there all bunched up, leaning over the plate, and wiggling your bat like an Apostle Paul threatening the Thessalonians, like you're gonna hit the ball over the Congregational Church there." Sherm pointed to the white church beyond the row of ash trees and the far street.

"Yeh, I suppose at that I do look kind of silly. Pa's said the same thing."

A dozen swallows had come out from their perches in the cow barns on the edge of town, and began working the baseball diamond and the outfield for flies and bugs. They swooped and dipped around the players, calling out their little cries, eeep, weeb, eeep. They flew in and out of the slanting low sunlight and advancing shadows. It was the wonderful magic moment of evening time at the end of a long sunny summer day.

Sherm gave Free's elbow a friendly pinch. "Why don't you stand in the box like Rogers Hornsby? Remember that story about him in the *Journal?* How he always stood back in the box, deep? And if the pitcher threw him an inside pitch he pulled it down the third base line? And if the pitcher threw him one on the outside corner of the plate he tried to hit the ball over the second baseman's head?"

"I remember."

"Good. Then stand up straight. Bat resting on your shoulder. Or even resting on the ground. Eyes on the pitcher. But otherwise quiet. Like a cat sitting a couple of feet away from a mousehole." Sherm with a laugh added, "Don't even wiggle the tip of your tail."

Free's solemn face broke into a smile. "I haven't learned how to wiggle mine yet, Uncle."

"I know. Now listen. Just as Lefty winds up, you wind up in the batter's box, your bat held way back, tall on your right foot, and then, when his arm comes around and the ball comes towards you, you pounce on the mouse and cowtail it out of here. All we need is a deucer and it's a tie ball game. Hear?"

Free nodded.

"All right. Find your pitch and kiss it on the nose." Sherm then gave Free a good clap on the butt and ran back to the coach's box near third.

As Lefty wound up, Free stood erect in the back of the batter's box, bat quiet, eyes fixed on the motion of the pitcher. As the ball began to dart towards the plate, obviously Lefty's hard one, Free balled up the muscles of his lean body, hung for a moment on his right foot with his left foot lifted, then stepped forward and swung. He got around on the ball good and drove it past Lefty's ears. The ball seemed to weave back and forth a little as it drilled its way up, and then, the fast spin of it catching air, it lifted like a small balloon shot out of a cannon, climbing, climbing. Still rising, it cleared the corner of the schoolhouse.

"My God! what a poke," Sherm whispered. "He caught it three inches from the end of his bat."

The ball finally found its height and leveled off and rode on.

Everyone fell silent, the Hello fans, the Bonnie fans, even the runners on the bases.

Finally the ball began to settle, and slid out of sight beyond the tallest ash tree, and then a second later was seen to hit the grass beside the Congregational Church and bounce against its big white double doors.

"Holy Toledo!" Sherm said low. Then Sherm woke up. "All right, you dummies, run! Run, for godsakes! Or Free will pass you up on the base paths and that'll be the third out."

Garrett, Jimmy, and Spider scored in a bunch. Then around third came long-legged Free, a funny happy smile on his tan-pink face, taking what seemed rod-long strides. The Bonnie boys erupted from their long plank bench, and the crowd behind them joined in and formed two walls of yelling whooping jumping celebrants. They swarmed around Free, almost blocking his path to the plate. Bonnie 12, Hello 11.

"What a wallop!"

"What a belt!"

"The old grand tour!"

Even Reverend Tiller got caught up in the uproarious excitement of the come-from-behind moment. His big smile almost crinkled shut his blue eyes.

Umpire Koltoff stood a moment in what seemed heavy thought, and then, after making sure Free touched home, turned and headed for his house across the street behind the backstop.

The Hello fans, crushed, eyes flicking in disappointed anger, quietly went to their cars and started the motors with bubbling roars, and drove off.

All except Ted Herman and Jabber Jurgens. Manager Herman

headed straight for Garrett and Jimmy and Sherm. Herman tugged at Garrett's shirt and turned him around. "How about a return game? Godalmighty, we've got to have revenge for this one."

Garrett threw a look at Reverend Tiller standing nearby. "Well, we can think about it."

"No thinking about it. How about this coming Sunday?"

"We can't."

"Why not?"

"We're not allowed to have fun on Sunday."

"Well, you have fun in bed on Sunday, don't you?"

Sherm almost choked. Ted Herman had almost said that dirty word.

Sherm remembered that two weeks before Reverend Tiller had preached about sloth in church, saying that too many young couples were not showing up for church on Sunday morning. "What are they doing on Sunday morning that they don't come to church?" Of course everybody knew what he was referring to.

Garrett laughed a crazy horse laugh one moment and turned solemn as an owl the next moment. "Really, we can't, Ted. It's against our religion. And besides, if we do have fun"—Garrett paused to throw a look at Reverend Tiller—"on weekends, we do it before midnight."

"Oh for godsakes. That's ridiculous. God didn't make the hours. We did. We made clocks and then we had hours. He made the day and the night for his way of figuring time. And he ain't gonna check your clock one minute before or after midnight."

Reverend Tiller stepped forward as if to make a comment; then, thinking it over, turned his back on Herman and Garrett and walked away. It was apparent from the way he held his shoulders that he had all he could do to keep from laughing.

Herman waved his arms in frustration. "Besides, what's wrong with fun in bed on Sunday morning? Didn't God tell you people, you of all people, to be fruitful and multiply? And fill the earth? Ain't that his work you're doing for him? He wouldn't say you couldn't do his work for him on Sunday, would he?"

Jimmy Wales was enjoying the conversation. As a Catholic he had no objection to playing baseball on Sunday. He was wise enough, though, not to say anything.

Garrett finally got control of his face. "Tell you what. We're awfully busy around now. Fellows are out cultivating corn. Some are getting ready to cut their alfalfa. Right after comes harvest time. We already got some games pinched in between our work. But as soon as we can we'll call you for a return game. Okay?"

"And you play it in Hello, you know. Where we'll have the home crowd around to root for us."

"We know. We know."

Herman shook his head. "Can you imagine. No fun on Sunday."

Sherm broke in. "Well, Branch Rickey of the St. Louis Cardinals won't go to the games of his own team on Sunday. He promised his mother he'd never play on Sunday or go see a game on Sunday. And then there's the great Christy Matthewson. He wouldn't pitch on Sunday either."

"That's nuts, is all I can say."

Afterwards Garrett remarked, "It was almost worth it to see our minister's face when Ted almost said that dirty word."

The next day the box score of the Hello-Bonnie game appeared on the front page of *The Bonnie Review:*

HELLO HOMEBREWS

	AB	H	2b	3b	HR	R	RBI
Sweep, ss	4	0	0	0	0	2	0
Meylink, 2b	4	1	1	0	0	2	2
Gorselman, lf	3	0	0	0	0	1	0
Jurgens, c	4	0	0	0	0	1	0
Cruellen, 1b	4	0	0	0	0	1	0
Cager, rf	3	0	0	0	0	1	0
Manning, cf	3	0	0	0	0	1	0
Herman, 3b	4	1	0	0	0	1	1
Coleslaw, 3b	0	0	0	0	0	0	0
Groten, P	3	0	0	0	0	1	0
	32	2	1	0	0	11	3

Errors, Coleslaw, 2. Doubleplays, 1.
Innings pitched: Groten, 8⅔; 9 hits, 6 strikeouts, 10 walks.

BONNIE BOYS

	AB	H	2b	3b	HR	R	RBI
F. Wales, 2b	4	1	0	0	0	1	0
Haber, 3b	0	0	0	0	0	0	0
Tollman, 3b	3	1	0	0	0	2	0
S. Engleking, ss	4	3	1	0	1	3	3
G. Engleking, lf, 3b	3	2	1	0	0	2	2
J. Wales, c	4	0	0	0	0	1	0
Bent, lb	4	0	0	0	0	1	0
Lawson, rf	4	1	0	0	1	1	3
DeBoer, cf	4	0	0	0	0	0	0
Alfredson, P	4	2	0	0	1	1	4
	34	10	2	0	3	12	12

Errors, Haber, 5.
Innings pitched: Alfredson, 9; 2 hits, 13 strikeouts, 6 walks.

	1	2	3	4	5	6	7	8	9	R	H	E
Hello Homebrews	11	0	0	0	0	0	0	0	0	11	2	2
Bonnie Boys	0	0	0	3	0	4	0	0	5	12	10	5

Chapter Nine

The Bonnie Boys played their next game at Hazard.

Manager Garrett was a little upset that Wimp Tollman and Jimmy Wales couldn't make it. Wimp's father said he needed the boy to help put up some alfalfa hay, and anyway didn't believe in letting his boy play ball away from home. And Jimmy had to work late at the First National Bank because the state bank examiners were in town.

Talking it over, Garrett and Sherm decided that Pete Haber could play in the outfield, with Garrett playing third base again; and they'd ask Pete's brother Harry Haber to catch for them. Harry had recently moved back to a farm east of Bonnie. Garrett had long wanted Harry to play for the Bonnie Boys. Harry was almost forty years old, but, man, how that fellow could catch. And hit? Harry was a really good sticker.

When the Bonnie Boys arrived at Hazard, they found that the Hazard Hoboes were already on the field taking batting practice. Hazard was even smaller than Bonnie, having only some three hundred fifty souls, but for some reason the little town and the farms around it produced some of Siouxland's better players. They were a tough bunch to beat.

The diamond, a twelve-acre pasture, belonged to a retired farmer who lived on the south edge of town. In between ball games the farmer ran several cows and a riding horse on it. Always just before a game, the old farmer hired several pool hall bums to go over the skinned part of the diamond as well as the outfield with shovels and a couple of wheelbarrows to scoop up the cowplops and the horseballs. The cows and horses were stalled in a small nearby barn. Also earlier in the day the old farmer would get out his old Fordson tractor and drag the skinned part as smooth as a black stove top.

Sherm and Garrett, after slipping on their spike shoes, walked onto the edge of the dirt infield.

Sherm bent over for a closer look. "Not a pebble in it. We should be able to play without an error."

Garrett said, "Yeh. That means there's no gravel pits around here anywhere."

Sherm lifted a shoulder. "Man, what a great evening to play ball. Cool. Not a cloud in the sky. No wind."

Garrett nodded. "The only thing I don't like, is, the sun sets behind first base. Spider better not throw to me to catch a runner. I'll be blinded."

Sherm said, "We'll have to work out some strategy for that. Maybe he can first throw to me and then I'll throw to you."

"Something like that." Garrett looked around some more. "Hey, they don't have a mound here. Free's gonna have to pitch out of a hole."

"Free's used to that, playing with his brothers on his dad's yard."

"Let's hope so. Well, let's get ready to tattoo that old potato. It's our turn to run through pregame practice."

While Free slowly warmed up with Harry Haber, Fritz Engleking hit grounds to the infielders, and outfielders Pete Haber and Sleepy DeBoer and Stiffy Lawson threw high flies to each other.

Sherm at shortstop kept reminding Garrett at third and Frankie Wales at second that on a dirt field a ground ball starts to die on the second bounce. "Don't be afraid to run in on it so you can catch it on the first bounce."

Around five-thirty the umpire, Jack Chestnut from Whitebone, showed up. It turned out that his buddy umpire couldn't make it. It meant Jack Chestnut would have to call balls and strikes as well as call the play on the bases.

Both teams assembled on their benches. Two men with rolling chalk boxes quickly laid down the white lines from home to first and beyond, from home to third and beyond, as well as the batter's boxes.

After Sherm and Garrett had penciled in the Bonnie batting order and had exchanged copies with the manager of the Hazard Hoboes, they began to speculate what Hazard players they might have trouble handling. When the Hazard players took the field first, both Sherm and Garrett watched them closely.

Garrett said after a while, "It's pretty much the same bunch we played three years ago."

Sherm said, "What about that guy at short?"

"He's new to me."

"Something about him I can't quite put my finger on. Like I saw his picture somewhere."

Garrett looked at the Hazard batting order. "Let's see who they got at short. Ah. Risberg."

"Don't know the name. But he's as smooth as glass out there. Look at how his glove is always in the right place. And look at how he fires the ball. Pegs it to first with no waste motion. Oh, and see how he tosses the ball to his second baseman to make the double play. Man, that's the way I've got to learn to play shortstop."

"I betcha that Risberg played pro somewhere."

Sherm looked through the crowd to see if he could find an old-timer who might know his baseball. The crowd continued to thicken as cars full of fans drove in from the country. Some of the fans climbed the stand behind the backstop, some sat on the hoods of their cars, and some, the older folk, stayed sitting in the cars. A local vendor carrying pop and candy worked the crowd. Loud talk, cheers, razzing increased. Finally Sherm spotted an old bowlegged fellow sitting alone on a folding chair and smiling to himself as though he knew something.

Sherm strolled over and kneeled beside the old man. "Say, kind sir, that Risberg at short there, where could I have seen him before?"

"How the hell would I know what you seen before?"

"What I mean is, Risberg's face looks familiar but I can't place it."

The old-timer rolled his brown beery eyes at Sherm, and scratched a gnarled hand through his grizzled head, as though to say Sherm had a lot of crust to bother him. Then, old cracked lips curling into a sneer, the old man went back to watching infield practice, in particular Risberg at short.

Sherm stepped over to where Free was warming up. "Boy, the manners of some people. I asked that old bastard there who Risberg might be and he wouldn't tell me."

Free held up throwing for a moment. "That's Swede Risberg."

"How would you know?"

"I saw his picture in the paper a couple of years ago. He once played for the Chicago White Sox and was part of their bunch who threw the World Series to the Cincinnati Reds in 1919. Sold out to gamblers. He was banned from professional baseball forever. After that some of the White Sox players of that year were known as the Black Sox."

"That means we'll be playing against a major leaguer."

"That's right."

"You ain't nervous about it?"

"I've already figured out how to pitch to him."

"How?"

"They always say that if a batter is gonna stick in the majors the last thing he has to learn is how to hit the curve. So no outdrops for Risberg. I'll throw him nothing but inshoots. On his fists. My inshoot is really squirting in today."

"I'll be jiggered." Sherm walked over to where Harry Haber was catching Free. "How's the kid throwing today?"

Harry Haber was dapper where his brother Pete was clumsy. Harry had a handsome head of graying hair, sharp gray eyes under very bushy black brows, and a wise old smile. "Ball jumps all over the place."

Sherm next went over to Garrett to tell him what he'd learned about Risberg.

Garrett's blue eyes opened. "A ringer then."

"Yeh."

Garrett got up from the Bonnie bench. "Come. We'll see about that." He and Sherm headed for Dubber DeMoor, the manager of the Hoboes, on the other bench. Garrett tapped Dubber on the shoulder. "What the heck you guys doing with a ringer?"

Dubber whirled around. His swarthy face flushed over. "Oh, you mean Risberg out there."

"Who else but? How much you guys paying him? Or is he paying you so he can play a little again after throwing the World Series to the Cincinnati Reds?"

The Hazard manager hardened up. "Look, our regular shortstop broke his arm cranking his Ford. So we had to get a sub from somewhere. Besides, Swede works near here and has relatives living in town."

"Two of our players couldn't make it either. But we didn't call in any ringers."

"Don't let your water get hot over it."

"It's kinda sneaky."

Dubber stood up. "Well, if you wanna make something of it, let's start the dance right now."

Sherm broke in. "Oh, shit, let's let the Black Soxer play. We'll beat them with him playing."

About then Umpire Chestnut stepped on the home plate and announced the batteries. "Omar Manderson and Tim Houghtaling for Hazard. Alfred Alfredson and Harry Haber for Bonnie. Play ball."

Garrett said, "By golly, there's another face I don't know. That pitcher of theirs. Manderson. He wasn't pitching for them the other time we played them."

Free had finished his warmup and had joined them on the bench. "Manderson was in the paper this spring. He tried out with the Minneapolis Millers and couldn't make it. He comes from around here all right."

Sherm watched Manderson throw his pre-inning warmup. "Got some swift. Looks like he's got control too."

The first three innings neither team scored. Both pitchers were tight with their hits and walks. There were no errors. Fortunately no balls were hit Pete Haber's way. It developed that catcher Harry Haber couldn't sit in a squatting position anymore, his stiff knees wouldn't let him, but he managed to bend over far enough to scoop up Free's big drops. Sherm struck out his first time up, on a quick breaking little curve, after he fouled off several rising fast balls.

When Risberg came up, Sherm became especially alert. From his position at shortstop Sherm could just make out Harry Haber's finger calls. Sure enough, Harry called for nothing but inshoots. Sherm rose on his toes on every pitch, but Risberg missed them all. Three pitches, three strikes. Free was really whizzing them in there. Red hot rivets titty-high.

In the top of the fourth inning, Pete Haber, of all people, ignited the Bonnie attack with a double. Sherm and Garrett followed with sharp singles. And then Harry Haber got hold of one, grunting mightily as he came around with his big black bat, and sent the ball spearing over the center fielder's head, and it rolled and rolled all the way to the fence along the railroad track. Harry despite his stiffened knees scored easily for a home run. Bonnie 4, Hazard 0.

Hazard rallied in the bottom of the fifth right after a long freight train came through. The engineer had let go with several rousing blasts and that seemed to throw Free off his rhythm as well as awaken the Hazard bats. Free walked two men and then gave up three singles. And wouldn't you know it, a ball was finally hit Pete Haber's way, and he completely misjudged it. It fell for a double. Hazard 5, Bonnie 4.

Sitting on their bench again, Garrett said, "From now on I'm gonna shift Pete around in the outfield, depending on who's at bat. If he'd 've caught that ball they'd only 've had two runs."

Harry Haber, sitting nearby, nodded. "Pete's a good sticker but he always had lumpy hands." He shook his head gravely. "Too bad for Free. Because he's been throwing nothing but spears and boomerangs."

Sherm said, "Free's sure got that Risberg eating out of his hand. Striking him out every time he's been up."

Harry Haber smiled. "The last time he struck out, Risberg said, 'Your long gears out there has got a fine screwball.'"

The sun kept sinking toward the horizon. Finally it slid behind the top of a gray metal grain elevator and then a huge purple shadow began to reach out toward the baseball diamond.

In the bottom of the sixth, Garrett moved Pete Haber to left field when he saw the Hazard cleanup man, a left-hander, come to bat. Sherm signaled for everybody to shift over to the right side of the diamond. Free took a long look at the burly batter and then wound up and really poured one in. Strike one.

"That's the way to shoot it to 'm, buddy boy," Sherm chirped from his position.

Again Free wound up as though to throw the ball even harder; and completely fooled the batter when a floater lifted from his fingers, the ball not turning once all the way to the plate.

"That's the way to get him to misunderstand you, Stretch old boy."

The next pitch, a high hard one, didn't quite fool the batter, and he came around on it in time to hit an opposite-field long drive.

Pete Haber took one look and called for it. "I got it! I got it!" He ran back for it with his strange loping galloping stride, thick lips and long face hanging loose. And miracle of miracles, just as he turned around, the ball landed on his chest, and hands grabbing at it here and there, he managed to keep the ball from falling to earth. Third out. Side retired.

Then Pete Haber further astonished people when he whirled and threw the ball at a single bull thistle at the edge of the field— and hit a rabbit sitting behind the thistle, knocking it over. Pete ran over, grabbed the rabbit by its ears, picked up the ball, and came trotting in to the bench with the rabbit and the ball in hand.

Garrett was almost beside himself. "What in God's name...?"

Pete said, "Damn rabbit was sittin' in the shade of that thistle laughing at me."

A good share of the fans, some Bonnie, some Hazard, heard Pete's remark, and broke out in wild wonderful laughter.

Pete laughed with them. He took the rabbit and walked over to a plump matron from Hazard and held it out to her. "You like rabbit stew? Here you are." He dropped the rabbit in her lap.

The startled woman looked down at the rabbit in her lap, then at Pete, then with a loud "Uggh!" flipped the rabbit out of the valley in her blue dress to the ground. At that point the rabbit came to, blinked, and, scooting, zigzagged under the row of cars on the first base side of the field, and disappeared.

Sherm shook his head. "There's nothing like the fun of country baseball."

Garrett cautioned his players sitting on the bench that when they were batting to keep their eyes peeled on the pitcher. Manderson had tried to quick-pitch him a couple of times. "If you're in the batter's box, stay awake, because if you're not paying attention he quick likes to whip one over on you."

In the top of the ninth, with one out, Free sent a screamer over the second baseman's head for a double. Frankie Wales next caught hold of one of Manderson's quick curves and drove it past the third baseman's glove. Swede Risberg, diving for the hole between himself and the third baseman, ticked the ball enough to bobble it up in the air, and caught the ball while lying on his back. No wonder he could be a star shortstop for the Chicago White Sox. Two out.

According to the lineup Garrett had made out, Pete Haber was up next. Shucks. It probably meant he, Sherm, wouldn't get a chance to hit a home run to win the ball game for Bonnie. But Fritz Engleking, who'd been keeping score, cried out that Sherm was up next, not Pete? What? How could that be? But Sherm was so anxious to hit a home run he decided not to question it. And when no one on the Hazard bench questioned it either, Sherm let it go.

Sherm had been watching Manderson closely and spotted something. Every time Manderson threw a curve, just as he wound up, he moved his thumb down towards his little finger. So. Sherm stepped into the batter's box, taking up a position some six inches closer to the plate than usual. He was going to hit that dinky curve. In fact it was as if he'd already done it.

Garrett called from the on-deck circle. "C'mon, Sherm, whale it out of here. You can do it."

After the Hazard catcher had given his signal to Manderson, Swede Risberg out at short moved two steps toward third. Aha. Curve ball coming. Manderson wound up, took a peek at where Free was standing on second base, then started his pitching motion. Sherm saw Manderson's thumb move down toward the little finger. Sherm stepped into the quick-swerving ball, caught it on the nose, and drilled a scorcher exactly over where Risberg had positioned himself. Risberg instinctively leaped for the ball after it had whistled past him. The ball kept drilling out until it had climbed a little above where the left fielder was standing, and then it took off, lofting up and up, becoming a tiny brown dot, and finally leveled off, rode on some more, and slowly dropped to earth. It kept bounding until it hit the east side of the old pioneer's little pasture. Sherm slowed down going toward first, and, after stepping on the bag, stopped to watch the ball roll. Then with a smile, he trotted around the bases, scoring behind Free.

Manderson, still in his leaning stance after his pitching motion, watched Sherm cross the plate. Then Manderson's shoulders sagged and his cherubic cheeks turned sad.

After the ball had been thrown back to the infield Swede Risberg ran over to have a talk with Manderson. He turned Manderson around so no one on the Bonnie bench could read their lips. Finally, after a good talking to, Manderson seemed to buck up some. Risberg gave him a hearty clap on the butt and ran back to his position.

After his first pitch to Garrett, a ball wide of the plate, Manderson got hold of himself, and proceeded to strike Garrett out on three swift hooks. Bonnie 6, Hazard 5.

As Free took his warmup pitches in the last of the ninth, Sherm led the happy chatter. Sherm had to force himself to think about the half inning ahead. The feel of his bat coming around, then of making contact as solidly as he had, of watching the ball take off and finally almost soaring out of sight, was still in him like a miracle and a marvel.

Then Free lost some of his pinpoint control. He threw three straight balls wide of the plate, and not with his usual zip. And grooved his fourth pitch. The batter hit a scorcher through the box that was too hot for Free to handle. Sherm was already moving at the crack of the bat and slid over to cut it off behind second. The ball shot faster then he expected and he had to leap and stretch all out to flag it. And just did nail it. In the webbing of his glove. The thought flicked through his mind that it was like there was another brain in his wristbone quick telling his fingers to adjust to the bad hop. He instantly righted himself and on the dead run half-wheeled himself around and fired a sidearm snapshot at Spider Bont. Left-handed Spider had to lean to the right side of first base, to his full length, and scooped it out of the dirt with a lifting flick of his first baseman's mitt. Batter out by a half a step. The Bonnie crowd cheered; even the Hazard fans applauded the play. Spider flipped the ball to Frankie Wales, who flipped it to Sherm, who flipped it to Garrett, in the old-time ritual of tossing the ball around the diamond after an out with nobody at base. Garrett then walked over and placed the ball in Free's black glove and told Free to keep chucking it in there.

"Now you got 'em where you want 'em. Two more outs to go and we can ride home with another scalp."

Free continued to pitch with an odd uncertain motion. Two pitches, two balls. One was an outdrop and the other was a screwball.

Sherm called from deep in the grass with a calming purr of sound. "C'mon there, buddy boy, show 'em you're king of the hill."

The Hazard coach at third mocked Free. "Ha, a girl could do better. C'mon, Enos boy, connect!"

When Sherm saw Harry Haber call for a fast ball down the middle, Sherm whistled, and cried, "Throw Enos the old slopball, Free boy." Frankie Wales on the other side of second base held his glove to his mouth and called, "Dink it in there, pitch, and Aunt Mary will never see it."

Free wound up and really put out. The ball came in letter high, and then took off a little, inside. Enos came around early and lifted a towering pop fly behind third base. It was obviously a foul ball.

Sherm easily outran Garrett for it. Sherm didn't have to worry much about colliding with left fielder Stiffy Lawson since moments before Garrett had waved him back to play Enos deep. But Sherm did have to worry about the barbwire fence beyond third. As he ran he was almost sure the ball would fall on the other side of the fence—unless the light breeze that had just sprung up would carry it back into the playing field. The wind was probably stronger up there than down on the field. Sherm remembered how the wind always seemed stronger up on the platform of a windmill when he climbed it to grease the blades than down on the ground. Sherm took a look where the fence was, and when he came to the fence ran tight alongside it with his back to the infield. He looked back over his left shoulder. Sure enough the ball, after reaching its height, started to descend in a slant toward the fence. Sherm put the socks into it. If he could catch this one there would be two out. He ran. Ran. The ball kept slanting south, down, down, until he could make out the turning seams.

Garrett came running behind Sherm. "Get it! Get it!"

Sherm could almost feel the pricky barbs of the fence reach for the skin on his pumping left elbow. Then, when the ball was almost in front of his eyes, level with them, he dove forward, recklessly, gloved hand outstretched. The ball dropped into the pocket of the glove. He tried to lighten his fall by making a car spring out of his body, head up at one end and feet at the other. His body bounced lightly, rocked a second, stilled. Ball still in the glove. Two out. Wow. Okay, Swede Risberg, did you ever make a play like that when you shortstopped for the White Sox?

The Hazard crowd applauded the catch even more than the Bonnie fans. Car horns honked loud and long. No matter how partisan country crowds might be, they knew their baseball, and knew when they'd seen a good play.

Free continued to throw out of rhythm to the next batter. He walked the man on four straight pitches. Next up was Swede Risberg.

Catcher Harry Haber called time, removed his mask, and walked out to have a chat with Free. Sherm and Garrett also ran up to put in their two bits worth of advice.

Harry Haber beamed an encouraging smile at Free. "You okay?"

"Sure." Free rolled his right shoulder.

"Those last pitches, it looked like you were hurting."

"It's this hole I've got to pitch out of. I can't seem to throw natural."

Sherm said, "You didn't really hurt your arm, did you?"

"No."

Harry Haber said, "This Risberg who's up next, we've been getting him out before, so we should have no trouble with him."

"Keep throwing him that inshoot," Sherm said, "Because I see you got a hop on the ball tonight. Harry?"

Harry Haber hoisted up his chest protector as if to scratch himself. A big blotch of sweat had shown up under both armpits. "Don't worry. We'll get him."

Everybody ran back to their positions.

Sherm picked up a little twig off the skinned diamond and threw it behind him. "Okay, my handsome uncle-sayer, throw him that old wicked one."

Sherm saw Harry give Free the signal. Inshoot. Good. Sherm saw Risberg glance down as though to take a peak at Harry's fingers. Then Risberg glanced out where Sherm was playing. That devil. Trying to steal the sign. A major leaguer would.

Free wound up and wheeled it in. The pitch headed for the middle of the plate, then jerked in over the top of Swede Risberg's level swing, just missing his hands.

"That a boy, Free. Let's give him another one just like it."

Risberg stepped out of the box, thought to himself a moment, narrowed his hard glittering eyes, finally stepped in again. He stood a little different from before. Harry gave the sign and again Risberg looked down as though to check to see if he had the trademark showing on his bat, but actually to catch the sign peripherally.

Free appeared to see what Risberg was doing. As he wound up, he set, pushed, the ball deeper in his right first, then, with a look at first to see what the runner was doing, threw hard, making the ball come deep out of his hand between his long finger and his ring finger. The ball seemed to leave his hand after he'd finished his pitching motion. It was spinning so fast the seams couldn't be made out. The ball darted for the center of the plate and then really jerked in. Risberg swung mightily and missed it a good half foot. The ball popped like a firecracker in Harry's pud.

Some fellow in the Hazard section with a raucous voice, seeing that his team was going to lose, let fly with a taunt. "Where'd you guys pick up that ugly mutt of a pitcher? The Bonnie boneyard?"

Then Sherm was surprised to see Harry call for Free's big outdrop. Hey. That was no good.

Free shook his head; he didn't want that sign. Again Harry called for the hook. Again Free shook him off. Yet again Harry called for the hook, thick brows gathering in two black knots behind his mask. And yet once more Free shook his head.

Sherm held up a hand. "Time!" He ran in to talk with Free. Garrett joined them. Sherm said, "What's Harry doing, calling for the hook?"

"I don't know," Free said. "But I'm not throwin' it."

Sherm called out, "Harry? Come up here a sec."

Frowning, Harry took off his mask and walked up.

Sherm said, "Free says he don't want to throw the hook."

Harry's brows worked like two black moths. "All night I've called for nothing but what Risberg calls screwballs. I thought it was time we figured he'd be looking for it. The last time, you know, he set himself for it. So I thought we'd finally feed him the big hook."

"No," Free said. "The way he swings, he kills hooks. But he can't hit the high inside pitch. Especially my inshoot." Free's jaw set out. "I throw the best inshoot in baseball. He's never even seen one like it in the majors."

Harry said, "Don't get the bighead, kiddo."

"Listen!" Free snapped, "I want to get that big league bigshot ringer. But I also know he's got muscles in his eyes. He'll hit my hook a ton because he was used to seeing it in the majors."

Garrett said, "Free's right, Harry."

"Well, by gum and by golly, Free's throwing that big wonderful hook of his next or I'm quitting right now." Harry made a motion as if to take off his chest protector.

"Now now, Harry," Sherm said soothingly. "You've called a great game so far. But Risberg will be wondering what we're talking about out here and he'll now be figuring he's gonna get the hook."

"No, he won't," Harry said. "He'll figure that Free shook his head because Free didn't want to throw yet another screwball."

Sherm saw the reasoning. "Well, all right. You better throw it then, Free. And really put the set in it."

179

Free let his shoulders drop. "All right. But if Risberg hits it, it's your neck, Harry, not mine."

Everyone ran back to their positions.

Sherm called out, "Give him the old screwball again, buddy boy."

As Free wound up, Sherm saw Risberg look over to where Pete Haber was playing right field; saw Risberg quick jump into another position as if he meant to hit one late to the first baseman.

Then the ball was on its way to the plate. It headed for Risberg's chin; then slid down for the low outside corner of the plate. Risberg's bat came around and caught the ball on the nose and sent a screamer out toward Pete Haber in right field. Pete didn't know what to do at first, run in or back up; finally got his legs tangled up and fell down. The drive soared over Pete's head, and when it finally fell to earth it bounded all the way to the fence alongside the railroad tracks. Risberg circled the bases easily with the walked batter scoring ahead of him. Hazard 7, Bonnie 6.

In vast disgust, Free sat down on the ground next to the pitching hole.

Harry stood stunned for a few moments; then took off his mask and chest protector, dropped them on the ground next to the Bonnie bench, and wordless headed for his car.

Both Sherm and Garrett approached Free. They knew he had a temper when finally aroused; also knew he was very strong. Finally Garrett said, "Well, we can't win 'em all. We're at least playing .500 ball."

Free swore like a crazed drunken drayman.

Risberg walked up. He looked down at Free. "Fret not, son. The score of this game won't be chiseled in stone."

Free glowered. "But it will be chiseled in italics in my memory."

"Actually, son, you're going to be a good pitcher someday. You got a major league screwball. And your big hook only needs more speed. And, you should throw your knuckler more often, if only to show a change of speed now and then."

Free asked, "What did you think we were talking about just before you hit it?"

Risberg laughed. "That your catcher finally called for the hook. Which I'd been looking for the whole game. I always was a sucker for the screwball."

"See! Son of a bitch."

Then Risberg turned to Sherm. "Have you ever thought of trying out for the majors?"

"I've dreamed about doing just that ever since I was in grade school."

"Well, you got the goods. Hands. Speed. Eye." A sardonic look moved out from the corners of Risberg's sad thin lips. "I think if I'd have kept playing you could have retired me."

It was what Sherm had long wanted to hear from a first-rate player. But Sherm kept a straight face. "Thanks."

Garrett had a wonderful smile for both Free and Sherm. "Well, what . . . about . . . that."

Chapter Ten

Sherm and Allie were sitting in Sherm's old Ford alongside the Little Rock River. They'd found their own lovers' lane when Sherm learned that his brother John had put in a lazy-man's gate in the very northeast corner of the farm. Going through the gate from the road and then carefully driving down the outside row of corn they could park near the deep swimming hole where they would be hidden from view. Dusk was turning from pink to brown.

Allie was nestled in Sherm's arms, cheek comfortingly warm against his, when he told her what Swede Risberg had said. It took several moments for it to sink in, and then, when she saw what it really meant, she slowly sobered over and withdrew from him ever so slightly. "Then you'll leave me here in this dump of a town and go play for the Chicago White Sox?"

"No, play for the Chicago Cubs."

"Same difference."

"I mean to take you along with me."

"Me live in the same town with that underworld crook Al Capone?"

"You won't be living next door to him, for godsakes."

"All of Chicago is corrupt. And he's the sign of it."

"Now now, let's not get into a swivet over this. I'm still a long ways from the majors."

"But the thought of you wanting to go there is just as bad as if you were."

Sherm tried to snuggle her back into his arms. "Come, my curly-haired love, we're not going to have a fight over this now, are we?"

182

"Maybe we are. Because I don't like it that you think it's a cinch I'll agree, just because you got me tight around the belly."

"Hey! Such language." Sherm leaned back to have another look at Allie. In the fading pink her beauty was like a dream. Was this sweet woman, with her long lanky legs and long wavy dark hair, going to turn out to be another Ma? Or even another Matilda? Were all women alike?

"Well, you can't blame me. I don't like being left behind. Or given no thought to."

"Sweetie, I've got it in me to do something important in life. And I want to do it before I'm thirty."

"What about me? You want to remember I'm three years older than you."

"So?"

"Well, by the time you've made it in the big leagues I'll be an old woman."

"Don't you trust me when I say that wherever I go you'll go with me?"

Allie sat stiff.

"After all the good times we've had, do you think I could forget you?"

"Sherm, you just told me a little while ago that this Swede Risberg once sold out to the crooks of Chicago. How can you trust him when he says you're a good ballplayer?"

"Must a man be considered a crook all his life just because he once made a mistake when he was young?"

"You know well enough that if you cross Scarface Al Capone he'll shoot you."

"You don't believe then that whoever touches one of God's servants touches the apple of God's eye?"

Allie scoffed. "How can you call yourself a servant of God if you play baseball on Sunday? What kind of witnessing is that, playing in front of godless thousands?"

"C'mere, babe, let me give you a champion kiss."

"Och! You men." The hint of wrinkles to come formed up around her eyes.

"Honey lady, you know what? I don't like it that every time I want to kiss you, you get real nervous. What's the matter? Did Cornie Taylor beat you up? Or something?"

With an effort Allie overcame whatever it was that was bothering her and she smiled a child smile. And then she kissed him. When that child smile pushed through that set hurt pattern in her face, she was adorable. "No. Of course not. I could've easy licked Cornie if he'd've tried something."

He smiled indulgently. "You probably could've." He took her face in his two hands and rubbed noses with her. "Look, love, let's neck awhile."

"You don't fuss around, do you?"

"Listen to that bird's love lullaby. In the gooseberry bushes below the riverbank here. Hear it? Listen."

Again a thrush fluted soft falling notes in the browning dusk. When would the fledglings break out of the spotted eggs? Eee-ooo-lay-lay.

Sherm could feel Allie listening, trembling a little. The smell of her freshly ironed yellow blouse was sweet to him. It reminded him of the time when, plowing, he'd stepped across the road to her house and found her ironing the shirts of her brothers in the kitchen. He remembered the smile of surprise that opened her face inside the hood of her long wavy dark hair, how after she'd caught sight of him she threw her head back causing her hair to swing back over her shoulders. He remembered too how when he first slid his hand over the sweet mound of her belly and then slid his hand up to cup her breast, she snapped at him with a laugh, sticking the hot iron almost in his face. "You cut that out!"

"Heart of my life," he said, "it'll all turn out all right. Just you watch." He slid his hand around her middle. "Come, a kiss please."

She held him off. "You men sure got it easy. You can run off and do anything you want. And start necking any old time you want and never have to worry when it is. While we women. . . ."

"While we women what?" When she didn't answer, he said, "Come, tell me, I'd like to know. How you really feel."

She blurted it out. "Haven't you ever wondered why it is that girls have to wash their underwear so much when they're in love?"

"I've never lived in a house where there was a young girl."

"And how about married women? Haven't you ever noticed that Matilda has a lot of her underwear hanging on the clothesline sometimes?"

"Now that you mention it, yeh."

"We women . . . well, we're just so terribly different from you men." Allie drew in a deep breath. "You're so lucky."

"You know what I don't like?"

"What?"

"You can't go through life with defeat always in your head. When you walk on the diamond you've got to figure you've already won. If you don't, you're licked before the first pitch of the game."

"There you go with your baseball again always."

"Well, then take just simple life. When you wake up mornings you better not have defeat in your head or you're already done for the day." Sherm chuckled. "After you've had your morning cup of coffee, that is."

"See? You can joke about it. While we girls can't."

"You smell wonderful. Like those stinky milkweed flowers."

"I like that. Stinky."

"I suppose you'd rather have me say a fancy word for stinky?"

"I sure would."

"Well, Allie, let's see now. It really is a perfume, you know. So, how about . . . the aroma of angels stinking up the place?"

"Of all things, how can an angel stink up a place? God in heaven isn't going to like that."

"How would you say it then?"

"How would I know what I smell like in your nose?"

Sherm snuggled her up close. "This isn't getting us anywhere. Come, a kiss please."

"It's gonna cost you."

"You mean, you charge money for them?"

Allie game him a light punch in the stomach. "Not money."

"What then?"

"You can be a gentleman."

"Sissy gentlemen don't have babies."

"What? Is that what you have in mind?"

"In a couple of years, yes."

"If you think that's what we're gonna try tonight, guess again."

"You mean, I can't get into your pants tonight?"

"I should say not."

"Then you've never been diddled?"

"None of your business."

Sherm managed to steal a kiss. "It wouldn't hurt to diddle a little, would it?"

"No." Allie quick collected herself. "I mean, yes, it would."

"You're a sweetheart, you know that."

"Now you're buttering me up."

"All the better to eat you, says the wolf."

"Now it's my turn to ask you. Sherm, have you ever diddled?"

"Would we get a kid if we diddled just a little?"

"You didn't answer my question."

Sherm sighed. "I never even came close." Then he started to laugh. And he told her what he and Free had seen one night in that patch of popcorn Father Cobden had planted near his Catholic Church.

Allie gasped. "You seen that? Allie Brewer and Dennis Nabor? Part naked?"

"You mean, their parts naked." He laughed. "Of course that ain't the first time I seen a girl naked."

"When? Where?"

"Right here. In the swimming hole below the bank here."

"Oh! You sneaked down here and watched us Pipp girls swimming here?"

"Suppose I told you I thought you were beautiful?"

"Then you did!"

He couldn't help but laugh out loud.

"That wasn't fair, Sherm. You could see me naked but I couldn't see you."

Sherm made a motion as if to unbutton his shirt. "Well, I'm ready and willin' to give you your turn right now, if that's what you want."

Abruptly she blurted a question he hadn't expected. "Would you think it wrong of me if we did it?"

His face wrinkled up. "Can't we wait with that question?"

"Would you respect me in the morning after?"

"Of course I'd respect you afters in the morning. And at noon. And at coffee-time around three. And at supper. Of course. Because I love you."

She asked it again. "Would you think it wrong of me?"

"Of course not!"

"That's easy for you to say. Since you want it so bad."

"Hey! How would you know that?"

"I know you men."

"Because your brother Bart is sex mad?"

"That's a terrible thing to say about my brother."

"You defend him?"

Silence.

"Allie, I've got to be honest about this. Sure, I've often day-dreamed about us. About how we'd go swimming in this swimming hole here. And afterwards we'd fall on the sand together."

Her soft brown eyes became as hard as garnets. "You can take me home now."

"Can't."

"Why not?"

"There's no way we can turn around here without running over some of my brother's corn."

"I wish you'd quit guying me. Because you can back up all the way to the road."

"Hey, I never back up. Don't know how. I always go forward. That's the only way a fella's gonna come out ahead."

"That's what my brother Bart says."

"Bart's the oldest in your family, ain't he?"

"What of it?"

"Being the oldest has made him kind of bossy, hasn't it?"

"If I said it did, would you be afraid to marry into my family?"

"Ha. I've got a funny sister, you know. That Joan. You probably should be afraid to marry into my family because of her then too."

"Then you do wonder about him?"

"It makes us even steven. And so long as they don't have to live with us, it'll be all right, I guess. There ain't a family on earth but what they don't have a black sheep of some kind."

What he said seemed to mollify Allie. She relaxed against him, and when he didn't take advantage of it, she turned and slipped her arms around his neck and gave him a long warm hug and kissed him. "I will say that, even if we don't see eye to eye, at least we don't fight much." She released herself from him. "Now, it's got real dark out and you better take me home."

"All right, my lady love, I'll back you all the way to the Pipp yard."

Chapter Eleven

The phone rang just as they were eating breakfast. Two longs. It made everybody jump.

John said, "Who would be calling us this early in the morning? Unless there's been a cloudburst somewhere."

Matilda was lifting the fried eggs out of a black frying pan with a turner and sliding them onto a platter. "Will you get that, John? I've got my hands full here."

John put down his fork. "Probably the President calling me from Washington, D.C., to have me help him save J. P. Morgan's knots."

Matilda snapped, "Watch your language. Even the littlest teacups have ears."

John rose to his feet and went over to the wall phone by the kitchen cabinet. He lifted the black receiver off its nickel hook. "Yeh?" He listened a moment, then held out the receiver to Sherm. "For you. It's the President all right."

Sherm spoke into the black mouthpiece of the phone. "Yes, Mr. President."

There was a laugh over the buzz of the line. "Hey, if it was that easy to be President, I'd run for that office." It was Garrett Engleking.

"You got my vote."

"Say, what I'm calling you about is, you know that game we was going to have with Alvord here tomorrow afternoon? It's been cancelled. They had a flood on Mud Crick there and everybody's too busy cleaning up the mess to want to play."

"Shucks. And here I was looking forward to hitting another homer for you. Only this time in the bottom of the ninth."

Garrett chuckled. "You're still gonna get a chance to do that. In a game that'll mean even more to you."

"How's that?"

"We're playing the Tennessee Rats instead."

"You mean that team of colored players that's been traveling through Siouxland? And winning all their games?"

"That's who. They had a game set with Amen, but Amen's best pitcher, Chizzle Van Citters, had a motorcyle accident. So Hoot Goodman, the manager of the Rats, called me to see if we had an open date."

"Hey, great. Tomorrow afternoon then. Saturday."

"That's it."

"That should be some game. I was reading in the *Sioux City Journal* where the manager of the Sutherland Saints said they had runners so fast they multiplied like rabbits on the bases."

"Yeh, and they got one hitter on the team, a fellow by the name of Nig White, who can hit a ball over the moon. He's supposed to have hit one at Hinton that they measured going more than five hundred feet on the fly."

"That'd be over our Congregational Church."

"At least," Garrett said.

"Well, we'll have Free walk him and strike out the rest."

"Something like that. Did you hear about their pitcher? Fellow named Vivien? Left-hander?"

"No."

"People say he has no bones in his pitching arm."

"Oh come on now."

"That's the rumor. He throws a down-and-away breaking ball to the right-hand batter like no one else in all of baseball."

"That's a bunch of bullshit to put the fear of God in us. Ha. Well, no matter, we'll get 'em."

"You tell 'em."

"I better hang up. My mouth is watering over so I can hardly talk. Matilda's fried eggs."

Matilda poured a second cup of coffee for her men and sat down. "Baseball again, I see. And that was a dirty word you just said too."

Sherm said nothing. Matilda was getting to be almost as bad as sister Ada against baseball.

John buttered up a slice of bread, liberally, and then slid an egg on top of it. "Did you say colored players?"

"Yep. Tennessee Rats."

Matilda sat down with a thump. "You mean to say you're going to play with those smelly creatures?"

Alfie spoke up from where he was sitting on two wish catalogs placed on a chair. "Domeny Tiller said in question school that Noah had dark skin and that God loves all his creatures. Everybody."

Matilda made a wry face as she helped herself to some spilling egg yoke.

"Out of the mouths of babes," John said.

Saturday turned out to be a muggy itchy day. Sherm hoped that by game time at two o'clock the sun would burn off some of the humidity. Instead it seemed to get worse.

Both teams watched each other during pregame warmups. The black players for the Rats had to make quick judgments about the white players for just that one game; and the white players for Bonnie had to see if they had the sand to cross bats with a famous traveling black team.

After watching them awhile, Sherm saw that the black players in their purple-striped gray suits weren't putting out much, just sort of lazing around, laughing at private jokes, sometimes falling to earth after running futilely for a ball, and lolling on their backs, legs up in the air, smiling hugely at the sun. When it was the Bonnie Boys turn for their last infield warmup, Sherm deliberately made it a point to dog it himself, appear lazy. He'd surprise them, show them, during the game when it counted.

Sherm noticed, as the Bonnie infield ran in to their bench, there still wasn't much of a crowd. There were only a couple dozen boys, several old ladies, and the wives and girl friends of the players. Sherm said, "Hardly pays to pass the hat."

Garrett said, "Before the game is over there'll be a crowd, don't worry."

Manager Hoot Goodman had been looking at the thin crowd too. The arrangement had been for the winner to take all of the gate. He ambled over to talk with Garrett. He had a jolly potbelly and a skin so dark it had the look of a ghostly black. "They told me this was a baseball town."

"It is."

"We won't be able to get the price of gas for our bus out of this town. You may have to put us up until we can raise the dough."

"Well, the town people'll be dropping around pretty soon. And later on some of the farmers."

"Maybe we should've played on Sunday tomorrow."

"Don't worry about it."

Hoot Goodman looked off to one side as though to make sure he wasn't tipping his mitt about what he was going to suggest next. "Ahh, how about fattening the take with a little side bet."

"What do you have in mind? Doubling who wins the game?"

"Oh, we know who's gonna win the game."

"I wouldn't be too sure about that."

Hoot smiled white. "Uhh, I was thinking about, say, a fifty dollar bet. We think we got a pretty fast man, and we were wondering if you've got a fast man."

A wily look came over Garrett's face. "We got a couple. How do you want to race them?"

"See who goes the fastest around the bases. Home plate around to home plate."

"Race two men around at the same time?"

"No no. We got a stopwatch. We'll time each man separate."

"Can I see your stopwatch?"

Hoot dug out an old worn watch.

Garrett and Sherm inspected it closely. Finally Garrett said, "How do we know if this thing is accurate? That you can't speed it up or slow it down?"

"If it's not accurate it'll be the same difference for both of us."

At that moment Garrett spotted Jackie Van Valkenburg sitting in the stands behind the backstop. "Hey, Jackie, c'mere a minute."

Jackie slid down off his plank seat and trotted around the backstop. "Yes, Mr. Engleking."

"Do you think your dad's got a second railroad watch at home? I know he's on the Bonnie-Whitebone run this afternoon. Would you go look? Ask your mom if we could borrow it for a couple of minutes."

"Sure, Mr. Engleking." Jack broke away on the dead run for his home up on the silk-stocking block just around the second corner from the high school grounds.

Hoot pushed out a thick purple lip. "You don't trust our watch?"

"Well, if we're gonna time 'em, I'd like to know exactly how fast our own man is. Be kind a nice to know if a man here in Bonnie broke the world record for going around the bases."

"Billy Sunday holds the record. Fourteen seconds."

"Whew!" Sherm whistled. "That's three-and-a-half seconds a base." Sherm wondered who Garrett had in mind to race against Hoot's man. Would it be Fritz, Garrett's brother? Or would it be the Bonnie shortstop, himself?

Jackie Van Valkenburg came running back. "Mom says you can use it for only a minute. I've got to bring it right back."

Garrett patted Jackie on the head. "Good boy. Now, Mr. Goodman. Let's hold 'em side by side, and when you start yours up I'll mark my watch in my mind and we'll see how accurate yours is. After all, a railroad watch should be the judge."

Three heads—two blonds, each with a baseball cap on, and a curly black-haired one, also with a baseball cap on—leaned together. Hoot started his stopwatch with an up snap of his thumb and hand, and Garrett and Sherm checked the motion of its second hand against the second hand of Van Valkenburg's Waltham railroad watch. When Hoot once again snapped his thumb down, Sherm and Garrett were pleased to see that the stopwatch was accurate. At least so far as they could judge.

"Okay," Garrett said. "your man runs first."

"No no," Hoot said. "When we hold these matches we always let the home team man run first to see what we have to beat. Do we use our fastest man or our second fastest."

Garrett held back a smile. He turned to his bunch. "Fritz, come up here." He explained what was wanted. Fritz's soft brown eyes warmed up.

Hoot said, "The way we usually do it, is, we have the runner take a practice swing with a bat in the batter's box at an imaginary ball, and then drop the bat and circle the bases."

Fritz nodded, went back and got a bat, and took up his position as a left-hander on the first-base side of home plate.

Hoot said, "When I say, go! you drop the bat and start to run, and I'll snap on the watch."

"Wait." It was Constable Koltoff. He'd just arrived to umpire the game, along with Deputy Sheriff Hasselmore. Constable Koltoff waddled in among them. "What's this?"

"We're having a side bet," Garrett said. "See who's got the fastest runner. Fritz here against one of their runners."

Constable Koltoff spotted the stopwatch. "You're gonna have a pistol start, ain't you?"

The appearance of the two badges sobered the black team.

Hoot's already dark face darkened even more. Hoot said, "Pistol start is okay by us."

"All right." Constable Koltoff lifted his pistol from his holster and aimed it at the sky. "Ready?"

"All set."

Bang!

In two steps Fritz was already going at full speed. He had short powerful legs and they pumped him forward like the reciprocating pistons of a steam engine. He hit the dirt so hard on each step he picked up small compact clods with his spiked shoes. Before the mind could adjust to his speed, he was around first base and heading for second. The strange hard beating sound of his shoes hitting earth made Hoot look up from his stopwatch a moment. Hoot's eyes widened, showing white. Fritz's arms worked like quick counterweights to his piston legs. Around second. Around third. Stompstompstomp. And then Fritz came down the last stretch. And with a lengthened stride hit home plate.

Hoot snapped down the stopwatch. "Holy sufferin' dogs," Hoot whispered. "Fourteen and one-fifth seconds." Hoot managed a sick smile as he looked around at Garrett. "Looks like I'll have to call on our fastest after all."

"It's your choice. Your man is next."

Hoot walked over to his bench. He talked awhile to his players. Finally he tapped the shoulder of a slender man. The player stood up, picked up a bat, and together the two walked up to home plate.

Garrett quirked his eyes at Hoot. "That your fastest now? Or do you still have another one up your sleeve!"

Hoot had to laugh. "He's our best, all right. I tell you, we never expected to run across a flying two-legged steam engine like you got there." He nodded at Fritz. "Man, you sure can run."

Fritz was sweating like he'd just stepped out of a shower with his uniform on. "I try my best."

Hoot rolled a little in his stance. "Looks like we lost the bet." He turned to the slender black standing next to him. "Well, Footsie, since we're not running Scat, it's up to you." Hoot smiled at Garrett and the umpire. "Gennelmen, meet Footsie Cooney, our premier shortstop."

Footsie for the first time looked up. He had a face so lean and drawn he found it hard to smile.

Hoot pointed. "Okay, Footsie, get set."

Footside ambled easy over to the plate. He moved so slow, so lazylike, it had to be fake.

Sherm watched it all closely. If Footsie beat Fritz's time, he'd have to run next.

Constable Koltoff once again held up his pistol. He fired. Bang!

The sleepy Footsie, swinging his bat and dropping it, was suddenly transmogrified into a haughty head-out hound. He seemed to lengthen a foot on his very first stride and by his second stride his muscles turned into fast-pouring syrup. He touched the earth so lightly he hardly kicked up little throws of dust. It was as if his spikes on each step barely punctured a small dried puffball.

"Gollies," Garrett whispered. "Looks like we've thrown away fifty bucks."

Sherm said nothing. He could feel himself filling up with heat.

Footsie swung out a little as he rounded first, and swung out again as he rounded second. Silence fell on the field. It became so quiet the five men standing around home plate could hear very clearly the swift light pattering of Footsie's toes on the base paths. Little boys standing along the third base line stood with mouths open. Around third Footsie came, lean face drawn as though in a death grimace, toes swifting past each other, and then, like a passing thought, he crossed home plate.

Hoot snapped down his stopwatch. "His best yet, by God! Fourteen even." He held the watch out for Garrett to see.

Garrett had been timing Footsie on the Van Valkenburg railroad watch. He held his head sideways. "Darn, you're right."

With a white smile, Hoot said, "I suppose now you're gonna tell me you got a faster man."

"Yep." Garrett turned to Sherm. "Well?"

Sherm said, "I've just changed to lighter oil." After all he was the son of parents who could claim they were of higher issue.

Garrett next turned to Umpire Koltoff. "Constable, you got another shell in that water pistol of yours?"

Hoot had to laugh. "I'll say this for you guys. You don't take it very serious you're gonna lose fifty bucks."

Garrett said, "Now whatever gave you that idea?"

Hoot said, "Well, nobody's ever beat Billy Sunday's record of fourteen seconds around the bases."

Sherm said, "Well, your man just tied it. So maybe this is the day when somebody's gonna break it."

"Ha."

Sherm picked up his bat and stepped into the batter's box on the right-hander's side. "All set, Constable. Let go with your roman candle firecracker."

Bang!

Sherm too by his second stride was in high gear. He ran more upright than either Fritz or Footsie. But he didn't swing out to round first base. He went directly at it already tipping to his left, leaning over so far he almost touched the ground with his left hand; hit the first base bag hard enough to jolt him hard left; in two strides had righted himself and sped for second base. Sherm ran so fast his legs looked like the flittering blades of a flying scissors.

A loud voice let fly from behind third base. "Look at that fellow run!" It was Free's father.

Sherm thought: "Alf must've talked Ada into letting him go see us play the descendants of Ham."

Sherm headed directly for second base, and again leaning inward turned it almost at a right angle, and in two steps was upright again heading for third.

The black players on the Tennessee Rats' bench slowly stood up to watch Sherm go.

Once more at third, Sherm, leaning in, took it at a right angle, hitting the base with his right foot, and in two strides was erect. For the first time he found himself leaning forward as though to pick up more speed. He churned his arms faster to hurry his swiveling hips. His eye automatically adjusted the length of his stride and he hit home plate with his right foot.

Hoot snapped down on his stopwatch, and gasped. "I'll be dog. He did break it! Thirteen and three-fifths seconds. That's impossible!"

Garrett looked up from his railroad watch. "Whatever it is, it beats your man."

"That it does. Goddammit. Fifty bucks shot to hell." Hoot looked around. "And still not much of a crowd. This is gonna be our worst day on the road."

Garrett held out his hand. "Pay up."

Hoot pocketed his stopwatch. Then from the back pocket of his purple-striped gray baseball pants he pulled out a battered wallet. Slowly his gray-edged fingers extracted four tenners and two fivers. "There goes our dinner money."

"Sorry."

Constable Koltoff turned to Garrett. "Where's your new game ball?"

"Pete?" Garrett called. "Dig that new ball out of our gunnysack."

"Will do," Pete Haber said. He reached into the sack and came up with a shiny square box. He opened it and took out a gleaming white ball and tossed it to Garrett. Garrett in turn handed it over to the umpire.

Looking around, Sherm saw that somewhat of a crowd had begun to drift in. Even some farm men had shown up.

The Bonnie team ran out onto the field while Free strolled over to the mound to take his warmup throws with the new ball. Spider Bont at first threw rollers to the infielders and in his usual easy-does-it manner accepted snap throws in return.

Sherm couldn't resist looking every now and then over at where Vivien, the black pitcher, was warming up behind the Rats' bench. Sherm could see why some people said he had no bones in his left arm. Vivien's throwing motion was like the slap of a wave on a lake beach, with the push of water sliding up the sandy shelf and ending with a little curl on itself. A couple of times when Vivien threw hard it reminded Sherm of the slap of a rug being shaken out.

When Free said he was ready, Constable Koltoff stood on home plate and bawled out long and loud: "Battery for the Bonnie Boys, Free Alfredson and Jimmy Wales! Battery for the Tennessee Rats, Phenomenal Vivien and Digger Jones! Play ball!"

Jimmy squatted behind home plate. "All right there, my fine-feathered pitchin' poet, let's really chuck now."

The first man up for the Rats was Footsie Cooney.

Sherm checked to see where the Bonnie infield was playing. Footsie just might want to bunt his way on. Sherm waved Spider at first up several steps; the same for Wimp at third. Holding glove to mouth, Sherm called to the Rats bench, "You boys better figure that all you're gonna get out of this game is some batting practice. Because we've already won."

Hoot, coaching at first base, smiled huge and white. "Pardon us, but we want to know if you've got insurance on those windows in the high school. We're liable to break a few."

Sherm had to smile in return. "Actually, for all the good it's gonna do you, you might as well have left your bats in your gunnysack."

Hoot gave Footsie several signals.

Sherm called loud and clear to Free. "I know you're a little wild at first, so concentrate on getting the ball over. Not like the last game when one of your wild pitches conked the batter standing in the on-deck circle because he looked like he was a little too anxious to bat."

Hoot cupped hands to mouth. "Just watch the ball, Footsie. And cut it in half like you're gonna swing a butcher knife through it."

Jimmy cast a dark look up at Footsie, then showed two fingers deep in his crotch between his knees for an inshoot. "Let's show him your dark one, buddy boy."

Free wound up with his long arm, reached back, then came around and let fly with a pitch that speared straight for the center of the plate; then, at the last moment, jerked in towards Footsie's chin. Footsie had already started his swing when, too late, he saw that the pitch was going to handcuff him. He finished his swing weakly. His eyes opened like a pair of full moons.

Jimmy cried, "He's got a hole in his bat!"

Sherm called, "Don't strike out the first man, Free my boy, or you'll jinx the game for us. Just let him hit it somewhere. We'll get it."

Jimmy next showed three fingers. Free snapped off his big outdrop. Footsie shortened up on his bat and leaned over the plate. He watched the ball carefully and at the last second bunted it to the right of Free, halfway between the pitcher's mound and first base. Free dove for it. So did Spider. When Free came up with it there was nobody covering first. Frankie Wales hadn't been able to get over fast enough. Base hit. The black boys cheered; the Bonnie bench glowered.

Sherm called time and ran in to talk to Free. He called in Jimmy from behind the plate and Frankie from second and Spider from first and Wimp from third. Behind his glove he whispered, "The next fellow up is Scat, their center fielder. He's fast too. He's gonna bunt for sure. So Wimp and Spider, you two play way in, almost halfway to the plate. And Frankie, you skedaddle over to first the moment you see him make a motion to bunt. Okay?"

The three infielders nodded.

Sherm next spoke to Free. "He's gonna bunt. So don't try throwing your high hard one. Just get it over the center of the plate and let him bunt. We'll challenge him to bunt. And get him. And remember, fellows, if you can, force Footsie at second.

Jimmy will yell where you're to throw it. And Jimmy, just call for Free's straight ball now."

As Free was about to start his windup, Sherm called out, "Okay, pitch boy, let's fake a wet one."

The white ball sailed in straight and true, knee-high. Scat did scrunch up to bunt, and laid down a beauty to Wimp. Wimp, already on the run, wringing both hands once as usual, scooped up the ball. Jimmy tossed aside his mask and yelled, "Second!" Wimp heard, whirled, fired a perfect screamer at second base. Sherm caught it on the run and stepped on second, forcing the runner. Base umpire Hasselmore jerked his right thumb up. "Runner is out!"

The Bonnie fans erupted. A few latecoming old-timers took off their hats and waved them. "That's showing those coons!"

Sherm noticed when Footsie slid into second that he hadn't tried any dirty tricks, spikes coming in high and aimed at one's face, or a rolling football block to knock one off the bag; hadn't even tried to kick the ball out of one's glove. Sherm smiled down at Footsie. "Thanks for coming in like a Christian."

Footsie smiled his gaunt smile. "If this'd been in the Negro league, or the majors, I might have come in different."

Sherm nodded. "Tell you something about that. I've already decided that should I ever reach the majors, and they come in kicking at me with their spikes, like Ty Cobb does, why, I'll get 'em the next time they come into second."

Footsie rose easily to his feet. "What'll you do?"

"I'm aiming the ball for their face, not first."

"Good luck. But you better do it in front of the home crowd."

"I know."

"That's partly why I came in like your Christian."

Sherm smiled again. "Hey, listen, I like to think we're all God's children, Ham, Shem, and Japheth. All of us should be busy witnessing for him. At all times."

Footsie brushed the dust off his purple-striped gray uniform, especially down his right side. "How come it's all right for your pitcher to throw curves?"

"You got me there. I'll ask my minister about it the next time we have a Young People's meeting."

"You do that. And write me a letter in care of Ham."

Sherm laughed. He looked at Frankie for him to watch second, what with Scat on first, then walked the ball in to Free. He saw that Free was scowling. "What's up?"

"Those slick devils are trying to bunt their way on."

Sherm placed the ball in the middle of Free's black glove. "That they are. And why not? They figure that with your long arms and long legs you probably ain't very quick."

"The son-of-a-guns." Free's armpits were soaked with sweat.

"Look. It's easier for a shorty to look quick than a long bird. Tell you what. When you finish your pitch and come down on your right foot, why don't you quick look to see what the batter may be up to? If he's gonna bunt. And where he's gonna lay it down. Once you make that out, go for that spot, and be there when the bunt gets there. Now, let's see how quick you are, at least between the ears."

Free looked at the palm of his hand. It ran with sweat. "See that?"

"Why don't you load up one side of ball with it? The ball will come into the plate like a hammer heavy on one end. Make sure you juice up the ball on the same side every time."

Free nodded, and Sherm ran back to his position.

The next man up was the first baseman, Goodtime Jackson. He was a tall fellow who'd allowed himself to get fat. He swung several bats warming up, threw two of the bats to one side, then stepped in with the biggest and longest bat. Jimmy called for an inshoot and Free wound up, with a careful eye on Scat at first, and threw. Goodtime swung mightily, and missed.

Spider cried from first, "Good pitch, pitch. He swung like an old woman through that one."

Jimmy called for the knuckler next and Free threw a perfect floater. It didn't turn once all the way to the plate. Right after he finished the pitch he set himself to jump either way for the possible bunt. Goodtime did bunt. He dropped it perfectly down the third base chalk line. The ball rolled some dozen feet, then stopped. There was no possible way Wimp was going to field it in time, nor for Jimmy to dart in from behind the plate to get it. But Free, anticipating, leaned in on the run and then, as he fell to earth, fired underhanded towards first. And beat Goodtime by a step. Two out. With Scat advanced to second base.

Sherm jumped up. Lord, what a snap throw.

The Bonnie crowd let out a roar. More and more people had

come to the game, and all joined in on the clamor. The stand behind the backstop had filled up and under the trees a crowd three deep ranged almost from home plate well past third. Ladies cooled themselves with waving fans and men with flopping straw hats.

Next up was the cleanup man for the Rats, Nig White. He wasn't a big man. He looked a little like a huge black ant, with a very thin belly, very thick thighs and buttocks, and surprisingly large forearms. As he stepped into the batter's box, he wiggled his big heavy black bat like it might be a slender horsewhip.

Sherm ran in. "Well, Free, here's where we find out if you can pitch in the majors some day."

"This the guy who hit that record homer at Hinton?"

"The same."

Catcher Jimmy came duckfooting up. "Well, Sherm, how do we pitch to him?"

Sherm said, "Let him furnish his own power. Call for nothing but floaters. Each one slower than the one before. Think you can do it, Free?"

"I think so. That last knuckler felt good when it left my hand."

"That's it then." Sherm ran back to his position.

Jimmy went back behind the plate and showed four fingers. Then with a glance up at Nig, he cried, "Okay, Freesy boy, let's give him a little Bonnie smoke."

Free wound up, threw a quick glance at Scat to make him take a step back to second base, then let fly with another perfect floater. The ball dappled in, began to waver, then wavered even more. Nig waited, and waited, finally swung. He came around so fast his bat whooshed. He just barely ticked the ball, and Jimmy hung on.

"Ah, just a tickey for our hero," Sherm cried. "Give him another, Free, my boy. He's gonna need a net to catch those butterflies."

Free knuckled in another floater. Again Nig fouled it, this time almost hitting his foot.

Jimmy noticed that Nig moved up several steps to the front of the batter's box. Nig meant to crack the ball before it began its last darting movement. Jimmy called for a hard inshoot.

Sherm whistled low to himself. Wasn't it dangerous to throw a fast ball to a fast-ball hitter? But he too had seen Nig move up in the box. Maybe it was the perfect call.

And Free saw why Jimmy was showing him two fingers. As Free came around and paused with a last look at Scat just off second, he set the ball deeper into his fist, and then let fly with his hardest thrown ball of the day and the one with the most spin. The ball headed for the plate, then jumped in and up. Nig, swinging mightily, missed it by a good foot. Three outs.

Again Sherm jumped. Wow. The kid was going to be able to hold 'em. The Bonnie Boys had a chance to win.

Frankie Wales was first up against Phenomenal Vivien. With his quick black eyes Frankie watched Vivien's every move. And it was very strange the way Vivien threw the ball. His supposedly boneless left arm worked more like a slack slingshot than an arm. The ball started out moderately fast and then, two-thirds of the way to the plate, slowed down and began to dance. It more fell downward over the plate than sailed over it. The pitch was over the plate, two feet high at the front of the plate and six inches high at the back of it. Frankie, after two strikes in a row, swung at a low pitch just inches off the ground and bounced it to shortstop Footsie. Footsie threw him out easily.

Wimp next up swung at the first pitch and also hit it to Footsie. Two away. As Wimp came past where Sherm was swinging his bat before stepping in, Wimp whispered, "He throws slop, for godsakes. That's not baseball."

Sherm nodded, and stepped in. Taking his cue from Nig, Sherm too stood in the front part of the batter's box. He also shortened up on his bat and made up his mind to swing lightly at the ball, punch it instead of crush it. Sherm cautioned himself to be on the alert for what could be Vivien's fast ball. Nig was the Rats' catcher and sitting behind home plate would certainly spot where he stood. Sure enough, Vivien wound up a little more elaborately, as though he were pulling back harder on the rubber band in his arm, and the ball did come in fairly fast. Sherm smiled. Well, Sherm decided to swing at it rather than wait to see what the next pitch might be. He caught it square and hit a streak straight at Vivien. Vivien might not have any bones in his left arm, but he did in his right arm. His gloved right hand flicked up in front of his face and with a whut the ball stuck in the middle of his glove. Great catch. Even the Bonnie fans cheered that one. Inning over.

So the game went. Inning after inning. 0 to 0.

The crowd continued to thicken. It got hotter and hotter out. There wasn't a soul there, either fan or player, but what he or she didn't have a spreading patch of sweat under each armpit. Tension mounted. Cheers came more in the form of quick chirps than loud cries.

Around the sixth inning, late afternoon clouds began drifting in from the west. The white cream-colored cumuli approached in parallel courses, with wide alleys of blue light. When the cloud shadows brushed over the diamond, everybody heaved a sigh of relief and pleasure. Eyes lifted heavenward to see if there was any rain in the rising vapor mountains.

By the end of the seventh inning Phenomenal Vivien still hadn't walked anybody, hadn't allowed a hit. There were no errors behind him. He was on the way to pitching a perfect game.

Some of the old grizzled baseball players in the crowd began to murmur. "Can't you bozos hit that rinky-dink junk? Why, some of the grade school kids could hit them girl pitches." "My God, if you call that pitchin', I think I'll go home and dig out my old glove and play again."

Nor had Vivien struck anybody out. Every ball had been hit on the ground to the infield. Smiling to himself, sometimes even laughing right out loud, Phenomenal Vivien toyed with the boys from Bonnie.

Meanwhile Free had been doing pretty much the same with the traveling blacks. In seven innings he'd allowed only two squib hits and walked three. There'd been two stolen bases, one by Footsie and one by Scat. What helped was that he was pitching into a southeast wind and it made his ball dart and dance all the more. His big sidearm curve, thrown at the batter's belt, sometimes swept completely outside the plate. His knuckler fluttered like a mindless brown moth. And his inshoot winked off sideways like a firefly.

Sherm muttered to Free, "Boy, if we win this one, it's gonna be just barely by our chin strap. That Vivien throws the ball so slow you can shake hands with it as it crosses the plate."

"Yeh, he mostly throws a push ball."

"Push ball? I never heard that one before."

"It's where you throw the ball so slow it pushes a cushion of air ahead of itself for it to slide off from. And God only knows which way."

The Bonnie Boys finally caught up with Vivien's easy-served dishes in the bottom of the eighth. Free, batting fifth in the batting order, decided to move up in the batter's box too. He stood with his feet wide apart and took a short hard rip at the ball. He caught Vivien's first push ball with the fattest part of his new long bat and drove it on a line straight for the southeast corner of the high school building. Before either the Rats' center fielder or the right fielder could decide which way it would carom, it bounced directly back toward second base. By the time Footsie raced over to trap it Free reached first safely.

Garrett next up also went after the first pitch by taking a short whack at it instead of swingin' for the long ball. He hit a grass cutter past Footsie. Free ran for second, and Garrett made first easily. Two on.

The Bonnie players took up the chant. "He's blowing up! He's blowing up!" The Bonnie crowd roared. "He's going sky high!"

Jimmy next up took up a position in the batter's box as close to the plate as possible, leaning over it as if looking to be hit with one of the soft push balls. For the first time Vivien looked worried.

Manager Hoot stood up. He pointed a finger at a lanky fellow sitting at the far end of the Rats' bench and, with a revolving motion of his heavy arm, motioned for him to warm up. Another player grabbed a catcher's mitt and strolled with the lanky fellow out on the grass beyond first base. Soon the lanky fellow was popping the ball into the reserve catcher's mitt.

Vivien got the first ball over for a strike on Jimmy, but then threw four balls wide of the plate. Bases loaded.

Hoot called time and with a belly-heavy swaying gait walked out to the mound. Nig and Footsie joined the conference. After some talk, Hoot took the ball from Vivien and patted him on the shoulder and sent him to the bench. He next signalled for his lanky pitcher to come in. Hoot then walked into the plate to tell Umpire Koltoff who the relief pitcher was.

Just before Spider stepped into the batter's box, Umpire Koltoff announced from home plate: "Count Dixey now pitchin' for the Tennessee Rats!"

A stir of amusement went through the crowd. Pete Haber cried, "A count no less. When is the king of the Congo coming?"

Count Dixey's first pitch was a ball. Footsie called softly from shortstop, "Fog it in there, Dixey boy." Dixey's next pitch split the plate for a strike. When Spider tried leaning over the plate, Footsie called in, "Loosen him up with a conker." And Scat called in from his position at second, "Chase him back with a duster."

Count Dixey hardly needed the advice. By his third pitch his control became plumb-line perfect. Two more pitches down the middle and Spider was called out.

Sherm sitting on the bench next to Garrett remarked, "Looks like the Count has really got a hummer there."

"You tell 'em. He's got a six-inch hop on it just as it climbs into the strike zone in front of the plate."

Stiffy Lawson was an old veteran ballplayer who'd seen many great pitchers come and go. He fouled the first pitch, a low line drive to the right into the box elder trees.

Sherm called, "Attaboy, Stiffy. Now that you got your eye on it, straighten out the next one into one of those high school windows.

Footsie called from short, "Come on, Countie boy, cut loose. Whang 'em in there."

For the first time Count Dixey took a full windup and wheeled it in. The ball jumped over Stiffy's bat. Strike two. Again the Count wheeled it in. Strike three.

Sleepy DeBoer stepped in next. He appeared to have awakened some. His blue eyes opened wide enough so they looked like a pair of petals from a foreget-me-not. Sleepy watched the first one go by and his eyes opened even further. He swung at the next one after it had popped into Nig's pud. Then Sleepy stepped out to have a think about what he'd seen so far.

The Bonnie bench, watching the Count throw, began to look a little sick. The Count had a lazy way of coming around. But his motion was deceptive. It was unbelievable to see how fast that ball could streak out of his easy flowing delivery. The color of his skin also caught their eye. Unlike the other black players he looked like he'd been minted out of old copper.

Sleep stepped in again, opening up his stance and moving his hands farther up the bat handle. It didn't help any. Sleepy swung completely under the third pitch. Three outs.

Top of the ninth. On Free's very first pitch, Sherm knew something was wrong. He ran in. "Throw your arm out, Free?"

"It's so darn hot and close." With his sleeve Free wiped running sweat from his eyes.

"Well, bear down, boy. Or don't you care?"

"Of course I care."

"You're lucky the batter didn't swing on that first pitch."

"It was a strike though."

"We don't have a relief pitcher like they do. So you gotta burn it in there."

Free responded with two blazing inshoots. One out.

"All right, you long-legged poet you, it's time you threw your secret pitch. That curly one."

Once more, though, on his first pitch to the next batter, Free threw awkwardly. The ball bounced in front of the plate.

Sherm trotted in. "What the heck, Free."

Free pointed down at where his left foot usually landed after a pitch. "That's where Vivien'd been landing with his foot and he's dug it all up."

"You sure that's it? Man, it looked like your arm was going to part company with your body."

Free called time, and waved his arm for Umpire Koltoff to come up and have a look, "I don't suppose the high school janitor's in the crowd? We could use a rake to level this off a little."

Umpire Koltoff shook his head. "I didn't see him." Umpire Koltoff began to work the sandy edge of the mound with the side of his heavy black shoe. Free and Sherm helped with their spiked shoes until they had the mound back to normal. Umpire Koltoff stomped on the soft dirt several times with his flat heavy black shoes. "There. That should do it."

Free tried several practice pitches. "Yeh. That's better. Now I dare to come down hard." Free then showed Umpire Koltoff the ball. "It's hard to believe this was white when we started the game."

"What are you trying to say?"

Free turned the ball over in his black glove. Grass stains and sand bruises had turned the ball into a dark green-brown. "See this side of the ball? Vivien must've had some sandpaper stuck to his belt. Because it's so sanded off here you can almost see the wound yarn underneath. And the leather here looks like a bunch of butterfly wings."

"Oho," Sherm said. "No wonder Vivien was so hard to hit."

Umpire Koltoff took the ball. "See this dark spot here? That's where you've been loading up the ball. With sweat. I saw you. So it's even steven. Let's finish this game. Play ball." Umpire Koltoff stomped heavily back to his position behind catcher Jimmy Wales.

Sherm ran back to his position far back on the grass.

Jimmy called for a knuckler. It floated in so slow and so still that the batter, had he wanted to, could have counted the stitches. The batter swung twice at the ball, the first time far too early, and the second time almost too late. He poked a bouncer towards Spider, and Spider easily outran him to first. Two out.

"Now!" Sherm called loud to his teammates, raising two fingers, "two out and one more to go. Then we go get 'em."

Free rolled his right shoulder several times, walked around the mound as though he were giving himself a good talking to, picked up the rosin bag and fluffed his sweating right hand with it, and then ascended the mound and leaned in for Jimmy's signal.

Jimmy called for a straight ball. "All right, Free old boy, let's give him one of your dipsy-doo snakes."

Sherm moved to his right two steps; thought it over as he tried to anticipate where the next batter might hit it; went back left a step beyond where he'd first positioned himself. As he did so, out of the corner of his eye, he thought he caught sight of a familiar curved waist in the crowd beyond third. He turned for a closer look. Hey. Allie Pipp. She must've talked her old man into taking her to town after all. Great. Now he himself could take her home. After he'd hit a homer to win the game. Great kisses coming.

Free wound up slowly, rose high on his toes, threw the ball from directly overhead, seemed to lean all his weight down into the ball, giving it a terrific backspin. The batter didn't allow quite enough for the hop on the ball and popped it up in the evening sky, high. Frankie Wales called for it, circled around under it, finally at the last second dived to his left and caught it falling to the ground. Three out.

Cheers from the Bonnie crowd were muted. There was still Count Dixey to face. And when the Count warmed up before the inning started, the Bonnie bench watched him with the narrowed eyes of cougars.

Frankie was first up in the bottom of the ninth. Flat-footed, he went after the first pitch. No use waiting for the perfect pitch to hit. The Count wasn't wasting any. Frankie smacked a daisy cutter deep in the hole to the right of Footsie. Footsie slid over easily, made a clean pickup, came up erect, and fired a strike to first base, the pitcher Dixey having ducked away to avoid getting hit. One away.

As Wimp stepped into the batter's box, Sherm said to Garrett,

"What a crackerjack out there at short. A guy can learn a lot just watching him. He's better than Risberg."

Garrett nodded. "Eight players like him along with a pitcher like the Count and you could beat the Yankees."

"Sure is a shame these fellows can't play in the majors."

"Not everybody believes we're all God's children."

Wimp also went after the first pitch and sent a trickler through the box. Count Dixey made a grab for it but missed. Footsie glided over and then at the last second dived for the ball. He caught it on the short hop while lying flat on his belly. Quickly jumping to his feet he still nailed Wimp at first by a step.

Everybody cheered the great play.

Sherm stepped in. He too decided to go after the first pitch. The Count hadn't thrown any curves so far. That meant the first pitch would be a fast ball right down the pike. Sherm made up his mind to swing several inches higher than what it looked like he should. That way he should catch the rising ball dead center. He also decided not to shorten up on his bat like both Frankie and Wimp had done, but grip it at the very end. He wanted the leverage so he could end the game with one stroke.

The Count wound up with his beautiful elastic limber motion. Around came the arm and the brown ball exploded toward Sherm.

Willing it, willing it, Sherm did swing higher than what his eye told him to swing. And he swung grunting, feeling the muscles in his forearms and his buttocks bulge up just as he connected, getting in that extra k-nick, a short sudden doubling of power. The sound of horsehide and ash wood colliding was loud and glorious. Sherm saw the ball jump away from his ripping bat, already rising. As he ran to first he watched it go. It rifled out, climbing, and then, catching at the air, it lifted up and up, and out, reaching a level some hundred feet high, and sailed over the first row of trees, then the next row of trees, and finally, unbelievably, it landed on the roof of the Congregational Church.

Everybody seemed to hold their breath until the ball hit the roof of the church. Then the Bonnie people leaped up, shouting, roaring. Men waved their hats. Little boys jumped up and down. Women shrilled and waved their fans. Car horns bleated.

As Sherm ran around third, he caught sight of Allie again. She was smiling like a vamp at him.

Free and Garrett and all the boys were waiting for Sherm. They mobbed him so that he had trouble finding the plate. The Bonnie boys had big round eyes and wide red open mouths. By God and by golly! they had beaten the famous Tennessee Rats!

In the midst of the melee Umpire Koltoff stood waiting importantly making sure that Sherm touched home base. When Sherm finally did touch it, he turned solemnly, and headed for home and supper and tea. Bonnie Boys 1. Tennessee Rats 0.

The Tenessee Rats meanwhile clustered around their bench. Slowly they took off their spike shoes. They tried to smile as they shook their heads.

Presently Garrett tugged at Sherm's arm. "Step over here a minute."

"Sure thing."

"You know what I'd like to do? I'd like to give Manager Hoot Goodman back half of our bet. Twenty-five dollars."

Sherm's eyes opened. "You wouldn't kid me, would you?"

"It cost them money to drive here. And they were a great drawing card, even though the crowd was a little slow coming at first. Your brother-in-law Alfred and our grocer Tillman passed the hat and collected more than a hundred bucks. Our biggest take by far this year."

"Oh, well. I suppose it is fair at that."

"Besides, these fellows are good scouts. Nothing mean or dirty. They played fair and square. Didn't argue once with the umpire. They behaved like real human beings. I'm all for baseball, no matter who plays it."

"Yeh, Footsie slid into second like a Christian that time I beat him to the bag."

"Then it's okay to give Hoot back twenty-five bucks?"

"Fine by me."

Garrett and Sherm walked over to where the Rats were getting ready to head for their bus.

"Hoot?"

"Yeh?"

Garrett got out his pocketbook and peeled off two tens and a five-spot and handed it to Hoot.

"What's that for?"

"Gas money. We didn't want you to think we were cheapskates. Take it."

Hoot took the money reluctantly. The three bills lay in his gray-edged palm. "That's mighty white of you boys."

"Think nothing of it."

Sherm added with a smile, "In the next life, if we should happen to get through the pearly gates, we'll probably all have gold skins."

Footsie winked with a lean smile. "Shucks. And here all my life I've been glad God made me black. Except of course I wisht he'd 've made my skin thicker."

All four had a good laugh.

Time to go home.

Allie was waiting for Sherm in his car. As he stepped in, she had a warm kiss for him. "How does it feel to hit a ball that far for the winning run against a slick team?"

"I can't think of anything sweeter."

She kissed him again.

"But I tell you something. A home run don't last very long. Fourteen seconds at the most. And then it's back to plowing corn."

Chapter Twelve

The next game was at Amen on a Saturday at six sharp. Starting at that hour gave the players time to get in the game before dark.

That morning the wind had turned northeast and by game time it had driven out the sticky itchy humid air and made the skies as clear as a drop of distilled water. All creatures perked up, horses, cows, chickens, grasshoppers, men and women and children, and the swooping riverbank swallows. Even old cars ran better.

When the Bonnie team arrived on the Amen diamond southwest of town, they found the home team warming up, the manager hitting grounders to the infielders and an old energetic man swatting very high flies with a long slim fungo bat to the outfielders. Already a big crowd had gathered. The plank bleachers behind the backstop screen were filled and the area between home plate and third, and home plate and first, was packed four deep, with still more ardent local fans arriving late. Cars full of baseball nuts were lined up beyond third and first.

For years there'd been bad blood between Amen and Bonnie on almost every count: dating, banking, business, religion, baseball. When on Saturday or Sunday nights the boys from Amen drove over to Bonnie to take out the Bonnie girls, fights, vicious ones, broke out. And vice versa. And the baseball game between the two towns often turned into brawls before the ninth inning, so that the umpires sometimes had to call the games in favor of one team or the other, 9 to 0. Once fisticuffs broke out so ferocious that the cornstable had to call out the fire department to cool off both the players and the fans. That night the dry cleaners had a lot of business.

Many times, because of their mutual hostility, the two teams provided lively paragraphs for the local newspapers. Once when Amen played at Bonnie, the Amen coach at first base pulled off a good one. He'd been taking some pretty mean razzing most of the game, and finally, in the heat, he took off his baseball cap to wipe the sweat off his forehead and exposed a dome that was completely bald. The Bonnie crowd erupted with laughter. Many choice epithets were thrown his way. A smile crept over his face and curled up his lips, and quite unabashed, swinging his cap low in a deep bow and pointing to his shining head, he said, "Ladies and gentlemen, the evidence of a misspent youth." The raucous laughter stopped for a moment, and then turned into admiration for his quip. And some Bonnie wit called out, "Pretty good there, Charlie. At least there's one good old sock in Amen who knows how to turn the other cheek."

On another occasion, when Bonnie was playing at Amen, Pete Haber suddenly stepped out of the batter's box and protested to the umpire that the Amen pitcher was throwing a drunk ball. Shrieks of derision broke out. The umpire waved his hands for quiet, then asked Pete what he meant. "A drunk ball?"

"Yeh," Pete said. "We all know the pitcher Fidgety Phipps is the town drunk. He always blows on the ball just before he throws it, and that makes for a drunk ball."

"Oh, come on."

"Just smell the ball once, ump."

The umpire smelled the ball. "Why, you fathead," he snapped. "It only smells of licorice."

"So that's what he's doctoring the ball with."

"Get in there and bat, you squirrelhead. You're lucky he ain't throwin' an emery ball."

"He's doin' something out there that ain't legal."

"Listen, you bright-eyed bushy-tailed farmer you, bat!"

Pete stepped into the batter's box, but then, thinking over what the umpire had just said, stepped out again. "Don't you call me bushy-tailed."

"Why not? Any time I see a guy with hair growing onto his ears, I think I can call him that."

"But you can't see my tail."

"Aha! Then you got a tail. Bat, or I'll call the game 9 to 0 in favor of Amen."

Sherm and the Bonnie Boys watched their rivals throw the ball around the infield. Sherm's eye fell on the first baseman. "Say," he said, nudging Garrett, "that's Art Cruellen from Hello out there."

"It sure as heck is. I wonder if they brought in any other ringers."

What about that old duffer along the left field line warming up with that kid?"

Garrett fixed sharp blue eyes on the gray-haired Amen player. "Stiffy, ain't that Smokey Joe Lotz?"

Stiffy had already spotted the fellow. "From Remsen. Looks like he's pitchin' tonight."

"Gollies," Garrett said. "He can be good some nights."

Sherm watched Smokey Joe too. "Look at how easy he's throwing. Sort of anty-anty-over."

Stiffy said, "That means he's still got a sore arm and has to warm up real slow before a game."

"Didn't he pitch for the St. Louis Cardinals once?"

Free had been listening. "Back in 1916. Lost three and won none. Was finally sent down because his shoulder kept acting up."

"See," Stiffy said.

Garrett said, "Well, we'll knock him out of the box the first thing."

Jimmy Wales showed up with a bandage wrapped around the palm of his catching hand. "Garrett, I don't think I should catch with this tonight."

"What happened?"

"I was cutting some salami and the knife slipped."

"Salami? Ha."

Jimmy couldn't look Garrett in the eye.

Sherm said, "So, Pussy, you had a fight with Florence Small. The one you said was like hosing a rainspout."

Jimmy flicked Sherm a black look. "Watch it. I don't want that nickname to get around. I wouldn't take kindly to being called Pussy during mass."

Garrett got out his lineup card. "You can catch a fly ball, though, can't you?"

"Sure."

"Tell you what we'll do. You and I'll switch positions. I'll catch and you play left field."

"Whatever you say."

"Think you can swing a bat?"

"I can at least bunt."

"That's good enough. Smokey Joe just might be slow enough afoot for you to get on if you lay one down."

After the Bonnie Boys had warmed up, the home team ran out on the dirt diamond. The Amen Tigers were a pretty good country team. They usually won most of their games by big scores. They had four good hitters of their own, and with Art Cruellen playing first for them, they could really rocket the ball.

Smokey Joe on the mound took several dozen warmup throws before he said he was ready. The Bonnie players started razzing Smokey Joe early, taunting him that he was throwing like an old washerwoman. Smokey Joe only smiled. Smokey Joe was a man of average height, but there was an air about him that he had been important somewhere. There was a classy style to his delivery. He threw sidearm, cross fire, and when he wound up it looked like he was going to throw towards home plate by way of third base. That kind of delivery caused many a batter, afraid of being hit, to step in the bucket just before he swung.

"Play ball!" the umpire at home plate cried. "Batteries for the Amen Tigers, Smokey Joe Lotz and Dubber Stob! For the Bonnie Boys, Free Alfredson and Garrett Engleking!"

The home crowd let out a roar of anticipation. There were so many fans from Amen that there was hardly room for the few Bonnie supporters who'd driven over. The Bonnie folk had to stand on the grass well beyond first base along the right field foul line.

Garrett shook his head at all the noise. "It's gonna be a roughty. We're gonna have trouble scoring from third."

"How come?" Free asked.

"That's right. You've never played here, Free. Well, no matter how often the umpire backs them up, these Amen fans actually lean over the third-base chalk line so you have trouble running past them trying to score. They'll spit on you. Curse you. They'll spill beer on you. Even once that I know of personally, they'll throw rotten eggs at you."

Sherm's chin stuck out. "We'll see about that."

"Now listen here," Garrett said. "We don't fight back. We smile. And take it. And hit the ball galley-west. It's the only way you'll shut 'em up."

Sherm looked over at where Free was warming up with Pete Haber. "Been wondering about him. He didn't look right that last inning against the Rats."

Garrett studied Free's motion too. "He'll be all right. He's young and strong. And today he's throwing against a good wind and his curve will jump all over the place."

"Doc Fairlamb told Free's dad he shouldn't let the boy do too much lifting too early. Long-geared guys like him don't get melded together like us shorter fellows do. Joints are soft and are slower to mature."

"He'll be all right." Garrett turned to the men sitting on his bench. He leaned forward so no one in the pushing crowd standing behind them could hear him. "Listen, whoever is coaching at first and third, give off a lot of signals as if they mean something. But in fact they'll mean nothing. I'm gonna let everybody make up his own mind what needs to be done. That'll muddle them up for at least half the game."

The first three innings nobody reached first. Both Smokey Joe and Free pitched no-hit ball. Smokey Joe's tricky deliveries and his perfect control made him hard to hit. Meanwhile Free's big outdrop and riding-high inshoot had the Tigers flailing air.

The crowd settled down, became silent at times, intent on watching a tight game of country baseball unfold.

The evening weather was perfect. Everybody took deep breaths, savoring mown grass and hay-scented air. The cool northeast wind felt good on the neck and bare forearms. The aromatic smell of summer-heated resin rising from the wooden bleachers was like a queen's perfume. The smack of a fast ball popping into the catcher's pud had the import of dreamy music. And the sound of hard ash wood striking taut horsehide became the lingering note of a prairie harp.

Just before it was the Bonnie Boys' turn at bat in the top of the fourth inning, Garrett again drew all heads together to give them some advice. "Listen. The trouble is, you guys are all trying to kill Smokey Joe's easy-looking pitches. Now this is what I want you to do. Shorten up on your bat and move up a foot in the batter's box. Then take a short quick poke at the ball. Nice smooth stroke. I want you all to go for singles. And you fast guys, you steal bases on that lazy windup of his. You hear?"

All heads nodded.

"All right then. Let's go knock him out of the box."

Frankie Wales, leadoff man, found one to his liking on the third pitch and lined it over the Amen shortstop's head. Wimp Tollman fouled off six pitches before he drew a walk. Sherm de-

214

cided to take Garrett's advice too and lashed a double just inside third base down the white left-field foul line, scoring Frankie and Wimp.

The Amen fans began to mutter. Several called for the Amen manager to change pitchers. The Bonnie fans beyond first base began to shout and wave their caps.

Free surprised Sherm. Free did shorten up on his bat, but he looked awkward striking out. It was obvious he was favoring his right shoulder. The boy was coming up with a sore arm.

Garrett ignored his own advice. He swung from his heels. He'd once been Bonnie's home-run hitter but this year still hadn't connected for one. Garrett seemed to have guessed right that Smokey Joe was going to finally throw a hard one with real smoke on it. Three innings had finally loosened Smokey up. Garrett caught the ball on the fattest part of his heavy bat and sent a screamer over the left-fielder's head. The winging ball kept rising for a dozen rods more and then slowly settled like a pheasant seeking cover in the far deep grass.

But when Sherm and then Garrett rounded third base and headed for home, they had to fight their way through a fanatic Amen crowd. The crazy nuts had burst across the white chalk line onto the diamond. Some tobacco juice landed in Sherm's right eye. A rotten tomato sploshed against his chest, almost obscuring the lettering on his uniform. Someone stuck out his foot and almost tripped Sherm. Sherm held his arm up over his face and like a halfback rammed his way through the swearing roaring melee and scored.

Garrett fared even worse. He not only was called every possible scurvy name a Siouxlander could think of, he was spat on, tripped, rotten-egged, kicked, and cursed down to the hottest part of hell itself. His long home run meant that the Amen Tigers would probably lose. Bonnie 4, Amen 0.

From then on it was a question if Free could hang onto the lead until the end of the game. He allowed two bingles in the bottom of the fourth but managed to strike out the side with his big outdrop. The outdrop seemed to be the one pitch he threw well. Against the brisk northeast wind he could start the curve out aiming it at the batter's head, and then have the ball swoop out and down and clip the low outside corner of the plate. The two singles were hit by Dubber Stob, the catcher, and Art Cruellen, the first baseman. Both reached out for the big curve and, though fooled by it, managed to catch the ball on the end of the bat and skim it over second baseman Frankie's outstretched glove.

In the bottom of the fifth the word on the Amen bench was, "Go after Free's first pitch." That first one was almost always a straight hard fast right down the pipe. Result: three pitches became three pop flies. Side retired.

The next inning Free had his problems. His control was suddenly off. He walked the first two batters on four pitches each.

Sherm called for the ball from Garrett, and then the two met with Free near the mound. Sherm said with a little laugh, "Well, my favorite uncle-sayer, I see you like to play with matches."

"What do you mean?"

"You just walked their two weakest hitters at the bottom of their batting order. And now you got their four best hitters coming up."

Free shrugged. Even in shrugging it could be seen his right shoulder was turning stiff.

Garrett said, "Listen, bud. We've got a four-to-nothing lead. They've got to catch up. So they're gonna take chances. The pressure is on them, not you. Just get the ball over and let 'em hit. Even if they're .300 hitters it means seven times out of ten they're gonna fail to get on base. Got it?"

Free nodded.

The Amen crowd began to chant. "Free the Freak is blowing up! Free the Freak is blowing up!"

Free turned red. "I'm no freak. I'm just big."

The Amen chant changed slightly. "Free the geek is starting to squeak."

Free growled. "You two guys get back to your positions. I'll show them."

Sherm gave Free a hearty clap on the butt. "Okay."

Free forgot the pain in his arm for the moment. Somehow. In the falling brown dusk he poured nine straight strikes over the plate, all of them fast jump balls. The three leadoff hitters didn't even get a foul off him. That shut up the Amen crowd for the moment.

In the bottom of the seventh, Amen finally did fashion a rally, which almost got out of hand. Two errors, both by Spider at first, two banjo singles, and two walks, produced three runs. And the bases still loaded.

The Amen crowd went wild. Right after Free had walked his second man, some wag with the voice of a braying donkey called out, "He's got 'em higher than that, boys! He's got 'em higher than that."

Garrett took off his mask and called time. He carried the ball out to Free. Sherm joined them. Garrett said, "You letting those muffs by Spider get to you?"

Free said, "There really should be two out by now. And only one run in."

Sherm placed a hand on Free's high shoulder. "We know. We know. The way Spider plays first is enough sometimes to break one's heart. And all because that sonofabitch thinks he's got to have his bottle of homebrew before a game to relax."

Garrett looked up at Free in a warm sweet way. "Remember when I worked for your dad?"

"Yeh?"

"How you and I once figured out how to get the hay rope back on the pulley with a sling full of hay hanging halfway up the new door?"

"I remember."

"Well, then let's get this rope back onto the pulley."

Sherm said, "You ain't maybe thinking to get into trouble on purpose so you can show off how good a pitcher you are?"

Free began to pace around, fighting mad.

Sherm said, "I heard on the sidelines a while ago there's a Chicago Cub scout in the crowd. And you know how much you and I want to play for the Cubs someday."

Free brightened up. "Really? You sure?"

Sherm nodded.

Free said, "Let me at 'em."

Sherm smiled. "Shoot it to 'em now, boy. Remember, we'd already won this game even before we started to play it. The Englekings never lose, you know, and you've got some Engleking blood in you."

As Free ascended the mound, the Amen manager coaching at first called out, "Let's keep the beans rolling now, boys! Let's knock that big geek out of there."

Sherm leaned in to see what Garrett was calling for. In the low slanting sunlight with its darker shadows it was hard to make out Garrett's fingers. Four of 'em showing? What? Knuckle ball?

And the fellow up a left-handed rinky-dink hitter? Used to hitting slop? Sherm thought of calling time to question Garrett's call. Sherm hitched up his shoulders once, twice; decided to let it go. He waited until Free started his windup and then shaded himself over near second base. The left-handed batter might just hit that slow ball through the box on the second base side.

Free threw a perfect knuckler. It hardly turned. It danced in.

The batter followed the pitch all the way and took a good swing at it, a short chopping whack. Sure enough, he hit a low liner past Free's feet toward the shortstop side of second base. Already leaning to his left by the time the batter swung, Sherm slid over smoothly and nailed the ball on the first bounce and caught the lead runner between himself and second base. The runner hesitated, not sure if he should dodge past Sherm or retreat back to second base. Before the runner could make up his mind, Sherm leaped at him, tagged him for the first out; then jumped on second base forcing the runner coming in from first; then threw a strike at Spider at first base. Spider leaned out with his big wide mitt. For that instant he looked like a broken wishbone. The ball smacked into the pocket of his mitt a split second before the batter's foot hit first base. Triple play. Bang-bang putouts.

There were shouts of glee and blaring car horns from the Bonnie section of the crowd. There were dismal groans from the Amen fans.

Sherm quick put on a face to show it was the usual kind of play for him.

In the top of the eighth Sherm got his third hit, a line single over short. But he was left stranded on first. Smokey Joe seemed to get better as the game went along. He'd finally got his old soupbone warmed up and was as loose as a goose. His sidearm fast one came knifing in better than ever and his big curve seemed to stop in midair in front of the plate as though he'd jerked it back with a rubber band. Except for that four-run fourth inning he had been masterful all evening.

In the bottom of the eighth, Free seemed to get his speed and his control back. Eight pitches and the side was retired. One strikeout. And two ground-huggers skipping across the skinned diamond out to Sherm.

Top of the ninth. Smokey Joe threw nine pitches and chalked up three strikeouts.

Garrett shook his head. "I was hoping we could add a couple of insurance runs in the ninth. But Old Smokey Joe is hotter than a depot stove out there."

Jimmy said, "That old son of a gun. He stares you down first, and then to make it even worse, just as he winds up, he sneers at you. Makes you want to take a baseball bat to him and hit him over the head."

Bottom of the ninth. Amen at bat. The fans clamored for a rally. And as luck would have it they almost got their wish. On his very first pitch, Free threw awkwardly again and hit the batter on the hip. One on. On his second pitch, a knuckler, the batter hit a wicked side-spinning grounder at Wimp. Wimp wiggled both hands once, twice, and fumbled the ball. Two on. Upset, Free walked the next batter on four pitches. Bases loaded. Nobody out.

Garrett took his mask off and called time. He walked out to the mound with a strangled look on his dust-begrimed sweaty face. "What in God's name is wrong with you?"

Free kicked at the dirt on one side of the mound.

"The first part of the game I almost needed a mattress to catch your fast ball. But now, heck, your Gramma could throw harder."

Sherm strolled up. He waggled his head at the revolting developing. "Well, Free, you're sure going out of your way to be the hero tonight. I suppose now you're gonna strike out the side." Sherm looked over to see who was up to bat next. "Their second, third and fourth batters too. The big guns in their batting order."

Free almost cried. "You can't imagine how sore my arm is. I can hardly grip the ball anymore it hurts so. If I'm not careful while Garrett's giving the signal, the ball'll drop out of my fingers."

"You ain't got three more outs in that arm?"

"I dunno."

Garrett stood thinking fiercely. "Well, we can't bring in Spider. That bully pitches okay when he's got a fat lead. But in a game as close as this one he'll blow sky high."

Free took off his glove and rubbed his right shoulder. "I think maybe I could still throw a pretty good submarine ball."

"Oh no," Garrett said. "No, not that. You sure you can't throw me a half-dozen more screwballs?"

"Inshoots? Maybe a couple more. Because now it's that outdrop that's wrecking my arm. To throw that one, I've got to hold my wrist and my elbow crooked when I snap my arm around. And that's hard on the elbow and hard on the shoulder here."

"Okay," Garrett said, "I'm gonna pretend that I'm calling for different pitches, but you and I will know, and Sherm here will know, you're gonna throw nothing but your inshoot. The way that pitch has been darting in on the batter I think we can still get 'em. Sherm, what do you think?"

Sherm considered the scheme. "Sounds good to me. All three batters coming up next are right-handers. That means I'll probably get the ball all three times."

The camaraderie of the three of them, Sherm, Garrett, and Free, seemed to revive Free. "Uncle, just like you say, I'm going to be that hero you want and strike out the side.

"Okay. It's all right to think that. But remember, you got seven fellows out in the field behind you who are just as anxious as you are to beat these devils."

Free nodded.

Garrett and Sherm ran back to their positions.

Garrett made the usual show of giving a hidden finger signal. Then he let fly with a cheery call. "All right, Free old boy, make 'em bite."

Sherm called from deep short. "Give him the one that goes up and down and then curlicues around."

The second man in the Amen batting order was their third baseman, Hi Faversham. He was the local blacksmith, a powerful man with huge forearms. He wiggled his bat like it might be but a long toothpick. He had unusually long arms for a man who was but five foot ten. When he swung the arc of his bat more than covered the width of the plate. He dug his spikes in deep and got set to slug the ball into the next county. He showed his white teeth in a devilish smile. He hadn't shaved that day and his black whiskers gave him the look that sometime during the day he might have wiped his face with a sooty hand.

Free wound up, rocked on his back foot, and, grunting mightily, fired. Sherm could see from his position that Free had really stuck that ball deep between his long finger and his ring finger. Wonderfully, the kid managed to get some smoke into it. The ball headed for the center of the plate letter high, then darted in towards Hi's neck. Hi swung, also grunting mightily. He caught the ball near the trademark on his bat and lifted a towering pop-up above Sherm.

"I got it!" Sherm cried.

"It's all yours, Sherm," Free called.

Jimmy came running in from left field and then slowed down when he saw that Sherm has his eye on the ball. The ball went up so high it caught the last full blast of light from the setting sun. "A tall can of corn, Sherm."

At last the ball came down. Sherm caught it easily, hardly moving in his tracks. The moment he caught it, he quick snapped looks around to make sure no runners would try to advance. The Amen crowd moaned. Then, pinching back a smile, Sherm brought the ball over to Free on the mound. He plopped the ball into Free's glove. "Well, it looks like you're only going to be able to strike out two this inning for that Cub scout to see."

Free couldn't help but grunt a short laugh. "I tell you, Unc, the way my belly feels I'll take a double play instead. And the heck with the Cub scout."

"Then your arm felt all right on that last pitch?"

"I forgot to think about it."

"Good boy. All we need is a couple more good pitches."

The next man up was the squat catcher, Dubber Stob. He had short thick arms and crowded the plate. Again Garrett put on a show of calling a certain pitch.

The Amen coach at third formed a trumpet around his mouth with his hands and yelled, "Okay, Dubber baby boy, let's plant the next one in Old Lady Kitchenmeester's potato patch!" The crowd took up the cry and repeated it. "In the potato patch! In the potato patch!"

Free looked all three runners back to their bases, wound up slowly, rocked once, twice, and let fly. And once more he threw the ball deep out of his hand between his long finger and his ring finger. The pitch headed for the outside part of the plate, belt-high; then squirted in toward's Dubber's chest. Dubber swung ferociously. And hit another towering pop-up. It was almost an exact duplicate of Hi Haversham's skyscraper.

"I got it!" Sherm yelled.

"It's all yours, Sherm," Free called.

Deep silence in the crowd. All runners ran back to their base. Then the ball descended, coming down faster and faster.

Sherm had to move back only three steps to catch it. Ball safely in his glove, he quick checked to make sure no runner thought of trying to advance a base.

Some Amen fans began to swear. "The lucky stiffs." "Bastards." "Godammit to hell anyway, why couldn't Dubber have straightened that one out?"

Sherm brought the ball to Free. He finally had a conquerer's smile for his pitching nephew. The boy was going to wiggle out of the pickle he was in. "Well, now all you can show that Cub scout is one strikeout in the bottom of the ninth. With the bases full."

Garrett called time and came running out. He was so excited he'd forgotten to take off his mask. With his ribbed chest protector on he looked like a knight with a jousting helmet pulled down over his face. "Free, you remember the next guy up, don't you?"

"You bet. Art Cruellen."

"He kills the big hook. Now, after I've called the pitch, I'm going to pretend that you're going to throw me that big hook. By shifting over to my right, behind the plate. That'll make one of his teammates warn him to look for number three. But don't you pay any attention to where I sit. You throw the ball, your inshoot, so that it'll wind up close to his throat. Okay?"

"Don't worry. I know exactly how to pitch to this bozo. I'm still disgusted with what he did to a nice girl in Hello. I was just a freshman at the Academy at the time and I've never forgot it. The dirty bastard."

Sherm ran back to his spot at shortstop and Garrett settled down on his heels behind home plate.

The Amen manager coaching at first base yelled, "Okay, Art, let's clean them bases!"

For once Free managed to glare at the batter as if he meant to skull him. Just as he wound up he made a motion with his right hand as if he were setting the ball in his fingers to throw the big outdrop; then at the last second, at the top of his windup, reset the ball deep between his long finger and his ring finger. With a tight grunt he let go. The ball headed letter high for the center of the plate; then, the last few feet, darted in. Cruellen swung. The ball rode in over the top of his big flashing swing.

Sherm called, "That a boy, Free. Now throw him another one of those fadeaways. He never saw the last one."

Cruellen stepped out for a moment; thought about what he'd just seen; then, a spidery squint forming around his eyes, stepped in again.

Again Free gave Cruellen the narrow eyes, daring him to swing at the next pitch. Free threw a riding inshoot that jumped up and in. And once more Cruellen with his big flittering swing missed it by at least half a foot.

Sherm was of half a mind to run in to remind Free they needed only one more strike to win; then decided against it. The boy at last seemed to have found his old-time rhythmic motion. Better not disturb him. At the same time a swift rising bubble of feeling spread in Sherm from his nose and eyes into his brain. He whispered to himself, as he rocked back and forth from one foot to the other getting set for the next play, "Ain't baseball wonderful. It's the most happy daring game in the world. So sweet and desperate."

Wimp at third finally let his farm voice be heard loud and true. "All right, Free, let's get him now! He swings like an old garden gate."

Cruellen tried to take a sidelong peek at Garrett below him to see where he was setting up behind the plate. Quite deliberately Garrett squatted over to the right behind the plate as if he were finally calling for Free's famed big outdrop.

The whole crowd, both the Amen and the Bonnie sections, fell into an echoless silence.

Sherm called once more. "Don't throw too hard now, boy. Don't overthrow. All we want is one more pitch out of your regular motion. Remember, the last of the ninth is the game."

Free didn't bother to nod. He knew what he was doing. He wound up pretending he was setting the ball in his hand for the falling slant and at the last second again reset it for the inshoot, grunting desperately as he threw. His last pitch was the fastest. The ball speared toward the plate, then curved in like the long bent blade of a scythe. Cruellen started to step forward to smash what he thought was going to be the falling outdrop, saw he'd made a mistake, tried to correct his stance as he swung, missed the ball by more than a foot. The ball rode high in over his hands. Strike three. Side retired. Bonnie 4. Amen 3.

Sherm threw his glove high in the air, then his gray baseball cap. The Bonnie players converged on Free yelling their heads off.

"Wow! Wow! Hurray for Bonnie! Ain't it something!"

"You tell 'em. We beat the great Smokey Joe Lotz! A major leaguer."

Some in the Bonnie contingent of fans almost fainted from the relief that their team had won.

Amen fans turned sullenly on their heels and headed home.

Sherm found Free in the melee. "You big lug you! Now for sure we're both going to the Cubs someday." Then Sherm pulled Free's face down and gave him a kiss.

Chapter Thirteen

It was after supper. The wall phone rang.

Garrett got up from his easy chair where he was reading the sports section of the *Sioux City Journal* and stepped into the kitchen. He lifted the black receiver from its nickel hook. "Hello?"

"This the manager of the Bonnie Boys?"

Garrett blinked at the two nickel bells above the black mouthpiece. "Sometimes."

"Ha. I know what you mean. This is Deacon Blake. Scout for the Chicago Cubs." Blake had the rough voice of someone who'd yelled a lot. "When you guys playing your next game?"

"This coming Friday evening. Why?"

"Where?"

"At Hello, Iowa. It's a grudge game."

"Where's the diamond there?"

"High school grounds. Why?"

"I hear you got a young pitcher with a good screwball."

"Yeh. I catch him sometimes."

"What time?"

"Six bells. Say, weren't you at the Amen game?"

"I thought of taking in that game, but the big boys in Chicago told me to go catch a Cowboy game here in Sioux City instead. So I missed your Amen game. Too bad. I wanted to do Smokey Joe a favor and watch him. He thinks he can still pitch in the majors."

"So that explains it. The Amen manager mentioned you might be there."

Blake's voice turned confidential. "By the way, do me a favor, will you?"

"Yeh?"

"Don't tell your kid pitcher I'll be there. I want him to pitch natural. I don't want him to throw with the bighead."

"Then you know he's only sixteen?"

"Only sixteen? I didn't know he was that young."

"Yeh. He's just a boy. And it could be we've let him throw too hard too early against grown men."

"You haven't let him ruin a good arm?"

"Well, he wound up pretty good the other night." Garrett reset the black receiver on his right ear. "By the way, there's another fellow you ought to have a good look at."

"Who's that?"

"Our shortstop. He's the best I've ever seen. He can play for your Cubs right now. He covers the field like a blanket."

"I'll look him over too."

Chapter Fourteen

In their pregame warmup at Hello, Sherm spotted something. Spider at first, Frankie at second, and Stiffy in right field made some sloppy throws and then stood around and laughed about it.

When they all ran in to their bench between third and home, Sherm asked Frankie, as casually as he could, "You and Spider out on a toot last night?"

"Nope." When Frankie smiled darkly handsome and turned evasive he looked like the very devil himself.

Sherm took a step closer to Frankie in a buddy way. Sure enough. Frankie stunk of homebrew beer. Homebrew beer on a person's breath always smelled like sour swill. "Okay. But just don't you guys on the right side of the diamond boot too many balls tonight. This is a grudge game for Ted Herman and his boys, and they're going to do everything they can to wallop us."

"Then you better give Stiffy hell too. We rode over with him here."

"Then you had some homebrew in his car?"

"What of it? Spider and I worked like dogs pitching bundles for Homer Fox. And you know Homer makes the best homebrew around."

"And Stiffy?"

"We had a little left for him when he picked us up."

Sherm's thin lips became slits. "Too bad we don't have three good subs."

"Or that you ain't the manager."

"Yeh." Sherm slowly shook his head.

Then he went over to where Free was warming up. "Well, highpockets, how's the old arm tonight?"

Free said, "So far so good. But I tell you something. Pitching bundles doesn't go good with pitching baseballs."

"Well, that's how it is playing baseball in the country."

"I should've probably had me a bottle of homebrew first before I caught my ride with Garrett. Since my dad makes the best homebrew around. No settlings."

"Heaven forfend!" Sherm exclaimed.

Free had to laugh. "Forfend? Uncle. And here you're the one who's always after me for using swear words."

Sherm said, "You want to remember I read Shakespeare too when I was a freshman at my academy. 'Now heaven forfend . . . the holy maid with child?'"

"Oh, Uncle Sherm, I don't know that much about girls yet."

"Good thing too. As well as not drinking. Listen. I just found out that Frankie and Spider and Stiffy had some of Homer Fox's homebrew before they drove over. And you know how potent Homer's brew is. It's practically whiskey the way he makes it."

"O-ee."

"That's why they been dropping balls out there during practice. Those pikers."

"Too bad we can't kick 'em off the team."

"That's what I say. Listen. What we gotta do tonight is make sure that nobody hits the ball to that side of the diamond. Keep the ball outside to left-hand hitters and inside on right-hand hitters. Make everybody hit the ball to Wimp and me. And to Garrett out in left field."

"I'll try to remember."

"Not just try it. Do it!"

"Uncle, warming up here, I notice I'm not all that accurate tonight. Though I'm throwing just about as hard as ever."

Sherm winced. Not accurate? Then the kid had hurt his arm. "Lord," he whispered, "now we've got to have luck."

Garrett came walking up. "I see they're not pitching Lefty Groten tonight. Which is too bad. Left-handers are socialists and how I love to crush them."

"So I noticed. Ain't that Rich Grower warming up?"

"Yeh. He pitched for Des Moines too in the Western League."

Sherm told Garrett then that Frankie, Spider, and Stiffy had each had a bottle of homebrew before they drove over. "I told Free to pitch in such a way that all balls get hit to either me or Wimp. Or to you out in left field."

"Shucks." A private thought wrinkled up the surface of Garrett's face. "And I so want to beat Herman and his bench."

Sherm pawed the ground with his spiked shoes. He turned to Free. "Listen, I know your arm bothered you a little at Amen the other night. Otherwise I'd tell you to strike everybody out. So what you better do is like I told you, pitch outside to the left-handers and inside to the right-handers. Let 'em hit in the early innings. Save your smoke for the eighth and ninth. Okay?"

Free nodded.

It was shock thrashing time and not many Bonnie fans drove over for the game.

But the red-faced Hello fans came out like an army of mad ants. Some six lines of the stretched out from behind the Hello bench all the way out to the trees along a sidewalk. Other Hello fans behind them sat on the hoods of their cars.

There was no wind. The sun shone down over a line of young cottonwoods on the west side of the diamond in a broad throw of warm light. It was a great evening for a game.

Thinking to throw the Hellow Homebrews off their feed a little, Sherm walked over to where Herman was standing in front of his team seated on their bench. "Ted, it's no use. All the coaching in the world ain't gonna help you much. I know you like a deadright straightforward man, so I'm telling you that you birds might just as well forfeit the game because we've already won."

Ted's dark brows lifted up his forehead a little, giving him the look of an owl that didn't like being interrupted by a hawk. "You don't even want us to get in a little batting practice?"

"If our pitcher strikes everybody out, that ain't gonna be much of a batting practice for you."

"What if Rich Grower throws a no-hitter? What are you gonna do for runs?"

"What? When I've made up my mind to hit at least one home run off him?"

"Five bucks says you don't."

"I don't bet with a Homebrew player." Sherm thought it not a little funny that the Hello players should be called Homebrews when three of his own Bonnie players were tipsy with homebrew. Sherm gave Herman and his bunch the circle of victory with his thumb and long finger, and then walked back to his own bench.

The two umpires Herman had hired were from Le Mars. They stepped up to the home plate while a grounds keeper quickly repaired the white-chalked foul lines where the pregame rituals had disturbed them. The leaner man with the sardonic swarthy face was Dr. Roger Maris and the burly man was Stub Adams, one-time great catcher for the Le Mars nine. Plate umpire Maris picked up a red trumpet and announced in a crackling authoritarian voice: "Battery for Bonnie, Alfredson and Wales! Battery for Hello, Grower and Jurgens! Play ball!"

The game began quietly. Grower had a good outdrop and had everyone in the Bonnie lineup swinging futilely at it. He struck out seven of the first nine batters. Free, throwing a lot of slop stuff, discovered he had good control of it. The Hello batters had been instructed by Herman to go after Free's first pitch, and except for a few fouls, they all hit grounders to either Sherm at short or Wimp at third. In three innings Free made only twelve pitches without allowing a hit.

In the top of the fourth, Sherm came up with two out. Sherm had been carefully studying Grower's pitches, and had finally made out that Grower wasn't sure of his control when he threw the hummer and so quite deliberately set his right foot an inch over to aim it the better. Sherm watched for the inch overset of Grower's right foot and, with the count one and one, spotted it on Grower's third pitch. Sherm swung easily and caught the ball square and sent it drilling out over the shortstop Sweep's head for a double.

Standing on second, catching his breath, Sherm watched to see how Free, up next, would go after Grower's pitches. He wasn't too surprised to see Free stand deep in the batter's box, deeper even than the famed Rogers Hornsby stood in it, and as far back as possible. But Sherm was afraid Free would be duck soup for Grower's big outdrop. Sherm waved his hands to get Free's attention and get him to stand closer. Free didn't see him.

Grower wound up and fired a fast ball. It missed the inside of the plate. Ball one. Again Grower threw a fast ball, almost at Free's chin. Ball two. The third time Grower wound up, Sherm saw him set the ball in his hand for the outdrop. Oh boy. But to Sherm's delight, as Grower came around with his arm, Free rode up on his right foot, then pointing his left foot strode toward second. Around came Free's long slim bat and caught the ball a foot above the outside corner of the plate and larruped a scorcher over the second baseman's head. A gen-u-wine Rogers Hornsby swing like Sherm had told Free before to take. The bounding ball headed for the gap in right field.

"That's the way to kiss that onion," Sherm shouted. And then Sherm took off and scored easily while Free pulled up safely at second base.

Grower stood behind the mound a few seconds, fumbling with the rosin bag, thinking over what had just happened. Two doubles in a row? Were the Bonnie Boys stealing signs somehow? Grower had a heavy square Frisian face and it could be seen he was biting his teeth tight to keep from cursing. Then, deep chin set out, he climbed the mound again and proceeded to strike out Garrett on three blazing fast balls, stranding Free on second. Bonnie 1, Hello 0.

The roof caved in on the Bonnie Boys in the bottom of the fourth. The first Hello man up hit a grass cutter past Wimp. Sherm darted to his right, made a spectacular stop with his bare right hand, stopped and set his right foot, then drilled a perfect throw across the infield to Spider at first. The throw had the runner beat by at least two steps. But Spider dropped the ball. Runner safe.

Sherm couldn't believe it. Sherm charged across the diamond past where Free was standing with a disgusted look on his face, and stopped a dozen yards in front of Spider. "What the hell, Spider! You got butterfingers or something? That ball was right in your gut."

Spider picked up the ball and tossed it to Free. He turned red. "Sun got in my eyes."

"Bull-shite! You're drunk."

"I'm dead sober."

"The sun ain't setting that far in the northwest."

"You wanna make something of it?"

The Hello team began to taunt Sherm and Spider. "The Bonnie Boys have lost their luck!" The Hello crowd joined in. "The Bonnie Boys play like old maids."

Garrett came hustling in from left field. "Hey, hey, you two. Remember where you are. And that you're playing baseball, not cops and robbers. Everybody makes an error now and then."

Sherm whirled around. "You don't drop a ball that's right smack in your glove." Then Sherm lowered his voice. "That's what we get when we let those boneheads drink homebrew before the game."

Garrett took Sherm by the arm and headed him back to his

position. "Let's not fight in front of the enemy. We'll get the next one in a double play."

"You hope." Sherm sneered at the ground. "I never did care much for Spider. Got all the tools to be a great player, but he pisses it away with his carelessness."

"Now now."

"Besides, I've never liked the way the eyelashes of both his eyes are slanted off to the left."

"Oh for goshsakes, Sherm, that's only maybe because he sleeps on his right side and the pillow keeps pushing them over all night long."

"It still makes him look shifty. Which is what he is."

The next man up hit a slow ground hugger to Wimp. Wimp ran in and snapped it up easily and whipped another strike to Spider. And, Spider dropped that one too. Two men on, first and second.

The Hello bench started up another yell. "The pitching poet is blowing up! Blowing up!"

Sherm gave Spider an awful face. "For godsakes, Spider, you don't have to go dropping 'em on purpose now."

Free turned to Sherm. "It's all right."

"No, it ain't all right. You better start throwing hard, instead of all that slop. You're gonna have to strike 'em all out if we're gonna win."

Gorselman the slugger was next up and Free threw him two hard inshoots. Free threw the second one harder than the first and the ball went in so fast its four seams didn't have time to catch at the air and move in. Gorselman came around late on it but caught it solid, a line drive straight at Stiffy in right field. Stiffy didn't have to move a step. The ball speared in directly at his belly and all he had to do was hold up his glove. But he dropped it, and the ball rolled behind him a dozen feet. Both runners scored and Gorselman wound up at second. Sherm was waiting at second when Stiffy finally threw the ball in.

Sherm glared out at Stiffy, and after a moment Stiffy looked away and scuffed at the grass with his spikes. Sherm carried the ball over to Free. "Arm okay?"

Free rolled his right shoulder around. "I think so."

"That sounds like it ain't. Well, at least try to strike out the next three guys so we get out of this inning only one run behind."

After a look at second, Free whipped in a darting inshoot. Jabber Jurgens with his short stout arms took a quick chopping swing at it and, lucky for him, caught it just right and lined a single out to Garrett. Gorselman, puffing, tongue out, rounded third and scored.

Cruellen got ready to bat next. He first waggled three bats around to make one bat seem lighter; then, discarding two of the bats, stepped in. There was a look on his face that he was out to get revenge for having struck out at Amen with the bases full.

As Free took the sign from Jimmy, Sherm saw that Cruellen had changed his batting stance. Cruellen had shortened up his grip on the bat and stood partly facing Free. Aha. That meant Cruellen was going to go after Free's inshoot with a short punching stroke like Jabber had. Sherm was about to yell a warning to Free, when he saw Jimmy looking up through his mask at Cruellen and then signal for an outdrop. Hey. All right. Good strategy. That Jimmy was one smart cookie.

Free didn't have a very good pick-off move to first but still threw over to Spider several times to keep Jabber from taking too much of a lead off first. Finally Free set the ball deep in his hand, and snapped off the biggest outdrop Sherm had ever seen him throw. Cruellen, set to go after the inshoot, was stunned to see the ball drop off the table on him. He missed it a good two feet. Cruellen, snarling to himself, stepped out of the batter's box to think over what had happened. Manager Herman called something to him from the Hello bench, and after a moment Cruellen nodded, and stepped in again.

Jimmy next called for a knuckle ball.

Cruellen was all set to go after the outdrop, saw that he was fooled, stopped his swing; then, starting over, managed to whack a low liner precisely in between Frankie and Spider at first. Both Frankie and Spider were slow in reacting to it. The ball rolled out past Stiffy. And Stiffy, to Sherm's horror, fell down face-first in the grass; then picked himself up and ran irregularly after the ball. By the time Stiffy retrieved it, Cruellen had circled the bases and scored. Home run. Hello 5, Bonnie 1. The hometown crowd roared, and jumped up and down, and waved their caps and hats, and yelled in happy derision at the hated enemy. "You've got 'em on the run now, boys! Let's bury 'em."

When the ball finally came back to the infield, Sherm ran over to catch it. Once more he glared out at Stiffy, and then at Frankie and Spider; and then, shoulders sagging, carried the ball to Free.

"Goddammit," Free cursed. "This is awful. It's as bad as that first game we had with them, when Pete Haber made all those bonehead plays at third."

Sherm said, "Easy does it with the swearing. Though I don't blame you. Actually, this is worse than when Pete made all those errors. Those three drunks with their dropsy."

"Or a bad case of fumblitis."

"It's almost enough to make a guy laugh in the face of hell the way Stiffy fell down. Then when he got up it was like he had his feet stuck in molasses."

"My arm is going out, Sherm."

"Wait. Just remember that first game with this bunch. How we came from behind and beat 'em twelve to eleven."

"What helped then was that we had the home crowd to cheer us on. And then Wimp finally came. But who've we got to replace those three drunks?"

"Yeh."

Free picked up the rosin bag and fluffed it over his pitching hand. "Goddammit."

Garrett came running in. He too was disgusted. But he didn't glare at the three culprits. "Look. Let's look at the bright side. What's five runs? We can still get 'em."

Sherm picked up a small pebble and threw it far over the row of young cottonwoods. "I suppose we can try."

"You tell 'em, sport," Garrett said. "Free, let's go after them now. Because you don't know how I hate to lose to Ted Herman. He's got one of the meanest stick-it-into-you tongues in creation." Then Garrett called Jimmy out to the mound. "Jimmy, I'm a little worried about Free's arm. So call for his sidearm hook. And now and then mix in his dancer. Throwing sidearm is almost submarine and that'll be easier on his arm."

Jimmy nodded. "I'd been wondering if I shouldn't do that." Jimmy smiled up at Free. "Long-gears here ain't got his usual stuff tonight."

Free narrowed his reddish blond brows at Jimmy. "Not even when I threw those couple hard ones?"

"Well, truth to tell you, Free, your ball ain't moving much tonight. Except when you throw the big drop."

Sherm asked, "Say, Free, you making sure you're getting the right spin on the ball? Like you used to do practising against the chicken coop with a tennis ball? Making the spin level like the

234

earth turns? Or like a top might spin? Instead of having it screw in nose-first?"

Free pushed out his lower lip. "That might be it. I'll make sure about that."

Garrett said, "But I want you to throw mostly submarine now. Your arm is too valuable to lose for just one game. Even if I do hate Ted Herman, that ain't enough of a reason."

Free nodded.

Sherm called over to Spider and Frankie, loud enough for Stiffy to hear too. "No more muffs now, you birds." Then Sherm walked back to his position.

Garrett and Jimmy also trotted back to their positions.

Free's new way of throwing puzzled the next three batters, and he struck them out on a dozen pitches. He also struck out four more in the next two innings. At the end of the sixth the score still stood at five to one in favor of Hello.

Top of the seventh. Sherm went after Grower's first pitch, a fast ball inside, and swinging close to his chest smacked the ball past Sweep's glove at deep short for a single. That brought up Free. Grower wasted two pitches throwing at Free's wrists to make sure Free wouldn't go looking for the big outdrop. But Free wasn't scared off. He caught Grower's third pitch, an outdrop thrown a little too high, and whacked it over the second baseman's head for another single. Sherm made third easily. The Bonnie bench and the small Bonnie crowd cheered lustily. "Now we got 'em on the run. Grower's blowing up!"

But Grower had pitched too long in the Western League to be flustered by a couple of hits. He backed off the mound, picked up the rosin bag and dusted his pitching hand, then coolly climbed the mound again and quite methodically struck out Garrett and Jimmie and Spider with nine blazing fast balls. Then it was the Hello crowd's turn to roar triumphantly. Score still stood, Hello 5, Bonnie 1.

Bottom of the seventh inning. The Homebrews finally solved Free's new delivery. They shortened up on their bats and swung for singles. Cecil Sweep started it off with a single to left. Meylink, the second baseman, whacked a liner past Wimp for a double. Gorselman stunned the Bonnie infield by bunting safely down the third base line, scoring Sweep, with Meylink going to third. Hello 6, Bonnie 1.

Sherm called time and ran in on the mound. Jimmy took off his mask and came up too. Sherm wrinkled his eyes shut. He shook his head at Free. "Those last couple of pitches . . . are you losing it submarine style too?"

Free gave him a very troubled look. "My arm is so sore I can hardly lift it." Free tried to show them, and with pain showing in his face couldn't quite raise his arm shoulder high.

"Goddammit," Sherm whispered. He looked at Jimmy. "Well?"

Jimmy's sly dark eyes looked left, looked right. He desperately wanted to beat the Homebrews too. "Actually, they've been lucky. Free's arm may be hurting, but underhanded he's still got good stuff left. He'd got good spin on in and the spin is coming in direct."

Sherm took several deep breaths. What to do, what to do. He wanted Free to have a chance at playing for the Cubs someday too. But oh how he hated to lose to that smartass Ted Herman. Sherm reached up and placed his hand on Free's shoulder. "Tell you what. Throw a couple of underhanded inshoots right at the next couple of batters. Make 'em worry a little up there."

Free shrugged his sore shoulder out from under Sherm's hand. "But I don't believe in trying to bean the batter. Walter Johnson the Big Train didn't either. It's not the Christian way."

"I know. I know." Sherm walked completely around the mound once. "Well, try your best. Just keep the ball in tight on the right-handers and away from the left-handers."

Free tried. He got Dubber to pop up to Sherm down the left field line. Free fisted Cruellen just enough to make him hit a dribbler up the middle. Sherm gobbled it up on the run and shot him down at first with a great throw. But on the play Meylink scored from third and Gorselman went to second. Hello 7, Bonnie 1.

Art Cager, the enemy right fielder, batting left-handed, hit a smash straight at Spider. Spider, slow to get his glove up, had the ball hit him in the gut. The ball rolled off a couple of feet. Cager crossed first safely, Gorselman scoring from second. Hello 8, Bonnie 1.

Third baseman Moss, a slender quick man, was up next. Free's arm finally hurt so much he lost all control. He grooved an inshoot down the middle. Moss caught it solid on the fat of his bat and hit it a ton. Even so it should have been caught. It went head high at Frankie, who had only to step off to his right. Frankie

236

reacted slow, and when he did reach out, it was too late. He'd come to a little like a sleepwalker. The streaking ball skipped out between Sleepy DeBoer and Stiffy and rolled into right-center all the way to the base of the high school building for a triple, Cager scoring all the way from first. Hello 9, Bonnie 1.

Garrett came hurrying in. "That's enough, Free."

Free stood with his right arm hanging like a broken wing. "That's all right with me. Boy, does my arm hurt."

Sherm could taste bile. For once he didn't join the powwow on the mound.

Jimmy took off his mask and came dragging over.

Garrett called Spider from first. Garrett asked for the ball from Free and placed it in Spider's big first baseman's mitt. "Well, Spider, here's your chance to shine."

Spider muttered, "Yeh, after the game is already lost."

"Just the same, I don't want Free to throw anymore. If it ain't already too late. Free, you take over first. We need your stick batting. That's why I bat you fifth." Garrett turned to Jimmy. "That okay with you?"

"If you say so."

"Listen. Cheer up. We still got two innings to get to Grower. Like we did against Groten in our first game with them."

"You hope."

"That's no way to talk. We'll catch up with Grower."

Grudgingly Jimmy told Spider what the signals were. "Just get the ball over. Don't show off. And don't let the runner catch you napping and steal home on you."

Spider nodded. "Let me at 'em."

When Free went over to first to take up his position he looked awkward. He kept moving around not sure where he should stand.

Garrett and Jimmy went back to their positions.

To everyone's surprise, weak-hitting Grower went after Spider's first pitch and hit a rising lick toward right field. Free jumped to catch it; saw he'd jumped too soon; jumped a second time and miraculously nabbed the ball in the tip of his glove at the end of his long left arm. Side retired.

Sherm made it a point not to sit with his teammates on the Bonnie bench, but stood off to the side.

Bonnie did manage a couple of hits in their half of the inning. After two were out, Spider and Stiffy each hit singles. Spider stood on second base preening proud and Stiffy on first managed a wriggly smile. Grower next walked Sleepy DeBoer, filling the bases. Then, quite calmly, Grower got Frankie to hit a weak comebacker to the mound.

In the bottom of the eighth Spider actually did pretty well with his strange spearing lefty slants. He struck out Sweep; got Meylink to hit a groundhugger in the hole behind Wimp which Sherm ate up; and, of all things, struck out Gorselman on three sharp-breaking curves inside. Spider couldn't resist beating his chest in monkey triumph.

Top of the ninth and Bonnie's last turn at bat. Sherm found himself seething mad at the disgrace of losing, all because of three half-drunk boys. He paced up and down behind the Bonnie bench. Then, just as Wimp, first up, was about to bat, Sherm stepped around in front of the Bonnie bench and said to Garrett, "I'm sick of your pussyfooting around, defending our three bung-eyed boys. I'm up next and after I hit a home run, I'm quitting. I'm not ever going to play for Bonnie again."

Hey hey," Garrett exclaimed. "Not so fast. Take it easy. After all, you and I sometimes have a bottle of homebrew ourselves. And that despite the sermon our preacher preached against it."

"But not before a game we don't. These guys"—Sherm pointed at Frankie, Spider, and Stiffy sitting in front of him—"had suds coming out of their ears when we started the game. And that's no good."

Garrett stood up. "Oh, don't be such a knocker."

Sherm turned to Free. "What do you say? You game to quit too after you've hit a home run your final time at bat? Just to show these drunks how much we wanted to win!"

"Sure. You know how my ma is death on drinking."

Garrett placed a hand on Sherm's shoulder. "Wait. Not so fast. What you don't know is that I had a call from a scout for the Chicago Cubs the other evening. He's right here in the crowd tonight watching both you and Free."

"What? A Cub scout has been watching Free and me play? With the way you bunch of dubbers played tonight? God! There goes our chance forever."

Garrett shook Sherm's shoulder. "Really. Take it easy. Let's first wait to see what that Cub scout says after the game. I'll introduce you to him."

"The way these guys flubbed the ball behind Free? Letting that poor kid throw his heart out?" Sherm leaned his nose within an inch of Spider's nose. "Do you realize you may have ruined Free's arm for the rest of his life? So he'll never have a chance to go to the majors?"

Spider had a lot of stud in him. "Him to the majors? That overgrown camel? Never."

"You clumsy calf yourself. You just never got used to drinking out of a pail, but had to go on sucking titty by way of the bottle." Sherm then went nose to nose with Garrett. "My mind is absolutely made up. I'm gonna hit a home run my last turn at bat for Bonnie. Then I'm done forever. Got it?"

Garrett turned white. He loved Sherm. "Please."

"Cousin, don't give me any of our family's smoochies."

Garrett finally got mad then too. "You know, I'm gonna have to take one of those bull-leaders I got in my store and hook it in your nose to control you."

Wimp first up in the top of the ninth hit the first pitch for a line drive single to the left.

Sherm up next counseled himself to get control of his anger. And instead use that anger to mash the ball. As Grower stepped on the mound and started his windup, Sherm watched him narrowly to see how he set his right foot. Sure enough, there it was. Grower set his foot an inch over towards first. It was going to be a fast ball. Sherm gripped his bat tightly and swung. He caught the ball on the thickest part of his bat. Like the quick flickering of three pictures shown rapidly after each other, he saw the ball strike his bat, saw the ball stop, saw the ball streak out. The ball had instant loft, soaring over the shortstop's head. He'd hit the ball so hard it seemed to suck air as it left the playing field. It rose high over Gorselman's head in left field, climbing, catching the late sunlight and turning from dirty light brown to tan, leveling off and clearing the first row of trees, then the next row of trees, then, descending, landing on the roof of Professor Brooks' white cottage.

As Sherm circled the bases and crossed home plate behind Wimp, he smiled sourly to himself. "That'll show everybody."

Sherm went over and leaned against the west end of the backstop. He watched Free step into the batter's box. He called out, "Okay, Free, my boy, now it's your turn to hit one."

Free stood deep and back in the box, waggling his long slim Travis Jackson bat.

Sherm was of half a mind to call time and tell Free what he'd spotted in the way Grower set his right foot; finally decided against it. Free had been hitting Grower pretty good as it was.

Grower set his right foot a certain way on the mound and Sherm instantly spotted it was going to be an outdrop, not a fast ball. Sherm whispered, "Free, watch it."

But as the pitch bent down over the plate low and outside, Free strode toward the second baseman and, arms extended, caught the ball just right. He swung with such speed that for a fleeting second it seemed the bat bent back like a willow switch. Sherm was standing in exactly the right spot to see the ball go. It zigzagged back and forth it was in such a hurry to climb. It rose and rose; and then to Sherm's astonishment it soared over the southeast corner of the high school roof, and then finally landed in auctioneer Meylink's houseyard.

Sherm jumped. Free'd done it too. "A box of Wheaties to that man!" Sherm shouted, aping an advertisement for a breakfast cereal he'd often heard over radio station WCCO in Minneapolis.

Free circled the bases with a serious face.

Grower watched him go, slowly turning on the mound as he did so, chin setting out.

There were no cheers from the Bonnie bench when Free joined Sherm near the end of the backdrop.

Grower was upset and showed it on his next two pitches to Garrett, missing the plate by a wide margin.

Manager Herman called from the Homebrew bench. "Don't give him a free ticket to first now, Rich. Remember what those birds did to us in Bonnie."

Grower did settle down. He struck out Garrett on three consecutive outdrops. Then he struck out Jimmy on three fast balls and made Spider pop up to third baseman Moss. Final score: Hello 9, Bonnie 4.

Game over, Grower came marching directly toward Sherm and Free. "Say, you guys. I've got to know something. You two hit me like you owned me tonight. What the hell's going on? Am I giving away my pitches?"

Sherm gave Grower a poker face. "No, Rich. It's just that we're both such good hitters."

"C'mon. You hit those pitches like you knew what was coming."

Sherm liked Grower and allowed himself a little smile. "I don't know what Free'd spotted in your delivery, but this is what I noticed. When you're going to throw your fast ball, you set your right foot an inch farther over towards first base than when you throw your big hook."

"I'll be damned." Grower's broad Frisian face opened as he suddenly understood something. "So that's why they started hitting me so hard in the Western League. Damn." Grower next turned to Free. "And how did you know when I was going to throw the outdrop? Because every hit you got off me was off that pitch."

Free pawed the sandy ground. "Well, I wasn't going to tell anybody. Not even you, Uncle Sherm. Because the minute a fella does, it ain't long before it gets back to the pitcher and then he makes adjustments. But . . . well . . . Mr. Grower, when you throw your outdrop, you set the ball so deep in your hand, your thumb sticks out a little. And as you come around with your overhand pitch, that thumb sticks out like a little rabbit ear. Against the horizon."

"I'll be a sonofabitch. That's just what I do. God, kid, you must have fast eyes."

"It's just that I noticed it. So I went after the outdrop instead of the fast ball. You see, I'm still a little slow coming around on smoke. I tend to hit the fast ball to right field a lot."

Sherm finally had to laugh. "You sneaky son of a gun, Free. Well, I'm glad to learn you're busy thinking when you play the game."

A voice behind Sherm broke in. "Baseball is a thinking man's game."

Sherm turned around.

A handsome fellow with a small potbelly stood smiling beside Garrett. He was dressed in a light gray suit and a red tie. He wore his gray felt hat tipped back, exposing a balding forehead.

Sherm said, "Do we know each other?"

"I'm Deacon Blake. I'm a scout for the Chicago Cubs. I called your manager the other night." Blake spoke in a raspy voice. "I asked him when Bonnie would play its next game. I'd heard Bonnie had a young pitcher with a good curve."

"Oh, yeh. Garrett mentioned you were here."

Garrett didn't say anything. He hardly smiled.

Blake went on. "Then your manager told me about you, Sherman. That you could hit and throw, could cover the field like a big blanket." Blake shook his head, smiling. "And I'll say that for you—you sure can do all three."

"Thanks."

"Have you ever thought of trying out for the majors? I think the Cubs might be interested."

"Thought about it? Ha." Sherm placed a hand on Free's high shoulder and shook it. "My buddy here and me have talked about nothing else but play for the Cubs."

"Really. Then maybe the Cubs could be in luck. You may not know this, but I heard that Old Man Wrigley is going to deal for Rogers Hornsby from the Boston Braves to play second. And they're thinking of moving Woody English from short to third. Woody they figure is better at third than at short. So they told all us scouts to be on the lookout for a shortstop. We're even scouting other major league teams with whom the Cubs might make a trade."

"The Cubs get Hornsby?" Sherm turned to Free. "Did you hear that? Our hero is going to the Cubs and I can play next to him. And he can teach you even more to hit like him."

Deacon Blake laughed.

Sherm said, "How do we go about this?"

Blake said, "I'll call the front office in Chicago about you. And they'll soon send you an invitation to join the rest of the Cubs on Catalina Island next March for spring training."

Sherm shivered he was so happy. "Free here too?"

Blake made a face, drawing the corners of his lips back into his cheeks. "Well, about Alfredson here. . . . " He paused. "You hurt your arm, didn't you?"

"It hurts now."

"Well, I tell you. The first couple innings I saw you throw a couple of good fast balls. And you've got a good hook. And your screwball is major league."

Sherm said, "That's what Swede Risberg told him."

Blake's eyes opened. "You pitched against him, son?"

"Yeh," Free said. "When we played Hazard this summer, he turned out to be their ringer from Sioux Falls."

"How'd you do against him?"

Free turned to Sherm. "You tell him."

Sherm said, "He struck out Risberg three straight times. And he had two strikes on him the fourth time up, when our stubborn catcher for that game decided to finish Risberg off with Free's big hook. Well, Risberg hit a homer off it. Free was mad. He wanted to pitch the inshoot again. But I guess he had too much respect for his elders. When he knew better."

"Good for you, son." Blake pushed out his lips in thought. "I tell you, Alfredson, you're a little young to be pitching against grown men. All the more so in the majors. Let me give you some advice. Next year, don't pitch a single inning. Play first base. You're a good hitter. And rest your arm for a whole year. Then when you're eighteen, I'll look you up again."

Free nodded. "Okay."

Grower tried out a smile on Blake. "Any chance the Cubs'll invite me out next spring?"

Blake gave Grower a slow look. "You had your chance. You don't have as much on the ball as you used to have with Des Moines."

"That's what I was afraid of. But you're right about Engleking here. He's the best at short I've ever seen." Then, shaking his head, he went to join his comrades celebrate their victory over Bonnie.

Blake turned to Garrett. "When's your next game? I want to see Sherman play one more time before I send in a report on him."

Garrett said shortly, "This was our last game of the season."

"Damn." Blake blinked to himself. He again turned to Sherm. "Tell you what. I think I will scout Smokey Joe Lotz one more time. See if he's got the stuff to be a reliever. He's pitching for Rutherland against Le Mars a week from this coming Sunday. Just before I drove up here from Sioux City, I heard Le Mars lost their shortstop in a car accident. I'll ask the Le Mars manager if he'd consider playing you. How about it?"

"Play on Sunday?"

"Yeh. You have trouble with that?"

"It's really against my religion. We're not supposed to have fun on Sunday."

"Sunday is our best day in the majors, you know. That's when we get our biggest crowds."

"I'd have to think about it."

"Can I call you about it, though? I'll have a talk with the Le Mars manager yet tonight on the way back to my hotel room in Sioux City."

"Yeh, you can call me. The bells on my brother John's telephone are beginning to sound a little tinny, but I guess the long distance operator can raise one more bingle out of them."

Blake laughed. "I'll be on the line for you then."

Chapter Fifteen

On the way home from the Hello game, Sherm had a talk with Allie about playing for Le Mars on Sunday.

Allie didn't have much to say. She loved him and anything he wanted to do was okeydokey with her.

"If I do go, Allie, would you care to come along with me?" Sherm kept a steady toe on the footfeed of his old Ford.

"What do you think? Of course."

"What are we going to tell your dad and ma?"

"Maybe you can think of something."

Sherm took the corner where Barry Simmons lived and headed west toward the Pipp homestead. "Tell you what. On the way home from Le Mars after the game, we can stop in and visit my mother in Jerusalem. That's where we'll tell your folks where we went."

"That's sort of a lie."

"I know it."

"And what will we tell them when you start playing for the Cubs every Sunday? In Al Capone's Chicago?"

"Free told me about a Parson Lewis who pitched for the old Boston Red Sox. He wouldn't pitch on Sunday either."

"Wouldn't it be a little different though for someone who was expected to play every day?"

"You're right. Pitchers work every fourth or fifth day. While a shortstop has to play every day."

Ahead and below lay the Little Rock River. The weak headlights of Sherm's old Ford picked up the red reflectors on either side of the iron bridge.

Allie sat apart from Sherm, against the door. She looked sad.

Slowly she shook her head. "I don't think I'm gonna like living in that godless Chicago."

"There's that all right. But first I've got to figure out what to do about Ma. I'm only nineteen, you know, and not yet of legal age. And she could stop me because I'm still a minor." Sherm drew back his lips in a deep grimace. "Man, is she gonna raise sand with me. Man."

When Sherm shut off the motor in front of the Pipps' house-yard gate, Allie said, "How about a piece of angel food cake and some hot chocolate?"

"Why not. I could even go for a dried-beef sandwich."

Allie slid over and slipped soft slender arms around him and drew his head down and kissed him. "With mustard too?"

"Not on the cake."

"You nut."

Soon Sherm was working on his second cup of hot chocolate. "It's like I told Ted Herman of the Homebrews once. There were two other guys who wouldn't play on Sunday either. Branch Rickey of the St. Louis Browns. And the great Christy Mathewson of the New York Giants. So maybe if I'm good enough I can maybe get a contract like that too."

Allie didn't like hearing any more baseball. "Dreamer."

They were sitting across from each other at the narrow kitchen table. A kerosene lamp on the wall above the table cast its soft amber light on them. Allie looked especially beautiful. Mary Magdalene must've looked like her.

Sherm slowly set his cup down. He leaned forward. "Listen, dolly girl. I've just simply got to do something important before I'm thirty. Because after that it's too late."

"But isn't it true we must keep the Sabbath?"

"But the real sabbath comes on Saturday."

"But we celebrate it on Sunday. It's also a day in memory of Christ's resurrection."

"But the other week I read in one of those filler pages in our *Bonnie Review* that some people say Sunday is only the day of the sun. Or, as the worldly people say, it's sin day. A day when they are off work and can have their most fun."

"That's blasphemy! It's a mockery of something that's very sacred to us."

"Nobody gets excited when we play catch on Sunday. Not even my sister Ada gets very hot about it."

"I doubt though if the Lord likes it very well."

"So what's the harm in me playing for Le Mars once on Sunday?"

"I'll pray for you, Sherman Engleking."

"And I'm not thinking so much either about all the money I'll make. It's just that it's such a joy to play the great game of baseball. It's the most glad be-all and the end-all of all things on earth that a man can do. You run, you scheme, you jump, you lay traps, you throw, you pretend one thing and do the other. You can throw your whole soul into it and it still isn't enough. There's always more yet to do to make it perfect. It's like kittens playing to learn how to mouse better. Ohh, it's great."

Allie's brown eyes melted under his eloquence. "Sherm, my love, if that's what you want to do, then that's what you should do. Go ahead and play a week from Sunday." She sighed. "You better get it out of your blood, or in your blood, one way or the other, or you'll never be happy."

Sherm called up Free the next evening, Saturday. "How's the old soupbone?"

"Not too bad. I could lift a cup of coffee with it this morning."

"Did you tell your dad?"

"Yeh. He just smiled. He said that when he used to pitch for Lakewood, he sometimes had a sore arm too."

Sherm looked down at the black mouthpiece of the wall telephone. He could see little tiny gray specks on it where people in talking into it had sprayed a fine mist of spit. "I got a favor to ask of you."

"Shoot."

"Can you keep a secret for a week or two?"

"Try me."

"I think I'm gonna play for Le Mars a week from Sunday. So Deacon Blake can watch me one more time."

"Oh."

"But I need batting practice. Do you think your arm could stand throwing me a couple dozen pitches? Say, Monday night after chores?"

"By then it should feel a lot better. But I tell you, Uncle, I mean to follow that Cub scout's advice not to throw hard anymore this year. Nor next year."

"I agree. I would just like to bat against your inshoot a couple of times. Smokey Joe was throwing us some of those at Amen the other week, and while I did manage to connect on a few, he actually was handcuffing me a little."

"That's probably because he threw a wrinkle ball."

"He what?"

"After that game at Amen, their catcher asked me how I liked trying to hit Smokey Joe's new pitch, the wrinkle ball. He'd noticed I didn't do too well at bat that night."

"What the heck is a wrinkle ball?"

Free laughed over the phone. For so young a kid he had a deep hearty laugh. "Go over and shake hands with Smokey Joe the next time you see him. Then you'll see why."

The next Monday night turned out to be a lovely evening. The sun was still up when Sherm took up his batting stance at a home-made plate on Free's yard. Free's father, Alfred, agreed to play a pretend first base and Free's brother Everett played shortstop. Sherm was to try to beat out bunts as well as hot rollers.

All went well the first half-dozen pitches. Sherm managed to lay down three good bunts and hit a comebacker to Free.

Of a sudden it seemed the Free was forgetting he had a sore arm. He was pitching as though Sherm was an enemy batter, was really trying to strike him out, not just make him hit the ball for an out. There was a narrowed glitter in Free's blue eyes.

Well well. Sherm decided to show him. Free came in with a really good outdrop that started for Sherm's head and then caught the low outside corner of the plate. Sherm missed it. So. Sherm stepped out of the box for a moment. "You're out to get me, eh?"

Free wound up again. Watching closely Sherm thought he saw Free stick the ball deep in his hand. Ah. Inshoot. Sherm prepared to step in the bucket and pull it down where the third-base line should be, into the cattle water tank. But to his astonishment the ball, instead of twisting in on his fists, abruptly darted straight down. That sonofagun.

Alfred couldn't resist it. He and Sherm had made their peace, but sometimes he still liked to put one over on Sherm, in this case having his son do it. "How do you like them potatoes, ha? I taught him that drop."

It made Sherm laugh, shortly. It pleased him to see how good Free really was. At the same time it made him wonder if he himself was major-league after all. Sherm picked up the ball where it had rolled after bouncing against the calf shed and threw it back to Free. "Okay, buster, throw me another one like that. But don't tell me when you're gonna do it."

Free turned away to hide a smile. He pretended to be walking around the mound to think over what to pitch next.

Everett with his sly smile called to Free. "Throw him that secret pitch. You know, the one you always get me out with."

Sherm shortened his grip. He became very wide awake inside his head. By God, if it was the last thing he ever did, he was going to hit the next pitch. Even if he had to hit it with his bare hand.

Free stepped his right foot into the little pitching hole he'd fashioned with his spiked shoes, didn't particularly set the ball in his hand in any way, wound up and threw. At the very last split second Sherm saw what it was. An open-hand palm pitch. It worked the air like a knuckler. Sherm resisted the impulse to swing early, resisted it some more, then as the ball came up, followed its flutter, and whacked it over Everett's outstretched glove.

"Aha!" Sherm cried. "That'd be a single in a real game."

Free let his right shoulder down. "Yeh. I guess it would've been. You lucky sucker."

So it went. Sherm managed to get two more acknowledged hits out of the next half-dozen pitches.

"Lucky," Free muttered.

Sherm said, "Just for the heck of it, Free, can you throw me a couple of those wrinkle pitches? You know, like you said Smokey Joe was throwing the other night at Amen? Because I'll be facing him again in Le Mars."

"I'll try. Though this old ball is so roughed up it probably already works like a wrinkle ball." Free became so lost in trying to come up with the new pitch that he forgot he was in a contest to see who was the better man. To throw the wrinkle ball a pitcher had to squeeze the ball between thumb and forefinger hard enough to wrinkle up one side of the leather cover. Ready, his arm came around smoothly.

Sherm instantly sensed an inshoot was coming. He opened up his stance, swung tight along his chest, and caught the ball dead center. The old ball speared off his bat straight into Free's face. There was a sound as though someone had thunked a pumpkin with his knuckles. Free's baseball cap flipped up and away from his head. The ball rolled one way, towards the barn on the left, and Free, tottering, fell the other way, on the right side of the pitching hole. Free hit the ground with a wumpf. And lay as still as a fallen telephone pole.

Since it was a kind of game they were playing, Sherm dropped his bat and ran for the pretend first base; then quick called, "Time out!" and ran towards the cattle water tank.

"Hyar!" Alfred yelled. "You hit my boy!"

"I know. Be there in a jiffy." Sherm picked up an empty slop bucket, dipped it full in the water tank, came running back, and spilled some of it over Free's face. When Free didn't come to right away, Sherm spilled another big splash over Free's face. Some green tank moss slid out with the water and caught in Free's sun-blond hair.

Sherm spoke sharply down at him. "Free!"

"Son!" Alfred barked.

Sherm spilled yet another splash over Free's face, emptying the rest of the slop bucket.

Free opened his eyes, shook his head, drops flying about. Then he sat up. "Where's the ball?"

Sherm smiled down at Free. He stepped over and picked up the ball and handed it to Free.

Free quickly tagged Sherm.

Sherm laughed. "Too late, buddy old boy. I ran to first and then called time. Then I ran to get the water."

"You mean, you acted like this was a real game instead of worrying about me?"

"What do you think you were doing, pitching the way you were?"

"I guess that's true."

"That's the fun of baseball. You test yourself against the best man around and yet you don't really fight him."

Free slowly got to his feet. He touched his chin gingerly. "Man, I already got a bump on it."

"So that's where it got you."

Free worked his jaw. "It ain't broke. So I guess I can still gnaw my way through a porkchop."

"Thank God," Sherm said. Sherm put his arm around Free's high shoulder. "I hope this won't make you gun-shy."

"Try me. You want to bat some more?"

Sherm laughed. "No. But that's the way to rebound." Sherm shook his head. "I probably shouldn't 've even asked you to pitch this little bit. To make sure your arm'll be back to normal a year from now."

"It will."

Later, sitting around the table in the kitchen, they all had some of Ada's aniseed-flavored hot milk. Sherm and Alfred were smiling about a big bump on Free's chin. It seemed to be thickening even more as they talked. Ada, Free's mother, didn't smile. She had a tender look for her oldest boy, and each time she leaned past him to pour him some more of the aromatic drink, she placed her hand lovingly on his shoulder.

Alfred lit his meerschaum pipe. "Too bad you boys weren't around when they played the game of *keatsen* in Sioux Center. When the Frisians first came over."

Sherm sat down his cup. "What's *keatsen?*"

"Frisian baseball."

Sherm drew up his nose in disbelief. "You don't mean to tell me now that the Frisians invented baseball too? The way you Alfredsons, all of you, like to brag about what great things the Frisians have invented is almost a mortal sin."

"Well, you should be proud too, remembering where your grandparents came from," Alfred said.

"How did those Sioux Center Frisians play their baseball game?"

"Well, the way my pa told it, in Friesland they had four bases like you do in America today. And they ran from base to base depending on where the ball was hit. And they used a ball with a solid center wrapped in cord and covered with leather like your ball. Some batters used a flat paddle for a bat, some used a thick leather glove. My pa says—that's your granpa, Free, your pake—he says he never saw such slick fielding in all his life."

"Hmp." Sherm wondered just what that slick fielding might have been like.

"Say," Free mused out loud, "I wonder if that word 'keatsen' is where the poet Keats got his name. After all, according to Pake and Uncle Romke, the Frisians were the boat people who brought their cousins the Angles and Saxons to England."

"So," Alfred said, "you might be playing for the Chicago Cubs next year. I wish I could see you."

Sherm threw a quick look at Ada. He wasn't sure he wanted her to know much about his plans for next spring, at least not until it was too late to stop him.

Chapter Sixteen

The following Sunday right after the morning church service, Sherm picked up Allie and headed for Le Mars. He took the King of Trails highway south out of Bonnie, zigged east to a mile north of Chokecherry Corner, then headed straight south through Sioux Center, across low rolling country, and finally over several considerable hills to swoop down into Le Mars. It was exactly one o'clock when he arrived on the diamond west of town. The game was to start at one-thirty.

The visiting team from Rutherland was already taking their pregame workout on the diamond, while the local Le Mars boys were loosening up along the third base line tossing the ball back and forth.

Sherm parked the car at the far end of a line of cars on the Le Mars side of the field. He watched the players on both sides a few moments, and then turned to Allie. "I better quick change from these Sunday duds into my uniform on the far side of the car here."

Allie had to laugh. "Suppose a car full of women drive up and park next to us?"

"Then they'll have a peek at the bare legs of one of the best-built men in all of Siouxland."

"Braggart."

Sherm deftly slipped out of his neat blue Sunday suit and into his baseball rags. He laced up his spiked shoes, caught his baseball cap on the back of his head, and reached into the trunk for his glove. "Well, Manager Joe McCarthy of the Chicago Cubs, here I come from Bonnie Doon, have you got some work for me to do?"

"Then you played that game too. We girls called it Lemonade and Ice Cream from New Orleans."

Sherm leaned into the car and gave Allie a kiss. "Wish me luck, honey, and we'll be on our way to Catalina Island next spring with the Cubs."

Allie loved him, and fashioned a smile for him. "Watch out for that wrinkle ball."

Sherm found the manager of the Le Mars Redcoats sitting on the far end of the players' bench. The man had a puzzled look on his fleshy red face as he was penciling in his lineup. Sherm got right to the point. "I hope Deacon Blake talked to you about me coming up from Bonnie to play shortstop for you."

The man looked up. "You Engleking?"

"That's right."

The man had a wide blond English moustache. "Good. Uh, where did you bat for Bonnie?"

"Third."

"That's where I've got you here." He stood up. "I'm Hap Moreton." He turned to the players on the bench beside him. "Fellows, this is Sherman Engleking. Up from Bonnie. Playing short for us today." Hap pointed them out for Sherm. "Booger here plays first. Scoop here at second. Nubbin on third. Our pitcher, Drury, is over there warming up with Jigger, our catcher. And those three at the end of the bench there are in the outfield, Bones, Pug, and Old Folks."

Sherm nodded at them in turn.

Twitch Pidcock, the manager for the Rutherland Saints, called over. "Okay, Hap. The field is yours."

Hap turned to his bench again. "Okay, gents. Let's look sharp out there today. No errors. Smokey Joe is a tough one to beat. Make one bad mistake and they can break the game wide open." He tossed a fungo bat to one of his reserve players. "You hang some flies to the outfielders. And I'll bang out some groundhuggers to my infielders."

After picking up several sizzlers and throwing the ball around the sacks, from short to first to third to second to home, Sherm saw that for once he was playing with real diamondeers. Booger at first was a regular acrobat the way he could do the stretch and snatch up bouncers. Nubbin at third was a demon for digging out mean shorthoppers, much like half-pint Wimp back home, except that he was smoother in his motions. And Scoop at second wasn't named for nothing—he seemed to be everywhere, flowing to his left or right and snaking up the ball and snapping it side-armed to first. While Jigger at home had a cannon for an arm the way he threw to second or third or first.

By the time the game started a big crowd from both Le Mars and Rutherland had filled the stands and had formed lines four deep behind third and first. The cars behind the lines of fans were also filled with cheering partisans.

Drury turned out to be a junk pitcher and an expert at nibbling the corners of the plate as well as a master of the change of pace. And while he rarely struck anyone out, he had every batter off stride so they hit mostly dribblers and pop-ups. He kept his in-fielders busy. The first three innings Sherm alone had six assists, all of them as easy as eating apple pie. No one reached first.

Meanwhile Smokey Joe also pitched masterfully. Along with his smoke, his wrinkle ball was bobbing all over in the strike zone.

In the top of the fourth, the leadoff man for Rutherland hit a creaser past Drury, the pitcher. Sherm darted over, reached down, and missed it. At the last second the ball seemed to have hit a pebble and bounced over his glove.

"Oh-oh," Sherm murmured. "I ought to have ate up that grounder." He looked over at the grandstands behind the back-stop. "Let's hope Deacon Blake was busy talking to someone beside him and missed that play."

On the very next pitch Sherm got a chance to make up for it. The Rutherland batter hit a smash headed for the hole between third baseman Nubbin and himself. Sherm gathered himself up into a muscled ball of power and threw his body at the low liner. Stretching his left hand as far as he could, he caught the ball in the very last inch of the webbing of his glove. He fell heavily on his belly, but in the next instant jumped to his feet and whipped the ball to Booger at first, doubling up the runner. Double play. Two out. Both the Le Mars and the Rutherland crowd cheered the play. It was baseball at its best.

"Gosh," Sherm whispered. "Now that play I hope Deacon Blake saw."

In the bottom of the fourth, Sherm came to bat for the second time with two out. In his mind's eye he saw again how Free pinched the cover of the ball powerfully between thumb and fore-finger to create the wrinkle ball. He watched Smokey carefully. Smokey had a way of smiling devilishly under the bill of his baseball cap on every pitch, so it was impossible to detect from his expression what he had in mind to throw next. If Smokey made an extra effort with thumb and forefinger, that was the ball to lay off. A wrinkle ball darted around too much. But if Smokey didn't work the cover of the ball that would mean his hard smoke and the pitch to go after.

Sure enough, on the first pitch Smokey lingered a mite longer than usual with the way he set the ball in his right hand. That had to be the wrinkler. It was. Sherm watched it drift away from the plate. Ball one. Sherm carefully kept a bland face. The next one would be the smoker. But once again Smokey took that extra split second before he wound up. Another wrinkler coming. Ball two.

Sherm made up his mind to go after the next one. And swing just an inch higher than usual on the raise ball. Around came Smokey's limber arm, and the ball speared in toward the center of the plate, and around went Sherm's bat as he stepped into the ball. He swung powerfully, his bat whipping around with great speed. He caught it right on the nose. In that quick darting moment he saw peripherally that the ball had connected some three inches from the end of the bat. The ball rifled up into the air a dozen feet above the Rutherland shortstop's glove, which came up too late, and then catching at the air, the ball rose, and rose, and skied up into the clear afternoon blue. There was a wonderful cry from the crowd as the ball, hit deep, kept rising. The full cry of the crowd also kept rising, until the ball arched over a row of trees far beyond the left-field board fence. Sherm circled the bases with a little smile to himself. As he came around third, the Le Mars bench lined up outside the white chalk mark to applaud him. Manager Hap Moreton greeted him at home plate with a bear hug. Hap's blond English moustache curved up at either end under his nose. "Wow. Did you ever tie into that one! Deacon Blake was dead right about you."

"Thanks."

Le Mars 1, Rutherland 0.

The boys on the Le Mars bench were finally convinced Sherm was all right. "Maybe we can beat Old Smokey at last."

Sherm's chest filled. He had to fight for breath. He picked up his glove and took a deep smell of it. He reveled in the aroma of the wet leather where he'd spit several times in the pocket of the glove to make it sticky. Behind him in the standing crowd he could smell someone eating a burnt hotdog covered with mustard.

Booger was up next, and Smokey Joe, incensed, grim, struck him out on three of the fastest pitches Sherm had ever seen. It was no wonder Smokey Joe had once had a chance to play for the St. Louis Cardinals in the major leagues, and why Deacon Blake was taking one more look at him as a possible relief pitcher. Maybe, it could just be that Smokey Joe and he would be playing for the Chicago Cubs next year.

Two more innings went by in tight tense baseball. It was thrilling. Except for short burps of cheers made for good plays, the crowd watched in throbbing silence. Sherm made two more glittering plays, once pegging a runner out from the hole in deep short, another time swinging behind second base and scooping up a grass cutter and throwing out the runner with a sidearm snapshot.

In the bottom of the seventh, Sherm was second up. Smokey Joe walked around the mound several times thinking to himself. There was a look on Smokey's face of a man wishing he could shoot the batter coming up instead of having to throw the ball to him. Smokey finally nodded to himself. He picked up the rosin bag, dusted his hand thoroughly, and ascended the mound. He wound up different from before. Instead of one revolution of his arm, he wound up several times, like a windmill whirling in a sharp breeze, and finally let fly at the plate. He missed it by a good foot.

"Thatty old eye there, Sherm boy."

Once again Smokey used a windmill windup and threw. Ball two.

On the third pitch, Sherm saw him pinch the ball, hard, with his thumb and forefinger. It would be a wrinkle ball. Just for the heck of it, and to show Deacon Blake he could hit anything, Sherm shortened up on his bat, and following the dancing ball all the way to the plate, took a short poke at it and connected, sailing a dying quail of a hit out to left field.

After Smokey got the ball back, he took several steps toward Sherm on first and said in a low gutteral voice, "You goddam lucky sonofabitch! A pip-squeak from Bonnie, that outlaw burg, trying to keep me from playing for the Cubs next year."

"Hey," Sherm said, standing erect on the bag, hands on his

hips, "if you ain't good enough you ain't good enough. Besides, who's to say we won't both be playing for the Cubs."

"You? Play for the Cubs? Not a chance of a fart in a whirlwind."

"I dare you to say that real loud."

Smokey Joe's gray eyes glittered for a moment more at Sherm. Then pulling the bill of his gray cap deep over his eyes, he went back to the mound and proceeded to strike out the next two batters. The score remained Le Mars 1, Rutherland 0.

Sitting on the Le Mars bench again, Manager Moreland asked, "Sherm, what was that all about between you and Smokey?"

"We just fanned some."

"What about?"

"Oh, he made a reference to my four-legged mother."

In the top of the ninth for a little while everything seemed to come apart. Just as Drury was about to deliver his first pitch, an old woman's shrill voice pierced through everything.

"Sher-mee! Sher-mee!"

Sherm was astounded. Speaking of the devil. Ma? Here? In Le Mars? At a ball game on Sunday?

"Sher-mee? My boy, you playing ball on Sunday? In this godless city?"

Then Sherm spotted Ma. She had just emerged from the crowd standing just outside the grandstand on the Rutherland side of the field. She pushed several people aside and came toward Sherm, crossing the white line between home plate and first plate, stomping on one leg and waddling on the other, face as dark red as an overripe plum, one hand pointing at Sherm, the other hand to her eyes as she fixed and refixed her spectacles on her nose, trying to make sure she was seeing what she was seeing.

Sherm glared at her from his position at shortstop. Now who in god's name had told her he was playing ball in Le Mars on Sunday? Allie? No, it couldn't be her. Matilda? No, because how could she have known? Brother John surely would not have told her. Aha. It had to be sister Ada. She'd somehow heard either Free or Alfred talk about it. Because Free knew. Son of a buck. But now . . . what to do about Ma?

"Sher-mee!" Ma came to within a dozen feet of him. "My boy, you come right home with me. Now! And we'll together get down on our knees and pray to God that you may be forgiven. Base-a-ball on Sunday!"

The crowd meanwhile had fallen into a choked silence. Here and there a weak titter escaped a fan.

Sherm made up his mind. He walked straight up to Ma and put his arms around her and gave her a big resounding kiss.

The crowd cheered. And laughed.

"Now, Ma, you don't understand. I have my reasons for playing this game today. It may mean a lot of money to me someday."

"Money? Money?" Ma's face turned a wild red. "What's money got to do with it when you may lose your soul to everlasting hellfire? You come right home with me."

Smokey Joe cackled derisive laughter from the Rutherland bench. "That's it, Ma, take that hick chick back to your nest. He's been trying to show me up all afternoon. And good riddance."

Sherm said, "See? You hear that, Ma? You've made a fool of me before all these—"

"What do I care what they think? I'm thinking of your salvation. You know you mustn't play on God's day—"

"Dammit, Ma! I'm going to finish this game. Who brought you here?"

"Well, yah, I got my husband Garland's nephew to bring me over. Pete Stanhorse."

"Did Step-Pa approve of you coming here?"

"No, he didn't. Because he knew he really wasn't your father. Sher-mee, think of what your own father would say about you playing ball on Sunday."

"He's gone now, Ma, and I have to live my own life. Now, don't you show me up anymore. Come." He put his arm around her and turned her around and headed her back. "You go to Pete Stanhorse's car and wait there until the game is over. Then I'll talk to you. Or, if you don't want to do that, go join Allie sitting over there in my car watching the game."

"Allie approved of you playing on Sunday?"

"No, she didn't. But I have to listen to my own conscience."

"But what if your conscience is wrong?"

"Now, Ma, that's enough." Sherm spotted Pete Stanhorse in the crowd near the grandstand. He steered Ma straight for him. "Here, Pete, you take care of my mother until the game is over. And don't let her get away. She's shamed me enough already today, you hear?"

Pete Garland nodded. He had the same big potato nose of

259

his uncle. He was thin and stooped. "I didn't wanna bring her myself."

"I don't blame you. Just make sure she don't interrupt the game again."

"I'll try."

Sherm ran back out on the diamond. The crowd cheered. There were several raucous hoots of derision from the Rutherland side of the field.

Sherm pinched his lips together as he leaned forward on his toes ready for whatever play came his way. "Now I've gotta make sure that Ma's coming here didn't discomboobulate me."

Drury once again got ready to pitch. He wound up and threw, and missed the plate a good foot. He proceeded to walk the first batter.

Sherm ran in to talk to Drury. Drury was a wise old baseball head and Sherm was a little hesitant to offer him advice. But it was the shortstop's duty to calm down his pitcher. Sherm raised his shoulders in apology, and smiled a smile he hoped looked sheepish. "Sorry about my ma, Pitch."

Drury smiled back. "Don't worry. I got one like that too." Drury had the look of a shrewd old owl who hadn't been able to catch most of the mice he wanted. There was a look of easy patience in his blue eyes. He lifted his baseball cap a moment and with two fingers combed back his gray hair. "For some reason I sometimes look like I'm blowing up in the ninth, and that's when I got my best stuff."

"Okay. Go get 'em then."

Drury's next pitch was perfect. The batter hit a crazy spinning ball to the second baseman. Handled right, it was a double-play ball. But Scoop booted it. Two men on.

"Oh-oh," Sherm whispered.

The next man up fouled off a dozen pitches and finally worked Drury for a walk. Bases loaded. Nobody out.

Hap Moreton called time and came trotting out. He waved Sherm and Scoop to come up as well as Jigger, the catcher. Hap's wiggling moustache with its two pointed tips looked like a pair of mice caught with their heads together in a trap. "Drury, goddammit, when are you ever gonna get over the ninth inning blues? One of these days you're gonna give me a heart attack."

Drury said, "Well, I threw a double-play ball. And you know, I'm not a strikeout king like Smokey."

"Goddammit, I know. I'd think of calling in Old Folks to relieve you but he ain't got much on the ball anymore. Except that he might have better luck."

"Well, it's up to you, Skipper."

Hap stomped around his four men, biting his lower lip, glowering at the Rutherland men standing on the three sacks.

Umpire Emory Stock came up from home plate. "Are you guys gonna finish the game? Or shall I call it nine to nothing?"

Hap said, "Hell yes we're gonna finish the game. Drury, give me that ball a minute. Oh, I ain't gonna take you out. I just want to touch that ball to change our luck. There. Now. Goddammit, pitch!"

Everybody ran back to their positions. Sherm remembered the time when Free had the bases loaded twice at Amen with nobody out. It would be tempting fate to expect Drury to wiggle out of the same kind of mess. Sherm looked to see who was up. My God. Their cleanup man, Cornie Tellinghouse, was already swinging a big black bat. He'd been known to hit the ball a country mile. He also had a tendency to pull the ball because of his quick swing. He wasn't a tall big man, just a squat broad man, with short powerful ham arms and a heavy butt. It was his heavy butt, working as a counterweight to his thick arms, that gave him distance. Sherm positioned himself on the grass in deep short, almost directly behind Nubbin the Redcoat, third baseman.

At the same time Sherm couldn't help but exult to himself what a joy it was to play in the complicated game of baseball. It was a thrill to be involved in great strategies, even with stick-in-the-mud players. Imagine what it was going to be like playing with the Cubs against star players! Sherm whispered to himself, "I just know for a God's fact that I'm going to do something wonderful, great, before I'm thirty. I can't wait."

Drury let go with a knuckler. It wavered toward the plate.

Tellinghouse timed the pitch perfectly it seemed. He hit a monster of a fly ball far over Nubbin's and Sherm's heads. Grand slam maybe?

Sherm ran to the third base line to watch it go. The ball rose very high, became small, slowly started to veer to the left, then veered faster as it started down, finally slanted over the foul line. At least Sherm was sure it had gone foul before it left the field.

The Rutherland bench began to roar that Tellinghouse had hit a homer.

The Le Mars bench yelled the long poke had gone foul.

The base umpire, Dennie Hensley, had run over to call it. But he was a little late, and he turned to home-plate umpire Emory Stock for him to call it.

Without hesitation, Umpire Stock pointed to his left, indicating it was foul.

The Rutherland bench went wild, as did their supporters. Some called Umpire Stock a "homer," meaning he favored the home team. Some called him a "crook." Some called him the "tenth man." Some called him "Blind Tom." One hoarse voice blasted through a bullhorn, "Let's string him up!"

Twitch Pidcock, the Rutherland manager, was so outraged he ran over to the man with the bullhorn, snatched it away from him, and blared out in the direction of the two umpires, "You don't rape this rube! I'm pulling my team off the field and you can have your game nine to nothing. Instead of one to nothing."

The Rutherland players couldn't believe their ears. What? Quit a game in which they had the bases loaded and nobody out? All the Rutherland players ran out on the field to protest their manager's threat. The three Rutherland runners, though, were careful not to stray from their bases.

Umpire Stock walked over and grabbed the bullhorn from Pidcock, then announced: "All Rutherland players will return to their bench or this game will really be forfeited. Now!"

The Rutherland players milled around him, trying not to curse him to his face.

Umpire Stock next bawled: "Twitch, get off the field and go take a shower!"

Pidcock turned purple. He hadn't appreciated having the bullhorn jerked from his grasp. He cocked his fist and knocked Umpire Stock down. Umpire Stock hit the ground with a whumpf, his mask flying one way and his ball-and-strike indicator the other way.

At that point, Manager Moreton ran out from the Le Mars bench to help restore order. He raised his hand, as if a priest out to bless everybody. "Now. Now. Let's calm down. After all, this is only a game. It ain't the World War."

Pidcock turned to Moreton. "You hired Stock on purpose for this game. You knew we never liked him. He's never, in his whole life, ever called a fair game against us. He's a homer pure

and simple. He knows who writes out the check for this game."
Pidcock next slugged Moreton so hard he fell down.

That brought all the Le Mars players over on the run. Fights erupted everywhere on the diamond. Fists popped on chins. Body slams were launched. Dust began to fill the air.

Naturally the fans from both sides were not going to stand or sit idly by either. Soon the whole field, diamond and stands, became a war zone.

A Le Mars cop, watching the game from his squad car beyond the last car on the Le Mars side, studied the riot for a few minutes; then, turning on his siren, roared into town. He called out the fire department, telling the fire chief it was a four-alarm case. A wild dangerous riot had broken out on the town baseball diamond.

Soon four fire engines showed up, sirens howling. They pulled up behind home plate, and unrolling their hoses, let fly powerful spraying streams of sprettling water at everybody milling around on the playing field. Fans were blasted down, both men and women. Players were blown down ass-over-appetite. It took a full half hour before all the fights were broken up, and the players returned to their proper places and the fans to the grandstand seats.

Throughout the whole melee, Sherm hadn't moved a step. He was a visitor there, and had no interest in the old-time rivalry between the two towns Rutherland and Le Mars. Besides, he had enough trouble afoot as a result of having quit the Bonnie team when they played Hello. He also noted that Smokey Joe hadn't stirred, either, from the Rutherland bench and had sat alone throughout the whole ruckus, smiling sardonically to himself.

Umpire Stock called both managers over for a private consultation. Both managers were soaked from head to foot and looked at the ground sullenly while Umpire Stock talked to them. By some miracle neither Stock nor Umpire Hensley had been hit by the blasting spraying water. Finally both managers, sneaking a look at each other, nodded their heads.

Umpire Stock walked over to home plate, stood on it, and announced through the bullhorn: "It has been agreed by both parties that the game will continue, that nobody will be banned from the playing field, manager or player, and that all players will return to where they were just before this unfortunate fracas started. The batter has one strike. No balls. Play ball!"

Sherm observed that parts of the diamond had little puddles of water. Luckily the dirt on the pitching mound was cork dry. At least Drury would have good footing. A strange smell rose from the soaked diamond. It reminded Sherm of wild roses in a roadside ditch on which rain had just fallen and from which dust had been washed. He checked his shortstop territory to make sure where the puddles were in case he had to make a play near or in them.

Drury still burned because of the long foul Tellinghouse had got off him. He wound up; paused with his hands closed over his belly and checked to see what kind of leads the runners had taken; then hurled his fastest pitch of the day. He groan-grunted, he threw the ball so hard. Tellinghouse hadn't expected a pitch that fast, was slow coming around, and missed it. Two strikes. That gave Drury the edge for the moment. Drury tried to tempt Tellinghouse with pitches off the plate a half-foot; changing speeds with a knuckler, then a curve that spun incredibly fast causing it to whip away from the plate, again a knuckler. Tellinghouse had a keen sense of the strike zone and let all three pitches go by.

With the count full, three balls and two strikes, the players on both teams watched narrowly, jaws working slowly on chews of tobacco or wads of gum. The fans sat tense.

Sherm called time. He trotted over to the mound. "Pitch, what's the real dope on this batter?"

Drury drew up his upper lip, for a moment resembling a bull that had encountered an alien smell. "He hits everything."

"Well, I noticed something. I think he's guessing up there. Sometimes he sets his back foot to pull the ball just as you wind up, sometimes he sets it like he means to hit up the middle. Just watch his back foot. You know, his right foot. And change your pitch accordingly."

Drury regarded Sherm with a wrinkled grimace. "Thanks."

"Think nothing of it." Sherm ran back to deep short.

Drury wound up again; paused to check to see how Tellinghouse was setting his back foot; fired. Tellinghouse had set his right foot to pull the ball.

Sherm quick took a step to his right.

Tellinghouse's black varnished bat flashed around and rocketed a screamer directly at where Sherm was leaning forward. Some dozen feet away from Sherm the ball started to rise, like a kite that had just caught the wind. From the moment it was hit, sound of wood on horsehide, Sherm knew it was going to be a riser. Sherm bent down farther; then leaped; then tried to leap another leap off the top of his first leap. His gloved hand shot up. There was a loud smack as the ball socked into the spit-greased pocket of his glove. One out.

Then, even as he was dropping back to earth, Sherm knew without thinking what to do. Out of the corner of his eye he'd caught Manager Pidcock's hit-and-run signal. All runners took one look at Tellinghouse's drive, knew it was another long one, at least fair and a double, probably even a homer, then put their heads down and took off. By the time Sherm landed the runner on second was directly in front of him. When the runner realized that Sherm had miraculously snared the ball, he tried to put on the brakes. But he'd hit a muddy spot, and slid, and fell down. Sherm ran up a few steps and tagged the runner. Two out. Then Sherm looked to see where the runner on third was. That runner too tried to put on the brakes. Too late. Sherm looked to see if Nubbin had run over to cover third. But Nubbin was frozen in his tracks by the screamer as well as by Sherm's catch. So Sherm ran over and touched third base, easily beating that runner. Three out. Triple play. Second one that summer. Except this one was unassisted. Game over. Le Mars 1, Rutherland 0.

The Le Mars crowd let out a hoarse roar of victory and joy. They poured out on the field, waving their arms, hugging each other, shaking each other's hands.

The Le Mars players stood around a minute or two, having some trouble understanding they had won, and that at the moment when all had looked black. They glanced at each other, gave each other a silly grin, and then all eight players, plus those on the bench, converged on Sherm and pounded him in happiness.

The Rutherland players said nothing. They left the field crushed.

The Rutherland fans turned their faces away from the diamond. With a polite smolder set in their eyes, and dreaming of future revenge, they headed home.

Deacon Blake sought Sherm out. He took him by the arm and led him off to one side. He was smiling. "Well, son, you've convinced me. You're ready for the majors all right. I'm writing the Cubs management yet tonight to tell them to invite you to their spring training on Catalina Island next March."

"I'll be there."

"I noticed how you kept your head during the hullabaloo.

That's too your credit. I also saw how you pickled Smokey's wrinkle ball."

"Gosh, I hope I didn't ruin Smokey's chances with the Cubs."

"You didn't. I'm going to tell Manager Joe McCarthy to invite him to Catalina too."

"I'm glad."

"That was your mother who interrupted the game, wasn't it?"

"Yeh, worse luck."

"So she's against Sunday baseball, huh? That's something you're gonna have to settle with your own conscience."

"I will."

"Very good. See you next spring."

Chapter Seventeen

Late October.

Sherm and John hustled out to the field to pick the fat hanging ears of corn with John's new red corn picker.

Picking corn the old way by hand had always been a grueling grind for several months. The brothers would be in the field before dawn and wouldn't be home until dark. It was rush rush up the corn rows, and rush rush down the corn rows, snapping off an ear here, an ear there, and without looking, throwing the ears against a bangboard. Often it was cold and miserable in drizzling rain or flying snow as they labored jerking their way from stalk to stalk. By the time the last ear was out they'd be thin and gaunt, losing as much as twenty pounds a season.

With the new machine they could ride, one of them up on the picker driving five horses, and the other in the three-box wagon driving two horses to make sure all the ears coming out of the picker fell into the wagon.

It was two above zero. They'd dressed in warm boots, mackinaws, blue woolen Scotch caps with the earflaps down, and a double pair of mittens. Their noses and cheeks slowly turned a raspberry red.

The morning was a drab one, windy, with heavy low gray-blue clouds, dust rising from the swinging horse hooves and the rolling heavy machine wheels, and mingled in with it the smell of coarse leaves from the cornstalks.

They picked two loads of corn and unloaded them into the corn-crib with an elevator, had a quick nine o'clock cup of hot coffee with cream and sugar, and then they were back to the field. They smiled at each other now and then about how easy it was with a modern machine to pick big loads in a big hurry. Inventors had finally got around to making work easier for the farmer. Corn picking would be a snap that fall. They'd easy have the corn out by the tenth of November.

On the second two loads it was Sherm's turn to sit on the steel throne of the corn-picking machine. Aiming the huge clumsy clamoring machine in such a way that the two long snouts of the snapping rollers always snared the single corn row exactly in the middle was a challenge. Luckily the horses had been trained earlier in the year during cultivating time to walk in the center of the rows. But riding down through the draws the rows weren't always straight and there the horses needed guidance. Sherm had to manipulate two sets of lines, one set to the lead team up front and the other set to the three horses in back. The horses didn't seem to mind working in the cold air, and all the chains and gears and rollers of the machine meshed with a low smooth roar.

After several rounds and having adjusted to the demands of driving the heavy machine, Sherm soon found himself thinking about other things. It still made him wince to remember how Ma had embarrassed him in front of that big Le Mars crowd, wince to the point where his lips, drawn back, worked up wrinkles into his cheeks. He recalled too how Allie, on the way back home from Le Mars, had smiled her wide smile in praise of his great playing, then the next minute had cried a little to learn that baseball scout Deacon Blake had told him he was ready to try out with the Cubs.

It also made Sherm wince to remember the look on John's face when he'd told him what Deacon Blake had said. John wished him well, of course. At the same time, though, it could be seen John wished he too could escape the hard work of the farm and make a living playing baseball. Sherm loved his brother. It was going to be hard to leave him.

Again Sherm let his eyes rove over the rolling corn picker to make sure all was running smoothly. He listened for suspicious squeaks. It was a new machine and they hadn't yet made out which parts needed the most oil and grease. The first couple rounds, while John drove, the horses had been skittish hearing the roar of the gears out of sight behind them. But after a while the horses had accepted the clattering racket and settled down.

It made Sherm smile to see how those revolving snapping rollers with their spiral grooves, down between the two steel snouts, could pinch the ears off the stalks. Sometimes the ears jumped up like they might be alive—yellow squirrels with jackets on—but because of the corn picker's high tin sides they always fell back into the moving slats, which pushed them inevitably over onto the husking bed where another set of rollers swiftly ripped off the husks.

Coming over the top of the hill, everything moving along smoothly, Sherm fell to thinking about what next spring might be like with the Chicago Cubs on Catalina Island. He pictured himself practising double plays with the great second baseman Rogers Hornsby. Hornsby was known to have the best across-the-chest throw to first to complete the double play. Just two days before, the *Sioux City Journal* had mentioned that the trade for Hornsby between the Cubs and the Braves was a cinch thing. Sherm also saw himself in fantasy watching how Hornsby took up his batting stance in the batter's box, how he strode into the ball and stroked it right or left.

But Sherm was sure he would have to play on Sunday. His name would appear in the box score printed in the *Sioux City Journal* and then the church was bound to learn about it. His church board was sure to call him on the carpet about it. He couldn't very well claim he had to play baseball for a livelihood and then argue it was like what the Scriptures mentioned, that if one's ass fell into a well on Sunday it was all right to haul that ass out. They'd argue that he could do something more practical for his livelihood. Baseball was only a game a man played for the fun of it. It was not necessary work. From the Cubs' point of view, Manager Joe McCarthy would require him to play every day. The pennant might be at stake. If he were a pitcher like Free, say, then perhaps he could ask McCarthy to so arrange it he didn't have to pitch on Sunday.

Rolling down a slope of land, out of the corner of his eye, Sherm spotted a cornstalk bobbing around in the husking rollers. Sherm watched it for a minute. He saw that it kept the husking rollers from cleaning off some of the ears, so that they went with the husks still on up into the little elevator and landed in the wagon John was driving. Couldn't have that. Carefully letting up on the lines a little, Sherm reached over with his left hand and caught the bobbing cornstalk at one end, and jerked at it. It wouldn't come. It seemed to have worked itself into the crease near the ball bearings. Sherm leaned farther over, hooking his right foot under a lever to keep from losing his balance, took a firm grip on the end of the cornstalk, and jerked, hard. At just that moment, the cornstalk decided to go down through the husking rollers; and it went so quick it almost took his hand with it. Miraculously the dangerous spiral grooves only licked at the end of his white cotton double mitten.

Sherm threw a look at John. He shouted, "That was a near thing."

John gave him a dark reproving look. "Be careful there!" he shouted back. "Or you won't be playing for the Cubs."

"Don't worry. I always come out ahead."

Just to be on the safe side, though, Sherm wondered what he should do in case his hand got caught in the husking rollers. He could kick out the trip to the main gears and so stop all the chains on the machine. Or he could kick out the lever that put the husking rollers in gear. If he was quick enough he could probably get them shut down before they damaged his hand much.

That noon as they were eating dinner, Matilda told John he'd better take off a couple of hours to take her to the Ladies Aid. It was her turn to give the program and she was not going to let corn picking stand in the way. "You boys are doing so well with that expensive machine you surely can bend a little and let me have some fun too."

Sherm saw an argument coming on. John's face had hardened over. Sherm offered up a little laugh. "Shucks, John, go ahead take her. We got those seven horses trained so well by now I can run the whole shebang alone. We'll hitch the two horses on the wagon with a tie strap to the outside horse on the machine. And do it in such a way the picked corn can't help but fall into the wagon."

John grimaced. "I don't like it."

"C'mon," Sherm urged, "when did we ever run into anything that either one of us couldn't handle alone?"

"Alone you really got to have your wits about you."

"I know. We've doubled up on work like that before."

"When?"

"Well, when we planted that very corn last spring. We had two horses on the planter and then behind us we had a lead strap back to another pair of horses pulling a two-section drag."

"Hmm. I still don't like it. But all right." John turned to Matilda. "I'm going to help Sherm get hitched up and watch him start out. Just to make sure it'll work."

It did work. As smooth as oiled glass. The horses, both those on the picker and those on the wagon, followed the rows perfectly. John only had to make one adjustment on the tie strap between the two sets of horses.

"Okay," John said. "But be careful, friend. I'll come home as soon as I can."

"You better hustle back to the house or we'll get burnt potatoes tonight."

Everything went perfect for two rounds. Sherm noticed as the machine clattered and rolled down the slow east slope that he was riding along the very spot where he and Free, while plowing a year ago, played their game of throwing clods at each other, and then had even wrestled in the stubbles while they let the horses go on pulling the plows down the field on their own. It was done as part of showing off so Allie Pipp could see them from her house across the road.

For the third round, he had to change wagons. That done he again started east across the field.

Sherm next got around to remembering how he and Free and Garrett used to will and will to win, will so hard they actually would win. Mind hot in their skull, rampant like a bull about to mount a heifer, they'd win despite wretched fielding by the rest of the team.

Back to Catalina Island. Sherm imagined himself matching wits with Charlie Root in batting practice. He'd study the way Root set his feet to throw the fast ball, watch for a bit of thumb when Root threw his outdrop the way Rich Grower did back in Hello.

In daydreams Sherm carefully took up an open stance in the middle of the batter's box, choked up on his bat a couple of inches. Charlie Root wound up and whipped it in. Fast ball. Too late Sherm saw he'd started his swing too low for a rising ball.

Sherm stopped the pretend pitch. He backed the ball all the way back into Root's hand to start over.

He could see drops of sweat on Root's nose and chin, could see sweat on the backs of his own hands, could smell the sweet rank aroma of the just-mown grass of the infield. Behind him Gabby Hartnett was chewing tobacco and spitting through his catcher's mask.

Sherm started Root's fast ball again towards the plate. Swinging an inch higher than usual, Sherm caught the ball on the fat of his bat and sent a screamer past English at third. Running to first, Sherm saw that Riggs Stephenson out in left field had picked up the ball on the first bounce. Glancing towards the bench, he saw a look of surprise spread over Manager Joe McCarthy's face.

Abruptly Sherm was back on his corn-picking machine. Something caught his eye. Another cornstalk was bobbing around on the husking rollers. He watched it for several moments. Damned thing was blocking some of the corn ears. Couldn't have that.

What with his attention being jerked back and forth between Catalina Island and the cornfield, he never gave a thought to what had almost happened earlier. When the husking rollers didn't clear on their own, he reached down his left hand and grabbed the jiggling cornstalk. At that very moment, just like before, the cornstalk decided to pass through the rollers. Before he could jerk his hand back, the husking rollers grabbed his double mitten. For a second it seemed the rollers would husk the double mitten right off his hand, leaving his fingers free. But the double mitten was new and tight over his wrist. Down went his hand, pulling at his whole arm, almost jerking him off his seat. Ow.

"Whoa!" he yelled, hauling back on both sets of lines with his right hand. Not even thinking about it, he did the right thing. His left foot kicked the trip to the husking rollers.

The horses, chilled, stopped.

But not quite in time. There was enough of his mittened hand caught in the rollers to stop the rollers instantly. But oh boy. He was in for it now. His hand was stuck.

He next kicked the trip lever to the main gears. That way

should the horses start up again, no part of the machine would turn over, including the husking rollers.

He stared down at his pinned hand.

"John sure ain't gonna like this."

Twisting around as far as he could on his steel seat, Sherm glanced back up the row towards the yard.

"Yeh, and I suppose John won't be back right away either. Matilda hasn't had much chance to gossip lately and she'll want to make up for the lost time and lollygag around an extra hour at the parsonage with those other women in the Ladies Aid."

Thank God the horses stood as still as the cornstalks around the machine. They appreciated the rest.

He glanced across the field toward Allie Pipp's house. He wondered if she'd been aware that he was running the whole operation alone. Perhaps she was ironing right then and was already looking across at him and wondering why he'd stopped. It gave him an idea. As best he could, even though he'd been pulled down a little into the machine by his caught left hand, he waved his right hand. He hoped she'd see it and interpret it that he was in trouble.

But after a while he gave up waving. It would be a miracle if she happened to be looking his way. If she was cooking in the kitchen she couldn't see him.

Sherm checked the road running past her place, looking east up along it to see if a car might be coming down it towards Bonnie. There wasn't. Nor were there any cars coming from the west.

Darn. Was he in a sweet pickle now. How in God's name was he going to get out of this one? This was worse than being behind eleven runs in the bottom of the ninth. He couldn't even bat to get out of it.

Just so the horses didn't move. But suppose something, a nervous rabbit having smelled a cougar nearby, spooked the horses, and the horses started running crossways across the tilled field, couldn't the jouncing throw the damned main trip back in gear? If so, he was a dead dodo. He's be sucked down into the husking rollers and come out the other side a nice pile of ground meat and crushed bone and be elevated up into the wagon.

He sat very still.

But maybe he wouldn't get sucked down into the machine.

Maybe, if he resisted powerfully enough, it would only rip off his arm at the shoulder. In that case though, he'd bleed to death before he could run for help.

No matter which way his trapped brain tried to think of something, come up with some clever idea, there was nothing.

Nothing.

He smelled blood. Oh God. That meant the hand was bleeding badly enough for the smell to come through the double mitten. Oh God. Just so the horses didn't smell that blood. Then they'd really go.

He sat very still for a long time.

"Hurry home, John."

Again he tried to wave his right arm out of his bent drawndown position. But in so doing he stirred up demons of pain in his left wrist just above where the husking rollers had him pinned.

Head hanging, he waited for John.

"My God, how am I going to get out of this mess?"

Slowly he turned stiff from the cold.

He let his right shoulder sag. His left shoulder slowly tightened up.

"Boy, is this a far cry from playing work-up like in the old days on the Christian School grounds."

He heard someone come brushing roughly through the standing corn to his left.

"John?"

"Sherm?"

It was Allie. Allie! She was banging through the corn rows coming in from the road. "What's the matter here, Sherm?"

Sherm's heart began to beat rapidly. He had a chance.

Allie came closer and stepped up on the bottom frame of the picker. "Sherm? Sherm!"

"Yeh."

"You got your hand caught in that thing!"

"Thank God you came."

"After I washed the dinner dishes, I looked out at your field here, wondering how you fellows. . . . Where's John?"

"He had to take Matilda to Ladies Aid."

"Then you were doing everything alone here?"

"Yeh."

She stared down at where his left hand disappeared into the husking rollers. "You need help fast. I'm gonna run back home and call the parsonage and tell Matilda to find John and get him out here."

"Your brothers ain't around somewhere?"

"They're all out picking corn too. On the north farm. Will you be all right until John comes?"

"No. How about you unhitching horses one by one. Before some critter scares them into a runaway."

"Oh, Sherm, you know I'm afraid of horses. And I hear John's horses are kind of wild and frisky."

"That's right. Then you better hurry and get hold of John. Or his hogs will have me for supper."

"Sherm." Then with a little crying yip, Allie started running back through the standing rows of corn toward her house.

Sherm again let his head hang. He probably was done for. John wouldn't make it in time. The horses were already getting restless.

He waited.

John came crashing down the corn row from the yard. He hopped up on the back of the corn picker. He stared with big wide white-circled blue eyes. "Just what I'd warned you about!"

"Yeh."

"Now what do we do?"

"How many wrenches you got down in that toolbox?"

"A lot of 'em."

"Well, you better start digging them out. We're gonna have to take the machine apart around the husking rollers so I can slip my hand back out."

John stared some more down at where Sherm's hand was caught. He started to shake. "Man, I bet that hurts."

"I don't feel a thing." Sherm stared down at his hand too. At that moment blood began to ooze up through that part of the double mitten he could see above the rollers. "But I'm afraid it's pretty bad."

"Sherm, Sherm. I should never have let you drive this whole shebang alone. It's all my fault."

"Hey hey. Ain't we farming in shares? Besides, what makes you think you wouldn't have done the same thing?"

"I suppose that's true."

One of the horses in the rear set of three looked back over its shoulder.

Sherm said, "We better get them five horses unhitched from this machine. I think maybe one of 'em has just smelled the blood. We can't have them start a runaway with me crucified to the machine like this."

"Oh God, no. Just sit tight there and I'll quick get them unhooked." Still shaking, fingers trembling, John unhitched the five horses one by one, little burps of sobs escaping him all the while. He left the horses standing free.

"About done?"

"Right now." John came running around behind the machine and began digging into the toolbox. He came up with several different wrenches. He tackled the first nut he saw.

"Wait a minute," Sherm said. "Let's think a little here. That's the wrong nut." Sherm leaned over to peer down into the shadows under the rollers. "We could use some sun, couldn't we?"

"Sure could."

Sherm finally made out what he thought were the key nuts. He leaned around and pointed with his right hand. "There, try that one first."

John opened the largest wrench and fitted it to the nut. He tried turning it, couldn't quite make it go. "Golly, Sherm, there's still paint on these nuts."

"Try harder. It's the only way we're gonna win this game."

"I know." John set himself at a different angle and pulled with both hands. The nut came loose. "There."

Sherm pointed again. "Try that nut next."

The next nut proved to be too tight. Groaning, face setting in a deep wrinkled grimace, John jerked and jerked. The nut just wouldn't budge. "Man, if that don't frost you."

"Take a hammer to it," Sherm advised. "Those nuts are factory tightened."

John jumped back to the toolbox and came up with a hammer and a cold chisel. He set the cold chisel at an angle onto one of the corners of the nut and tapped it with the hammer. It came loose.

Sherm tried to move his caught hand. Still tight. "Got a little crowbar in there? Or a long screwdriver? To pry those rollers apart?"

John found a heavy screwdriver and tried parting the vicious toothed husking rollers. "Darn, can't quite get the right leverage."

"Hmm. Let's see. Too bad we ain't at the end of the field so we could use a loose fence post. Hey, I know. Take off one of those ash singletrees and try that."

Jumpy, John hurried to get a singletree. In a moment he was back. Carefully inserting the singletree between where the ends of the rollers stuck out, he finally had the leverage, and hanging his whole body on it, opened the jaws of the rollers.

Sherm slowly drew his hand out. "What an alligator that machine turned out to be."

John climbed the machine up behind Sherm. He stared down at the mangled mass of cotton mitten and crushed hand. "Look at it begin to bleed."

"You ain't got some old rag in that toolbox we can wrap it with."

"No, but I got a shirt I can take off." Quickly John removed his mackinaw, then his gray flannel shirt. Shivering, he slipped his mackinaw back on, then took the shirt and wrapped it gently around the bloody lump. "Somehow we got to keep you from losing too much blood."

Free of the machine at last, Sherm started to climb down from his steel throne. Then, for a second, he blanked out; almost fell down. He gripped a lever with his right hand and, somehow, with a buzzing in his ears and strange tinglings sweeping up out of his neck and over his face across his eyes into his brain, he managed to hang on. Then his brain cleared and he was back on the corn picker. Gingerly he finished stepping down to earth.

"You all right?"

"Hey, I'm no chicken fighter."

"Now to get you to the hospital in Hello."

"What about the horses?"

"I mean for us to take the half-filled wagon back to the yard, you nut. And tie the hitching straps of the five horses to the rear of the wagon."

"Now you're thinkin'."

They arrived trotting on the yard.

John said, "You get your butt into the car there in the garage. I'll quick run to the house and tell Matilda. She can put the horses away. And do the milking tonight."

"Better yet, tell her to call Harry Haber next door. And Fritz

Engleking across the road from Harry. They can do the milking."

Sherm walked into the garage and angled himself into the front seat of John's Ford. He held his arm carefully against his chest. He saw where blood had also worked its way through the folds of John's flannel shirt. Red stains also showed on the front of his mackinaw.

John came running back, with Matilda cantering after him. John climbed into the car on the driver's side.

Matilda puffed. "But. . . . But. . . . "

"Got no time to talk now. Get those horses in the barn. Little Alfie knows where to hang the harnesses. And then call the neighbors to help you."

"But. . . . But. . . . " Her blue Frisian eyes bugged out as she finally caught sight of the bloody bundle Sherm was hugging to his chest. "But you won't know what doctor to see there."

"You're wrong as to that. Remember when Alfie fell off the roof of the hog house and he broke his collarbone? I shot him straight into Dr. Mars."

"You men . . . the way you get into these awful accidents!"

"Get them horses in the barn before they get restless." John stepped on the starter of his Model T Ford. Still warm, it rumbled up instantly. He backed it out of the garage. Then, tires digging little trenches, they roared off the yard.

The mangled hand began to hurt worse with every mile.

Entering Hello, Sherm had trouble to keep from fainting. The big bundle of wrapped shirt had turned completely scarlet.

John pulled up to the emergency entrance in the rear of the Hello Hospital. He stopped the car and ran around to open the door for Sherm. He helped Sherm out, slammed the door behind him, and helped him, gently, crying a little, into the hospital.

A buxom nurse in white with a strong chin and bold wide brow saw them coming in. "What have we here?"

"Hurry, nurse," John said. "This fellow tried to wrestle with a corn-picking machine. And lost."

"Follow me into the emergency room." She pointed to a rolling gurney. "Get on this. I'll call Dr. Mars."

Within seconds, Dr. Brander Mars, a black-browed slightly bowed man wearing a stiff white smock, came quietly into the emergency room. He looked down at the bloody mess lying on Sherm's belly. "Corn-picking machine, eh? When will you derring-do blokes learn to keep your damned fingers out of moving machinery. Christ!"

Sherm was a little startled by the doctor's language. "Well, you don't need to swear." Sherm tried to sit up.

"Lay down. Your Lord ain't going to object to strong language when it comes to pointing out your stupidity."

"Oh, I wasn't objecting to you calling on Christ. It's just that around horses and baseball players I never heard about daring-dos."

"Ah, a joker too, eh? Good." Dr. Mars began to unwrap John's flannel shirt from Sherm's arm. He turned to John. "How come you didn't put a tourniquet on his arm? You farmers are some of the best amateur inventors on earth, and yet you don't have the sense to take off your belt for a tourniquet." He turned to the nurse. "Get one."

Soon Dr. Mars had a rubber band snugged up tight around Sherm's upper arm. He finished unwrapping the hand. He stared down at the torn double mitten. He leaned over for a closer look. "Nurse, get the orderly. I want this man up in the operating room right now. Pronto."

John touched Dr. Mars on the elbow. "How does it look to you?"

"Not good."

"Can I go along and watch? I can push him up there."

"Okay. Nurse, lead the way for this man."

Soon the nurses had Sherm undressed and in a hospital gown and up on the operating table. The strong-chinned charge nurse spilled something into a thick wad of cotton. There was the strong sweet smell of chloroform . . . and Sherm was gone.

When Sherm came to, he asked, "Doc, do you think my hand will be healed by the time I try out for the Chicago Cubs next spring?"

Dr. Mars' black brows came down and his dark eyes narrowed to glittering slits. "No."

"No?"

"I was able to save your long finger. But the other three fingers were severed from the palm. Mashed off, actually. And they were all chewed up like they'd gone through a meat grinder."

"I see," Sherm said.

John bristled. "Cripes, Doc, you don't have to be so brutal."

Dr. Mars shrugged. "Well, he's going to know eventually when we unwrap the bandages."

John said, "But you could have said it in a more Christian-like way."

Sherm said, "It's okay, brother. I like for my doctor to be all western-honest, like horseradish mustard."

"But I still don't like it," John said. "Our example of Christian life should be enough to shame even doctors into having better manners."

Dr. Mars ignored John. He looked down at Sherm. "Your thumb was okay. So eventually, when that long finger heals, and you do all the right exercises, you'll be able to grip things again. In fact, that single remaining digit will become a powerful finger. You'll be able to drive a car. Work with a shovel. Even milk a cow, if you use a stripping motion."

Sherm felt sick to his stomach. Three fingers gone? Somehow he managed to work up a little smile. "Well, at least it's better than having lost the whole hand."

Dr. Mars smiled. "You'll do."

"What the heck, what is, is. And the only way I'm gonna be able to live with it, is to figure that this is already water in the ocean, waiting to be sucked up into the next wall of clouds coming over."

"Good Lord," Dr. Mars whispered. "I have me a philosopher on my hands."

Ma came barging into Sherm's room. She was blubbering red in the face. "Sher-mee! Sher-mee. My sweet boy! My sweet boy."

Sherm had been napping. The sickening sweet smell of chloroform still lingered in his nostrils. Sherm hated it when Ma turned goosey and teary-eyed. "After what happened today, you better not call me boy any more. I'm now a crippled old man."

"Och! Sher-mee. The mother who bore you always has the right to call you her sweet boy."

Sherm couldn't help but give her a part-devilish look. "Looks like you had your way after all, Ma. I'm sure the good Lord arranged this accident for your sake."

"What? Are you blaming me now for your own foolishness?"

Sherm turned his head and looked out the window of his white room. He saw where the blue flies of autumn lay dead in the dust on the windowsill. "Oh, Ma, let there be peace between us."

"Amen," Ma whispered.

The door burst open again, and tall gangling Free came charging in, with a protesting nurse tugging at his elbow. Free snapped, "Let me alone. I have a right to see my favorite uncle."

"But that doesn't make you one of his immediate family."

"The heck with that. Uncle Sherm and I are closer than brothers."

Sherm could almost laugh. "Hello there, uncle-sayer. Don't be rough on my favorite nurse."

Free looked down at the thick white bundle of bandages around Sherm's left arm. "How is it?"

"Well, it looks like the Cubs won't win the pennant next year."

"You mean, you won't be able to play ball anymore?"

"Oh, I guess I'll be able to play some softball. Maybe."

"But no more hard ball?"

"No."

Free drew up a white chair and sat down with a thump. "I guess that makes two of us."

"How's that?"

"My arm is still sore enough so I can hardly pick corn."

"Now for sure the Cubs ain't gonna win."

Ma sat looking at her son and grandson, crying; at the same time somehow beaming with pride.

Sherm glanced down at his bundled-up left hand. "I once thought I might be able to make a homer out of my life. But now it looks like it's only gonna be a single."

"Can you farm, though?"

Sherm looked out of the window again. The sun was just setting. "I could go west and take the mischief cure."

"Fat chance of that with Allie around."

Soon the charge nurse chased both Ma and Free out of Sherm's room.

Sherm was given a light supper of broth and tea. His mangled hand began to hurt more and more. He could feel his heart beating in it, slow swollen thumps. There were even swift little spurts of hurt where his three fingers used to be.

Sherm looked at the dark window once more. "I feel like I've died." He nuzzled his head in the stiff white pillow. "And I guess at that I've lost the one true life I always wanted to live."

Chapter Eighteen

It was after supper. The dishes were washed and the children had already been put to bed. John sat in his swivel chair repairing a leak in his red rubber boots with some innertube patching from his Ford. Matilda was darning a pair of John's brown woolen socks. And Sherm had taken off the bandages from his left hand and was exercising his long finger according to Dr. Mars' instruction.

Sherm had to be careful with the exercising. Dr. Mars had cut away too much skin and what was left was too tight. When Sherm worked the finger much at all, the tight skin broke and various stringy white scars always bled a little. But the doc was right about one thing. Sherm's remaining finger was getting stronger by the day and it wouldn't be long before it would be as strong as his thumb.

The three of them sitting around the white kitchen table didn't say much. A pan of skim milk to be made into a chocolate drink simmered on the back of the kitchen range.

The phone rang two longs. Their ring.

Sherm, to be useful at something, quickly got up and picked up the receiver of the wall phone. "Engleking here."

A weeping voice sounded in his ear. It came at him despite the hum of a long distance line. "Sherm-mee. Oh, Sherm-mee, something awful's happened." For some reason, Ma was speaking his name with an extra M in it.

"What now, Ma? Did Garland fall into the privy?"

"Oh, if only that were true, if I could choose."

Matilda looked up from her darning. "Now what kind of language is that with your mother. And that over a party line."

Sherm winked over his shoulder at Matilda. "Well, I always was a rubbernecker's delight."

"What? What?" Ma shrieked in his ear.

"Ma, I was talking to Matilda a second. Now, what's the matter in Jerusalem?"

"Oh, Sherm-mee, Garland's gone."

"What!"

"He's gone."

"He run away with some young girl?"

"Even that would be better than what happened."

"What did happen?"

"Garland and me were sitting here listening to Walter Damrosch and his 'Musical Appreciation Hour' over the radio, with Garland smoking his pipe in his rocking—"

"For godsakes, Ma, get to the point."

"—chair, when he gave up a deep sigh, and then he slipped out of his chair to the floor. Dead."

"Not really!"

"Yes, my boy."

"Did you call a doctor?"

"When the doctor got here he was dead all right."

Sherm stared at the two shiny bells on the wall phone. In many ways, Stepfather Garland Stanhorse had been a warmer father to him than his own father, Alfred. "Just a minute, Ma. Hold the phone, will you?"

"Ya, Sherm-mee."

Sherm turned to John. "It sounds like our second pa just died." Sherm repeated what Ma had just told him.

John stood up. "By jiggers, what a woman. She's outlasted two husbands. I always did say she was a toughie."

Matilda stood up in turn. "You Engleking men! Always joking. Even with death around."

John waggled his head. "Ah, Matilda, it's just our way of handling tough times."

"It's scandalous! I'll never understand you men."

Sherm broke in. "John, I'm not of much use to you here with only one hand. Why don't I drive down there yet tonight. Somebody better stay with her. Then when I find out when the funeral's gonna be, I'll call you."

"Do that."

Sherm turned to the phone. "Ma? Ma, I'm coming right down."

"Good, my boy. Good."

Sherm hung up the receiver. He turned to John. "Could you take Allie along? We're engaged now, you know. She's family."

John nodded. "Of course."

On the day of the funeral the weather turned cold, around zero, with occasional flakes of flying snow. John and Matilda, and Allie, drove down to Jerusalem in John's old black Ford.

Everything went smoothly at first. Ma was strangely stoical. She didn't cry during the short service in her house. She didn't cry during the longer funeral sermon in church.

Sherm watched her, wondering what was going on inside that head.

A caravan of seven cars rolled slowly out to the graveyard on the northwest edge of town, led by the black hearse and a car full of pallbearers. Stanhorse's nephew Pete with Ma sitting beside him drove directly behind the pallbearers, with John driving behind them. Sherm sat in front with John, and Allie sat in back with Matilda. The other cars were filled with curious old couples humbly thankful that they hadn't yet been called up.

They gathered around the grave. The undertaker opened the back of the hearse and the pallbearers lifted out Garland Stanhorse's coffin and carried it to the open grave and set it on several tight ropes.

Reverend Haan cleared his throat. To Sherm, the sound of it was exactly like the sound of a rooster clucking up his flock of hens around him.

Ma stood near the head end of the grave, with Sherm and John on either side of her, holding her by the arm to support her should she have one of her fainting spells.

Reverend Haan removed his glove and picked up a clod of yellowish-black dirt from the mound cast up by the gravediggers.

"Dearly beloved in Christ," Reverend Haan intoned, "we stand here in the sight of God, beside the grave of a beloved man, a Christian, about to commit his mortal flesh to eternal dust, from which he will someday rise on Judgment Day, to join all rejoicing saved ones in heaven."

Reverend Haan gave the clod a pinch and it broke up into crumbles of dirt. He sprinkled the crumbles on the coffin as the undertaker lowered it into the vault of the grave.

"For dust thou art—"

"Hahhk!" It was the sound of someone sucking in a deep breath, so long and so deep it seemed a chest would explode. There followed a series of yips, as if ripped out of the throat instead of expelled out of it. "Ahch! Ahch! Ahch! Ohhh Garrlandd! Gladly would I join you in death! Yes. Yes. Let them bury me with you! What do I want life for now? I want to join you, right now, in everlasting glory in heaven."

Before either Sherm or John caught on what Ma was up to, she broke free of them and hurled the bulk of her body down into the grave, landing belly first with a wallowing thump on the coffin, which for a second sounded like it had cracked partly open.

Reverend Haan never got around to saying: "—and unto dust shalt thou return." He stared past his gold-rimmed spectacles at the sprawled body on the coffin below. "In the name of heaven," he murmured.

"Ma!" Sherm cried.

"Ma!" John cried.

"I don't believe this," Matilda exclaimed.

Allie's soft deer eyes filled with tears.

Both Sherm and John leaped down into the grave, their legs straddling her body.

Ma reached her arm around the coffin and hugged it. "Garrlandd, my love, take me with you. As you rise up into glory."

John said, "Sherm, can you grab her legs with your one good arm?"

"Sure thing."

John leaned down and put his arms around the upper part of Ma's body. "Now. You too, Sherm, up she goes."

Grunting, with Ma protesting, they heaved her out of the grave and onto the edge of the spilling mound of dirt.

"Okay, somebody. Grab her up there and hold her until we climb out."

Quickly two of the nearest pallbearers tugged at her and helped her sit upright.

Then Sherm and John climbed out of the grave.

Sherm wanted to console her but didn't know how. He'd never hugged her much. Nor did John know how.

It was Allie, with her long dark curly hair, with her loving patient hands, who lifted Ma to her feet, and brushed the dust off her clothes, and put her arms around her, and murmured, "Now, now, it's all going to be all right. Time, Mother, time. Sherm and I will always be here to comfort you. Together we have him at least."

E N D

Roundwind